Praise for t
Jo

"Pure gold."
—*Atlanta Journal-Constitution* on
The Arrangement

"Romance writing at its very best."
—*Publishers Weekly* (starred review) on
The Guardian

"Fast paced, highly readable . . .
a bold, bright heroine."
—*Library Journal* on *The Gamble*

"A cast of convincing and likable characters . . .
with suspense and a believable romance."
—*Booklist* on *Golden Girl*

"Four stars! . . . A subtle sense of humor and
a bit of suspenseful 'whodunit' blend
for an enjoyable read."
—*Romantic Times* on *Someday Soon*

"Skillfully written with passion, compassion,
humor, and a terrific cast of characters."
—*Rendezvous* on *Royal Bride*

HIGH MEADOW

JOAN WOLF

WARNER BOOKS

An AOL Time Warner Company

WARNER BOOKS EDITION

Cover design by Diane Luger
Cover illustration by Alexa Garbarino
Hand lettering by David Gatti

Warner Books, Inc.
1271 Avenue of the Americas
New York, NY 10020

Visit our Web site at
www.twbookmark.com

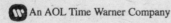 An AOL Time Warner Company

Printed in the United States of America

First Paperback Printing: February 2003

10 9 8 7 6 5 4 3 2 1

For Jay and Pam

1

$\mathcal{F}$ inish your milk," Kate said, and the doorbell rang. Ben started to get up, but she held up a hand. "I'll get it."

The little boy subsided into his chair. "Can I have another cookie?"

The kitchen was redolent with the smell of the quick bake oatmeal-raisin cookies she had just made, and she helped herself to one as she answered, "One more, if you finish your milk." She looked at the German shepherd lying on a mat in the corner of the sunny kitchen, and said, "Cyrus, stay with Ben."

Before she left the kitchen, she glanced from habit out the window, which gave her a view of the stable. The wooden barn looked peaceful in the September sunlight, with a few horses' heads hanging out the opened top of the Dutch doors on their stalls. As she walked toward the front door of the old farmhouse, the doorbell rang again. "I'm coming, I'm coming," she muttered, put her hand on the knob, and opened the door halfway.

The man outside had the kind of good looks generally associated with movie stars. His hair was streaked with blond, and his eyes were deeply and purely blue. He smiled, showing perfect white teeth.

Shit, she thought. Her fingers closed tensely on the door-knob. *My God, he hasn't changed at all, the rat.*

"Kate!" he said.

"What are you doing here, Marty?"

He shrugged. "I'm home, and I thought I'd come and see if Colleen was around."

"You haven't been home in eight years," Kate said. "We were all rather hoping you were dead."

"Kate," he said reproachfully. "I didn't walk out on Colleen, you know. She walked out on me. Anyway, as I said, I'm home, and I'd like to see her. Is she around?"

He can't see Ben, Kate thought in alarm, and she moved a little to block Marty's view of the hall. "Didn't you know? Colleen's dead."

His eyes widened. "What?"

Kate said bitterly, "You really must have cared about her, Marty. In all these years, you never once asked your parents about how she was doing?"

She started to push the door closed.

He wedged his foot against it. "How long has she been dead?"

Kate thought she heard the scrape of a chair against linoleum in the kitchen and replied rapidly, "Seven years. She died in a car crash. So you can go away, Marty. And don't come back. My mother will be even less happy to see you than I am."

She pushed the door again. She was a small, slender woman, but she had a lot of upper-body strength. Marty's foot held firm.

A clear treble voice said from behind her, "Who's that man, Mommy?"

Damn. Damn. Damn.

"Nobody," Kate said firmly. "Go back to the kitchen, Ben." Then, to the man in front of her, "Good-bye Marty."

Cyrus materialized at her side.

Marty looked warily at the dog, but held his ground. "Why are you so anxious to get rid of me?"

Kate's voice took on a sarcastic note. "That's easy enough to answer. I don't like you. You took my sister away from us, then you abandoned her. Get lost, Marty. We don't want you here."

"I told you, she left me," he repeated.

They stood at impasse, the door half-open between them, Kate acutely conscious of Ben still in the hall behind her.

Sensing her distress, Cyrus growled softly deep down in his throat, and moved closer to Marty. "You'd better go," Kate said warningly. "I can restrain him for only so long."

His eyes still on Cyrus, Marty said, "She left me for another man, Kate, but I was ready to let bygones be bygones, so I came to see her."

Kate's voice was contemptuous. "I guess she finally found out what a worm you were. Too bad she didn't listen to me and Mom before she ran off with you."

From behind her Ben said uneasily, "Should I call 911, Mommy?"

Still keeping her pressure on the door, Kate turned to give her son a reassuring smile. "No, Ben. That won't be necessary. The man is leaving."

Marty looked from the dog to Ben. "This is your son?" he asked.

After a fractional hesitation, she returned, "Yes."

He looked at her hand. "I don't see a wedding band."

From the hallway a small, strained voice said, "My mother died. Mommy is my mother now."

Once more she turned to Ben. His large, luminous brown

eyes were very dark, and Kate felt a surge of fury that he had to be subjected to this. She said crisply, "Ben, go back to the kitchen. I'll keep Cyrus with me."

Ben hesitated, his eyes going from the man in the doorway to Kate, then back again to the man in the doorway. Suddenly, breathlessly, he asked, "Are you my father?"

The words hit Kate like a punch in the stomach.

"No, Ben," she managed to answer steadily. "Marty is not your father. Now do as I say and go to the kitchen."

Mercifully, Marty remained silent as Ben did as he was told and retreated to the kitchen. Cyrus remained beside Kate, his eyes focused unwaveringly on Marty, who finally spoke. "So he's Colleen's child."

His voice sounded oddly triumphant.

"He *was* Colleen's child," Kate said. "I adopted him after Colleen died. And don't get any ideas, Marty. He is not your son. Colleen was quite clear about that."

A muscle flickered in his cheek. "Who was his father then?"

"I don't know, and I'm not interested in finding out. Ben doesn't need a father. He has Mom and me, and he doesn't need anyone else. So go away, or I'll sic Cyrus on you."

Marty was carefully not looking back into the dog's eyes. "How old is Ben?"

"None of your business."

"I can get it from the Records Office here in town, Kate. Stop being so obstructive."

If Marty went to the Records Office, someone in the town clerk's office would be sure to find out what he was doing, and news would spread that he was Ben's father. Kate struggled to contain her rage that this scumbag had the power to disrupt her relationship with her son, and said coldly, "He will turn seven next month."

"Thank you." He removed his foot from the door. "Well it was nice seeing you, Kate. Say hello to your mother for me."

"Drop dead," Kate said, and slammed the door in his face.

She took a moment to pat Cyrus reassuringly and collect herself before she walked back to the kitchen to join Ben. He was sitting at the old oak table, his empty glass of milk in front of him, and his arresting dark eyes were troubled. He waited for her to speak first.

She sat at the table across from him. "That man was once a friend of your mother's. He isn't very nice, Ben, and I don't like him."

"Did my mother like him?"

Cyrus went to his mattress under one of the windows. Kate had opened it before, and the crisp white cotton curtains rippled in the breeze.

"She was fooled by him, but then she found out how bad he was, and she didn't like him anymore."

"Oh," Ben said.

Kate took a deep, steadying breath. "Ben, why did you ask him if he was your father? Haven't I told you that your father is dead?"

He made no reply, just regarded her out of those large, long-lashed eyes.

"Didn't you believe me, Ben?"

"Yes."

"Then why . . ." She broke off. She already knew the answer to her question. He was hoping. No matter what she had said, he was hoping that one day his father would come. *Damn.*

She spoke in the most normal voice she could muster. "Soccer practice starts today. Nana will be home soon to take you. Why don't you go and change your clothes?"

"Okay."

He was so quiet and cooperative that he worried her.

Damn Marty Lockwood, she thought with helpless rage as she watched her son's small figure leave the kitchen. *Damn him.*

The first thing Marty did after he left Riverton Farm was to go to the Glendale Public Library. He sat at a computer, connected to the Internet, and typed in the keyword *Daniel Montero*. An hour later he left the library to return to his parents' Cape-Cod-style house. There he carefully composed a letter, which he mailed directly from the post office.

Two weeks later he received the response he had been hoping for. "May I speak to Martin Lockwood?" a man's voice asked when Marty picked up the phone on the third ring.

"I'm Martin Lockwood." Marty's heart skipped a beat. The man had spoken fluently, but his voice had a distinct Spanish accent.

"I'm calling for Daniel Montero. He would like to meet with you."

Marty's heart began to hammer. "That can be arranged."

"Mr. Montero lives in Greenwich. Would it be possible for you to come to his house?"

"Yes," Marty said smoothly. "Of course."

"Shall we say tomorrow at noontime?"

"Give me the address," Marty said, "and I'll be there."

He was still going over the speech he had prepared the following day as he walked up the flagstone path to the clapboard-and-stone single-floor house that belonged to the New York Yankees ace pitcher. The house was not lavish, for Greenwich, but the gardens framing it were magnificent. A small fountain played in the shrubbery-enclosed area that was surrounded by the drive.

I'm the one with the upper hand here, he told himself as he pressed the bell button. *I have to remember that.*

The door was opened by a slender, dark-haired man who looked to be in his fifties. Marty introduced himself.

"Yes. Come in." The voice was the same as the voice on the telephone the previous day. Marty stepped into a high-ceilinged front hall with polished bare wood flooring and yellow walls and looked around. "Come with me, please," the man said briefly, and Marty followed him out of the hallway and down a wide hall that led toward one of the wings. The man pushed open a door, said to the occupant inside, "Daniel, Martin Lockwood is here," and gestured for Marty to enter.

Marty strode forward and found himself in a comfortable and well-furnished office. It was a medium-sized room, with French doors giving a view of the gardens and a free-form pool outside. The large rolltop desk was golden oak, as was the computer station and the floor-to-ceiling bookcases. The man who was sitting behind the desk swiveled around in a large coffee-colored leather chair and Marty found himself looking at one of the most famous faces in all of American sports.

Daniel Montero said, "Stay, Alberto," and the man who had escorted Marty went to take a seat in a comfortable leather armchair. No one asked Marty to sit down: both men just looked at him.

Boldly, Marty stared back at the man he had come to see. The Yankee star's bronzed, clean-cut face was familiar from the newspapers, but the large brown eyes were even more remarkable in actuality than they appeared in photos.

"So," Daniel Montero said, "you wish to blackmail me."

Still nobody asked Marty to sit down, so he crossed his arms over his chest and replied with the words he had rehearsed, "As I wrote, I am in possession of information that you have a son who is being raised in ignorance of who his father is. If I inform the child's adoptive mother of your identity, she will most certainly demand a huge sum of money from you. What I am asking for my silence doesn't begin to compare with what you will have to pay in child support over the next eleven years."

Daniel Montero's face was calm and unreadable. "Why do you think this child is mine?"

"Because I know that eight years ago you had an affair with a girl named Colleen Foley." A trace of bitterness crept into Marty's voice. "I know this because she ditched me so that she could be with you." There was no flicker of recognition on Daniel's face at the mention of Colleen's name, and Marty continued defiantly, "Ten months after she started to sleep with you, Colleen had a baby. I saw him the other day. He looks just like you."

"Can this be true, Daniel?" the man named Alberto asked.

The Yankee pitcher's face remained calm and unreadable. "I remember Colleen. It was the spring training after I graduated from college. We were together until I left Florida to go to one of the Yankee farm teams. She told me she was going to go home." There was no trace of an accent in his voice.

"She did go home," Marty said triumphantly. "She went home and she had a baby. Then she was killed in a car crash. Her sister adopted the boy and is bringing him up. She doesn't know who the father is."

For the first time, a flicker of expression crossed Daniel's face. "This is difficult to believe."

Marty said, "I'm sure I can get some pictures. Once you see him, you'll know he's yours. Colleen had blond hair and blue eyes. This boy has straight black hair, like yours, and his eyes are like yours as well."

Marty brought out his *pièce de résistance*. "Once I give Kate your name, she can get the court to order DNA testing to prove paternity. Believe me, once that's done, you won't be able to get off the hook."

Daniel said slowly, "And you are telling me this because you think I will pay you to keep my identity a secret, so I will not have to pay child support to my son's adoptive mother?"

Marty smiled. "That's right."

"How fortunate for this child that he does not have you for a father," Daniel Montero said. "I, on the other hand, am perfectly willing to support him—and his mother—if it can be proved that he is in fact my son."

It took Marty a moment to digest the implications of this statement. The smile left his face and he stared at Daniel in outraged disbelief. "You *want* to pay for this child? But you don't even know him!"

"If he is my son, then I am responsible for taking care of him." He leaned slightly forward. "Where may I find him?"

Marty's brain churned frantically as he tried to find something to salvage from the wreck of his perfect plan. A glitter in Daniel's eyes alerted him to a possible alternate course. "It will cost you to find out," he said.

The glitter became even more pronounced. "You would blackmail me for this information?"

"Yes," said Marty, sure he was onto something now.

Daniel fitted his fingers together and said, slowly and deliberately, "In that case, let me tell you what I will do, Martin Lockwood. I will give your name to the police and tell them to arrest you for attempted blackmail. Then I will hire a private detective, who will search out the whereabouts of my son. You said that Colleen's sister is raising him, and that her name is Kate. I do not think it will be very long before he is located."

Shit. Marty thought furiously. *I told him too much.*

"Kate will refuse to see you," he said.

A straight black eyebrow lifted. "You told me she would sue me for child support."

"She's more likely to get a restraining order to keep you away from him," Marty said. "If you want, I can arrange for you to meet the boy away from her."

"A restraining order will avail her nothing if he is indeed my son. Nor am I going to sneak behind her back." Daniel stood up and the full force of his splendid physical presence dwarfed even Marty's good looks. "Now, are you going to tell me where I can find this Kate and my son?"

Checkmate, Marty thought bitterly, and gave Daniel Montero Kate's address.

2

It was the seventh inning, and the Yankees were up by two runs, but Daniel was in trouble. He had loaded the bases by giving up two walks and an infield hit, and Boston's biggest slugger was coming up to the plate. There was furious activity in the Yankee bullpen, and when Daniel glanced over at the dugout, he saw the pitching coach on the telephone.

Shit, he thought. *Mel is going to take me out.*

Then the manager himself was walking to the mound. Daniel cursed long and fluently to himself in Spanish as he stood with an impassive face and watched Joe approach.

"I think you've lost a bit of concentration," Joe said, holding out his hand for the ball. "Let's let Mike finish this up."

It killed Daniel to give up the ball. When he got into a mess, he wanted to be the one who got out of it. "I am sorry, Joe," he said stiffly as he handed the ball to his manager. Joe patted him on the shoulder as he walked by. The crowd gave him a standing ovation, which he forced himself to acknowledge by tipping his cap.

He sat by himself in the corner of the dugout, and no one came near him. Everyone in America knew that Daniel Montero hated to come out in the middle of an inning.

And against Boston! he fumed to himself as he squinted into the sunlight on the field. *I couldn't even get the damn ball over the plate! What the hell is the matter with me?*

Daniel knew the answer to his own question. He was meeting after the game with the private investigator he had hired to dig up information about Kate Foley, and he couldn't seem to keep his mind from straying to that future conversation.

I have a son. Every time he said those words to himself, sheer joy bubbled in his chest and stomach. After two years of thinking it would never be possible . . . he had a son. It was like a miracle.

On the field the batter hit a line drive down the left field line. The third baseman, who was playing on the line, snagged it, and the inning was over.

Daniel stood up and shook the hand of the pitcher who had relieved him and saved his chance for his twentieth win. Wins had seemed of the utmost importance to him just a few days ago. He was in a contest to win the Cy Young Award for best pitcher in the American League, and the more wins he rang up, the better his chances of getting the trophy over Boston's ace. Daniel had won it twice, and Boston's pitcher had won it twice, and Daniel wanted to be the one who went to three.

But that was a few days ago. Now all he wanted was to go down to the clubhouse, change into street clothes, and go home so he could meet with the private investigator. He was stuck, however, because of the significance of this possible win.

Twenty-two minutes later, the game was over and the scoreboard flashed the news that this was Daniel Montero's twentieth win. The crown went wild, and he had to step out of the dugout and tip his cap. Then his teammates were giving him high fives, and slapping his back, and looking so genuinely pleased for him that he felt guilty that he could not be more wholehearted in his response.

Finally, the team went down to the clubhouse, and Daniel steeled himself to be polite to the reporters who were already gathered around his locker, which was marked by a brass plate bearing his name. He had been born into a privileged Colombian family, and his mother had instilled in him from early childhood the necessity of courtesy to those beings less fortunate than himself.

"Did it make you mad to have to come out?" the reporter for the *Daily News* said as Daniel approached.

Daniel flashed his famous grin. "Not at all, Felipe. You know how much I appreciate Mike's help in the middle of an inning."

Everyone laughed, and a television reporter asked the next question. It was a full hour before Daniel was able to extricate himself from the clubhouse and get into his car to drive home.

Alberto met him in the hallway of his house in Greenwich, and said, "He's in your office."

Daniel did not want his secretary and his father's old friend to see his face when he was talking to the private investigator. Alberto saw too much sometimes, and there were some feelings a man wanted to keep private. "If you don't mind, I'll handle this alone, Alberto," he said.

"Of course."

Daniel walked quietly to his office door, inhaled deeply, and pushed the door open. The man inside got to his feet as he came in. "Congratulations," Joseph Murphy said. "Twenty wins. That's terrific."

Daniel held out his hand. "Thank you."

The two men shook, and Daniel looked into shrewd blue eyes that were on a level with his own. The other man's thick six-foot-two-inch frame carried considerably more weight than he did, however.

"Won't you please sit down," Daniel said.

Murphy resumed his seat in the leather armchair, and Daniel went to sit in the chair in front of his desk. He swiveled around to face Murphy, and said, "So, tell me what you have found out."

"There isn't a whole lot to tell," the detective replied. "Katharine Foley lives a quiet, structured life. She has custody of her sister's child . . ."

Daniel's heart leaped with hope. "Custody? I was under the impression that there was a legal adoption involved."

"There is."

Damn. Daniel's heart settled down. A legal adoption would make matters more difficult for him.

The detective went on, "The sister died in a car crash when Ben—that's the kid—was only six months old. Katharine adopted him, but she and her mother have raised him together. As far as I can discover, there's been no sign of a boyfriend since she took on the boy." Murphy lifted an ironic eyebrow. "She's not exactly a hot number, Mr. Montero."

That was good news. He did not want his son being raised by a hot number.

"How does she support him?" he asked.

The detective settled his burly frame more comfortably in his chair. "She teaches riding, and she buys and sells horses."

He stared incredulously. "And she makes money at this?" His father bred Andalusian horses in Colombia, and in Daniel's experience, horses were money-losers, not money-makers.

"She didn't when she first started the business, but she does now. Her mother's a schoolteacher, and she supported them for the first few years, until the business turned around. Now the business pays its own bills, with enough left over to live on."

"She must be a genius, to make money on horses," Daniel said with genuine wonder.

"Apparently she's a pretty smart businesswoman," Murphy agreed. "You said you wanted a report on her finances, so I got you a copy of her last tax statement." For the first time he opened the briefcase on his lap, took out a paper, and passed it to Daniel.

The number that Daniel saw typed under *net income* was decent. It was not in the same stratosphere as his income, of course, but it was enough money for a woman and a child to live on. Daniel frowned as he put the tax statement on his desk.

"Horses are a lot of work," he commented. "Where is Ben while this Katharine is working?"

"You asked me to find that out, and I did. When Ben was a baby, Katharine took care of him while her mother was at school. She did the stable work and teaching when her mother was at home. Now that Ben's in school, she has more time for the business, which is one of the reasons it's been making more money."

"What grade is Ben in?"

"He just started second grade."

Second grade. Daniel shut his eyes. *I have missed so much time.*

A little silence fell.

Murphy said, "I have a picture of the boy if you would like to see it."

If I would like to see it? "Yes," he said, his voice not quite as steady as he would have liked. "I would like to see it."

Once more the detective opened his briefcase. "It's only a newspaper photo. It appeared in the local rag last year. Apparently Ben's first-grade class went pumpkin picking, and the paper carried the story." He handed over a photocopy of the newspaper article. "You can see why they chose Ben for the picture. He's a good-looking kid."

Daniel stared down at the photograph and into a pair of huge, long-lashed brown eyes. It was like looking at a picture of himself when he was seven. Ben's dark hair was styled in the cut that Daniel had seen on the sons of his friends, but the face was the same.

Shaken, he looked up to meet the eyes of Joseph Murphy. "He looks very much like you," the detective said softly.

"Yes." Daniel inhaled and blew out slowly though his nose. "I have only just learned of his existence."

Murphy nodded, his blue eyes speculative. "He appears to be a perfectly normal, happy little boy. Katharine has done a good job with him."

Daniel nodded. "If I can prove that he is mine, can I claim the legal rights of a father?"

Murphy said, "You'll have to consult a lawyer, but I'm sure the court would award you visitation rights."

Visitation rights. The words sounded so cold. What he wanted to do was scoop his son up in his arms and never let him go.

"Have you met Katharine yourself?" he asked the detective.

"Yes. I stopped by the farm pretending to be looking for a place to board my horse. She's a beautiful woman. It's hard to believe she doesn't have a boyfriend, but apparently she doesn't date. She runs the stable and takes care of Ben."

Daniel spoke to the detective for fifteen more minutes, but the salient information had been delivered. Then he wrote Murphy a check.

The detective said hesitantly, "Usually I don't pester my famous clients, but would you mind giving me your autograph? My son is a Little League pitcher, and he idolizes you."

Daniel smiled. "Of course I will give you an autograph. I even have a picture I can sign for you."

Murphy's eyes lit. "That would be great."

Daniel pulled open several of his desk drawers. "Let me see, I think I saw some in here the other day . . . Yes, here it is." He took out a photo of himself in his Yankee uniform, signed it, and handed it to the detective. Then he courteously walked Murphy to the door and let him out to collect his Camry, which was parked on the circular graveled drive.

After Murphy had driven off, Daniel went along to the family room, where he knew he would find Alberto. He heard the sounds of a familiar voice as he approached the door and entered into the room to the notes of Luciano Pavarotti finishing up an aria from *La Boheme*.

"The Three Tenors again?" he said teasingly as he walked to one of the comfortable cushioned sofas placed at right angles to the stone fireplace.

Alberto got up from his seat between the speakers and went to turn the CD off. "So?" he said, as he sat across from Daniel on the matching sofa. "The news is good. I can see that in your face."

"Here is a picture of the boy." Daniel reached forward, the photocopy of Ben's picture in his hand.

Alberto took it and studied it for a moment in silence. "Lockwood was right. The boy is yours. You looked just like this when you were his age." He looked up from the picture and smiled. "Daniel, I am so glad."

Daniel's return smile was radiant. "So am I."

"After that terrible news two years ago, to find that you already had a son—it is like a miracle."

Daniel remembered vividly his emotions when the doctor had told him that his bout with mumps had probably left him unable to father a child. It was one of the reasons he was still single at the age of twenty-nine. How could he ask a woman to marry him when he could not give her a child?

"Your mother and father will be ecstatic," Alberto said.

Daniel leaned forward. "I've been thinking about this, and I want him to live with me, Alberto. I want shared custody. I don't want to be just a weekend father."

Alberto looked grave. "I understand your feelings, Daniel, but what will his mother have to say to that?"

"She's not his mother, she's his aunt. I'm his father. Surely the court would give heavy consideration to my claim."

"Daniel, think before you take this case to court." The gravity that was always present in Alberto's brown eyes was even more pronounced than usual. "The welfare of the child must be your prime consideration. It will not be good for him to be the center of a contested custody case."

Daniel stared at the floor and didn't reply.

"If you go in armed with lawyers, you will make an enemy of the mother. It would be far better to make her a friend, far better for her to willingly let you be a part of the boy's life than to throw a lawsuit at her. After all, she is a single mother. She cannot have had an easy time of it. She may be glad to have the help of a man in raising her son."

"I don't want to be a weekend father," Daniel repeated.

"Perhaps she will even agree to shared custody, but not if you threaten her, Daniel."

Daniel's eyes glittered. "I didn't say anything about threatening her, Alberto!"

"You spoke of lawyers. In America, that is always a threat."

After a moment, Daniel said with resignation, "True."

"I am certain that everything will work out happily, Daniel. I am only trying to suggest that you give it time. Get to know the mother. Get to know the boy. You are a very persuasive man. Rely on yourself, not on the lawyers."

Daniel nodded. "All right," he said soberly.

Alberto stood up. "And now, if you don't mind, I am going to put on some more music."

"Something happy," Daniel said. "I don't want to hear about Mimi's frozen hand again."

"How about Beethoven's Ninth?"

"Excellent."

Alberto went to change the CD.

3

$\mathcal{K}$ate waved good-bye to the school bus that was taking Ben away, then she and Cyrus went to the barn. She had already been there earlier to feed the horses and turn them out.

The woman who helped her muck out stalls in return for riding time for her children had just come in. "Morning, Diane," Kate said, as she went to tack up Shane, her own horse, for a riding session. The radio was set, as usual, to the local National Public Radio station, and classical music filled the barn as Kate bridled and saddled her horse.

She was never happier than when she was riding, and her session with Shane went very well. After she had turned him out, she tacked up two clients' horses to ride and school, then, at ten-thirty, she taught a lesson to a client from Darien, a woman who had been showing her horse in Amateur Owner jumper classes this season. The horse was a nervous Thoroughbred, which Kate had been training as well. However, the chestnut, which went around quite calmly for Kate, was still unreliable for his owner to ride.

I should never have bought a hot Thoroughbred for Nancy, she thought. *Her hands are just too heavy.*

When the session was over, she spoke to the owner about

changing horses. "Sometimes a particular horse-rider combination just doesn't work out. It's not your fault, it's not his fault, it's just one of those things."

"I just feel so stupid that I can't ride him," the client said with frustration. "He's wonderful for you!"

"You're an excellent rider, Nancy, but to be honest, he requires an extraordinary amount of tact. I'm beginning to think he needs a professional ride. I wonder if Adam Saunders might like him."

"You mean the eventer?"

"Yes."

"You mean he might *buy* Aladdin?"

"He might be interested. Should I give him a call?"

"Then I'd have to look for another horse."

"We'll get you something a little calmer this time. I know of a nice Hanoverian that's coming up for sale."

"Well . . . maybe that's a good idea, Kate. I'm getting awfully sick of careening around out of control."

"It's a little harrowing to watch you, I must admit."

"Okay. Why don't you get in touch with Adam Saunders then and see if he's interested?"

"I'll do that," Kate promised.

Nancy went home, and Kate cleaned and refilled all the water buckets, then she moved the privately owned horses from the four single-horse paddocks back into the barn and put out the second group of privately owned horses. Next she taught a beginner lesson, after which she went to the house for lunch and to make some phone calls about another horse she was hoping to sell. Then it was back down to the barn to finish mucking out stalls, to clean the bathroom and to bring her own horses in from the two fields where they had enjoyed an all-day turnout.

At three-fifteen, she and Cyrus were at the front of the

drive to meet the school bus. After Ben had had his snack, she took him down to the riding ring with her. Her mother was going to go grocery shopping after school and would collect him when she got home.

Four riders were warming up in the outdoor ring, which was enclosed by a post-and-rail fence. Kate paused for a moment to savor the picture presented by the four velvet-helmeted girls and their glossy horses outlined against the blue September sky.

How lucky I am to be able to work at what I love, she thought.

"Can I ride my bike, Mommy?" Ben asked.

Kate frowned. She fought a constant battle between her heart's need to keep Ben safe and her understanding that she had to give him room to breathe. "All right, but stay off the driveway, Ben. People will be coming in for the next lesson, and you can be hard to see. Ride in front of the house."

"Okay," her son promised blithely, and went off toward the old stone barn, which was now used as a storage facility. Kate watched him for a moment, then shook her head as if to clear it and turned her attention to her students.

Daniel Montero parked in front of the house fifteen minutes after Kate had started her lesson. When the doorbell drew no response, he decided to walk in the direction of the clear, crisp, feminine voice that was coming from the direction of the riding ring he had passed on his way in. As he was crossing the driveway, a boy on a small two-wheeler bike came flying toward him. Daniel held up his hand and the child skidded to a stop. With his heart hammering so hard he could scarcely think, Daniel looked at the vivid, dark-haired boy who was his son. He managed to say, "Perhaps you can help me. I am looking for Katharine Foley."

"That's my mom," the child replied. "She's at the riding ring. She's teaching a lesson, though. You'll have to wait if you want to talk to her."

"That's okay." Daniel seemed to have forgotten to breathe and forced himself to inhale. "I don't mind waiting."

"Would you like to watch me ride my bike?" The child's dark eyes were bright and fearless as he regarded Daniel.

"I would love to watch you ride your bike," Daniel replied.

The child—his son—cocked his head and regarded him curiously. "Do you know you look like Daniel Montero? My friend Connor has his baseball card."

"Do I?" Suddenly, Daniel was frightened. What would he do if his son was a Red Sox fan? Before he could allow himself to contemplate the awfulness of this possibility, he asked, "Do you like the Yankees?"

The big brown eyes sparkled. "I *love* the Yankees. I went to a game this year for Connor's birthday. Connor's my best friend, and his dad took us to see the Yankees play in Yankee Stadium. In the *Bronx*."

Daniel breathed a fervent, *Thank God*. "I hope they won."

"They did." Ben, who had been standing with his bike, now hopped on and rode around in a circle in front of Daniel. As he rode, he said, "Connor's dad bought us both Bernie Williams shirts. Isn't that cool?"

It broke his heart that his son had to rely on another boy's father for treats. *Not anymore,* he vowed silently.

"Very cool," he agreed.

"Do you like the way I'm riding?"

"Very much."

"I got this bike for Christmas."

"Er . . . did Santa Claus bring it for you?"

The circling figure stopped and Daniel looked into a

supremely scornful brown gaze. "Santa Claus is for babies. I'm not a baby."

"No, you're not," Daniel agreed. "You know, there's something else that you might find cool. I *am* Daniel Montero."

The soft, pink, little-boy mouth dropped open. "You are?"

"Yes. And I have to be back at Yankee Stadium for tonight's game, so I hope I will have a chance to talk to your mother soon."

"If you're lying, you'll get in trouble with Mommy," Ben warned. "She *hates* liars."

"I'm not lying, son." The word felt so good coming from his lips.

"Mommy!" Ben dropped his bike and began to race down the path in the direction of the cool, crisp voice. "Mommy, Mommy, Mommy! Daniel Montero is here to see you!"

Daniel followed the flying figure and emerged from the trees into the area of a sand-riding ring. The four riders in the ring were staring at him, as were the three women sitting on one of the benches that flanked the ring. The dog standing next to the slim girl in the middle of the ring began to bound toward him, barking furiously.

"Stop!" Ben screamed. "It's all right! Mommy, call Cyrus!"

The voice to which Daniel had been listening earlier commanded, "Cyrus, come."

By now the dog had reached Daniel, and he said calmly, "It's all right, guy. Come on, let's go meet your owner."

"It is!" he heard one of the girls in the ring squeal. "Oh my God, it *is* Daniel Montero!"

"Everyone walk," the black-haired girl in the center of the ring called, and the horses slowed from a trot. She crossed to the fence, looked through it at her son, and said, "Ben, what on earth is going on?"

The little boy grabbed Daniel's hand and pulled him closer to the fence. "Mommy, Mommy, look. It's Daniel Montero, and he wants to talk to you."

The feel of that small hand in his, so warm and alive, made him want to weep, and for the first time he looked at Katharine Foley. She had the same color eyes as Colleen, but her chiseled features did not have the sweetness of Colleen's less-perfect face. Her look was distinctly unfriendly, which surprised Daniel. He was not accustomed to being looked at in such a way by beautiful young women.

"Daniel Montero?" she said in that crisp voice of hers. "The baseball player?"

At least she knew who he was. "Yes. I am sorry to interrupt you, Miss Foley, but there is a matter of the utmost importance that I must discuss with you."

Her eyes went from Daniel's face to Ben's, then back again to Daniel. The flush of color that had been in her cheeks drained away, and her eyes widened.

She knows, Daniel thought triumphantly. *She sees how much we resemble each other.*

"Just a moment," she said, and climbed lithely out of the ring. "I'll get someone to take over my lesson."

A blue heron flew overhead as she walked toward the big wooden barn that lay across the stable yard from the riding ring.

Ben said, "Can I have your autograph, Daniel?"

"Of course."

Ben grinned, showing a gap where he had lost a tooth, and said in a distinctly satisfied voice, "Connor is going to be mad that he wasn't here."

At this point, the four girls in the ring had lined up on the other side of the fence from him, and the three mothers from the bench had come over. "We don't mean to intrude," a short-haired blond said, "but I had to tell you how much I admire your pitching."

He made a response and tried to pay attention to what the women and girls were saying to him, but all he was conscious of was the child whose hand still clung to his. He wanted to snatch Ben up, put him in the car, and take him home. Immediately.

He was signing his name on pages from a notebook the blonde had produced from her purse when he saw Kate returning with a tall, brown-haired girl at her side.

"Jean will take over the lesson," she said to the mothers. "I'm sorry, but it sounds as if this is important."

The mothers, who normally would have said that they were paying for Kate's instruction, not Jean's, exclaimed that they understood perfectly.

"We'll go to the house," Kate said to Daniel in a tense voice.

"Can I come too, Mommy?"

"No!" There was a hint of panic in Kate's voice.

Daniel said, "I need to speak to your mother in private, Ben. But I will see you again, I promise."

Ben scowled but did not protest. *He has been taught to listen to authority,* Daniel thought. *That is good.*

They walked back up the path in silence, Kate going first, flanked by her dog. She was not a tall woman, but there was something about her slender, perfectly straight back and the set of her head that told Daniel she would not easily be intimidated.

As they came closer to the house, Daniel noted that the white paint was peeling in a few places and thought that perhaps Katharine and her mother did not have the money to keep up such a large piece of property. He followed Kate up the three steps to the front porch and then into the unlocked house.

"Is it wise to leave your door open?" he asked as he closed the door. "It isn't visible from the riding ring. Anyone could walk right in and rob you, and you'd never see it happen."

"This is Glendale, Connecticut, not Central America, Mr. Montero," she replied coolly as she led him into a large living room.

Little bitch, he thought. "I am not from Central America, Miss Foley. I am Colombian."

"Oh, that must be why you're paranoiac about security."

Keep your temper, Daniel. He did not reply.

She did not sit, nor did she invite him to take a seat. She stood in front of an old stone fireplace, folded her arms across the chest of her red sweater, and said, "Why do you want to see me?"

Before he answered he looked around the room, trying to imagine what it must be like to live in this house.

It was a comfortable room, done in blue and white, with well-worn cushioned furniture and a landscape and some hunting pictures on the walls. The mantel held a very nice-looking clock, and there was an entertainment center as well as two large bookcases along the walls. The sofa and love seat and armchairs all had lamps in position to make reading comfortable.

A nice room, he thought. *A homey room. A good place for a boy to grow up.*

"I am here because I am Ben's father," he said, answering as directly as he had been asked.

"I don't believe you," she shot back. But he could see from the look in her eyes that she did.

He decided to try charm and produced his most beguiling

smile. "Please, Miss Foley, may we sit down? I would like to explain to you how my arrival here came about."

She looked as if she wanted to refuse, but said, "All right. You can sit there." She pointed to a blue slip-covered chair.

He sat. She continued to stand. He increased the wattage of his smile. "Please," and he gestured toward the chair that was closest to his.

After a brief hesitation, she sat and faced him, her straight back not touching the chair. The dog flopped down in front of her. "So? What do you want to tell me?"

"Eight years ago, when I was at spring training in Florida for the Yankees, I met a girl named Colleen Foley."

Her naturally pale skin went even paler. Instinctively, he put out a hand toward her, but she shook her head, and said, "Go on."

He kept his eyes on her face. "Colleen was not getting along with the man she was living with, and I invited her to move in with me. We were together for two months, then the Yankees assigned me to a Class A team in Minnesota. Minnesota did not appeal to Colleen, and she decided that she would rather go home. I think the adventure of being on her own was wearing thin. She missed her mother."

The aquamarine eyes he was watching blinked twice, as if holding back tears. She said grittily, "If what you say is true, then why didn't Colleen tell you about the baby?"

He shook his head in puzzlement. "I have been thinking about that ever since I learned of Ben's existence. The only answer I can come up with is that she didn't think I would be able to help her. After all, I was nothing but a two-bit Latino minor-league player. Most of us didn't have enough money to buy a new shirt."

She didn't say anything.

He went on, "In my case, she was mistaken. My family is

well-off, Miss Foley, but I didn't want to seem different from the other players, so I lived as they did. She probably thought the only thing I would do was offer her money for an abortion."

Still she was silent, her body rigid, rejecting him. He said, "If your sister had lived, I am quite sure she would have let me know about Ben. She would not have deprived the boy of having a father to take care of him."

She said angrily, "Ben has been very well taken care of."

His charm slipped a little. "I'm sure he has been, but he has lacked a father. Every boy needs a man in his life, Miss Foley, and I want to be there for Ben."

She said tonelessly, "I want your story confirmed by DNA testing before I say a single word to Ben about this."

He nodded reassuringly. "I perfectly understand, and I am willing to have the testing done."

A little silence fell. She was looking at him the way she might regard a sworn enemy at a peace conference that had been forced upon her. He said with genuine bewilderment, "I should think you would be delighted to discover that Ben has a millionaire father. Why are you acting so hostile?"

She lifted her chin. It was a very determined chin, he noticed, in contrast to the softness of her unlipsticked mouth. "I don't give a damn about your money." She pointed a finger at him. "I don't know you. I know nothing at all about the kind of man you are, and I don't like the idea of a perfect stranger walking into Ben's life and having influence over him."

"I am his father. I wish nothing but good for him."

"I won't know that you're his father until the DNA testing is done."

"I will have the testing done, but both of us know what the

result will be. Ben is the twin of what I looked like at that age."

Her eyes narrowed. Their color was much more striking against her black hair and brows than it had been against Colleen's fairness. "So you say."

"My mother could show you the pictures to prove it."

There came the sound of a door opening, and Kate called, "Mom, is that you?"

"Yes, it is, dear. What are you doing at home? I thought you had a lesson."

"Can you come in here, please?"

"Let me just put this ice cream in the freezer."

Daniel and Kate sat in tense silence until a woman walked in through the living room door. Then Kate said in a hard voice, "Mom, this is Daniel Montero. He says he is Ben's father."

"Ben's fa . . . ?" Daniel looked into a pair of shocked blue-gray eyes.

He stood up. "Yes, Mrs. Foley. I just learned of Ben's existence, and I have come to introduce myself."

She stared at him for a moment. "You look like him."

"Yes. And I have agreed to submit to DNA testing, which I'm sure will be conclusive."

"My God." The woman's face broke into a radiant smile. "But this is wonderful! Ben has a father!" She crossed the floor to him, holding out her hand. "I'm Molly Foley, Ben's grandmother. Did Kate say your name was Daniel?"

Kate's voice cut across his reply, "He is Daniel *Montero,* Mom, the baseball player." She might have been informing her mother that he was Daniel Montero, the convicted felon.

"The Yankee pitcher?" Molly said.

He shook her hand and smiled reassuringly into an older version of Colleen's face. "Yes, I am the Yankee pitcher, Mrs. Foley."

"Good heavens," Molly replied. Cyrus had come over to greet her, and she absently petted his head. "However did you find out about Ben?"

"Good point," Kate said in the same hard voice. She also stood up. "I'd like to know the answer to that question too."

Daniel turned to her and said, his own voice invincibly courteous, "I learned of his existence from a man named Martin Lockwood."

A look of infinite disgust flitted across her face. "Marty." She pronounced the name as if it was a curse.

"He is not a particularly savory character," Daniel agreed. "He came to see me a few days ago in order to blackmail me. Apparently he was under the mistaken apprehension that I would not be happy to learn that I had a son, and that I would pay him to keep the news a secret from you."

Kate frowned. "Why would you do that?"

"So I would not have to pay child support. At first, he was dismayed to learn that I was perfectly willing to pay child support to my son, but when he discovered that I was pleased about the child's existence, he tried to blackmail me for your address."

Molly said despairingly, "I will never know what Colleen saw in that boy. He was bad then, and he's bad now."

Daniel said, "Colleen had grown sick of him by the time I met her. That's why she moved in with me."

Kate took a step in his direction, like a duelist getting ready to attack. "Why were you glad to learn about Ben? Marty was right in thinking that most men wouldn't want to find out they had an illegitimate son they would have to support."

He shrugged easily, and replied, "Then I suppose I am different from most men." He had no intention of telling her about the mumps.

She did not look as if she believed him.

"How *did* you find our address?" Molly asked. "Did you pay Marty his blackmail?"

It was his turn to look disgusted. "I would never pay blackmail. I told him that I would report his extortion attempts to the police if he didn't furnish me with your address."

Molly glanced at his left hand. "Are you married, Daniel?"

"No, I am not."

"Is Ben your only child?"

"As far as I know," he responded truthfully.

Kate once more folded her arms across her chest. "So you're feeling guilty that you have all this money and you want to share some of it with your son. Fine. Send me a monthly check, and I'll bank it for his college education. But stay out of our lives."

"Kate!" Molly cried.

Daniel shook his head. "It's not going to be as easy as that, Miss Foley. Through no fault of my own, I was deprived of the company of my son for the first seven years of his life. Now that I have found him, I am going to make up for lost time."

Molly laughed softly. "My, Connor will be so jealous."

He flashed her a genuine smile, the devastating one that could not be faked. "Ben has told me about Connor."

Kate said, her voice brittle, "I have to get back to my lessons. If you will leave the name and number of your attorney with my mother, our attorney will get in touch with him. Except for the attorneys, I do not want anything about this conversation to leave this room. Have I made myself clear, Mr. Montero?"

Fire and ice, he thought. He had heard those words before

but had never understood what they meant until he looked into Katharine Foley's cold eyes and saw the fire burning deep inside them.

He thought that it was going to be awkward if she continued to be so hostile, and replied as mildly as he could, "You have made yourself perfectly clear, Miss Foley. I will abide by your request."

She nodded. "Very well. We will be in touch."

"Through our lawyers."

"Yes. Through our lawyers. I don't want you near Ben until I have proof of paternity."

"May I at least say good-bye to him today? I told him I would see him before I left."

Molly said, "Of course you may say good-bye to Ben, Daniel. Go on back to your lesson, Kate, and I will get the information you want."

"All right." Kate shot her mother a dark look, did not look at all at Daniel, and walked out of the room.

4

As the door closed behind Kate, Molly sighed and motioned Daniel back to his chair. "You must excuse my daughter's abruptness; she is not a person who accepts change easily."

"She seems to dislike me," he replied with honest bewilderment.

Molly felt a flash of amusement that he was clearly so unaccustomed to the kind of treatment he had just received from Kate. Then her amusement died, and she sat in Kate's chair.

"The people Kate likes are the people she loves, and there are only a few of us," she said. "Now, tell me about you and Colleen . . ."

He was wonderfully kind. He shared several funny stories and spoke of Colleen with affection. He never once implied that theirs had been a relationship of convenience for the both of them, but Molly was adept at reading between the lines, and she saw the truth for what it was.

At twenty-two, Daniel must have been gorgeous, but he had been too young and, Colleen would have thought, too poor to play the role of good provider. Colleen had come home to her mother and sister for that security.

Tears stung her eyes. She laughed a little shakily and said, "I loved my daughter very much, but responsibility was not one of her strong suits."

"She was beautiful and charming," he said. "And very young."

What a nice young man, Molly thought.

She said, "You really do look remarkably like Ben . . . or should I say that Ben looks remarkably like you?"

He grinned. "Either way is all right with me."

She folded her hands in her lap. "The DNA testing must be done for the sake of legality, I suppose, but it seems clear enough that you are Ben's father. There is the timing, as well as the resemblance."

"Let's be honest," he replied dryly. "The DNA testing must be done for the sake of your daughter, Mrs. Foley. The law does not require genetic proof."

"Well, then, yes, it must be done to satisfy Kate." She frowned and chose her words carefully, wanting to make clear to him what Kate had done for Ben. "The day my daughter turned twenty-one, she started the legal process to adopt Ben. Unlike Colleen, Kate is a very responsible person, and she has built her life around that child. Ben knows about Colleen, no one has lied to him, but in every way except by accident of birth, Kate is his mother."

He nodded gravely. "What have you said to him about his father? I'm sure the question must have come up."

Her clasped hands tightened. "Yes, it did. We told him that his father was dead."

His face became very stern. "I thought you said you didn't lie to him."

She took a deep breath. "If you look at the situation objectively, Daniel, you will see that we acted in Ben's best interest. We knew nothing about who his father was. All

Colleen told us was that it wasn't Marty—for which I thanked God every night. What were we to tell Ben? That his mother slept with an unknown man and that was how he was conceived? We couldn't be so brutal. Every child needs to feel that he was wanted, so we told him his father died before he was born, and that was why Colleen came home to us. He accepted the explanation. After all, his mother had died. Why not his father, too?"

Daniel's stern look had not lifted with this explanation. "One day he will start to ask more questions."

"I know that, and I have been dreading them." She smiled at him. "But now we won't have to cross that bridge. Ben will have a father after all."

"Yes," he replied emphatically. "He will." There was no wave in the lock of black hair that had fallen across his forehead; it was as shiny and straight as Ben's. He went on, "I want him to know the truth. I want him to know that I didn't learn of his existence until one week ago. I don't want him to think I have neglected him all these years."

"I can understand that."

The strong fingers that were resting on the arm of his chair tightened. "Will your daughter understand as well? Or will she try to poison his mind against me?"

"Kate is the most truthful person that I know. She is incapable of dissembling. She will tell Ben the truth."

He lifted a sardonic eyebrow. "If she is incapable of dissembling, then she won't be able to disguise the fact that she can't stand me. It's not going to be easy to start a relationship with Ben if he thinks his mother hates me."

"Kate doesn't hate you, Daniel. How could she? She doesn't even know you." Molly didn't like having to defend her daughter, and her voice came out sharper than she had intended.

"She pointed that out. She said she didn't like the idea that someone she knew nothing about would be in a position to influence Ben."

Molly gestured with her hand, and said mildly, "Surely her reservations are only natural."

He shook his head in disagreement. "If she truly loves the boy, I should think she would be glad to know he has a father. It's not natural for a boy to be raised by two women. He needs a man in his life."

The fact that Molly agreed with this statement didn't mean she liked hearing it from his lips. "I think you will find that Ben is a perfectly normal little boy," she said. "And I have always thought that it would be beneficial for both Kate and Ben if she got married."

"Why isn't she married?"

She looked for a long moment into the lean, proud face of her grandson's father. Then, "Why aren't you married?" she returned.

Nothing about his face changed, and she had a swift insight that, unlike Kate, Daniel was quite adept at dissembling. He said, "I just haven't met the right person."

"Neither has Kate," she shot back.

He gave her a charming smile. "I am looking, Mrs. Foley. I go out with women. Does Kate go out with men?"

Molly sat straighter in her chair, and said evenly, "Kate runs a training and lesson stable, Daniel. She starts work in the barn at six o'clock in the morning, and she isn't finished until she does her last barn check at nine o'clock at night. The time she does not spend with the horses and clients, she spends with Ben. She hasn't much time for socializing."

He looked skeptical. "Does she need to work that hard?"

"Yes, if the farm is to produce the sort of income it produced last year. I wish she didn't have to work so hard, but she does."

He said grandly, "Well, money will no longer be a problem. I will be happy to take care of the mother and the grandmother of my child."

Molly leaned forward in alarm. "Daniel, please don't try to play King Cophetua riding to the rescue of the beggar maid and her mother. Believe me, nothing would outrage Kate more. She loves what she does, and she is very good at it. If you want to be friends with Kate, and surely that is the desirable course of action, don't offer her money."

He said stiffly, "I didn't mean to insult you, Mrs. Foley."

She smiled. "I know you didn't. But Kate is fully as proud as I'm sure you are yourself. Would you like a stranger coming in, asserting claims to your child, and offering you money?"

He gave her a charmingly rueful look. "No."

"Of course you wouldn't. If you treat Kate the way you would want to be treated were you in her situation, she will come around. She loves Ben very much, you know. She wants him to be happy."

He nodded slowly.

She changed her tone, and said briskly, "So, then, why don't you give me the name and phone number of your attorney, and we will start the proceedings needed to establish your paternity."

He gave her a blinding smile and reached for his wallet. "I have his card to give to you."

That smile could qualify as one of the wonders of the world, she thought with amusement as she reached out her hand to take the business card he was offering.

She walked with him down to the riding ring and watched while he said good-bye to Ben. The little boy was ecstatic at meeting one of his heroes and chattered all the way back to the house, and the whole while she was putting away the groceries, about the wonders of Daniel Montero.

Ben did his homework while Molly made dinner, then the two of them ate together, with Molly putting a plate in the refrigerator for Kate to eat when she came in. Ben had a bath and watched the two Nickelodeon shows he was allowed to watch in the evening, then sat at the kitchen table with his Legos while Kate ate her dinner. Then Kate listened to him read a book and put him to bed.

Molly braced herself for the inevitable storm as she heard Kate coming back downstairs. She had put the Yankee game on after Ben's shows were finished, and she lowered the sound as her daughter came into the room.

"I am going to kill Marty Lockwood," Kate said. "I am going to eat his heart in the marketplace."

Her eyes were glittering. She meant it.

Molly sighed. "Eating Marty's heart won't make Daniel Montero go away, Kate. The damage has been done."

"Damage?" Kate said dangerously. She sat on the blue sofa and glared at her mother. "I thought you thought it was wonderful to find that Ben has a father."

Molly prudently turned off the ball game. "We always knew that Ben had a father, dear."

"Don't play word games, Mom." Kate ran her fingers through her short, feathery hair. "What are we going to do?"

Molly answered calmly, "We're going to have the DNA testing done, and when Daniel's paternity is established—as it will be, Kate,—we will tell Ben."

"Ben will be thrilled." The expression on Kate's face was bleak.

Molly leaned a little forward. "Ben will take his cue from you, dear. If you act as if you don't like or trust Daniel, then

Ben won't be able to feel thrilled. The signals that you send to Ben about Daniel are very important, Kate." She held her daughter's eyes, and said slowly and clearly, "He should not be made to feel guilty about being glad he has a father."

Kate scowled. "Mom, we don't know a damn thing about this man—other than that he's a good pitcher. He looks good, I'll grant you that, but so did Marty look good once. For all we know, Montero's the most morally corrupt person in the world. Colleen's record for picking men was not exactly stellar."

"I know he's kind," Molly said. "He told me about Colleen, and he said nothing but good things about her."

Kate made an impatient gesture. "There's nothing bad to say about Colleen—except that she had terrible taste in men."

"She had his baby and never told him. Clearly he isn't happy about that."

"Yes, and the more I think about it, the stranger I find it that he should be so determined to latch on to Ben. If he wants a kid so much, why doesn't he get married and have one?"

"He told me he hasn't found the right person to marry yet."

Kate snorted. "Then he's been looking in the wrong places."

A little silence fell as Molly regarded her daughter. At last she said quietly, "Perhaps he's like you. Perhaps he hasn't had the time."

Kate's lip curled. "I seriously doubt that, Mom."

This line of discussion was going nowhere, so Molly changed the subject. "The DNA test is going to be a match. Anyone who looks at Ben and Daniel together would know that. You are going to have to face the fact that Ben has a father, Kate. And maybe that's not a bad thing. You know I have always thought it would be good for him to have a man in his life."

"He has George."

"George is your friend, not Ben's."

"George is always very nice to Ben." Kate sounded a little defensive.

"He's nice to him, but the two of them have nothing in common. All George knows and talks about is horses, which is why you find him so fascinating. Ben is just not that interested in horses, Kate."

"I need to find a Western barn for him. Once he sees that other boys ride horses, he'll become more interested."

"He is interested in playing soccer and in the spring he wants to play Little League. Those are Ben's interests."

"Let's not fight, Mom."

"I wasn't fighting. I am merely trying to point out that Daniel Montero is not going to go away, and you are going to have to deal with him. It's not his fault that he never knew about Ben."

Kate stared at her short-nailed, ringless hands. "Maybe Colleen never wanted him to know. Maybe she knew something about him that we don't know."

"Like what?"

Kate looked up. "Maybe he deals drugs. He's Colombian, you know."

Molly said with real indignation, "I can't believe you just said that."

A little color stained Kate's cheeks. "What's your problem, Mom?"

"What would you have said to someone who called your father an IRA terrorist just because he was Irish?"

For a long moment the two women stared at each other.

Then Kate said, "Oh, all right, so he's not a drug dealer because he's Colombian. But that doesn't mean that there isn't something unsavory about him that Colleen knew and we don't."

"You are determined to dislike him, aren't you?"

Kate didn't reply, but the expression on her face was not encouraging.

"Honey, it's very important for Ben's sake that you don't appear to dislike Daniel. Let the child be happy that he has a father."

Still Kate said nothing.

Molly tried again. "Love is not just about giving, you know. It's also about giving up. I know it will be hard for you to share Ben, but he won't love you any less."

"This isn't about me, Mom! It's about Ben. Do you know how terrified I am that he is going to be hurt by this man? He's a new toy for Montero just now—a kid who looks just like him. But what happens when Montero gets tired of him, or when he gets married and has other children and doesn't have time anymore for Ben? Ben's heart will break, that's what will happen." The thinly sculpted bones of Kate's face looked to be pressing against her finely textured skin. "I don't trust this man, Mom. I think he's going to hurt my child, and there doesn't seem to be a damn thing I can do about it."

"Oh, honey." Molly went to sit beside Kate on the sofa and put an arm around her tense shoulders. "Try not to think like that. He seems to be a nice man. He went to the trouble of seeking Ben out, after all. And I like what I saw on his face when he was saying good-bye."

None of the tension left Kate's shoulders, and the set of her mouth looked scornful.

Molly dropped her arm. "Well, there isn't anything we can do until the DNA testing comes back."

"No," Kate agreed. "There isn't anything we can do." All of the scorn had left her voice. She sounded desolate.

5

The Yankees clinched the American League East on the day that Daniel got the results of the DNA test. His attorney phoned him while he was driving to the stadium for the game.

"It's positive," Luis Sanchez told him. "The boy is definitely yours."

After that, the game was an anticlimax. The good thing about clinching, Daniel thought, as he drank champagne in the celebratory clubhouse, was that the remainder of the season's games didn't mean very much, and he thought that Joe would give him some personal time if he needed it.

The following morning, Daniel got on the phone and called his parents in Colombia. His father picked up the phone first.

Daniel said in Spanish, "Papa, I have some news for you. I have discovered that I have a son."

"What? Are you certain? How did this happen?"

He drew a deep breath to steady his voice and related the entire story, concluding with the positive DNA identification. His mother must have walked into the room halfway through his explanation because he could hear his father relaying some of the information to her.

"But this is wonderful news, Daniel! Have you seen the child?"

"Yes. He looks like me."

His father said to his mother, "He looks like Daniel." Then to Daniel, "Have you spoken to the aunt? How did she take the news?"

In the background his mother exclaimed, "How could she be anything but happy?"

Daniel thought of Kate's hostile face and winced. "She's . . . cautious," he replied.

"I can understand that. She doesn't know you."

"You would like her, Papa. She's a riding teacher."

"Really?" Sharpened interest colored Rafael Montero's voice. "What kind of riding does she teach?"

"I'm not sure, Papa, but I will find out for you."

"Do that. Wait a moment, your mother wants to speak to you."

Daniel braced himself and when he heard his mother's voice he said as calmly as he could, "Hello, Mama."

"Daniel, I am so excited! I have a grandchild! How old is he? Does he really look like you?"

"He's seven years old, Mama, and he looks very much like me."

"I can't wait. I will see him when I come for the World Series."

"We aren't in the World Series yet, Mama."

"You will be. You are always in the World Series. Oh, I am so excited, Daniel! Can you send us a picture?"

Daniel blew out his breath and looked at the painting of his parents' ranch that hung upon his office wall. "I'll try. Can I speak to Papa again?"

"Certainly. I am so happy for you, my son."

"Thank you, Mama. I'm happy for myself."

His father came on the line. "Daniel?"

"Papa, my relationship with Ben's family is very delicate just now. We have to work out custody arrangements . . . Ben hasn't even been told of my existence yet."

His father cut in, "If you are asking me to keep your mother home, forget it."

Daniel sighed. "Oh, all right."

"We'll wait until the World Series. You should have things settled by then."

"I hope so."

As soon as Daniel hung up, he rang his attorney. Luis was out of the office, his secretary informed Daniel, but she would have him call as soon as he got in.

Daniel pulled up some figures on the computer for his charitable foundation, but he sat staring at them sightlessly, his mind involved with thoughts of Ben.

I wonder if I could get joint custody? Ben could live with me during the off-season and with his mother for the rest of the year.

This pleasing fantasy kept him occupied until the phone rang, and he picked it up to hear his lawyer's voice say, "I've set a meeting for tomorrow at eleven in the office of Miss Foley's attorney in Glendale. I think it would be best for all of the principals in the case to get together and see if we can come up with a solution that will be in the best interests of the boy. Miss Foley and her mother will be there, and I'd like you to attend as well, Daniel."

"Of course."

"The feeling I got from Miss Foley's attorney was that she was prepared to be reasonable about money."

Daniel made an impatient gesture. "The money is not the issue with me, Luis. The issue is that I want shared custody of my son."

"What do you mean by shared custody?"

"I mean that he will live with me from November through January. I have done some reading on this subject and the courts appear to be granting such custodial solutions more frequently these days."

"The boy goes to school, Daniel. You can't just shuffle him back and forth from one school district to the other."

This was one of the things he had just been thinking about. "That wouldn't be necessary. Glendale is not that far from Greenwich. I will drive him to school and pick him up."

"I don't know, Daniel. I think you may be asking for too much. What about asking for one day a week and one weekend a month?"

Daniel scowled.

"Daniel?"

"That's not enough."

"We want to settle this amicably, Daniel. This is not something you want to end up in court. It won't benefit you, and it won't benefit the child to have a custody battle emblazoned all over the newspapers."

"We won't know if Miss Foley objects to shared custody unless we ask her."

"Fair enough. I'll draft a letter and fax it to John Burnham, Miss Foley's attorney. But think about another custody arrangement that you can live with, Daniel. I simply cannot see Miss Foley turning the boy over to you for three straight months a year. And you must ask yourself, will the child want to be without his mother for such a long period of time?"

"He could see her! We both live in Fairfield County."

"He's only seven years old. Seven-year-olds need their mothers. I know because I have one."

Silence.

"If I hear anything back from Burnham, I'll let you know."

"All right. Thanks, Luis."

"You're welcome. And good luck at the game tonight."

"Thanks."

"See you tomorrow."

The two men rang off.

Daniel was still staring at the screensaver floating across his monitor when the phone rang again. He picked it up, as he sometimes did, and said, "Hello."

A woman's voice said, "I would like to speak to Daniel Montero, please. This is Kate Foley calling."

Daniel's mouth went suddenly dry. "This is he."

"I suppose you have heard the results of the DNA test, Mr. Montero."

"Yes, I have."

"I have told Ben, and he wants to see you. Could you come to the house this evening?"

Daniel took a deep, steadying breath. "I have a game this evening, Miss Foley. But I could come to see Ben right after school."

"I suppose that would be all right." Her flat tone did not bespeak enthusiasm.

"W . . . what did he say when you told him?"

"He had a lot of questions. I told him that Colleen had never given us your name, nor had she told you about her pregnancy. He is having a hard time understanding why she did that. Otherwise, I would say he is delighted."

His son was delighted. Daniel smiled. "What time does Ben get home from school?"

"The bus stops at our house at three-ten."

"I'll be at the house before three, then."

"All right. I'll pick him up at the bus as usual and bring him back to the house. You can see him then."

"All right."

"I just have one further thing to say, Mr. Montero."

"What is that?"

"If you ever hurt Ben, you will have me to deal with. And I will make you pay."

She sounded deadly serious.

"I would never hurt Ben, Miss Foley." He tried to project his sincerity into his voice.

"Good. I'll see you tomorrow at about three." And she hung up.

Telling Ben about Daniel was one of the hardest things Kate had ever done in her life.

"I have something to tell you, Ben," she had begun when he was sitting up in bed the night before, waiting for her to listen to him read.

He looked at her warily. Something in her voice must have cued him that what she was about to say wasn't pleasant.

She forced a smile, and said, "It's good news, honey, so take that worried look off your face."

His eyes brightened. "Is Daniel Montero coming back to see you again, Mommy?"

She was sitting on the bed, facing him. He was so close, but somehow he seemed far away from her. That man had already come between them. She cleared her throat. "Actually, Ben, Daniel Montero is coming back to see you."

Ben's eyes opened wide. "*Me?* Why would he want to see me?"

This was it. "You know how Nana and I have always told you that your father was dead?"

"Yes."

"Well, we told you what we thought was the truth. But it seems that we were wrong. Your father is alive, only he didn't know that he was your father until recently."

Ben's eyes were enormous. "My father is alive?"

"Yes, Ben, your father is alive. And"—she drew another steadying breath—"he is Daniel Montero."

Ben stared at her blankly. "Daniel Montero is my father?"

"Yes, Ben."

Ben shook his head, as if to rid himself of a pesky insect. "But how can that be, Mommy? I don't understand."

"I will try to explain it." Kate picked up her son's hand. "Colleen, your mother, and Daniel Montero were lovers. This means that they lived together like married people, only they weren't married. Colleen got pregnant, but she never told Daniel. She thought he was too poor to help her, so she came home to Nana and me. But she never told us the name of the man whose baby she was carrying. Nana and I assumed he was dead." She looked at him worriedly. "Are you getting this?"

His fingers were tense in her hand. "Colleen was having me but she never told Daniel?"

"That's right."

"But why would she do that, Mommy?"

"Daniel was only a minor-league player at the time, Ben. She must have thought he was too poor to help her."

"But didn't she know that I would need a father? And why didn't they get married?"

Kate felt like weeping. How could she possibly explain this situation to Ben and make it sound as if his parents had had his best interests in mind? She said carefully, "I don't know why they didn't marry, Ben. You'll have to ask Mr. . . . your father . . . that question. All I can tell you is that Colleen came home to Nana and me, and we took care of her until you were born. Then, when Colleen died, I adopted you. But you know that part."

His face was slightly flushed. "She never told him? Even after I was born, she never told him?"

"Ben . . ." She drew a deep breath. "Colleen died when you were only six months old. If she had lived, I'm sure she would have told him eventually."

Once she found out how much money he was worth.

Ben's eyes were very bright. "Was Daniel mad when he found out?"

She said cautiously, "Mad about what?"

"Mad at Colleen that she didn't tell him."

She replied honestly. "I think his main feeling is happiness, Ben. He is so happy to learn he has you for a son that he doesn't have any room inside to be angry."

Ben's face suddenly lit, as if a lamp had been turned on inside him. "Daniel Montero is my father. Mommy! Just wait until Connor finds out."

This conversation was going through Kate's mind as she sat at a conference table in her attorney's office awaiting the arrival of Daniel Montero and his attorney. She had sent an electric Ben off to school this morning with the promise that she would try to arrange a meeting between him and Daniel, and the warning not to say anything to anyone—not even Connor—until "things" had been decided.

Daniel came in, conservatively dressed in a navy blue blazer, white shirt, blue tie, and gray trousers. A slender man of medium height, with brown hair and golden brown eyes, accompanied him. The second man introduced himself to John Burnham as Luis Sanchez, Mr. Montero's attorney. Then Daniel shook hands with Mr. Burnham, and the two newcomers came over to greet and shake hands with Kate and Molly.

Daniel seemed to fill up the room. *It's because he's so much bigger than anybody else here*, Kate thought as she watched him take the chair directly across the table from her. But she had a feeling that he filled up most rooms; there was something about him that commanded attention, and it wasn't just his size.

John Burnham started the conversation. "I received your fax yesterday, Luis, and I have to tell you that the terms are unacceptable. The Foleys will not agree to joint custody."

You're damn right, Kate thought. Every time she thought of Montero's nerve in asking for joint custody, her blood boiled. But John Burnham had assured her that, without her agreement, Daniel had almost no chance of obtaining such a ruling. So she watched him carefully as he received the news.

For the briefest of moments, he looked stricken. Then he pulled himself together and turned his eyes to her. "You have had him for the first seven years of his life," he said. "Surely you will not begrudge me a share in the years to come?"

Her attorney spared her the necessity of answering. "Miss Foley did not say that she begrudged you a share, Mr. Montero. She said she will not give you joint custody."

Luis Sanchez said smoothly, "Then you are willing to agree to some custody-sharing arrangement?"

Kate knew that she could not keep this man out of Ben's life. She knew that she was going to have to trust him with her son. But she wanted those occasions to be strictly limited.

Burnham replied, "We are willing to allow Mr. Montero visitation rights. He may have the boy one weekend a month, and he may see him one day during the week as well. That is our best offer. Take it or leave it."

Kate's eyes went to Daniel's face. It was a polite mask of

attention, but she had seen that stricken look. What was he thinking?

Luis Sanchez did not even glance at Daniel. "Let Mr. Montero have the boy every other weekend, and we'll take it."

Kate said directly to Daniel. "You play baseball on the weekends. What are you going to do? Leave him with a baby-sitter?"

His brown eyes met hers, and she felt a little thrill of something go through her. He was trying to stay calm, but he was angry. "I don't play baseball November through January, Miss Foley. That's why I wanted full custody during those months."

Kate's eyes narrowed. "If you think I'm turning my son over to you for three months, you're crazy."

Luis Sanchez spoke in a soothing voice, "We understand your feelings on this matter, Miss Foley, and we have dropped that request. But surely Daniel could have the boy every other weekend during the months of November, December, and January."

"And for a few weeks in the summer as well," Daniel put in. "He can visit my parents' ranch in Colombia."

Fear knifed through Kate. "Ben is not going to Colombia," she told Daniel. "They kidnap anything that moves down there. The son of a big baseball star would be a temptation to all of the factions who use kidnappings to extort money."

Daniel's eyes began to glitter in the same way Ben's did when he was angry. "Your mother has had the pleasure of her grandchild's company for seven years. My mother deserves the right to get to know her grandson as well."

Kate opened her lips to reply, but Molly's voice overrode hers. "Of course she does, Daniel. But Kate is right. Colombia is too dangerous just now. Perhaps your parents could visit you for a few weeks in the summer and Ben could stay at your house right here in Connecticut."

"Mom!" Kate gave her mother an outraged look.

Her mother put her hand over Kate's. "Daniel is right, dear. His parents deserve to have some time with Ben. In fact, I am glad that they feel this way about an illegitimate child."

Kate's, "Don't call Ben that!" clashed with Daniel's, "Don't speak of him that way!"

Molly smiled. "Very well. But I think we have to give Daniel a few weeks of Ben's summer vacation, dear."

There was little Kate could say; her mother had cut the ground from under her feet. She gave Daniel a dark look. "All right. As long as he stays in Connecticut."

"I will respect your wish in that regard, Miss Foley." He turned to John Burnham. "Perhaps I could have him for a few weeks in the winter as well."

"Ben is in school," Kate said quickly.

"I will drive him to school and pick him up."

"I'm giving you enough time already," she said fiercely.

Luis Sanchez said, "I don't think it is unreasonable for us to ask for another few weeks, Miss Foley. In most custody cases, the noncustodial parent does get to spend vacation time with the child. Mr. Montero's vacation happens to fall in the winter."

Kate looked at her own attorney. "Can we put in the agreement that Ben has to agree to these 'visits'?"

Luis Sanchez answered, "That is not usually part of a custody arrangement."

"I don't mind," Daniel said.

Luis said, "I don't think it's a good idea, Daniel. There is nothing to stop Miss Foley from influencing the boy to say he doesn't want to spend time with you."

Daniel's eyes met hers. "I don't think she would do that."

"Why not?" Kate shot back.

"Ben told me that you hate liars, and you would have to lie to him to turn him against me."

Kate's narrow nostrils quivered.

"Very well," Luis Sanchez said. "We will accept the stipulation."

Damn, Kate thought unhappily. She had given Daniel more time than she had intended to.

John Burnham said, "In regard to child support."

Luis Sanchez sat straighter. "Of course we will agree to pay a reasonable child support. Do you have a sum in mind?"

"Miss Foley would like Mr. Montero to establish a college fund for Ben and to deposit enough funds in it so that Ben's education will be paid for."

"Of course," Daniel said impatiently.

"And the child support?" Sanchez said.

John Burnham looked from Kate to Molly, his mouth set in a grim line. "The Foleys do not wish to receive any money from Mr. Montero for Ben's upbringing. I might add that they do this against my strongest advice."

Molly said, "Daniel can buy him presents and take him shopping for clothes if he wishes, but Kate and I are perfectly able to pay for his needs."

"Are you serious?" Luis Sanchez asked with disbelief.

"Perfectly serious, Mr. Sanchez," Molly said.

"It's ridiculous," Daniel said. "I have a lot of money. I want some of it to go to my son."

You want to buy him, you mean, Kate thought.

"Do you know how expensive a college education is

today, Mr. Montero?" Molly asked humorously. "You will be contributing greatly if you send him through school."

Daniel leaned forward. "You yourself told me that your daughter has to work very hard to make the money needed to support your household, Mrs. Foley. Well, she will not need to work so hard if you will let me help you."

Kate felt stabbed in the back. "How could you say such a thing, Mom? I work hard because I want to. I have a successful teaching and riding barn, and I'm proud of what I've done. I'm not taking any handouts from anyone."

"I'm not anyone. I'm Ben's father, for God's sake!"

Unfortunately, Kate thought bitterly. "I know you're his father. We just established your rights to see him, remember? But I'm his mother. I have been taking care of him just fine for seven years, and I shall continue to do so without your help. I do not want any money from you, Mr. Montero. Is that clear?"

They stared at each other, and the roused hostility between them seemed to spark in the air. Kate felt suddenly breathless. She had a sudden insight that he would make a formidable enemy, this man. The clean bones and planes of his face suddenly looked very hard, and his eyes had begun to glitter.

"Very clear," he said.

A little silence fell, then Luis Sanchez said, "If that is all, then, I suggest I get the legal paperwork started. I'll fax a copy for you to review, John, before we have them drawn up for signing."

Daniel turned away from Kate. "Mr. Burnham, you can't allow your client to do something as foolish as accepting no child support from me."

Didn't he hear what I just said? Kate thought incredulously. When she spoke in that tone of voice, she was used to people listening.

Burnham replied, "Believe me, Mr. Montero, I feel even more strongly about this than you do. But I've known Kate since she was a small child, and once she makes up her mind, a blast of dynamite won't change it. She doesn't want any child support."

Kate said through her teeth, "My mother and I are perfectly capable of supporting Ben. We did just fine until you came along, and we don't need your money."

Molly stood up. "Thank you so much, John, but I need to get back to school. I'm giving an exam to my juniors this afternoon."

Kate stood up as well. "And I have a client coming for a lesson."

The two women stood poised, as if ready for flight.

"I will be by at about two-forty-five this afternoon to meet my son," Daniel said.

"Fine," Kate snapped, turning her back on him and walking out of the room.

6

$\mathcal{M}$olly arrived at the big brick building that was Glendale High School without remembering how she got there, her mind had been so preoccupied during the drive. Gil Stapleton, a science teacher, was standing near the back entrance, inhaling a cigarette. "Haven't you kicked that habit yet, Gil?" Molly asked as she drew abreast of him. "Do you enjoy huddling out here with all your addicted students?" Molly had lost her husband to lung cancer and had absolutely no tolerance of smoking.

"That's the key word, Molly. Addicted. Believe me, I'd stop if I could."

Molly cast him the skeptical look of a nonsmoker and went into the building. She signed in at the front office, collected her mail, and headed for the teachers' room to run off copies of the test she was giving in a half an hour. As she stood next to the copy machine, watching it spit out the papers she needed, her mind once more went back to the morning's meeting.

They had been lucky that Daniel had been reasonable about the custody arrangements. And Kate had surprised Molly by agreeing to let Daniel have Ben for a few weeks in the winter, although she had added the stipulation that Ben had to agree. She must understand how much Ben needed a father; nothing else would have made her agree to such an arrangement.

Molly understood the reason behind her daughter's over-protectiveness of Ben. Kate was not someone who gave her heart often, and two of the four people she had loved in this world had died and left her. The loss of a father and a sister would have been difficult and painful for anyone, but for Kate, whose emotions were focused so much more narrowly than most people's, the deaths of Tim and Colleen had been devastating. They had turned her daughter, who had been an utterly fearless child, into a tigress always in defense of her young.

Molly sighed. She sometimes felt the same overprotec-tiveness for Kate that Kate felt for Ben. It wasn't safe to shut out the world and give your love to so few people. Kate knew many people, but they existed on the periphery of her emo-tional life. She loved her dog and her horses more than she did any person who wasn't Molly or Ben. *It isn't safe*, Molly thought again as she went into the bathroom to comb her short blond hair.

She was evening out the papers she had run off when the teachers' room door opened and a young man walked in. He said, "Hi, Molly. I covered your second period class for you. Whew! They're a lively bunch."

"They are, but they're good kids. Not terribly interested in English literature, unfortunately."

"We played charades. They had to act out the title of a book or a play or a poem they've read during their high school English career."

Molly laughed. "I'll bet they loved that."

"They had a blast."

"Thanks, Ken, for covering. I had to meet with my attorney this morning."

"No problem," the young man replied pleasantly.

Ken was one of the numerous men who had asked Kate out only to be rejected because she "didn't have time." He was a nice young man, and Molly liked him. Unfortunately, he was now engaged to someone else.

They remained chatting about a film Ken had seen the previous evening, then the bell rang, and Molly went off to give her test.

Daniel drove up the long, narrow, tree-lined driveway of High Meadow Farm and parked his Mercedes. He sat for a few minutes, trying to collect himself.

He had told his manager about Ben the day before and had gotten Joe's permission to be late to the park. So here he sat, the man who had pitched the Yankees to three World Series championships, shaking in his shoes at the thought of meeting a little boy.

He had been trying all day to imagine what Ben must feel like, but his imagination had been unproductive. *Will he be pleased? Will he be angry? Will he have picked up on his mother's dislike of me?* All of these questions went through his mind, but he could answer none of them.

At ten to three, Kate came out of the house, followed by her dog. She crossed to the car, and Daniel got out. She looked up at him, and her boyishly cut hair shone blue as a raven's wing in the sunshine.

It was a true black, Daniel found himself thinking, unlike his own, which shone brown in the light.

"Come on in," she said impatiently. "There's no point in sitting out here like an unwelcome suitor."

He went with her back to the house, thinking, *But I am unwelcome. You've made little attempt to hide that fact.*

He followed her in the front door, then into the comfortable blue-and-white living room. She said, "I'll go and collect Ben from the bus stop. You can wait here. I'll send him in when we get back. When you've finished talking to him, you can come into the kitchen. Ben usually has a snack when he gets home from school."

"Do you always wait for him at the bus stop?" he asked curiously.

"Usually I do, and if I'm tied up with something, I send Cyrus." At the sound of his name, the dog lifted his head and looked at her.

"I'm going now," she said.

He watched her leave the room. She was wearing jeans, a long-sleeved blue shirt, and laced brown paddock boots and, from the back, with her short hair and slender frame, she could have been mistaken for a boy.

Not from the front, however, he thought. No one would ever mistakenly think that face was masculine.

It was fifteen minutes before Daniel heard the front door open. Then there was the sound of a dog's nails on the bare floor, and Kate said, "Go on into the living room, Ben. I'll be in the kitchen if you want me."

A floorboard creaked, then someone was opening the living room door. Daniel stood with his back to the windows, his heart in his mouth, as Ben came into the room.

"Hello," the little boy said shyly. "Mommy says that you're my father." He was dressed in jeans, sneakers, and a striped and collared knit shirt.

Daniel held out his hands. "Yes, I am, Ben. And I'm so happy that I've found you."

Ben crossed the room toward Daniel's welcoming arms

and allowed himself to be embraced. But Daniel felt the stiffness in his son's small body and did not attempt to hold on to him. He released him and smiled downward. "Why don't we sit? I imagine you have some questions you would like to ask me."

Ben's beautiful, little-boy face was grave. "Yes, I do."

Daniel sat on the blue-and-white patterned sofa and drew Ben to sit beside him. "Shoot," he said.

"Why didn't you come before?" Ben said.

Daniel had known this must be coming and had done his best to prepare an answer. "Let me tell you a story that may help explain why I didn't," he said.

Ben's eyes were trained on his face. "All right."

With difficulty, Daniel refrained from touching his son. He began the story he had thought up on the drive to Glendale. "Once upon a time there was a beautiful young girl who ran away from home because she wanted adventure. But the man she ran away with wasn't Prince Charming. He didn't take good care of her, and she decided she didn't want to stay with him. Then she met another man who she liked better. This young man was a baseball player, and he liked her, too. So she left the bad man and went to live with the baseball player." He looked down into Ben's grave eyes. "Are you getting this so far?"

"Is my mother—Colleen—the beautiful young girl?"

"Yes."

"And you're the baseball player?"

"That's right."

Ben nodded. "But if they liked each other so much, why didn't they get married?"

"They were both very young, Ben. They didn't think they were ready for something as serious as marriage. But then the young girl—Colleen—found out she was going to have a baby."

"Me."

"That's right. You. And knowing that she was going to be a mother made her grow up very fast. She realized that she had to have a home and security for her baby, and she decided that the best place to find both these things was in her own home with her own family. She thought the baseball player was too young and too poor and too . . . frivolous . . . to marry."

Ben's fine, straight brows drew together. "What does frivolous mean?"

"It means he wasn't serious. All he thought about was baseball. He wasn't interested in anything else. She didn't think he'd be a help to her."

For the first time, Ben's gaze fell away, and he looked at his feet. "Is that true?"

"Is what true?"

"That you wouldn't have been a help to her."

"No, it's not true. I would have helped her. But she didn't know that, Ben."

"Would you have been glad that you were having a baby?"

Daniel looked at his son's bent head. "Yes," he said. "I would have been glad."

Whether that was true or not, he didn't know. What he did know was that his son needed to hear those words from him.

Ben lifted his head. A little color had crept into his pale face.

Daniel said, "So what happened was that Colleen left the baseball player without telling him she was having a baby and went home to her mother and her sister. They took excellent care of her and her baby and then, when Colleen died, her sister adopted you as her own child."

"Mommy."

"Yes. Your mommy."

"But how did you find out about me?"

"The man that Colleen ran away with and later left came to your house one day and saw you. He saw how much you look like me, and he guessed what had happened. He was the one who told me about you."

For the first time normal color returned to Ben's warm olive skin. "Do we look alike?" he asked shyly.

"You look exactly as I did when I was your age. One day I'll show you some pictures."

Ben's eyes sparkled. "Then you really are my father?"

"I really am your father. And I am sorry that I wasn't around for you before, but I hope you'll let me be part of your life now. I'm so happy that I found you."

Ben smiled and Daniel's heart swelled. "I'm happy, too," Ben said.

This time when Daniel embraced him, the small body relaxed and leaned against him. Daniel buried his lips in the shiny dark hair and shut his eyes to hold back tears.

"Can I call you Daddy?" Ben asked into his shoulder.

He relaxed his arms and looked down into Ben's face. "I would love it if you would call me Daddy."

The little boy gave an excited jump. "Can I tell my friends who you are?"

"Certainly."

"Wow," Ben said. "This is so cool."

Daniel laughed a little shakily. "Your mom and I are working it out that you can spend one day a week and two weekends a month with me," Daniel said.

"Oh." The word sounded startled. "Then you're not going to live with us?"

Daniel felt a pain stab his heart at those artless words. "I can't live with you, Ben. Your mom and I aren't married. And I presume you want to continue living with her, not with me."

"You lived with Colleen, and you weren't married."

"That's true, but this is different."

"How?"

Daniel tried to speak calmly and logically. "Your mother and I hardly know each other. It will be better if we live separately, and you come to visit me."

"I know. Like Andy's parents," Ben said sadly. "They don't like each other either."

"I didn't say I didn't like your mother," Daniel said hastily. "I just said I don't know her."

"Maybe Mommy can come to visit you, too. That way you'll get to know each other."

"We'll see," Daniel temporized. "Right now the important thing is for you and I to get to know each other."

"Can I come watch you pitch?"

"Of course you can. In fact, I'm due to pitch Sunday afternoon. Would you like to come to the game?"

Ben clapped his hands. "Yes! Yes! Yes!"

"Great. Tell you what, let's go into the kitchen for a snack and you can tell your mom about coming to the game Sunday."

"Okay." Ben jumped to his feet. "Do you like milk and cookies?"

"I love milk and cookies."

"Or you could have a cup of coffee. That's what Mommy does."

"Coffee would be great."

"Come on," Ben said. "Let's go."

*   *   *

Kate was sitting at the kitchen table drinking a cup of coffee when they came in. One look at Ben's radiant face told her that the interview had gone well. She forced a smile and thought, *Please God, let this man turn out to be a good father to Ben.*

"Guess what, Mommy! My daddy said I could come to his game on Sunday. He's going to pitch!"

"I hope you will come too," Daniel said quickly. "And your mother as well. I would like to take you all out to dinner afterward."

I need to get to know this man, Kate thought. *I need to find out if I can trust him with Ben.*

"Thank you," she said to Daniel. "That would be very nice."

"Can we have some cookies?" Ben asked. "We're hungry."

He was so transparently happy with his marvelous new "Daddy" that Kate's heart cramped with fear. Could this man possibly realize the treasure he was plucking so casually out of her home? "Of course you can have some cookies. Do you like oatmeal-raisin, Mr. Montero?"

"Please call me Daniel. And yes, I like oatmeal-raisin."

"I want milk, but Daddy wants coffee."

Meeting the sparkling eyes of her son, Kate smiled. "Coming right up, my lord." She sketched a bow. "Will there be anything else I can get for you?"

Ben laughed. "No. You're so funny, Mommy."

Ears pricked, Cyrus followed her as she went to the counter to get cookies out of the cookie tin. "Cyrus gets a cookie, too," she heard Ben inform Daniel.

"As he should," Daniel replied gravely.

"Do you have a dog, Daddy?"

It seemed that Ben could not use that term enough. *I didn't realize how much he missed having a father.*

"I don't have one now, because I'm away so much. But I had several dogs when I was growing up."

Kate set the last cookie on the plate and turned to bring them to the table. "Mommy says it's not fair to have a dog if you're gone all day," Ben said. "Dogs need company."

"That is true, and that's why I don't have one. I do have a cat, though."

Kate put the plate of cookies down and looked at him in surprise. He did not seem to be the kind of man to have a cat.

"What's his name?" Ben asked.

"It's a her, and her name is Annemarie."

"Annemarie?" Kate said. "That's an odd name for a cat."

"She doesn't think so."

Kate laughed. "I imagine not." She brought a glass of milk for Ben and a cup of coffee for Daniel. For some reason she felt better knowing that he had a pet. "Do you take milk or sugar?"

"No, thank you."

She refilled her own cup and joined them at the table. "Do you have homework, Ben?"

"Just a little. I can do it after dinner."

"All right."

Ben looked from Kate to Daniel then back again to Kate. He beamed. "Now I have a family like everybody else."

Kate looked at Daniel and thought she saw a glimmer of amusement in his eyes. She said woodenly, "I'll inform the school and the parents of Ben's closest friends of what has happened."

"Thank you . . . Katharine."

"My name is Kate."

He shook his head. "Your name is Katharine . . . Katharine Foley."

"But everybody calls her Kate," Ben said around the cookie in his mouth.

"I believe I shall call her Katharine," Daniel said. He smiled at her. "A special name for the mother of my son."

Kate stared at him suspiciously. She didn't trust either his smile or the sudden warmth in his voice. He was trying to charm her, and she didn't like it. "Call me whatever you like," she said.

He finished his coffee. "Unfortunately, I have to be going. My manager gave me some time off, but I should be getting to the stadium as soon as possible."

"What time are you supposed to be at work?" Kate asked curiously.

"I usually get there between three and four. I do some throwing and they have a big spread of food, and I eat."

"I'll wear my Yankees hat on Sunday, Mommy," Ben said.

Once more she looked into his big sparkling eyes. *I have to make this work*, she thought. *For Ben's sake I have to be friendly to this man.*

"Would you like to walk me to my car?" Daniel asked Ben.

"Yeah!"

"I'll call you about Sunday," Daniel said, looking at her.

She nodded and watched as the two of them left her kitchen together. They both carried their heads the exact same way.

7

Kate stood next to Ben, her eyes focused on the solitary figure on the pitcher's mound. It was the eighth inning, there were two strikes on the man at the plate, Daniel was throwing a perfect game, and the crowd was on its feet, screaming for a strikeout.

He went into his windup, an incredibly fluid motion, and delivered the pitch.

"Ball two!" the umpire called.

"Damn," Kate said out loud.

"Damn," Ben repeated.

"You can't say that word until you're eighteen," Kate said automatically.

The stadium was packed, and all around them people were yelling words of encouragement to Daniel. The late-September day was warm enough for Kate to have taken off the cardigan of her blue sweater set, and the smell of beer and hot dogs was in the air. Ben's face was sticky from the cotton candy he had eaten earlier.

"What a fantastic way to end the season," the man next to Ben said to Kate. "A perfect game!"

When Kate was a child she had watched baseball games with her father on television, and she had really gotten into this one. When inning after inning had passed, and Daniel had not given up a hit or a walk, she found herself rooting for him as wholeheartedly as the people all around her.

Daniel went into his windup and the roar of the crowd seemed to shake the stadium. The pitch went in, and the man at the plate swung mightily. "Strike!" the umpire called, and the crowd went wild.

The inning was over and as Daniel approached the dugout he looked up at Kate and Ben, who were sitting behind it, and gave them a cocky grin. Ben grinned and waved back, and Kate smiled. The man next to Ben said, "Do you know Montero?"

Ben replied importantly, "He's my daddy."

Kate set her jaw and prepared to endure humiliation. The whole of New York knew that Daniel wasn't married.

"Well congratulations, youngster," the man said. "Your daddy is pitching a whale of a game."

"I know," Ben said. "It's *perfect*."

The man's curious gaze fixed on Kate. "The suspense must be killing you."

Kate looked at him through a wall of ice. "I'll survive."

"Ah." The man immediately took his eyes off her and fixed them back on the field. "Let's hope the Yankees can score another run here," he said to Ben. "One–nothing is a pretty tight game."

"Derek will get a hit," Ben said confidently.

Derek did in fact get a hit, but the following batters couldn't advance him beyond second base. Consequently, Daniel went into the ninth inning pitching a perfect game with a one-run lead.

Kate could not believe how involved she was with this stupid game. Her heart was beating hard, and her stomach was tight with tension. *Come on, Daniel*, she exhorted him silently. *Come on.*

The first Baltimore hitter bounced a weak grounder to the second baseman, who threw him out.

One down, two to go, Kate thought. Her hands were clenched into fists at her sides. The entire stadium was standing, and Ben climbed onto his seat so he could see over the person in front of him.

"He's got it," the woman behind her said jubilantly. "Nothing can stop him now."

Shut up, you idiot, Kate thought fiercely.

The next batter had hit a deep fly ball to left the last time he was up. "Careful, Daniel!" the man next to Ben called.

"Strike him out," Ben yelled.

Just don't let him get a hit, Kate prayed.

"Ball one," the scoreboard flashed. It was far too noisy to hear the umpire.

The next pitch was a strike, then Daniel delivered two more balls. The crowd yelped indignantly when the last pitch was called a ball, but the umpire's ruling was the law. The entire stadium tensed as Daniel delivered the three-one pitch. If he walked the batter he would still have a no-hitter, but he would have blown his perfect game.

The umpire's right arm went up, signaling a strike.

Now the count was full, and the crowd began to roar for another strike. Daniel sent in a slider, and the batter fouled it off. The crowd quieted until he went into his windup once more. The next ball was a fastball, a cutter that came in on the hands of the left-handed hitter, who swung at it futilely, missing completely.

Two out. The crowd was ecstatic.

Kate felt sick to her stomach. *This is ridiculous*, she

thought, but she couldn't seem to help herself. *He looks so alone out there.*

Strike one, the umpire signaled.

The batter fouled the second pitch off, then Daniel threw a low slider, but the batter didn't bite. The count was one-and-two, and Daniel was one strike away from pitching a perfect game.

The next strike was the pitch with which he had been getting out batters all afternoon, a high inside fastball. The batter swung late and managed to fist the ball off the handle of the bat. It flared into the air toward the shortstop. The standing crowd held its breath in anticipation. The shortstop jumped as high as he could, and the ball floated over the top of his glove to land just behind him on the outfield grass. It was a hit.

"Noooooo!" the crowd roared.

On the mound Daniel stood perfectly still as the left fielder picked up the ball and fired it into first. Then he turned around to face the plate and signaled for a new ball.

Kate, who admired grace under pressure above anything, was profoundly moved. Ben was crying. Kate leaned over and said close to his ear, so she could be heard above the roar of the crowd, which was still standing, "He's going to win this game for his team, Ben. Just watch. He won't let them beat him. And that's what really counts."

The first two pitches Daniel threw were balls and the crowd groaned with each call. "He's rattled," the man next to Ben said. "Can't really blame him. He lost a perfect game on a cheap hit that just cleared the infield. No wonder he's upset."

The third pitch Daniel threw was over the plate and the scoreboard pronounced the speed to be ninety-five miles per hour.

"Wow," Ben said, when Kate informed him of this.

The next pitch was a slider, which the batter went after and missed. Two balls and two strikes.

"Just throw it over, Daniel!" Kate yelled.

"Strike him out, Daddy!" Ben contributed.

Daniel, who usually liked to move the game along, took longer than usual before he finally went into his windup. His arm came around, the ball flew toward the plate, the batter swung. And missed.

Pandemonium reigned. The scoreboard announced the pitch to have been 97 mph. The catcher was embracing Daniel, and the rest of the infield was clustered around him, slapping his back. The crowd's ovation was deafening and, as he walked toward the dugout, Daniel looked up at Ben and Kate and tipped his hat. He smiled.

Good for you, Kate thought, and smiled back.

They had dinner at a Norwalk restaurant that was known for its casual atmosphere and terrific food. Kate, who had been afraid Ben was going to be subjected to terrifying elegance, was both relieved and pleased.

"Too bad Nana couldn't come," Ben said as he looked around with satisfaction. "She likes to eat out."

"I'm sorry too," Daniel said.

"She had to go to a special meeting at the high school," Kate said. In fact, she suspected that her mother had invented the need for her presence at the meeting so that Ben could have some time with just his mother and father.

A young waiter came over to take their drink orders. "What a bummer, Daniel," he said. "And it was such a cheap hit, too."

"These things happen," Daniel said philosophically. "That's why it's so difficult to pitch a perfect game."

Kate said she would have white wine, and Daniel ordered a bottle of chardonnay for the two of them. Ben ordered Pepsi.

Daniel said, "My father instructed me to find out what kind of riding you teach, Katharine. He breeds Andalusian horses—mostly for dressage."

"Does he?" Kate was delighted. "I've always ridden hunt seat, but lately I have become more and more interested in dressage. In fact, I've been working on it with my old Thoroughbred, and he's doing quite well."

"Does your father have a farm like us?" Ben asked.

"He has a ranch."

"Is that where you grew up?" Kate asked.

"No, he didn't buy the ranch until he retired ten years ago. When I was younger he was active in politics. In fact, he was Colombia's ambassador to the United Nations for eight years. I spent a great deal of my childhood living in New York, which is how I learned to play baseball."

"Did you play Little League?" Ben asked quickly.

"I did."

"Mommy doesn't like Little League." Ben gave her a dark look.

"I think it borders on being abusive," Kate said to Daniel a little defiantly.

"All organized sports for children have that danger," he agreed easily. "But I think it's important for children to play sports. A sport teaches mental discipline as well as physical agility and strength." He looked at her seriously. "It all depends on the coach. A good coach will get the best out of all his players without being abusive."

Kate, who knew a few riding instructors whose methods she deplored, reluctantly agreed.

Western. I did get Ben a Western saddle, and he has ridden occasionally, but he prefers his bike."

"I ride horses," Daniel said to Ben. "My father—your grandfather—rides horses. I think that is a narrow point of view to say that men don't ride."

Ben looked thoughtful. "Will you ride with me?"

"If your mother will lend me a horse, I will be glad to ride with you."

Kate was experiencing conflicting feelings. She had always been disappointed by Ben's lack of interest in horses, and any sign of notice on his part was very welcome to her. On the other hand, Daniel seemed to be worming his way into every aspect of her life. The last thing she needed was to have him hanging around all the time.

"Of course I can lend you a horse," she said. "There are some nice trails through the water company property near our farm."

"Yes!" Ben said, clenching his fist.

Daniel sipped his chardonnay. "That would be wonderful. It will have to be early on a Saturday or a Sunday, I'm afraid. I don't have any days off until the post season."

"Saturday," Ben said immediately. "My soccer game is on Sunday morning."

"And that is another bone I have to pick with organized children's sports," Kate said. "Sunday morning should be for church, but every sport schedules games on Sunday."

"Most Catholic churches have Saturday afternoon masses," Daniel pointed out.

"How do you know we're Catholic?"

"You're Irish, so I just assumed it. Was I wrong?"

"No. And that's what we do—go to church on Saturday afternoon. But I like going to church on Sunday."

"I'm sure you've had horse shows to go to on Sundays."

She had, of course, but she wasn't pleased to be reminded of that. He was very effectively shooting down all her arguments against organized sports for children, and she didn't like it.

"Can we go next Saturday?" Ben asked eagerly.

"I am sorry, Ben, but next Saturday I will be in Toronto for a three-game series. Perhaps we can do it the Saturday after that."

"Okay," Ben said.

Thank God he plays baseball, Kate thought. *Otherwise, he might just move in here*. Out loud she said, "I teach on Saturday mornings but I'll send someone along with you to show you the trails."

"I'm disappointed," Daniel said. Kate's glass was still half-full, so he poured the rest of the wine into his own glass. "I was hoping you could come."

Kate had an unerring instinct for phoniness and gave him a suspicious look, thinking he was once more trying to charm her. The brown eyes that met hers looked perfectly sincere. She shrugged. "Maybe you can convince Ben that it isn't unmasculine to ride a horse."

He laughed softly, deep in his throat. "I will try," he said. "I promise I will try."

Molly was reading a book in the living room when the baseball game threesome returned. Her eyes went immediately to her daughter's face, and relief surged through her when she saw that the hostility she had been dreading was not there.

"You should have come, Nana," Ben cried. "Daddy almost pitched a perfect game. And look! He gave me the last ball he threw!" He held up a baseball in his right hand.

"Let me see," Molly said admiringly, and took the ball

from him. "I heard all about the game on ESPN," she said to Daniel. "I'm so sorry, Daniel. To have come so close! And the hit wasn't even a good one."

He shrugged. "That's the way it goes."

"Sit down," Molly said. "Would you like an after-dinner drink?"

"Mom. He's driving." Kate sounded annoyed.

"A swallow of brandy won't hurt him."

"We had wine with dinner."

Daniel said with amusement, "Thank you, Molly, but Katharine is right. I've had enough to drink, thank you. But I would not mind another cup of coffee."

Now Kate looked annoyed. Clearly she thought it was time for him to go home. Ben, on the other hand, was thrilled. "Can I show you my baseball cards, Daddy?"

"I'd love to see them," Daniel said.

Molly said, "I'll fix the coffee."

Kate said, "I'll help you."

The two women went into the kitchen. "How was your day?" Molly asked as she filled the coffeemaker with water.

"It wasn't too bad," Kate said a little grudgingly. "The game was exciting, and he picked a pretty good restaurant. Ben ate a hamburger."

"That's good." Molly measured coffee into a filter.

"Enough is enough, though. You didn't have to offer him a drink, Mom. We've already devoted the whole day to him."

"Didn't you get along with him, Kate?"

"We got along okay. He's pleasant enough, I guess."

From most young women, this would not be an encouraging comment. Molly knew that from Kate it was a compliment. She said, "I offered him a drink because I thought Ben would like him to stay for a little."

Kate sighed. "I guess I'll just have to put up with him if he makes Ben this happy. He was in heaven all day."

"Daniel seems to be a very decent man."

"I hope to God he is, Mom, because it will break Ben's heart if it turns out otherwise."

"Shall we have coffee in the living room or out here in the kitchen?" Molly asked.

"In the living room. Ben has probably got his baseball cards spread out all over the place."

"Why don't you take in the cups and saucers, and I'll bring in the coffee when it's finished."

"All right," Kate said, and proceeded to pile cups onto a tray. Molly watched her daughter's slender back as she left the kitchen, and the smile she had been holding back dawned. Kate had not once said that Daniel was stupid or boring.

We're making progress, Molly thought hopefully. *We're making progress.*

8

Three weeks went by and the Yankees were in the middle of the postseason playoffs. Most of the games were played on an evening before a school day, or on the West Coast, but Ben was able to attend the two Sunday afternoon games they played at the stadium.

The *Daily News* broke the story after Ben's second visit. *Daniel Finds Lost Son*, the front-page headline read. Inside was the story that Daniel had given the reporter who had sniffed out the connection between him and Ben. It was essentially truthful, with the exception that Marty (who remained unnamed) was portrayed as a goodwill ambassador, not as a blackmailer.

Two days before the World Series was due to start, Daniel arrived home from practice to find his parents having a drink with Alberto in the family room.

"Daniel," his mother cried with delight as she jumped up to embrace him.

He gave her a generous hug, then held her away so he could look at her. "Mama. You look wonderful." Victoria Montero was fifty-five years old and looked forty. She had large brown eyes, dark brown hair, and a classically proportioned face. Her sense of style had made her famous in UN circles when her husband was the Colombian ambassador. She had a ton of charm and was a little spoiled.

"Daniel." His father came to hug him as well. Rafael Montero's good looks were of the craggy type; his son resembled his wife more than him.

"How was the trip?" Daniel asked them both.

His father answered, "Apart from all the security delays, it was fine."

Victoria said, "Have a drink, Daniel, and then you can tell us all about Ben."

Daniel turned to Alberto, and said, "Would you mind telling Maria that she can serve dinner whenever she is ready?"

"Of course not," Alberto replied.

Daniel moved toward the small table of drinks that had been set up in the corner of the room. He poured himself some scotch, which he diluted with water, then went to sit on the sofa directly across from his parents. They looked so expectant that he had to smile. "I don't know what I can tell you that you don't already know, Mama. He's a great kid. I'm very lucky."

Victoria rested her clasped hands on her lap. "And what is the mother like?"

Like no one else, Daniel thought wryly. He took a swallow of scotch. "Things are a little tricky between me and Katharine right now, Mama. The story about my finding Ben has just broken in the newspapers, you see, and she is having a difficult time dealing with the publicity."

His father said, "How can the publicity be anything but good? She has certainly done nothing wrong."

Daniel put his glass and coaster on the glossy wood coffee table that was placed between the two sofas. How to explain Kate's reaction to his parents? "The press have made a sentimental soap opera out of the story," he said. "She finds it offensive."

"It's a happy story," his mother said. "What's wrong with that?"

You'd have to know Katharine to understand, Daniel thought. He tried to explain, "She hates anything that's phony, and she thinks that all the hearts and flowers the press is rolling out is phony. And she's right. She did an excellent job of raising Ben until I came on the scene. I am not the knight on a white horse the papers have been portraying me as. Plus, she is a very private person. She doesn't like to see her affairs—or her picture—spread out all over the newspapers. And I really can't blame her." He sighed. "If she had the choice, I think she would simply erase me from her life."

"That must be a new experience for you," his father said dryly.

Daniel grinned. "Yes, Papa, I must admit that it is. She loves Ben, however, so she puts up with me for his sake."

"Is she pretty, Daniel?" asked his mother.

"She's beautiful," Daniel replied simply.

His mother and father exchanged a look.

"Does she have a boyfriend?"

"No. She runs her stable, and she takes care of Ben. That's about the extent of her social life."

His very social mother said lightly, "My, but she sounds boring."

Boring? he thought incredulously. He had never met anyone less boring than Kate. "She is one of the most competent women I have ever met. She's not boring."

"How old is she?" Victoria asked.

"Twenty-seven."

"She's beautiful, twenty-seven, and she does nothing but

take care of her horses and her child. Is she perhaps a lesbian, Daniel?"

Outrage shot through him. "Of course not! What a thing to say, Mama!"

"These things happen, you know. And you must admit that she sounds odd."

"She's not odd. She's . . . unique."

His father said, "Well, I am looking forward to meeting her. I would like to see her horses."

"And I'm looking forward to meeting my grandchild at last," his mother said.

The only grandchild I will ever have. The words were unspoken, but they resonated in everyone's mind.

Daniel said, "I will call Katharine and ask if you can come tomorrow after school. Alberto will take you. I have to be at the stadium for practice."

"You've been playing baseball all your life," his mother said impatiently. "How much practice do you need?"

"Leave the boy alone, Victoria. It's his job," Rafael said. The words sounded automatic, as if he had said them many times before.

Victoria said, "Well, you may be busy, Daniel, but your father and I will have plenty of time to devote to Ben. Perhaps we can pick him up after school and take him around with us. There must be things like a children's museum in the area."

Daniel picked up his scotch and took a swallow. "Ah . . . well, Mama, I'm afraid you might not see Ben as often as you'd like. He has school for most of the day, of course, and then he has soccer practice two afternoons a week."

"We will go to watch his soccer practices," Rafael said genially. "And in the evening we can take him to the World Series game with us."

"Ben won't be going to the World Series games, Papa."

"*What?*" Victoria said.

"As you know, Mama, they're night games, and Ben has school the next day."

"That's ridiculous," Victoria shot back. Her large brown eyes flashed. "A little boy who has just discovered his father, and that father is playing in the World Series, should be allowed to go to the games."

"Katharine doesn't see things quite that way," Daniel said.

His father gave him a shrewd look. "Is she trying to keep the boy away from you?"

"It's not her doing, Papa," Daniel said defensively. "It's that my baseball schedule constantly conflicts with Ben's schedule. It's very frustrating."

"What do you mean?" his mother asked.

"I'm free in the mornings, but Ben is in school. He is free three afternoons after school, but I am either due at the stadium for practice or I'm out of town. I get to take him out Saturday morning, if I'm in New York, and go to his soccer game on Sunday morning. I feel as if I never see him."

"Most of your colleagues see very little of their children during the season," his father said. "It's part of the price you pay for being a major-league ballplayer."

There was a white line around Daniel's mouth. "Most of my colleagues have known their children since birth. They aren't trying to make up for seven years of neglect."

Rafael said, "You did not neglect Ben, Daniel. You didn't know about him. That is a very different thing."

"I know, Papa. But put yourself in my shoes. How would you feel?"

Rafael sighed. "Like you, I suppose."

Victoria was still outraged that Ben would not be coming to watch Daniel play. "Rules are all very well," she said, "but there is a time when all rules deserve to be broken. Ben can miss a few days of school if he is too tired the following morning, but he should be allowed to go to the World Series games."

As Daniel was in complete agreement with this sentiment, he did not reply.

"Does he want to go?" Rafael asked.

Daniel looked wry. "Yes, he does. And it is a sore point between Katharine and me that she will not allow him to go. So don't mention it, Mama, please, or you will make the situation worse."

His father said, "She has been the boy's mother for almost his entire life, Daniel. You must respect her wishes."

"I know, Papa."

His mother said, "Well I think her wishes are unreasonable. That poor little boy. She probably won't even let him watch the games on television."

Alberto came back into the room. "Maria is ready to serve dinner, Daniel."

Daniel stood up and watched as his father held out a hand to his mother to help her to her feet. "I'm sure Maria has outdone herself for you, Mama," he said genially, changing the subject.

"Your mother has already been in the kitchen to check on the menu," his father said.

Victoria said with dignity, "I did not go in to check. I went to say hello to Maria." She took her husband's arm, and the four of them went down the hall to the dining room to eat Maria's famous *Ajiaco de Pollo Bogotano*.

Kate's eyes widened as they rested on the face of Victoria Montero. Surely this woman was too young to be Daniel's mother! But she was smiling and holding out her hand and saying in a charmingly accented voice, "I am so pleased to meet you, Miss Foley. We are so happy that Daniel has found his son."

"How do you do, Mrs. Montero," Kate said, shaking hands.

"And I am happy to meet you as well." Rafael Montero's voice was deep, his face was craggy, and his arrogant, hawk-like beak was a harsher, bolder version of his son's proud nose. He was carrying what looked like a large album.

Kate looked up at him. Clearly Daniel had got his height from his father. "I am happy to meet you as well, Mr. Montero." She gave a brief hello to Alberto, whom she had met before, and said, "Won't you please come in? Ben should be here any moment. You must have been just ahead of the school bus."

They all went into the living room, and Kate noticed Victoria's quick scan of the room. Daniel's mother was dressed in a beautiful beige cashmere pantsuit while Kate wore her usual jeans, boots, and sweater. Her back stiffened.

When they were seated, Rafael said, "I must thank you, Miss Foley, for being so gracious to my son. I am sure you must feel that he has disrupted your life."

Kate was surprised. It was the last thing she had expected him to say. She actually gave him a smile. "Yes, it has been rather . . . disruptive . . . but Ben is so happy to have a father that I can't complain."

The front door opened, and the adults in the room turned instinctively toward the living room door. Cyrus came trotting in and froze as he saw the newcomers. Kate snapped her fingers, and the dog came to her as Ben walked into the room. Everyone stared silently at the handsome, dark-haired boy, then Victoria began to weep.

She said in Spanish, "Rafael, oh Rafael, it is like looking at Daniel again!"

"*Sí*," he said.

Kate got up and went over to her son. "Ben, these are your father's parents—your grandparents." She led him to stand in front of the sofa where Victoria and Rafael were sitting side by side. "This is Ben."

"Hello," Ben said shyly.

Tears were flowing freely down Victoria's cheeks. "You look just like your father," she said and, ignoring Ben's politely extended hand, she enveloped him in a perfume-scented embrace from which Ben emerged with his hair ruffled and his cheeks reddened.

Rafael said a little gruffly, "In Colombia we do not shake hands with our grandchildren," and he also hugged Ben, although not as violently as his wife. During these embraces, Kate had returned to the love seat.

Ben gave Kate a look that was a cry for help.

"Come and sit down," she said, patting the cushion next to her, and Ben scurried to her side. She looked at Daniel's parents. "What would you like Ben to call you?" she asked.

"Grandmama and Grandpapa, of course," Victoria answered immediately.

Kate nodded, and mentally gave Victoria a good mark. She did not look like the sort of woman who would relish being called *Grandmama*.

Victoria gestured to the album, which Rafael had placed upon the coffee table. "I brought a picture album of our home in Colombia, and there are also pictures of your father when he was a little boy. Would you like to look at it?"

The wary look disappeared from Ben's face. "Yeah!"

"Well why don't you come and sit between me and Grandpapa, and I will show it to you?"

Ben shot Kate a look, and she nodded. He got up and went to join his grandparents on the sofa. The three heads bent over the picture album, and Victoria said, "This is our home in Bogotá, where your father was born."

Kate looked politely toward Alberto, who was sitting in the blue-flowered armchair, and he said, "No lessons this afternoon, Miss Foley?"

"I have a lesson in about a half an hour," she said. "I'll go down to the ring when my mother comes in."

"I have not yet had the pleasure of meeting your mother," he said pleasantly. "She is a teacher, I believe?"

Kate replied and continued the conversation with Alberto with half of her attention while the other half was focused on the threesome on the sofa. Ben appeared to be enjoying the pictures enormously.

Fifteen minutes later, Molly walked in, and introductions were performed.

Mom looks every bit as young as Daniel's mother, Kate thought loyally as she looked at her mother's pretty, fair-skinned face. Molly kissed Ben and shook hands all around before going to sit in the solid blue armchair.

Kate looked at the clock on the mantel. "I'm sorry, but I have a lesson I must give. I'll leave you in the care of my mother."

She was hoping she could just slip out quietly, but the Monteros insisted upon shaking her hand again and saying how much they appreciated her kindness, etc., etc., etc.

Finally, Kate was on the drive walking in the direction of the riding ring. For Ben's sake she was pleased that the Monteros were so interested in him; she was not so pleased on her own behalf. It seemed to her that her life and her home were becoming awfully cluttered with people since Daniel Montero had declared himself to be Ben's father.

Back in the living room, Molly watched the rapt face of her grandson as he pored over the picture album. He looked up at her, eyes sparkling. "There's a picture of Daddy in his Little League uniform, Nana. We should show it to Mommy."

Molly forced a smile. The last thing she wanted to see was a battle between Kate and Daniel over whether or not Ben should be allowed to play Little League. There was enough tension right now over whether or not he should be allowed to attend the World Series games.

She said to Alberto, "I understand you are Daniel's secretary, Mr. Carrillo."

"That is right," the slender, elegant-looking man replied. His dark hair was shot through with gray, and there was a grave look in his brown eyes that she found very appealing. "I took on the position a year ago to help Daniel out temporarily, and I have stayed longer than I planned. I will be returning to my post at the University of Bogotá in January, however. Like you, my vocation is to teach."

"Really?" Molly was surprised and pleased. "What is your subject, Mr. Carrillo?"

"Mathematics."

"You have my respect," Molly said. "I never understood anything after multiplication and division."

"What do you teach, Mrs. Foley?"

"English, which includes both literature and grammar."

"I am quite fond of the romantic poets," he said.

"Are you really? Do you have a favorite?"

"Wordsworth."

Wordsworth was one of Molly's favorite poets. She smiled.

"Nana, look at this," Ben said. "It's a picture of Daddy in a cowboy outfit."

Molly went to stand behind the sofa so she could see the album, which was resting on Victoria's lap. In the picture Daniel looked about twelve years of age and was dressed as a gaucho, with chaps and hat and furred vest.

Molly laughed. "He looks as if he's enjoying himself."

"We were visiting the ranch of a friend, and he was having a grand time chasing around after cattle," Rafael said reminiscently.

Victoria turned the page, and they went on to the next picture.

Later that evening, after Ben had gone to bed, Molly and Kate sat in the living room, and Kate said, "Don't you think it's odd that Daniel's mother and father should be so gaga over Ben?"

"Why should it be odd?" Molly put down the paper she had been correcting. "You and I are certainly gaga about him."

"It's odd because of the circumstances. Look at it objectively, Mom. A man finds out he has had an illegitimate child with a woman he knew for a couple of months. All right, if he's a good guy, he'll want to make sure that the kid has everything he needs. But would his parents want to meet the kid? Would they ask the kid to call them Grandmama and Grandpapa? I think it's definitely odd."

Molly frowned. "I suppose, when you put it that way . . ."

"That's the way it *is*."

"Perhaps it has something to do with Colombian culture, this reverence for a biological child."

"I don't think so."

"Well, what do you think, then, dear? Do you think Daniel and his parents have some nefarious reason for being nice to Ben?"

"Of course not."

"Then why are you so concerned with their reasons? We should be grateful that they feel the way they do and that Ben has such a wonderful addition to his family."

"I don't know about grateful," Kate said sardonically.

"Why not? Surely it is better that he have more people to depend on than just you and me."

"These people's interest comes with a price, Mom. *Grandmama* made one or two comments about Ben's not going to the World Series that I didn't appreciate. Just about the last thing I want is Daniel's mother butting into my relationship with my son. It's bad enough that I have to put up with Daniel."

"Daniel has backed you up on your decision, dear. He hasn't tried to undercut you."

"You must do as your mother wishes." Kate mimicked Daniel's deep voice. "He hasn't exactly thrown himself heart and soul behind me, Mom."

"He doesn't agree with your decision, but he is supporting you. I think he has done very well."

"You like him a lot, don't you?"

"Yes, I do. He seems to be an admirable young man, and I don't agree with your decision either, Kate. I think Ben should be allowed to watch his father pitch."

Kate's delicate, winged brows, which looked as if an artist had painted them with a fine brush, drew together. "You never said that before."

"Like Daniel, I try not to come between you and your son. And I agree with you that Ben should not be allowed to go to all of the games, but I think he should go Thursday, when Daniel pitches. He can miss school on Friday, or he can go in late."

Kate didn't reply, but got up and carried her teacup into

the kitchen. Molly went back to correcting papers. She had put the ten o'clock news on when Kate finally came back into the room. "All right," she said from the doorway. "Ben can go to the game on Thursday night."

"I think that would be good for him," Molly said, refraining from commenting on Kate's unusual change of mind.

Kate sighed and sat beside her mother on the sofa. "He's been . . . sad . . . that he can't go. If he had been mouthy, or angry, or just about anything else, I would have stuck to my guns. But he's just sad. I can't bear to see him that way."

Molly smiled at her daughter. "I know how it feels. I once refused to let you go to the National Horse Show with your father because it was on a school night, and I gave in, too."

Kate grinned. "I remember that. Daddy wanted me to see the Puissance Class."

"It didn't hurt you to go to the horse show, and it won't hurt Ben to go to the game."

"Probably not." Kate stretched her arms over her head. "I think I'll call Daniel and tell him I've changed my mind. He'll have to see about tickets."

"Good idea," Molly said.

"Do you want to come too, Mom?"

"I'd love to come."

"Okay, I'll tell him to get three more tickets."

Molly smiled at her daughter's back as Kate left the room.

9

*D*aniel was running down the street. Sweat poured down his face, and his heart thundered in his ears. Behind him, in the car from which he had just escaped, lay his father's chauffeur, shot in the head.

He ran, waiting for the bullets that would blast into his unprotected back, wincing away from the bullets that would kill him. It was three o'clock in the afternoon, in a residential neighborhood of Bogotá, and his car had just been ambushed in the street by four thugs in a Mercedes. He pounded down the pavement, twenty-one years of age, strong and athletic and running for his life.

He awoke with a start in his own bedroom in Greenwich, Connecticut. His heart was hammering in his ears, and he was covered in sweat. *Dios*, he thought. *I have not had that dream in years.*

He switched on the light next to his bed and sat up, his back against the mahogany wood of the headboard. *Where did that come from?*

It had been eight years since the henchmen of drug lord Pablo Escobar had tried to kidnap Daniel from the streets of Bogotá, and he had thought the experience was behind him. He had survived, most probably because the kidnappers had

had orders not to kill him. Angel Santos, his father's chauffeur, had not been so lucky. Rafael still paid a regular pension to Angel's wife and children.

Perhaps it's having Ben, Daniel thought as he listened to the slowing of his heartbeat. *Children make you feel so vulnerable. Didn't someone once say that he who has wife and child has given hostages to fortune?*

The adrenaline was still pumping through his body, and he knew he wasn't going to go back to sleep anytime soon. Thank God he wasn't pitching tonight. The way the rotation had fallen out for the World Series, he was due to start the second game tomorrow night, which would make him available to pitch the fifth game should the series go that far.

According to his mother, Ben had enjoyed looking at the picture album and had said he would like to visit Colombia. *That's probably it*, Daniel thought. *The idea of Ben in Colombia was what provoked the dream.* For the first time, he understood the fear he had heard in Kate's voice when she had said Ben could not go to visit his parents. For the first time he took comfort that Ben would be staying right here in civilized little Connecticut, with his school and his soccer and his dream of playing Little League baseball.

A line of moonlight was slanting in through the not-quite-closed blinds, and he slid down onto his pillow so it would not shine directly into his eyes. His thoughts drifted to Kate.

He had never met a woman like her. She was beautiful, but she seemed oblivious to her appearance. He had never met a woman with fewer feminine wiles. Her weapon was her intelligence; not once had she tried to influence him by using sexual attraction.

She was full of intensity, but he thought she was yet unawakened to sexual passion. She was like the sleeping princess in the fairy tale, waiting for the right man to come along and kiss her into life.

"I haven't had time." It was her single excuse for the narrow life she led. She hadn't time for a boyfriend, hadn't time to go to the movies, hadn't time to shop for nice clothes, hadn't time to talk on the telephone with friends. What time she had left from Ben she devoted to the stable and her horses.

And she appeared perfectly content. That was what amazed Daniel. She didn't appear to need anything more than what she had.

He had been elated to learn that she had decided to allow his son to come to the Thursday night game. He knew that part of her original decision to keep Ben home had been her dislike of the publicity that would inevitably surround their attendance. The cameras would focus on Ben and Kate, who made a devastatingly attractive mother-son duo, and, just in case there was someone in the universe who hadn't heard it by now, the announcers would drag up the story of how he and Ben had found each other. There was nothing Daniel could do to stop the cameras from rolling or the announcers from talking or the papers from reporting. It was the price he paid for being a star.

He had never before minded the public life he led. He had privacy in his home, which was why he lived in Greenwich, and if the papers wanted to announce the name of every woman he dated, he hadn't cared. It hadn't mattered that much.

He didn't feel that way anymore. Now he wanted fiercely to protect his family from the spying eyes of strangers. But the only way to do that was to withdraw from the world, and that wouldn't be healthy for Ben.

It was the solution Katharine would have chosen, but Daniel didn't think it was healthy for her either. She needed to be drawn into life, not be given more of an excuse to back away.

What would it be like to have Katharine here in bed with me?

His response to that thought was instantaneous.

Good God, he thought, half in amusement and half in dismay. *Now I'm never going to get back to sleep.*

With a groan of resignation he got out of bed and headed for the shower.

The last notes of the "Star-Spangled Banner" floated through the stadium, and the crowd cheered lustily. Then the players put their caps back on, the crowd sat down, and Daniel got ready to pitch.

Originally, Daniel had got three seats for his mother, father, and Alberto, and then, when Kate changed her mind, he managed to get three more seats directly in front of his parents. Rafael and Victoria were sitting in their original seats, but Alberto was sitting next to Molly and Ben was directly behind Kate, because she was small and wouldn't block his view.

This was the first World Series game Molly had ever been to, and the electricity of the crowd amazed her. The Yankees had won the opening game the night before, and the fans were hungry for another victory.

How does he do it? Molly thought, looking at Daniel as he threw his warm-up pitches. *How can he function in the middle of such mass hysteria?*

The crowd quieted as the umpire put on his mask and crouched behind the catcher. Daniel sent in the first pitch, and the umpire's right arm went up, signaling a strike. Ben yelled, "Yeah!" and Molly turned to smile at him. His small face was aglow, and she felt her heart swell.

Thank God it was Daniel and not Marty, she thought.

Daniel retired the side in order. In the bottom of the first the Atlanta pitcher put two men on with walks, but the Yankees couldn't advance them.

And so the game progressed. Daniel didn't give up a hit until the fifth inning, but he got the next man to hit into a double play. As they entered the seventh inning stretch, the sole run in the game was a homer by Bernie Williams.

"Doesn't this team ever get Daniel any runs?" Kate asked in amazement. "I have been to three of his games and the most runs they have got him is two."

Rafael leaned forward. "He got better run support during the season, Kate. But you've been at the playoff games where Daniel is pitching against the best pitchers. There are fewer runs on both sides."

Alberto smiled.

"What is so amusing?" Molly asked.

He said softly, "Oh, I just find it entertaining to listen to Rafael spout baseball talk. He has become quite an expert. When I think of how unhappy he was that Daniel wanted to play baseball and not soccer, I have to smile."

"I didn't know that," Molly said in surprise. "His parents seem so proud of him."

"They are, Mrs. Foley. They are very proud of him. But, unlike Venezuela, Colombia is not a baseball country. Soccer is our sport, and Daniel was very good at soccer. But when Rafael was assigned to the United Nations, and the family came to live in New York, Daniel discovered baseball. After that, soccer was something he played in the fall while waiting for the baseball season to start again. It took a while for Rafael to adjust."

Molly smiled into the thin, sensitive face of the man sitting beside her. "Please, won't you call me Molly? As I explained earlier to the Monteros, we are used to informality in America."

He smiled back. His smile wasn't as spectacular as Daniel's, Molly thought, but it had great warmth. "If I call you Molly, then you must call me Alberto."

"Certainly," she said. "Alberto, have you known Daniel for a long time?"

"I have known him since he was born. Rafael and I were friends at the university, and we have remained friends ever since. We used to fantasize that Daniel would marry my daughter Elena, but the two of them had other plans."

"I didn't know you had a daughter."

"Yes, she lives in Bogotá. Her husband is the president's press advisor."

"Have you any grandchildren?"

"A girl and a boy, four and two."

Molly smiled. "How lovely." She wanted to ask about his wife, but didn't want to sound pushy.

He volunteered the information. "My wife died three years ago from cancer."

Molly almost reached out to put her hand on his, but at the last moment she restrained herself. "I am so sorry. I know how it feels. I lost my husband to lung cancer ten years ago."

They looked at each other with the sympathy and increased interest of people who have known suffering.

"However do you come to be working for Daniel?" Molly asked.

"His previous secretary decided to go back to school for an MBA and left him in the lurch. I had been trying to write a novel, but between my duties at the university, and the demands of my grandchildren, I never seemed to get any time. So when Rafael suggested that by helping Daniel out I would get some time to write, I decided to try it. I took a sabbatical from the university and came to America."

"A novel! But I thought you were a math teacher."

A look of quizzical amusement came over his eyebrows and eyes. "Is it so impossible for a math teacher to write a novel?"

Molly laughed at herself. "Of course not. Do forgive me. How narrow-minded I must sound."

"It's all right. You are not the first person to have such a reaction."

"And have you gotten the time to write while working for Daniel?"

"Yes, I have. I write in the mornings and devote the rest of the day to his business. It has worked out very well. In fact, the book is finished."

"That's wonderful. Are you pleased with it?"

"I think I am. I am so close to it that it's hard to say if it's wonderful or terrible. I am going to send it to a publisher I know in Bogotá and get his verdict."

"Mom, the inning has started."

Molly looked at the field, where a Yankee batter was digging in at the plate. "So it has." She turned back to Kate and noticed the TV camera zooming in on her daughter's face. Prudently she didn't mention it to Kate, who hated being filmed.

"It isn't just because of me," Daniel had told her the other night when they and Molly had been sitting over tea in the farmhouse kitchen. "You're a very beautiful woman. It's your own fault the cameramen love you."

His tone had been quiet and dispassionate, and Kate had not stiffened up at his comment on her looks. "It's your fault that they found me," she had retorted, and he had smiled and agreed that he must take the blame for that.

"Get a hit for God's sake," Kate said to the man at the

plate and, as if he had heard her, the second baseman drove a long single into left.

"Good hit," Rafael called from behind Molly.

"Get another one," Victoria shouted.

"Yeah, don't let him just die there on first base," Kate muttered. "Move him over."

The next batter bunted the runner to second, to the approval of the stands. Then the leadoff man was up, and he worked out a walk. The shortstop came to the plate.

"Come on, Derek!" Ben screamed. "Hit a home run."

The pitcher quickly got ahead one ball and two strikes. Jeter proceeded to foul off the next five pitches, then the pitcher left the sixth pitch in the middle of the plate. The *crack* of the bat would have brought the crowd to its feet if it hadn't already been standing. The ball was drilled down the left field line, and the crowd held its breath to see if it would stay fair or go foul.

It went into the stands to the right of the foul pole and the stands went wild: Three Yankees crossed the plate.

"Four to nothing," Kate crowed. "At least that gives Daniel something to work with."

As it turned out, Daniel did not need the extra three runs. He pitched eight innings of shutout ball, then Joe went to the Yankees ace reliever to finish off the game in the ninth, which he did.

When the game was over, Daniel came out of the dugout and Ben raced to the fence to talk to him. Kate followed. They spoke for a few moments, then Kate came back to report, "Daniel said that one of the security guards will see us to our cars. Let's get moving, Ben is tired."

"No, I'm not," Ben protested.

"Yes you are, you just don't know it yet," Kate returned.

Victoria laughed. "I used to say the same thing to Daniel."

Kate smiled. "Mom used to say it to me. It must be one of those universal mother things, passed down from generation to generation."

Alberto came back to them with a security guard in tow. "This gentleman has kindly offered to see us to our cars."

Molly put her hand on Ben's shoulder, and they all began to move up the stairs.

By the time they got home, Kate was tired. When she got into bed she fully expected to fall asleep instantly, but an hour later she was still awake, with pictures from the game going around and around in her mind.

This is ridiculous, she told herself. *I have to get up at five-thirty to feed the horses. I need to get my sleep.*

But still the image of Daniel, standing on the mound in solitary splendor, kept running through her mind.

How does he throw the ball so hard? He's a tall man, but he's not huge. He's not at all bulky. He's muscular like a cat, not a bodybuilder. Where does he get the power to throw so hard?

Ben had loved being at the game. She was glad she had changed her mind and let him go. *If a father for Ben had to turn up, I suppose we could have done much worse than Daniel. If only he wasn't such a celebrity! That damn camera was all over us tonight.*

Not that Ben cared. The more he was on television, the more he liked it. He evidently had become as big a celebrity in his school as Daniel was.

And *that* Kate didn't like. She wanted her son to have a normal childhood, with the chance to grow up in a normal way, and this had become more difficult with the addition of Daniel to the family. Of course, it was also normal for a boy to have a father, so she supposed Daniel had added something as well as taken something away.

Once the World Series is over he's going to want to be with Ben all the time. Maybe he can do some riding with him. Ben enjoyed himself that time they went out on a trail ride together. Maybe Daniel can convince him that riding is a masculine thing to do.

Kate had vowed not to force her son to ride if he didn't want to, but deep in her heart she couldn't understand why anyone wouldn't want to experience the deep joy of being one with a horse. She was offering him this tremendous gift, and it killed her that he wouldn't accept it because of some stupid sexist prejudice.

I should get Rafael to ride with him, too. Kate had had a few wonderful conversations with Daniel's father, and Rafael had promised to give her a dressage lesson when she could find the time. Kate had every intention of finding the time as soon as possible. Rafael had impressed her enormously. He had actually studied with Nuno Oliviero in Portugal, and he was training a young rider to be on Colombia's next Olympic team. Kate planned to take advantage of every bit of his knowledge that she could access.

I'll have to ride Shane. What a shame that Rafael didn't bring one of his Andalusians along with him. Kate had seen pictures of some of Rafael's horses and had been awed by their proud, powerful beauty.

I should have Ben watch while Rafael gives me a lesson. He thinks his grandpapa is great. Let him see that Grandpapa thinks horses are as important as baseball.

Gradually, her thoughts slowed down and became less logical. An hour after she got into bed, Kate finally fell asleep.

10

The following day Kate spent part of the morning in her office with George Murray, who had been her closest friend for fifteen years. She was having a schooling show for her students at High Meadow at the end of the month, and George, who owned a neighboring farm, had been helping her to plan it.

"You ordered the ribbons?" he said, going down the checklist in his hand.

"Yes."

"And you've arranged for a caterer?"

"Yes."

"The judge is booked?"

"Yes."

"Do you have a farrier on call?"

"No. Joe can't do it that day."

"Hmm." George squinted at her, his light blue eyes fanned by a nest of sun wrinkles. "I suppose I can tack on a shoe if it comes loose."

"That would be great, George."

"How is that Thoroughbred gelding going for Nancy Kakos?"

"He's not. She's got too heavy a hand for him, and he has no patience for it. She needs a Warmblood."

"I know someone who's selling a nice Hanoverian."

"Millie Aldridge?"

"Yep. You've heard about it, I guess."

"I've started to look around. But I've also got to sell Aladdin. Nancy needs the money to buy another horse."

"It's not as easy to unload a hot Thoroughbred as it is a Warmblood."

"Tell me about it. I was thinking of Adam Saunders. Aladdin is really talented, but he's not the sort of horse a professional would buy for a client."

"You did."

"Yeah, and it didn't work out."

"You're just a sucker for Thoroughbreds, Kate. You get that from your dad."

"Dad always said that no other breed has the heart and courage of the Thoroughbred."

"Arabian lovers would dispute that."

"There were some notable occasions when they did," she retorted, and they both laughed.

"Did you hear that Tom Walker's mare foaled last night?"

"No. Did it go all right?"

"Went fine. A little filly."

"How nice."

They gossiped for another ten minutes, then George left. Kate leaned back in her chair, closed her eyes, and let the peace of the office enfold her. *How many hours have I spent in this room with Daddy and George just talking horses?* She opened her eyes and looked at the old armchair where George had been sitting. She pictured the scene in her mind, her father sitting behind the desk, George sitting in the armchair, and herself at seven years of age, sitting on the chair in the corner, drinking a cup of hot chocolate and listening to the men talk.

Everything I know about horses I learned in this room.

Kate had been devastated when her father had died. She had spent her life as his shadow, following him around the barn, watching him handle horses, teach horses, teach people how to ride horses. Tim Foley had been a charismatic Irishman, and people and horses had gravitated to him as naturally as flowers moved in the direction of the sun.

Unfortunately, Tim had not been as good a businessman as he was a horseman. When he died, Kate and Molly had discovered that the farm functioned on a month-to-month basis, and to cover the bad months Tim had dipped into the savings account he had established when he sold twenty acres of farmland to a developer. By the time he died, the savings account was almost empty.

Kate had wanted to take over running the farm immediately, but Molly had insisted that she go to college. So for three years she had gone to Southern Connecticut, living at home and teaching lessons when she could. Then Colleen had died, and Kate had quit school to take care of Ben. It was then that she had devoted herself to building up the business.

The single, most profitable thing Kate had done was to replace boarding horses with school horses and dramatically increase the lesson program. "School horses not only pay for themselves, they bring in money," she had told George. In her father's day, the emphasis had been on boarding and training horses; Kate threw her energies into the school, and the change in direction paid off. She didn't have the prestigious clients that her father had attracted, but she had dozens of kids taking lessons and paying a good price to do so. The business was in the black.

I'd like to have Aladdin for myself, she thought. Shane,

her own horse, with whom she had won numberless ribbons when she competed as a junior, was eighteen, and she basically just kept him in shape. She would love to have a younger horse to work with. . . .

Stop, she thought. *I can't afford to buy Aladdin, and keep Aladdin, while I still have Shane. And I would never ever sell Shane. So stop daydreaming and get back to work.*

She turned on her computer and was entering check payments when she heard a knock. "Come in," she called, and the door opened to admit Daniel. "What are you doing here?" she asked in surprise.

"I came to see you."

"Oh." Kate regarded him warily, wondering what new request he was likely to spring on her. "Come in and sit down."

He was dressed in jeans and a black T-shirt and he put her in mind of a panther as he prowled over to the chair recently vacated by George. He smiled. "Don't look like that, I've only come to thank you for letting Ben go to the game last night. It meant a lot to me."

Kate switched off her computer. "You're welcome, but you didn't have to drive over here to tell me that."

"I wanted to."

She looked into his eyes but all she saw there was honesty. She smiled as well. "I'm glad I let him, too. I just wish the damn television would leave us alone."

"I'm sorry about the television, Kate. I'm so used to it that I barely notice it anymore, but I can understand that to a private person like you it must seem like an invasion."

Kate held up a single forefinger. "That's exactly the word. Invasion. Everyone is entitled to some private space, and the press invades that. It's horrible."

His smile became a little crooked. "I know this will be

hard for you to believe, but there are people who actually crave publicity."

"Then they must be people with no sense of self-worth," she said flatly.

His smile died. "There are people in this world, Kate, with so little sense of self-worth that they use other people—or sometimes ideologies—to give confirmation to their very existence. They can be very dangerous, people like that."

His hair had fallen across his forehead almost to the straight black lines of his brows. His brown eyes were sober as he added, "You, on the other hand, are a remarkably self-sufficient person. You seem to need no one other than Ben and your mother."

"That's not true," she replied, feeling as if she had somehow been put down. "I need Cyrus. I need my horses and my stable. I need George."

His eyebrows flew up. "George? Who is George?"

"George is my best friend."

He scowled. "Why haven't you mentioned him to me?"

"There wasn't any reason to."

"If he's your best friend, then Ben must know him."

"Of course he does."

"You know I want to learn all about the people whom Ben knows."

Kate's patience snapped. "Don't be ridiculous. Do you expect me to make up a list of all the people whom Ben has encountered in his life and submit it to you?"

"No." She could see him making an effort to sound reasonable. "But if this man is your 'best friend,' then he must be more important to Ben than just a chance acquaintance."

Kate said conversationally, "Do you know, one of the things I have liked about you, Daniel, is that you're never stupid. Don't make me change my mind."

There was a moment of tense silence, then his face relaxed. "I'm sorry. It's just that I feel so bad that I missed the first seven years of Ben's life that I get a little carried away trying to catch up. Besides, I thought you didn't have time for a boyfriend."

"A boyfriend?" She stared at him as if this word had suddenly come out of the abyss.

"George."

She laughed with genuine delight. "George isn't my boyfriend, Daniel. He's sixty-eight years old!"

His jaw dropped. "And he's your best friend?"

"Absolutely. I can always count on George—and he can always count on me. If that isn't being a best friend, then I don't know what is."

He gave her an odd, searching look, then said, "Sometimes I think you're the most simple person I ever met, and other times I think you're the most complicated."

"You're pretty complicated yourself," she said.

"I'm an ordinary man, but you are definitely not an ordinary woman."

He looked so serious as he said this that she didn't know how to respond. Instead she said, "Can I ask you something, Daniel?"

"Sure."

"Why is Ben so important to you?"

He looked amazed. "What kind of a question is that? He's important to me because he's my son."

She looked down at the old green blotter on her desk, and said carefully, "I can see that you would want to make sure that he is all right, and that the people raising him are good people. I can see that you would want to share some of your wealth with him. But why this obsessive need to get close to him? Most men in your situation would not feel that way."

"I am not 'most men.' "

"You just told me you are an ordinary man. Well, ordinary men would not embrace an illegitimate child the way you have embraced Ben."

He looked at her for a long moment in silence. Then he said slowly, "I will tell you why, Kata, but I don't want you to tell anyone else."

The way he pronounced her name sounded like *Cotta*.

"All right."

He said, "A few years ago I had mumps, and the doctors told me that I would never father a child."

There was pain in the large brown eyes regarding her, and Kate realized how hard it must be for him to reveal this information to her. He was such a splendid man, young and strong and beautiful. How it must have hurt to learn of this disability. How happy he must have been to learn of Ben.

"I see," she said quietly. "That explains it, then. I wondered."

"It is not something that is general knowledge."

She felt a sudden surge of fierce protectiveness for him. "It's nobody's business," she said. "But I'm glad you told me."

He wasn't looking at her. "What you said about my *obsessive need* was right. You deserved to know the truth."

"Your parents know, obviously."

"Yes." His eyes focused on the hunting paperweight on her desk. "My mother thought she would never have a grandchild. So, please, indulge her interest in Ben."

Kate nodded. She wanted to go and put her arms around him and hold him close and tell him that it didn't matter, that he would adopt children and love them as much as he loved Ben.

Good God, she thought in horror. *What is wrong with me? He would hate that kind of sympathy.*

She said, "I will try to be a little more . . . accommodating . . . Daniel."

"You have been very accommodating," he assured her. "The problem is not with you but with me. I never seem to have any time to spend with Ben. I'm always playing baseball!"

She laughed at the look of frustration on his face. "That's true, but the season will soon be over. What do you do when you're *not* playing baseball?"

"I spend some time in Colombia with my parents. I shoot some commercials. I do some charity work. I relax. It's only for a couple of months; we have to report to spring training in February."

She said with alarm, "I don't want Ben going to Colombia."

"I understand, Kata. I will keep him home in January, and drive him back and forth to school, just like a regular daddy."

"Is it really necessary for Ben to live with you during January? Why can't you simply visit him here?"

"I want to live under the same roof with him. I can't explain it, but it's very important to me."

"It's just that all of his activities are right here in Glendale. He'll have birthday parties to go to and things like that. It would be much more convenient not to have to keep driving him all the way from Greenwich."

"Are you inviting me to stay with you for January?"

She stared at him in surprise. The idea hadn't entered her mind. Her brows drew together as she thought it through.

It might not be a bad idea. I'm not comfortable losing custody of Ben for a month, and that wouldn't happen if Daniel stayed here. Of course, he'd be under my feet all the time.

Still, he doesn't irritate me too badly, and it sounds as if he'd have enough things to keep him busy. And Ben would be here under my eye, eating properly, getting his homework done and getting to bed at a decent hour.

She said cautiously, "Would you like to do that?"

"If it's all right with you and your mother, I would love to do that."

"You wouldn't expect me to entertain you?"

He smiled. "No. I realize you are a busy woman, Kata."

"We do have a guest room. Let me talk to Mom and get back to you about this."

"Fine." He got to his feet, looking very tall in the confined quarters of her office. "I brought a few carrots for Abraham," he said, referring to the horse he had ridden on his trail ride with Ben.

"He's out in the back paddock. I'll show you."

"There is no need to disturb yourself. I know the way. Then I have to be getting home. We fly to Atlanta this afternoon."

"Well . . . if you're sure."

He nodded. "Go back to your bookkeeping, or whatever it was that you were doing."

"Good luck in tomorrow's game. When do you pitch next?"

"Wednesday, when we come back to New York. That is, if the series goes that long."

"Maybe it won't. You're ahead two games to nothing."

"I know, but the Braves can be very tough in Atlanta, and we have three games there."

"Well, good luck."

He grinned at her. "Thank you. Give my love to Ben."

"I will."

Daniel finished feeding carrots to all of the school horses that were turned out in the back paddock, then made his way back to his car. As he turned down the state road that would take him back to Greenwich, he thought about his interview with Kate.

I can't believe I told her. Was I crazy?

Not only had he told her, he was not feeling uncomfortable that he had told her. Somehow it had just seemed the natural thing to do. Her question about his feelings for Ben had needed to be answered, and you just did not look into that direct, aquamarine gaze and lie.

Her response had been perfect. She had accepted the fact for what it was, recognized that it validated his behavior, and put it aside. If she had commiserated with him, he would have hated her.

If any other woman had confided in me about her best friend George, I would think she was trying to make me jealous. But not Kata. That thought never crossed her mind.

He grinned as he thought about her delighted laugh when he had accused her of having a boyfriend. *Any other woman would have seen that I was jealous and played me along. But not Kata.*

He knew she hadn't planned to invite him to stay at High Meadow. The look of utter surprise on her face when he had mentioned it had given her away. He thought he had been very clever to suggest it, and was pleased that she was considering letting him come.

She drew him. He had grown up with people who felt passionately and who expressed those feelings with ease and fluency. Kate was different. Her feelings were deep and concentrated, and she shared them with very few people, but no one who had been in her company would doubt that she had them. She was like a tiger in the zoo, controlled, con-

fined, yet dangerous in her very passivity. He remembered
how she had once warned him that if he did anything to hurt
Ben, he would have to deal with her. She had been serious,
and he had taken her seriously. To hurt Ben was to hurt Kate,
and she would retaliate.

He thought that being a guest in her house for a month
was going to be very interesting.

11

$\mathcal{B}$en went into school late on Friday, and when Molly went to pick him up at soccer practice, she found herself preceded by Alberto and Daniel's parents. They all smiled and greeted her as she joined them.

"We decided at the last minute to come, and it was too late to phone you," Alberto said apologetically. "I can easily take Ben home if you have other things to do."

"This is what I do on Friday afternoons," Molly said comfortably. "Don't worry about it."

"Ben is a marvelous player," Victoria said enthusiastically. "It is almost like watching Daniel all over again."

"Ben is not Daniel, however. He is himself." Molly thought it was necessary to make this point. She didn't want to see Daniel's parents try to push Ben into a preexisting mold.

"We know that, Molly," Rafael said gravely. "And there is one way in particular I am hoping that he differs from his father. I would like to see my grandson choose soccer over baseball."

"He certainly seems to like it," Victoria said, and they all fell quiet as they watched Ben dribble the ball down the field in a drill.

"He loves all the running," Molly said, when Ben had finished. "Boys have so much energy! I thought Kate was full of fire when she was a child, but Ben even beats her."

Rafael laughed. "He is a healthy boy. Of course he has energy."

Alberto said, "My grandson is the same way. Never still. His sister can sit and draw, but not him. He must be racing his trucks all over the room."

Molly laughed. "That sounds familiar—although Ben can play with Legos for hours. He loves to build things."

"That is interesting," Alberto said. "Perhaps he will grow up to be an architect or an engineer."

"He'd like to be a rocket engineer, I think. He's into all the space stuff."

The subject of their conversation had been running across the field while they spoke, and now he pulled up beside them. "Grandmama, Grandpapa, my coach wants to meet you. Would you mind coming to say hello to him?"

"Of course not."

"Do you want to come, Nana?"

"I already know your coach, Ben. Take your grandmama and grandpapa and Alberto."

"No, no," Alberto said. "You go, Rafael and Victoria. I will remain here with Molly."

He and Molly looked on as Ben escorted his grandparents across the field to where his coach was huddling with the team.

"It is good of you and your daughter to be so welcoming to Daniel's parents," Alberto said. "It means a great deal to them to get to know their grandson."

Molly remembered Kate's words about how unusual she found Daniel's parents' behavior, and said carefully, "To be truthful, I have found it a little surprising that they care so much. Not many parents would be so pleased to discover they have an illegitimate grandchild."

There was the briefest of pauses, then Alberto said, "We have a great sense of family in Colombia."

He was looking out across the field and Molly looked at his profile. It was calm. *Kate was right*, she thought. *There's more here than meets the eye.* There was no way she could pursue this train of thought without being rude, however, so she let the subject drop.

"Are the Monteros going to Atlanta with the Yankees, Alberto?"

"Not unless it looks as if the team will win the championship down there. So we will be around all weekend, getting in your way." He gave her a rueful smile.

"Nonsense," Molly said lightly. "You won't be in our way at all. I have Ben all the time. I certainly don't grudge the time he spends with his other grandparents."

"And your daughter? Is she as . . . forbearing?"

"Kate feels as I do, that it is in Ben's best interest that he become acquainted with all of his extended family."

He looked at her, a faint smile in his usually grave eyes. "You are a very nice woman, Molly Foley."

To Molly's great surprise, she blushed. *Good God. Is it that long since I received a compliment?*

"Thank you," she managed to say.

"You're welcome. I was wondering if you would care to see a movie with me on Sunday night?"

Molly had to tighten her jaw to keep it from dropping open. "What movie?" she said stupidly.

"I saw that *Jealousy* was playing in the local art theater. I never got a chance to see it when it was first out, and I prefer to watch films on the big screen rather than the television. But perhaps you have already seen it?"

"Actually, I haven't. I would love to see it, though. It's one of those movies that I would like and Kate wouldn't."

"Daniel saw it and said it was wonderful."

"Nana!" Ben was racing across the field in their direction. "Grandmama wants to know if I can go out with them for ice cream?"

"I'll look up the times and call you tomorrow," Alberto said.

Molly said, "Fine."

The following morning Kate had just finished feeding the horses when Rafael came into the barn. She smiled when she saw him. "Now I know you're a true horseperson. No one else would get up at this hour to give a lesson."

He was dressed in khaki pants, collared shirt, and soft suede jacket, and he smiled at her words. "I don't have to get up like this at home, I must confess. I have a man who feeds for me. You can't do all the work of this stable by yourself?"

"I do as much of it as I can. Labor is one of the biggest costs involved in running a business like this, and I save where I can. I'm lucky to have a woman who does stalls in exchange for lessons and riding time for her kids, and that's a great help. And my friend George is great about fixing things, so I save on labor that way, too."

"Who takes care of the horses?"

"I do all the turnout and I have a few high school kids who groom for me after school. Boarders do their own tacking up here."

"Are you telling me you run this barn with no paid help?"

"I pay the kids who work for me," Kate said defensively.

"But my dear girl, you yourself must work from sunup to sundown."

Kate laughed. "I work later than sundown in the winter.

It's a pretty busy life, but when I look around here and see all my healthy, happy horses, it's worth it."

They both paused to listen to the soothing sound of horses munching on hay and crunching on grain. Then Rafael said, "Is there anything I can do to help you before we start?"

"No. I'll give them a chance to eat, then put them out after our lesson. All I have to do is tack up Aladdin."

Rafael followed her to the stall. "Is this your horse?"

"No, my own horse is eighteen, and I decided that it would be better not to use him. This horse belongs to a client of mine. She pays me to train him, so our session will be a lesson for him as well as me."

They chatted easily as Kate put the saddle and bridle on Aladdin, then they walked together into the indoor ring, which they reached through a double door in the back of the barn.

"This is very nice," Rafael commented as he looked around. Kate's father had built the indoor arena many years ago with high windows all around the top of the walls to let in the light. The year before he died, he had had several skylights installed as well, so there was much less feeling of enclosure than there often was in similar indoor arrangements.

"I'm going to have to replace the footing next year, which is a huge cost, but it will have to be done. It's okay for now, though."

Rafael nodded. "To start with, let's lower your stirrups two holes."

Kate had a wonderful lesson, then Rafael got on and showed Kate how to get Aladdin to soften through his back. When he got off, he said, "You need to get a dressage saddle if you're serious about doing this work. I'm amazed you were able to do what you just did while you were sitting in this."

"This is Aladdin's saddle. My own saddle is better," Kate said.

"Is it a dressage saddle?"

"No, it's a flat hunt seat saddle."

"If you want me to give you another lesson, borrow a dressage saddle. You'll be amazed at the difference."

"Would you give me another lesson?"

"Of course. By the way, this is a very nice horse—for a Thoroughbred."

"You don't usually like Thoroughbreds?"

"I like them for racing, but they are not built for dressage. Their necks are set too low and their hindquarters are meant to push out, to run, not to come under, for collection."

"That's true, but Aladdin has a wonderful stride."

"He does. But you must ride one of my Andalusians to really feel what collection is like. Come to Colombia with Daniel, and I'll open your eyes."

Kate surprised herself by thinking, *I would love to do that.*

She managed a smile. "That is very kind of you Rafael, but Daniel must have told you that I have strong feelings about taking Ben to Colombia. There is just too much going on there right now."

"I agree that it would not be a good idea to bring him to Bogotá, but he would be safe on the ranch."

"I would be a nervous wreck the whole time."

He sighed. "I suppose I cannot blame you. My poor country, what a tragedy she has become. And it is all because of the drugs."

He sounded so deeply sorrowful that Kate did not know what to answer. She finally said, "Come up to the house and have some breakfast."

He shook his head, as if awakening from a reverie, and accepted with his usual courtesy.

*   *   *

That evening the Foley and Montero families gathered around the TV set in Molly's living room to watch the third game of the World Series. Molly was surprised by how conscious she was of Alberto. It wasn't a sexual thing, or at least she didn't think it was. It was more a hyperawareness of his presence and his movements.

What did he mean by asking me out to the movies? Is it a date?

It had been ten years since Molly's husband had died, and she hadn't been out with a man since. She had thought that all that sort of thing was finished for her. Her sole responsibility now was to her daughter and her grandson. Nor had she ever met a man who interested her enough for her even to think about going out with him.

Alberto Carrillo interested her. She scarcely knew him, yet when they spoke she had a feeling that on some deep, unspoken level, they understood each other. She thought he was a man of deep sensitivity, and that appealed to her.

Molly's marriage had been a marriage of opposites. What had been between Tim Foley and her had been passion, not like-mindedness. The passion had been powerful enough to keep her in a marriage that in some ways had been frustrating. She loved poetry; Tim loved horses. She was quiet and deep feeling; Tim was fiery and outspoken. Yet they had had a successful marriage, and she had been devastated when he died.

Now she found herself interested in Alberto, who was everything that Tim had not been. Alberto, she thought, was more like her.

The game did not go well for the Yankees from the start. Their pitcher gave up five runs in the first three innings, and the Yankee hitters had a hard time getting the ball out of the infield. The game ended much as it had begun, with the score five to nothing in favor of Atlanta.

"Daddy should have been pitching," Ben said for perhaps the twentieth time. "He wouldn't have given up a single run."

"Unfortunately, he cannot pitch every game, *niño*," Rafael said.

Alberto turned to Molly, and said softly, "One good thing about the loss is that I will not have to trek off to Atlanta tomorrow. We can still go to the movies."

Molly smiled.

Kate said disgustedly, "They are the sorriest-hitting bunch of ballplayers I have ever seen."

"The other pitcher threw a superlative game," Rafael said objectively. "It is not that the Yankee hitters are so bad, but that the Atlanta pitcher was so good."

Molly thought with a flash of something like panic, *How on earth am I going to tell Kate that I'm going to the movies with Alberto? What will she think?*

Rafael said firmly, "We should be going, Victoria. Ben needs to go to bed, and Kate has to get up very early in the morning."

"Very well." Victoria turned to Ben, who had been sitting beside her on the sofa, and gave him a kiss and a hug. "Now remember, you are all coming down to Daniel's house tomorrow afternoon to watch the game with us. And I expect you to stay to dinner afterward."

Kate said formally, "Thank you, Victoria."

"Who will feed the horses?" Molly asked.

"George said he would let the last turnout in and feed them."

"Molly and I will not be staying to dinner," Alberto said pleasantly. "We are going to the movies. We will get something to eat after the film is finished."

Kate, who had got up to shut off the television, whirled around to stare at her mother. She looked shocked.

"*Jealousy* is playing at the York," Molly said with an outer semblance of ease. "You know how I have always wanted to see it, and you haven't been interested."

"Raphael and I saw it in Bogotá," Victoria said. "I'm surprised you missed it, Alberto. You will like it. It's very good. But why don't you stay for dinner and go to the movie afterward?"

Alberto smiled. "I don't think so, Victoria."

Kate's stare went from her mother to Alberto then back again to her mother. Molly fervently hoped she wasn't blushing.

"Do not let us interfere with your plans, Alberto," Rafael said smoothly. "By all means, go to the earlier movie."

Ben yawned hugely, and all of the adults turned to him, grateful to focus on something other than Alberto and Molly. "Time for bed, *niño*," Rafael said. "It's after eleven."

"All right," Ben said. He yawned again. "I have a soccer game tomorrow morning, Grandpapa. Are you and Grandmama coming?"

"Of course we are coming."

"Good." Ben looked satisfied. "I like having a big family," he said.

Two tears rolled down Victoria's face. "We like it, too."

Kate took charge. "Ben, go upstairs and change into your pajamas. I'll be along in a minute."

The little boy left the room and all the adults began to migrate toward the door, stopping in the front hall to don jackets and coats. The minute Kate had closed the door on her guests, she turned to her mother. "What is this about you and Alberto going to the movies together?"

"There's nothing more to say about it, Kate. Alberto asked

me if I would like to see *Jealousy* with him, and I said that I would. End of story."

"But . . . is this a *date*, Mom?"

"What if it is?"

Kate stared. "Well . . . I don't know what to say."

"Don't you approve of my going out with Alberto?"

Clearly she didn't. Clearly she also knew she couldn't say so. "Don't be silly, Mom. You can go out with whomever you want."

"Thank you, dear." Molly went over to the coffee table and began to gather glasses. "Just because you like living like a hermit doesn't mean that I have to like it, too." On that note, she took the glasses into the kitchen. A few moments later she heard Kate on the stairs, going up to put Ben to bed.

12

$\mathscr{K}$ate liked Daniel's house. The furnishings were clearly very expensive, but the overall effect was warm and welcoming. Daniel wasn't there, of course, so his parents acted as host and hostess.

First Victoria took them all on a tour of the house, which had four bedrooms, four baths, Daniel's office, a large living room and dining room, and the family room, where the only television in the house reposed.

It was a very nice house, with lots of windows letting in lots of light. But Kate was pleased by its relatively modest size. Clearly Daniel didn't feel the need of owning a large mausoleum to demonstrate his worth. Ben was especially taken by the swimming pool, and Molly wished she could see the gardens when they were in bloom.

As they settled in front of the television to watch the game, Kate kept an eye on her mother and Alberto. She was still shaken by the fact that they were going out together after the game was over.

Mom never wanted to go out before. She's been perfectly happy with me and Ben.

Maybe she really wanted to see the movie. I should have

gone with her when it first came out, then this issue would never have come up.

She watched the two of them and noticed that they seemed to be on terms of easy friendship. *How on earth did Mom get to be so buddy-buddy with Alberto? I thought they hardly knew each other.*

Alberto turned to say something into Molly's ear, and she laughed. *Mom looks so young. God, what if she decides she wants to marry him?*

This was a disturbing thought to Kate. In some ways she was still like a child, never looking very far ahead, thinking that things would go on as they always had. She had never been one to deal well with change, and a change as overwhelming as her mother's marriage was frightening.

Good grief, she scolded herself. *Mom is only going to the movies with the man. I'm jumping ahead of myself by worrying about them getting married!*

The Atlanta pitcher retired the first two Yankee batters, but the third batter got a double and the fourth batter got a long single to left, which sent the man on second home. The Yankees were on the board.

"Hooray," Kate said. "It's nice to know that they *are* capable of scoring a run every now and then."

Unfortunately, the Braves got the run back in the bottom of the first and the score held until the sixth inning, when the young Yankee second baseman hit a home run into the left field stands. The Yankees in the dugout all came out to shake his hand and the camera focused for a few moments on Daniel.

"There's Daddy!" Ben cried excitedly.

Daniel was wearing his hat and his jacket and his lean dark face split into its marvelous smile as he shook his young teammate's hand. Kate felt something stir inside her as she watched him. Then she frowned and clamped down on whatever that unfamiliar emotion was.

"It's hot in Atlanta," she said. "Why is Daniel all wrapped up in that jacket?"

"He's keeping his arm warm," Rafael replied. "He may have to pitch Wednesday in New York, and he doesn't want it to stiffen up."

Kate nodded.

The Yankee pitcher tired in the bottom of the eighth and loaded the bases. Joe Torre brought in his top reliever, but the first batter sliced the ball down the left field line and two runners scored. Then the next batter hit a long double, scoring two more. The score was five to two, and that was what it stayed until the game was over.

All the people in the Montero living room were disappointed, and they commiserated with each other as the sports announcer gave a rundown of the game.

Rafael said, "The good thing is that I would like to see Daniel pitch again, and if the Yankees had won today and tomorrow, the series would be finished in Atlanta. Now they're tied, and no matter what happens they have to come back to New York, and Daniel will pitch."

"My poor nerves," Victoria said. "I think the mother of the pitcher must suffer the most."

"I think you're right, Victoria," Kate agreed. "There is more pressure on the pitcher than on any of the other players."

"I'm going to be a pitcher when I grow up," Ben declared. "Just like Daddy."

Kate was stunned. "I thought you wanted to be a fireman," she got out.

"No, I'm going to be a pitcher."

"Perhaps you will be a soccer player, eh?" Rafael said with a smile.

Ben's eyes sparkled. "No. I'm going to be a pitcher. And I'm going to pitch for the Yankees."

Molly said placidly, "That would be nice, dear. But first you have to grow up."

"I'm seven already, Nana."

"I know. And in fifteen years, when you get out of college, you can decide what you want to be."

Ben looked a little daunted. "Fifteen years is a long time."

"I know. But it will go by fast."

Alberto said, "The movie starts in half an hour, Molly. Perhaps we should be going."

Kate's eyes swung from her son to her mother. Was that a flush of color in Molly's checks? *Is Mom blushing?*

Alberto fetched his own jacket and Molly's white boiled-wool jacket and the two of them went out into the cool October evening.

The film was engrossing and as they walked back into the lobby, Alberto said quietly, "I can see why Jonathan Melbourne got the Academy Award. That was a very powerful performance."

"Yes. It was . . . disturbing," Molly said. "Did you read the book?"

"I did, and I must admit I didn't think it could be filmed. So much of the action was interior. But Melbourne was brilliant."

"I must admit I haven't read the book. I have so much reading to do for school that I don't have much time to read for pleasure."

"What are the books that you teach in school?" Alberto asked.

The conversation continued easily as they drove to the restaurant and had a leisurely dinner. Molly found Alberto very well versed in English and American literature and was embarrassed that she knew so little about Latin American fiction.

"I have been meaning to read Isabelle Allende for years, and I haven't gotten around to it yet," she said apologetically. "You must think me very parochial."

"I would never think that," Alberto returned. "I think you get so much pleasure out of your own literature that you haven't felt the need to look elsewhere."

Molly smiled. "How nice of you, Alberto."

"I am a nice man, remember?"

"You are a nice man."

They smiled at each other. "Tell me about your grandchildren," Molly said, and the ensuing conversation lasted all the way back to the door of Molly's house.

Kate was waiting in the living room when Molly went in. She had a book in her lap, but she looked up the second Molly came in the door. "How was the movie?" she asked.

"It was wonderful," Molly replied, going to sit in one of the blue-and-white chintz chairs. "Jonathan Melbourne was fantastic."

"How was Tracy Collins? It certainly wasn't her usual kind of film."

"She was terrific, actually. She gave a sense of depth to the character that I don't think was actually there in the script."

"Did Alberto like it?"

"Yes."

"Did you have a nice dinner?"

"Yes."

"Where did you eat?"

"The Firelight. And don't ask me what I had to eat, Kate. You sound like a mother cross-examining a teenager on her first date."

Kate's aquamarine eyes look startled, then she smiled ruefully. "I'm sorry, Mom. You just took me by surprise. I didn't realize you even knew Alberto very well."

"I didn't, but we had a chance to get better acquainted over dinner. I like him."

"Is this serious, Mom?"

"Kate—I've gone out with the man once. Let's not get carried away, please."

"But you like him."

"I like him. That doesn't mean we're going to elope."

Kate laughed. "I'm sorry, Mom. I suppose I do sound as if I'm cross-examining you. It's just that . . . well, you've never gone out with men before."

"Like you, I've been too busy."

There was a little silence, then Kate said soberly, "Daniel coming into our lives has upset things more than I thought he would."

"He's been good for us. The both of us were so exclusively involved with each other and with Ben that it wasn't healthy."

Kate's eyes flashed. "Of course it was healthy! How can you say otherwise? Look at Ben. Have you ever seen a healthier, happier child?"

"It might have been good for Ben, Kate, but it wasn't good for us."

Kate's jaw looked stubborn. "What's good for Ben is good for me."

"Not necessarily, dear," Molly returned mildly.

"Do you think you'll go out with Alberto again?"

"If he asks me."

"Oh."

"Is Ben in bed?"

"Yes."

"I'll just peek in and see if he's awake."

"Mom . . ."

"Yes, dear?"

"I was talking to Daniel the other day about his having custody of Ben for January, and he suggested that he might move in with us for the month. What do you think about that?"

"What do I think about Daniel living with us for January?"

"Yes."

"I don't know. What do you think?"

"I was thinking it would be good for Ben to be able to stay home. This way we can make sure he's being taken care of the way we want. Daniel might let him stay up too late, or eat bad things, and he might not be on top of Ben's homework, either."

Molly looked thoughtfully at her daughter and didn't reply.

"We do have a guest room, and he shouldn't get in your way; you have a private bathroom in your bedroom."

"He would have to share the other bathroom with you and Ben. Does he know that?"

"I don't think that will bother him. Daniel isn't the kind of man who hangs around the bathroom a lot."

"How do you know that?"

Kate shrugged. "He just isn't the type."

Out of your vast experience with men, you have come to that conclusion? Molly thought ironically. "Well, if he still wants to come when he knows about the bathroom situation, it will be all right with me."

"Okay. Then I'll tell him he can come."

Molly was at the door when she remembered something. "By the way, I mentioned to Alberto that we found it a little odd that the Monteros were so interested in Ben, and he said that Colombians have a great sense of family."

There was a moment's pause, then Kate said, "That's probably it, then."

Molly looked at her daughter, who refused to look back. *Kate knows something she isn't telling me.*

"Don't wake up Ben if he's asleep."

"I won't." As Molly climbed the stairs she thought, *I wonder if Kate realizes that she has just made a decision that puts her loyalty to Daniel over her loyalty to me. And that is something she has never done before.*

Instead of being upset by Kate's defection, Molly was pleased. She was also pleased by Kate's desire to have Daniel live with them for January. This was a course of events her daughter would not even have contemplated a month ago.

Kate is warming up to Daniel.

She looked in Ben's room, where a night-light gave dim illumination to the blue walls and the poster of Daniel that hung over his bed. He was sound asleep. Molly looked at the small, dark head snuggled into the pillow and felt such tenderness swell in her heart. How lucky they were to have this child.

"Thank you, Colleen," she whispered, bent and touched her lips lightly to the tousled hair on the pillow.

She went along the corridor to her own room, the room she had shared with Tim for twenty years and had slept in alone for the past ten. She switched on the light, went over to her dresser, and looked into the mirror that hung over it.

There were lines at the corners of her eyes and at the corners of her mouth, and she didn't look young anymore.

I'm not as pretty as I used to be. Does Alberto find me attractive?

Kate was attractive. Kate was beautiful. Anyone looking at Kate would classify her as a heartbreaker. Yet, to her knowledge, Kate had had exactly five dates in her life.

Can Daniel possibly realize how innocent Kate is? How could he? No young woman of twenty-seven is as clueless as she is when it comes to a man-woman relationship. It was always horses with Kate, and her father encouraged her. Then he died, and she shouldered the business. Then Colleen died, and she shouldered the responsibility of Ben.

I wonder if I should explain Kate's circumstances to Daniel?

She stared sightlessly at her image in the mirror as she contemplated this question. *No*, she finally decided. *Better keep out of it. Better not to intrude.*

She glanced at the calendar on her dresser. She had a mammogram scheduled for after work tomorrow. *Better remind Kate that I'll be home later than usual. She'll have to take Ben to her first lesson.*

Suddenly and hugely, Molly yawned. *I'm tired. I think I'll get into bed and read for a bit.* She yawned again and turned to go into the bathroom.

13

The Yankees won the Monday night game and returned to New York leading the series three games to two. If they won the Wednesday night game at the stadium, they would be World Champions; if they lost, they would have to play another game.

Daniel was pitching the Wednesday game. Kate spoke to him on the phone on Tuesday, when he got home from Atlanta, but the first time she saw him was when he took the mound at the stadium on Wednesday night. She watched him the whole time the "Star-Spangled Banner" was being played, watched him standing erect and solitary on the pitcher's mound, his black hair uncovered to the evening breeze, and something stirred inside her. *He's an amazing person*, she thought. *He's a father Ben can be proud of.*

The stadium was quiet while the notes of the national anthem were sung magnificently by a Metropolitan Opera star; then, as "the home of the brave . . ." died away, the fifty-thousand-plus crowd erupted into cheers. The sound was deafening, and Kate continued to look at Daniel, who had begun to throw his warm-up pitches.

He's going to win. I know he's going to win.

He pitched a perfect first inning, three men up, three men

down. In the bottom of the first, the Atlanta pitcher also retired the side in order. This evenhanded matchup continued until the fourth inning, when the Yankees got two hits but failed to score. In the bottom of the fourth, Daniel walked a man, thus blowing any chance for a perfect game. As the seventh inning started, both pitchers were throwing no-hitters, and the fans were going wild.

"This is unbelievable," Kate said to Alberto, who was sitting next to her. "Why is it that when Daniel pitches, the other pitcher seems to be inspired?"

He smiled. "It does seem that way, doesn't it?"

Daniel walked the first man he faced in the seventh and the next man up sacrificed him to second. The catcher went out to talk to his pitcher, and the two of them conferred until the umpire went out to break up the meeting.

Daniel threw the next pitch, and the batter hit it off the handle of the bat, flaring it into short left. Kate shut her eyes, it looked so much like the kind of dinky hit that had ended Daniel's bid for a perfect game.

The left fielder caught the ball at his shoe tops and fired to second, doubling up the runner. The side was out.

Kate found herself screaming with all the rest of the insane fans. Next to her, Ben was jumping up and down.

On his way off the field, Daniel waited for the left fielder to catch up to him, then gave him a light punch on the shoulder. The left fielder grinned, and the two men jogged to the dugout together.

In the bottom of the seventh, the Atlanta right fielder made an error, putting the Yankee leadoff man on. After a passed ball advanced the runner to second, the batter hit a long fly ball into right field that the right fielder made a leaping jump to catch, robbing the hitter of a home run. The man on second took third on the out.

When Kate saw the ball flying toward the right field stands, she almost had a heart attack. Now the Yankees had one out and a man standing on third.

A long fly will get him in, Kate thought. *You have to get him home!* Kate urged Bernie Williams in her mind. *You have to get him home!*

The count went to three and two before Bernie connected solidly and sent the ball into center field. It didn't quite make it to the fence, but it was enough to send the man on third racing home. The relay throw went into the plate and the umpire spread his arms. Safe. The Yankees had scored a run without getting a hit.

The two teams went into the eighth inning with both pitchers throwing no-hitters, but with the Yankees ahead one to nothing.

"This really is unbelievable," Alberto shouted to Kate above the roar of the crowd.

Kate and Ben had been holding hands, jumping up and down, yelling "Yes! Yes! Yes!" She turned to Alberto with a dazzling smile. "Isn't this great?"

Alberto said, "If they can keep it up, it will go down as the greatest game ever pitched."

The eighth inning went by uneventfully in the field, but in the Yankee bullpen their ace reliever began to throw.

"They can't be going to take Daniel out?" Kate said incredulously. "He's throwing a no-hitter."

"In a game as close as this, Torre regularly brings Rivera in," Alberto said.

"That's not fair!" Ben cried. "Daddy is pitching great."

The woman in front of them, who was the wife of one of the other starting pitchers, turned and said, "He's probably just getting Mariano ready in case Daniel gets into trouble."

It seemed as if she was right, because it was Daniel who

came out of the dugout to make the trip to the mound. If he got the next three outs without allowing a run, the Yankees would be the World Champions.

The ovation he received as he walked to the mound was thunderous. Kate felt tears sting her eyes as she watched him pick up the ball and straighten up to throw.

At one time she had thought he looked small out there on the mound all by himself, but he didn't look small to her anymore. Instead he seemed to dominate the entire stadium, his whole being radiating joy in the game and confidence in his own strength and skill.

It's how I feel when a get a perfect movement from one of my horses, she thought in sudden enlightenment.

The first batter hit a little dribbler to the third baseman. One out.

The second batter walked. Groans came from all over the stadium. In the bullpen Rivera got up and began to throw again.

The third batter hit a soft liner to the shortstop. Two out.

The fourth batter went to a three and two count before he swung and missed. Three out. The stands went wild.

On the field the Yankees were mobbing Daniel. Daniel's family was hugging each other, and his mother was crying.

"Aren't you happy, Grandmama?" Ben asked when he saw her tears.

"I am so filled with happiness that I am crying," Victoria responded with a laugh. "Come here and give me a hug."

They didn't get to see Daniel, as he had told Kate to take Ben home as soon as the game was over. Ben didn't want to go, and Kate herself was reluctant to leave the scene of Daniel's triumph, but Molly hated crowds and wanted to get away before the general rush to leave the stadium. So they departed while most of the crowd was still celebrating in the stands.

Kate put the radio on for the ride home, and it was there that they learned Daniel had been named the series Most Valuable Player.

"Hooray," Ben shouted from the backseat. "Daddy is the MVP! Daddy is the MVP!"

"He deserves the award," Kate said as she pulled onto the Major Deegan Expressway. "I certainly wouldn't give it to any of the Yankee hitters."

"Wait till I get to school tomorrow," Ben crowed. "All of the kids will be so excited. Daddy pitched a no-hitter!"

"I thought you were taking tomorrow off," Kate said.

"No way! I have to go in, Mommy. I have to tell everyone about the game."

Molly said, "I feel sorry for the poor opposing pitcher. He pitched a no-hitter, and he lost. What a feeling that must be."

"It must be terrible," Kate said cheerfully. A car cut in front of her and she frowned and said, "Idiot."

"Daddy said that now that baseball is over he'll have more time to spend with me," said the voice from the backseat. "He said he would take me to a basketball game at Madison Square Garden, Mommy. And to a hockey game too."

"That's great," Kate said.

"He said he would take me to the Museum of Natural History to see the dinosaurs."

"You've been to the Peabody in New Haven. They have dinosaurs."

"But Daddy says this museum is *huge*. And they have a planetarium that shows pictures of the sky."

Ben continued to rattle on in this vein for a while, and then his voice slowly dwindled away. "He's asleep," Molly reported.

Kate made the turn for the Merritt Parkway. "You know what, Mom? I think we're in for a long haul of 'Daddy says . . .'"

Molly laughed. "He's so happy to have a father, and I know he's been disappointed that he hasn't seen Daniel as much as he wanted. It will be good for the both of them to have time together."

"I guess," Kate returned.

"Daniel really was magnificent tonight."

"The man knows how to pitch," Kate agreed.

"Have you told him that he can stay with us for January?"

"Not yet."

"I hope a month under the same roof with Ben doesn't cool his ardor for fatherhood."

Kate replied soberly, "I don't think that it will. I think Daniel is in this for the duration, Mom. I think we can trust him not to hurt Ben."

"What makes you say that, dear?"

Kate hesitated, then said, "It's just a feeling I have."

"I have the same feeling," Molly replied. "I think he's a good man, Kate, and I think we're lucky he came into our lives."

In the darkness Kate smiled, but she didn't reply.

That night, as she lay in bed, she thought about the conversation with her mother and she thought about why she hadn't told Molly about Daniel's bout of mumps.

He asked me not to tell anyone, and I'm simply honoring his request.

But Kate had never counted her mother as an "other person." Molly was almost an extension of herself, and as such Kate had never shied away from confiding in her. A month ago she would have told Molly Daniel's secret without hesitation, confident that the information would go no farther.

But there was no denying the fact that she felt she would be betraying Daniel's trust if she confided in her mother. *He's obviously supersensitive about this issue. He would never have told me if I hadn't asked him to explain his interest in Ben.*

But he had told her. And Kate was happy that he had trusted her enough to tell her. And she wasn't going to do anything to violate that trust.

He's a good guy, Daniel, she thought as she drifted off to sleep.

That night she had a dream that she was a child again, shopping with her mother. They were in a store like Macy's and it was Christmastime. She was walking next to Molly, keeping close to her red coat, when her attention was distracted by a statue of a horse in the china department. She stopped to look at it, and when she turned around again, Molly was gone. Panic gripped her heart. Where was Mommy? She stood in the middle of the aisle, looking up at all the coats that were passing her by, but none of them was Molly's coat. *Mommy! Where is Mommy?*

She struggled against her panic, and woke up, her heart pounding. *It's all right*, she told herself as she stared, wide-eyed, around her dark room. *It was just a dream.*

It was a dream she had had before. In fact, she had once asked Molly if she had ever gotten lost in a store when she was a child, and Molly had said no. So Kate didn't know where the dream came from, but it was truly terrifying.

She lay in bed, waiting for her heartbeat to slow. *I must have gotten lost one time, if not in a store than someplace else. Mom just doesn't remember.*

It was the only way she could account for this occasionally occurring dream. After a time her heart quieted, her breathing slowed, and she went back to sleep.

14

Daniel found Kate washing water buckets when he stopped by High Meadow the following afternoon. He frowned as he saw her at the sink, with her sweater sleeves rolled up and wearing bright yellow rubber gloves, vigorously scrubbing the inside of a bucket.

"Do you do this every day?"

"Of course,". she returned. "Do you think I'd allow my horses to drink out of dirty water buckets?"

"I mean, don't you have someone who does this for you?"

"It's much cheaper if I do it myself." She continued scrubbing but gave him a smile. "Congratulations. Not only did you win the World Series, you did it pitching a no-hitter. The game was great."

Every other woman Daniel had known would have given him a hug and a kiss. Not Kate. She just continued scrubbing her buckets.

He grinned. "Thanks. Poor Belaveau. He pitched a no-hitter, too, and he lost."

Kate said sardonically, "True. Once again, the Yankee hitting was notable for its absence."

"If you notice, Kate, the guys always manage to get what

we need to win. Even without a hit last night, they scrambled and got a run home."

Kate began to rinse out the bucket. "I guess. We heard on the radio on the way home that you got the MVP. Ben was ecstatic. I wanted him to stay home from school today, but he insisted on going in. He wanted to brag."

His son wanted to brag about him. That felt good.

Kate was going on, "He won't be home for another hour. You're a little early."

"I came to see you."

"Oh?" She looked at him with a lifted eyebrow. "What's up?"

How could a woman wearing yellow rubber gloves manage to look so attractive? He cleared his throat. "Did you talk to your mother about my staying with you for January?"

She put another bucket in the big sink and began to scrub once more. "Yes, and it's okay with Mom. Are you sure you want to do this?"

"Yes."

"Okay then. You can have your custody month at our house. I must warn you, Ben is already talking about playing basketball."

"Basketball? How can kids his size possibly reach the basket?"

"These days they start kids in organized sports almost as soon as they can walk," Kate said.

He asked mildly, "How old does a child have to be before you take her for riding lessons?"

Kate stopped rinsing the bucket and stared at him. "Eight," she said after a minute.

"I rest my case."

After a moment she gave him a reluctant smile. "Point taken."

"I'm celebrating my win and my freedom today, and I was wondering if you'd like to go out to dinner with me this evening?"

She finished rinsing the bucket and put it on the floor with all the other clean buckets. "I teach until eight."

"We'll go out after eight then."

For the first time since he had met her, she looked a little flustered. "What is this going out to dinner deal? First Alberto asked Mom, then you ask me. I don't get it."

"How can anyone who looks like you be so clueless?" he asked in amazement. "Haven't you ever dated at all?"

"I went to my junior and senior proms. It was a big deal for Mom that I go, so I did."

"Your last date was your senior prom in high school?"

She replied defensively, "I once went out a few times with a guy from college. But he wasn't interested in horses. I haven't had time for dates since I got Ben."

"Your mother would have watched Ben for you if you wanted to go out."

"But I didn't want to go out. When you get up at five-thirty in the morning and finish work at eight o'clock at night, you're too tired to go out."

"Well, come out to dinner with me tonight. I like horses."

She bit her lip. "Is this a date?"

"Yes."

"I don't know if that's a good idea, Daniel. I don't think you and I should get involved. I don't think it would be good for Ben."

"It would be great for Ben. Oh come on, Kata, lighten up. Going out to dinner with me doesn't constitute a permanent commitment. We'll just be two people who like each other having dinner together. I promise I won't try to kiss you."

The prettiest pink color stained her cheeks. For once she didn't have a comeback.

"What do you say?" he urged.

"Perhaps your parents could come with us."

He regarded her with amusement. "Do you really need chaperones?"

The pink in her cheeks got deeper. "I suppose I sound very silly. It's just that you took me by surprise."

"I really want to celebrate the World Championship and the no-hitter. Please, won't you come out with me?"

"You must have plenty of other women you could ask."

"I don't want to go out with another woman. I want to go out with you."

She regarded him uncertainly. He waited. At last she said, "Okay, I'll come. Where do you want to go?"

"How about Antonio's?" He named a well-known and expensive restaurant in Greenwich.

"Do I have to get dressed up?"

"Just don't wear jeans."

"Okay."

"Can I do something for you around here? Do you have any stalls that need to be mucked out?"

She gave him a doubtful look. "Do you know how to muck out a stall?"

"I do indeed. Although my father uses straw, not wood shavings."

"He gave me the most marvelous lesson the other day!" she said enthusiastically. "You never told me that he studied with Nuno Oliviero!"

He looked at her lit-up face and thought, *One day you are going to look like that for me.* "I didn't? How could I have forgotten that?"

"I can't imagine," she retorted. She finished rinsing the last bucket and started to fill it with water.

He was horrified. "Are you going to fill all of these buckets and carry them by yourself back to the stalls?"

"They won't do the horses any good sitting here by the sink."

"They're too heavy for you to carry. You should fill them after you put them in the stall."

"How?"

"Don't you have a long hose?"

"It's a bigger pain in the neck to unwind and rewind the hose. It's easier to just fill the buckets from the sink."

She had finished filling the first bucket and went to lift it out of the sink. "I'll do it," he said firmly.

"I do it every day, Daniel."

"Well you won't do it while I'm here. You fill the buckets, and I'll carry them to the stalls."

She gave him a long, level stare, and he waited. He was trespassing on her territory, and he knew that was dangerous. But he was simply incapable of watching her lug those heavy water buckets.

"All right," she said at last. "It will be faster that way."

He didn't realize how much he had feared being dismissed until she spoke, and relief flooded through him. He didn't say anything more, but lifted the water bucket out of the sink and began to walk with it into the barn.

"Be sure you attach the handle to the fastener in the stall," she called after him.

"I will," he called back, and proceeded on his way.

Daniel went home, and Kate brought the horses in from turnout. Then she went back to the house. The phone rang as she walked in the door and she picked it up in the kitchen.

"Hello?"

A woman said, "May I speak to Molly Foley, please?"

"She's not here just now. May I take a message?"

"Will you please ask her to call Dr. Barnes when she gets home?"

Kate felt the bottom drop out of her stomach. Dr. Barnes was her mother's gynecologist. "All right."

"Thank you. I'll be here until five."

"I'll tell her."

Kate hung up and collapsed into a chair at the kitchen table. *Mom had a mammogram on Monday. Something must be wrong. That was Dr. Barnes herself.*

Like a sleepwalker, she went down the driveway to the bus stop to pick up Ben. She established him in the kitchen with milk and cheese and crackers, all the time listening for the sound of the door opening. As soon as she heard it she ran to intercept Molly in the hallway.

"Mom. Dr. Barnes called about twenty minutes ago. She wants you to call her right back."

Molly put down her canvas school bag and stared at Kate. "Did she say what it was about?"

"No. But you had a mammogram on Monday. Didn't they read it at the Mammography Center?"

"No, they don't do that anymore while you wait. Is Ben in the kitchen?"

"Yes."

"I'll call from upstairs then."

Kate went back into the kitchen and tried to act normally as she listened to Ben tell her about what had happened that day in school. Finally, she went with him upstairs so he could change into play clothes. She went to knock at the closed door of Molly's bedroom.

"Mom?"

"Come in, dear."

She pushed open the door and entered the pretty peach-colored room to find Molly sitting on the side of the queen-sized bed, her hands folded in her lap. "Did you talk to the doctor?"

"Yes." Molly looked at her. "Evidently there was something that looked like a calcification on the mammogram that they want to check out further. She's sending me to a surgeon for a biopsy."

"Shit," Kate said.

"It doesn't mean it's cancer, Kate."

"Of course it doesn't. But it's scary all the same."

Molly said soberly, "Yes, it is."

Kate sat next to her mother and hugged her hard. "It's going to be all right, Mom. You have no risk factors for breast cancer. No one in the family has ever had it, you don't smoke, and all you ever have is an occasional glass of wine. You're going to be fine."

Molly nodded. "Dr. Barnes is going to make an appointment for me with a surgeon she recommends."

"Do they have to operate to do a biopsy?"

"They must, or she wouldn't be sending me to a surgeon."

Kate picked up her mother's hand and held it tightly. "I'll always be here for you, Mom. You know that, don't you?"

Molly turned to smile at her. "I do know it, Kate. Now try not to worry. The chances are it's only a false alarm."

Daniel picked Kate up at eight-thirty, and she got into the car reluctantly. She had wanted to call the date off so she could stay home with her mother, but Molly had insisted that she go out.

It didn't take Daniel long to figure out something was

wrong. Almost the first thing he said when they had been seated by a reverential waiter was, "What's wrong, Kata?"

"How do you know that something's wrong?" she parried.

"You're not a hard person to read."

"Great."

He said mildly, "If you don't want to tell me, okay. What would you like to drink? Is wine all right?"

Paradoxically, the moment that he said she didn't have to tell him, she wanted to. She twisted her napkin in her lap, and said, "Mom has to see a surgeon about her mammogram. They found something on it, and she has to go for a biopsy."

His face became very grave. "Oh, Kata. I am so sorry. But it could be nothing, you know. A teammate of mine's wife had to have a biopsy last year and everything was fine. The same thing may happen to your mother."

"God, I hope so."

The waiter came over, and Daniel ordered a bottle of wine. Then he said, "My mother had breast cancer, you know."

Kate stopped twisting her napkin. "She did?"

He nodded. "Five years ago. It was picked up on a mammogram."

"And she's okay now?"

"She's fine."

"Did they do a mastectomy?"

"No, they just took out the lump."

"Did she have to have chemotherapy?"

"Yes, she did."

"Oh God, Daniel. I am so scared."

"It's a very scary thing. But you don't know that it's cancer, number one. Number two, the survival rate for breast cancer when it's caught early is very high."

"How do we know that Mom's was caught early?"

"Because it was picked up on a mammogram. She didn't feel a lump herself, did she?"

"No."

"So it is quite probably in the early stages—if it's cancer at all."

Their wine came, and the wine steward opened the bottle and poured a little for Daniel to sip. He nodded, and the steward filled Kate's glass, then Daniel's. The waiter came over and asked if they were ready to order, and Daniel told him to come back.

"How is your mother taking the news?"

"Like Mom always takes bad news: calmly and bravely."

He nodded. "Have you told Ben?"

"No. We'll tell him if we have to, but he doesn't need to know anything yet."

He nodded. "My parents didn't tell me until the cancer diagnosis had been made, so at least I didn't have to go through all the agony of waiting to find out. When does Molly see the surgeon?"

"Monday."

He nodded and took a sip of his wine.

She said, "I'm sorry to pour cold water over your celebration, Daniel. I wanted to cancel our dinner, but Mom wouldn't hear of it."

"I'm glad you came and don't worry about my celebration. We did plenty of celebrating last night in the clubhouse."

She said in a rush, "Do you know what the worst thing about all this is?"

"No. What?"

"I think I'm more afraid for myself than I am for Mom. I mean, what would I do without Mom? She's a huge part of my life. Losing her would be like an . . . amputation."

He looked in her eyes, and said calmly, "I don't think you're going to lose your mother, Kata. Women get breast cancer at an alarming rate, but only a small percentage die of it."

She drew a deep breath and exhaled. Then she took a drink of her wine. Then she looked at Daniel and smiled. She hadn't intended to tell him about Molly, but now she was glad that she had. "Thank you. I feel better."

"I'm glad. You'll let me know if I can do anything for you?"

She nodded.

"Did Ben really want to brag about me to his friends?"

"Yes, he did. I was going to let him take the day off, but he insisted on going in to school."

He smiled that wonderful smile that always made her want to smile back. "That makes me happy."

"Will you be going to Colombia for a while now that you're finished with baseball?"

"I don't think so. I think I will spend some time with Ben."

She brought up a subject that had been on her mind. "Do you think you could ride with him more frequently, Daniel?"

"Of course. We had fun that one time we went out."

"It's not that I want to turn him into a professional rider, but he is missing out on so much because of this prejudice he has about boys riding."

He grinned. "You are merciless about other sports, Kata, but when it comes to your own it's a different story."

"May I take your order now, Mr. Montero?" It was the waiter, and his arrival saved Kate from having to respond.

15

*M*olly went out to dinner with Alberto on Saturday night, but she didn't say anything to him about her mammogram. Instead she asked him questions about Colombia and, in listening to his replies and becoming involved in the ensuing conversation, she managed to forget for a short time the cloud that was hanging over her head.

Monday morning at ten o'clock she reported to the surgeon's office in New Haven, the pictures from her mammogram under her arm. She was not as nervous as she thought she would be. Her naturally sanguine temperament had asserted herself, and she was inclined to believe that everything would be all right.

After a ten-minute wait, she was taken to an examining room, where she met the surgeon. Dr. Rose was a tiny woman in her midthirties, and she smiled at Molly. "I've looked at your mammogram, and now I'd like to examine your breast," Dr. Rose said, and Molly lay back upon the table.

She was shocked when Dr. Rose felt a lump.

"You mean, you can actually *feel* something?"

"Yes." The doctor picked up Molly's hand. "There. Can you feel it yourself?"

Molly wasn't sure.

"It seems to be a fairly good size," Dr. Rose said.

The bottom fell out of Molly's stomach. She had been assuming, because it was picked up on a mammogram, that it would be small. "That doesn't sound good," she managed to say.

"It may be fine," the doctor said, "but we're going to need a biopsy to know for sure. I'd like you to go for an ultrasound first, though. That will let me see even more precisely exactly where this mass is."

"Okay," Molly said faintly.

"If you like, I can stick a needle into the lump and aspirate some cells. I think it's big enough for me to do that, and if the cells come back positive for cancer we can go right ahead with the operation without having to do a biopsy first."

My God. The lump is so big that she can stick a needle into it.

"Sure," she said. "That sounds sensible."

Molly was feeling numb as she got back into her car and headed toward school. *It really might be cancer*, she kept thinking. *It really might be cancer.*

That afternoon, while Ben was changing into play clothes, she told Kate about her visit to Dr. Rose. "She talked about doing a lumpectomy," she said. "Apparently they are as safe as mastectomies, and you don't have the disfigurement to deal with."

"But you don't know for sure that the lump is cancer?"

"No, I don't know for sure."

But Molly was beginning to suspect, and when she went the following day for an ultrasound, her suspicions deepened. At first the radiologist had been very reassuring, telling her he did many of these screenings that turned out to be nothing. But he sang a different tune after the test was over and he had looked at the results.

"You can't tell for sure what it is until you have the biopsy results, but I often get a pretty good idea from the pictures I take, and I have to say, Mrs. Foley, that this looks like cancer."

Molly grimaced. "That wasn't what I wanted to hear."

"And I may be wrong. I've seen things that look exactly like cancer turn out to be benign, and things that look harmless turn out to be cancer. As I said before, only the biopsy will tell for sure."

Molly's appointment had been for later in the afternoon, so instead of going back to school she went home. Kate had not come up from the barn yet, so Molly went to check the answering machine. There was a call from Dr. Rose asking her to call back.

Molly did.

The doctor herself came on the line. "We did manage to get a reading on those cells I took out, and they are cancerous."

Molly felt numb. "So what's the next step?"

"The next step is to get a date for surgery. It will be done at Yale-New Haven Hospital, and they have a nursing unit in the hotel across the street where you can stay overnight much more comfortably than you would in the hospital. Some family member can stay with you if you like. You'll be able to go home the following day."

"And you'll be doing a lumpectomy?"

"That's right. The lump is about two centimeters long, so it's fairly big, but I think the lumpectomy is the way to go. I'll also take the sentinel node and a few other lymph nodes from under your arm, to make sure it hasn't spread."

"You're sure a mastectomy wouldn't be better?"

"In your case, it isn't necessary right now."

"Okay," Molly said numbly.

"I'll have my office book the surgery date and get back to you. Also the hospital will be calling you with information and instructions."

"Okay," Molly repeated.

"I'm sorry the diagnosis turned out to be cancer, but we're going to make you better, Molly."

"Thank you, Doctor," Molly said.

"You'll be hearing from my office soon."

"Okay. Thanks again."

Molly put down the phone and sat staring into space. *It's really true. I have cancer. I have to have an operation and maybe chemotherapy and radiation. I might even die.*

Her stomach cramped. *Suppose the Church is wrong? Suppose there is no afterlife? Suppose when you die you just cease to exist?*

I can't imagine myself ceasing to exist. I can't imagine the brain and the bundle of feelings that are me just disappearing forever, blown out, like a candle.

I shouldn't think this way. At least I know that Kate will be fine. She doesn't need me anymore, and Daniel will always make sure that she's all right financially. Ben will be fine, too. It's not like I'm a young mother leaving young children, like Debra Winger in Terms of Endearment. *I can go without fearing for the ones I'm leaving behind.*

Alberto. What will he say when he hears the news? He lost his wife to cancer. Will he stop seeing me because of this? Do I care if he stops seeing me?

Kate's voice came from the front hall. "Mom? Where are you?"

"Here, dear. In the kitchen."

Kate came in the room dressed in her usual jeans, paddock boots, and sweater. "How did the ultrasound go?"

"I just heard from Dr. Rose, and the cells she got from the tumor turned out to be cancerous."

"Oh, Mom," Kate said. "Oh, Mom." She came to put her arms around Molly, and the two women stood for a long moment, embracing each other in silence.

At last Kate said fiercely, "It's going to be okay. It's going to be okay, Mom. I just feel that it is."

Molly felt tears well in her eyes and made a heroic effort to force them back. Kate was scared enough already. She didn't need to see her mother cry.

Kate held her tighter, as if she sensed her mother's turmoil. "Daniel told me that his mother had breast cancer five years ago. And look at her now! She looks fabulous."

Molly managed a laugh. "She certainly does."

"Maybe you could talk to her, Mom. You know, get the scoop from the inside and all that."

"Perhaps I will." Molly stepped away from her daughter, and Kate looked anxiously into her face. "We'll see this through together, Mom. Like we always have."

"I know, dear. And that's a comfort to me."

"So what's next?"

"Dr. Rose will operate and take the lump out. She's also going to take out some lymph nodes to make sure it hasn't spread."

Kate nodded. "When? And will you have to stay in the hospital?"

"I'll have to stay overnight."

"That's not too bad."

"No, I really don't think it will be. I've done a little reading, and thousands and thousands of women have had this procedure and been cured. Did you know that the breast cancer rate was one in eight?"

"One in *eight* women gets breast cancer?"

"That's right."

"God." Kate frowned as if a sudden worrisome thought had crossed her mind. "What about your health insurance, Mom? Will it cover the operation?"

"I'll talk to the Glendale Teacher's Association representative at work, but I think we'll be all right. One of the men on the staff had a prostate cancer operation, and he said the insurance covered practically everything."

"Well, that's good."

"Try not to brood about this, dear. It's a lump, which the surgeon is going to remove, then everything should be okay again." She glanced at the kitchen clock. "You're late picking Ben up at the bus stop."

Kate too glanced at the clock. "Oh my God. See you in a few minutes, Mom," and she ran out the door.

Molly went upstairs and sat on her pretty flowered quilt and stared into space. *Tim,* she thought. *Are you able to hear me? I remember when you were first diagnosed you told me that you weren't ready to die. But by the time the cancer got through with you, you were. Will it be like that for me? Right now I want to hang on to life with both hands and my teeth, too, if necessary. But if this thing can't be stopped, I'll probably end up ready to let go like you were.*

The ringing of the telephone interrupted her thoughts. She picked it up, and it was Alberto. He wanted to know if she would like to go into New York with him next Saturday to see the new show at the Metropolitan Museum of Art.

Molly wanted very badly to go but, "I can't, Alberto. Kate has a horse show here on Saturday, and she needs me to keep an eye on Ben."

"How about Sunday then?"

"Sunday would be fine."

They made arrangements, and Molly hung up the phone. *If I'm going to have surgery, I'll have to tell Alberto. There are some things you just can't hide.*

On impulse, she unbuttoned her blouse and looked down at her breasts. Molly was not a vain woman, but she knew she had very nice breasts, and she had been proud of them. *Poor thing*, she thought sorrowfully, looking at the creamy white breast cupped in its plain Warner's bra. *What will you look like when the surgeon gets finished with you? How much will be left? She said the tumor was big.*

Down below she heard voices in the kitchen. *Kate and Ben*, she thought, and went to change her clothes so she could go down to join them.

Daniel came in as the three Foleys were sitting around the kitchen table having oatmeal-raisin cookies as a snack. Molly invited him to join them.

"Where are your parents?" Kate asked.

"They had a reception to go to in New York. Some of my father's old diplomatic friends."

Kate said, "No, you can't have another cookie, Ben. You won't eat your dinner."

"I always eat my dinner," Ben responded indignantly.

Suddenly Kate smiled. "You do. All right, one more."

The three adults talked about the horse show Kate was having on Saturday until Ben left to go and change into his play clothes. Then Daniel said, "How are you doing, Molly?"

"I got the bad news today, Daniel. It's cancer."

His face became very grave. "I'm so sorry. You're in for some unpleasant months, Molly, but I'm sure you'll be all right. Did Kate tell you that my mother had breast cancer?"

"Yes, she did. And your mother is certainly the picture of health today."

"She is perfectly healthy. And it has been five years since her tumor was discovered."

Molly and Daniel discussed Victoria's treatment as Kate looked on. *It's amazing how comfortable Mom and I feel with Daniel. He really is becoming a part of the family.*

Her mother asked her a question, and she answered.

How long have we known him? She counted back in her mind. *Since the beginning of September. Almost two months.* She looked at Daniel's face as he listened to what Molly was saying. *It's because he's Ben's father that we feel so comfortable with him. They look so much alike that it's like talking to a grown-up Ben.*

Daniel asked her a question, and she blinked and asked him to repeat it.

"What is Ben going to be for Halloween?" he asked.

"A baseball player," she answered wryly. "His soccer coach also coaches baseball, and he gave Ben a uniform to wear for the party."

"Is he going trick-or-treating?"

"No. The houses here are much too far apart, and no one wants their kids walking around these narrow streets in the dark. One of his friends' parents are having a Halloween party, and that's where he's going."

"I never thought of a baseball uniform as a costume," Daniel said with amusement. Absently, he reached for another cookie.

"Neither did I. But he insisted that was what he wanted to be."

"I thought that Ben and I might go riding on Saturday," Daniel said, and bit into his cookie.

Kate finished her coffee and put the cup down. "Saturday's no good, I'm afraid. I'm having a horse show here."

Daniel swallowed the cookie and stared at her. "You never told me that."

Kate lifted an eyebrow. "The subject never came up."

"It didn't come up because I didn't know anything about it."

Kate said a little impatiently, "It doesn't involve Ben, Daniel. Although he does hang around the caterer's stand for most of the day."

He was frowning. "How many people are you expecting for this show?"

"It's just for my own students. It gives them a little competition, and we end the day with a costume show. The owners dress up their own horses, and the lesson kids get assigned a school horse and get together on a costume. It's a lot of fun. Some of the costumes last year were terrific. But I need all of my horses that day. Perhaps you and Ben could go out for a ride on Sunday?"

Slowly he nodded. "We could do that. Then perhaps Ben could come back with me to my house for dinner. My parents are leaving on Monday."

"I'm sure he'd like to do that."

"You and your mother are welcome also."

Molly said, "Let your parents have Ben to themselves, Daniel. Kate and I will stay home."

Daniel smiled at her. "You are very thoughtful, Molly."

This would be so nice, Kate thought, *if only Mom didn't have cancer.*

16

*D*aniel's phone rang at five in the morning, and he answered it groggily. Kate's voice, sharp and urgent, came over the wire. "Daniel! The judge for my show just called, and she's sick; she can't come. Do you think your father could possibly act as judge today?"

He answered, his voice a little thick, "If you hold on, I'll go ask him."

Daniel got out of bed, thrust his feet into an old beat-up pair of slippers that he loved, went down the hall to his parents' room, knocked, and pushed open the door. His father instantly leaned up on an elbow, and Daniel beckoned to him. Rafael, wearing a pair of burgundy pajamas with his initials embroidered on the pocket, came out into the hall.

"I have Kata on the phone. The judge for her show is sick, and she wants to know if you could take her place."

Rafael frowned. "I am a certified dressage judge, but Kate does not teach dressage."

"It's just a show for her students, Papa. It doesn't count for points or anything. And she's really in a bind."

"Where is the telephone?"

"Come and use the one in my room."

Rafael followed his son back into his bedroom, and

Daniel handed him the phone. "Of course I will be your judge," Rafael said to Kate. "At what time should I be there?"

There was a minute of silence. Then Rafael said, "I am happy to be able to help you, Kate. I will see you a little before nine."

He hung up the phone.

"That was nice of you, Papa," Daniel said.

"Kate is family. Of course I will help her."

"That's how it feels, doesn't it?" Daniel said a little dismally. "Like we are all family."

"Yes. I think it is very nice."

"And that's how Kate regards me. As family."

Rafael sat on the side of the bed. "Do you want to be more than family to her, Daniel?"

"Yes."

Rafael looked sober. "You should think about this, my son. If you become romantically involved with Kate, and it doesn't work out, there could be bitterness between you that would not be good for Ben. It might be easier to stay as just family."

Daniel made an impatient gesture with his hand. "But I'm not her brother, or her brother-in-law, and it's simply impossible for me to feel that kind of a relationship to her."

There was a small silence, then Rafael said slowly, "I have spent some time with Kate during and after our lessons, and she is not like most other women her age. In some ways she is still extraordinarily young."

Daniel went to sit next to his father on the bed. "She's clueless about sex, you mean. I know that. How she has ever managed to remain so impervious in a society that worships sex, I will never know."

Rafael smiled. "Her world has been her horses and Ben.

She is very focused on her job, Daniel, so focused that there has been no room for romance."

"You would think she would show a little awareness that I am a man!" Daniel said.

"She has Ben, so her maternal needs are being fulfilled, and she has not yet discovered physical passion. But when she does, I think she will become singularly focused on the man who awakens her. Which is why I say go carefully, Daniel. Kate is not someone to play around with. With her, it will be very serious."

Daniel stared at his slippered feet. "I think it might be serious with me, too, Papa. She is unlike any woman I have ever met. And my feelings for her are different from what I've felt for other women."

"Are you thinking of marriage?"

"I might be." He turned to look at his father. "It would be the best thing for Ben."

Rafael shook his head. "Don't marry her for Ben's sake, Daniel. It has to be for your sake, or it will be a disaster."

Daniel sighed. "I hear you, Papa."

"Very well. Now let me go back to bed to get a few more hours' sleep before I have to judge this horse show."

Daniel accompanied his father to the show and when they pulled into High Meadow, the stable yard was overflowing with cars, and cars were starting to be parked along the driveway as well. There seemed to be dozens of girls of all sizes and shapes, wearing jodhpurs and riding jackets, running purposefully between the outdoor riding ring and the barn.

"A busy place," Daniel remarked to his father.

"Yes. Let's find Kate and let her know we're here."

They found her talking to an attractive blond woman and a little girl who looked to be about nine. As soon as they came up to her she broke into a smile. "Rafael! I can't thank you enough for doing this. I was at my wit's end when, suddenly, I thought of you."

"We'll go and register then," the blond woman said.

"Yes. Jean will have a list of all the classes I've entered Ashley in."

As the woman and the child turned away, Rafael said, "What kind of classes are you having, Kate? And do you have a set of judging rules to give me?"

"It's just equitation classes, Rafael. I've grouped the kids by ability, and it's just a matter of who looks like the best rider to you. There are eight ribbons in every class, so most of the kids will get some kind of a ribbon. If someone's been left out, I'll let you know so you can award her a ribbon in their last class."

"Is it all children?"

"This morning it is. After lunch we have the adult classes. I have two divisions, Pleasure and Hunter under Saddle. Each division will have three classes; the Hunter under Saddle has one jumping class and the rest are flat. Just pick whoever looks the best to you."

"Do I have to give each rider a written score, like in dressage?"

"No. But keep your notes so that if someone asks you why they got the ribbon they did, you can tell her."

"All right."

So far Kate had not spoken a single word to Daniel, and now he said, "Hello."

"Oh . . . hello, Daniel. Sorry, I didn't mean to ignore you." She gave him a polite smile. "Did you come to watch your father judge?"

Girls had been chasing Daniel all of his life. He looked at Kate's face, at the clear modeling of her cheekbones, the fine line of her eyebrows, at the politely smiling mouth that looked as if it had been drawn by an artist's brush, and he thought, *Damn it, stop looking at me as if I was your cousin or something.* Out loud he said, "I came to see if I could help you."

Her face lit up. "Do you think you could organize the parking? There will be more cars coming in, and I need someone on the driveway to direct them to park on the lawn. If the driveway gets blocked up, we're in trouble."

She wanted him to stand on the driveway and park cars. "All right," he said.

She picked up something in his voice, because she hastened to assure him, "You don't have to if you don't want to. I'm sure I can find something else for you to do."

She made him sound like a petulant child who had to be kept occupied. "Don't be foolish. Of course I will direct cars for you."

A grateful look was his reward.

But I don't want gratitude from you, Kata. I want something very different.

A man's voice called "Kate!" and Daniel turned to see a tall, thin man with an incredibly weathered face, approaching them.

"George!" Kate said. "Thanks for coming."

The man's light blue eyes were focused on Daniel. "Introduce me, Kate," he said abruptly.

"George Murray, this is Rafael Montero, who is going to be our judge, and this is Daniel Montero, Ben's father."

George held out his hand first to Rafael and then to Daniel. As he shook hands, Daniel could feel the older man assessing him. "Pleased to meet you," George said. Then, to Kate, "I thought Pam Jenkins was going to judge for you."

"She called me at four o'clock this morning to say she

was sick. I didn't want to ask you to substitute because you judged the last show, and I think the kids should have a variety. So I called Rafael and he accepted."

"Kate tells me you're a dressage trainer and rider," George said to Rafael.

"Yes. But she assures me that all I have to do is pick the riders I think do the best."

Daniel said, "If I am to help park cars, I had better get out to the driveway."

She gave him a quick smile. "Thanks a million, Daniel."

"Not at all," he said, and went on his way to do the most boring job at the whole show.

He wasn't alone for long. Gradually a stream of people came out to the driveway holding their programs and asking him to autograph them. In between showing people where to park, he obliged. Ben also spent fifteen minutes with him, talking nonstop about the Halloween party he had gone to. But he eventually got bored and went back to the show.

As the flow of traffic slowed, one of the adult riders lingered to talk to him, and Daniel allowed her to engage him in conversation. Her name, she told him, was Nancy Kakos, and she was riding in the adult division later in the afternoon. She asked him all the usual questions about what it was like to be the Yankees' top pitcher, and he responded by asking her what it was like to be Kate's student.

"She's a wonderful teacher," Nancy said. "She's very demanding, but she also understands your limitations. And she's honest. For example, the horse I have now is too much for me, and Kate is going to sell him, and not charge me a commission, because she was the one who bought him for me in the first place. Most trainers would charge a commission on the sale of the horse and the purchase of the new horse, but Kate won't do that."

She should, Daniel thought. *She's supposed to be a businesswoman for God's sake.*

They continued to chat. Nancy was a pretty woman, with hazel eyes, brown hair, and a warm smile, and Daniel allowed himself to bask a little in the familiar sunshine of feminine attention.

When it was time for her first class she invited him to come and watch. As there had been no cars by in the last fifteen minutes, Daniel decided that he had done his duty for the day, and accepted.

The adult classes were being held in the outdoor ring, and Daniel found a place along the rail and looked for Kate. His father came out of the barn carrying a clipboard and when he saw Daniel, he waved. Daniel waved back.

A group of women and one man on horseback gathered outside the gate that led into the ring.

Where is Kate?

At last he saw her, coming around the side of the barn with George. The two of them were deep in conversation.

Kata, Kata, Kata, he thought with rueful amusement. *What do I have to do to get you to see yourself as a woman and me as a man?*

There was a microphone set up in the indoor ring, but the outdoor ring didn't have any. As Daniel watched, George ducked into the ring and went to stand next to Rafael in the middle. "Riders in the ring, please," he boomed in a voice that reached everyone in the immediate vicinity.

Someone opened the gate, and the riders came in single file. Most of them began to trot around the perimeter of the ring, warming up before the class started, and Daniel looked assessingly at Kate's students and their mounts.

The horses were lovely. Nancy was riding a particularly

striking bay Thoroughbred, and he wondered if that was the horse she had said was too much for her.

He felt Kate come up to his side. "Thanks a million for parking the cars, Daniel. I know it's a thankless job, and I appreciate your helping me out."

He bent to give Cyrus a friendly pat. "Not at all. Where is Ben? I saw him for about ten minutes before he got bored and went away."

"The last I saw of him he was eating a hot dog. My mother is in charge of him for the day, so I really haven't been keeping track."

"How is your mother doing?"

"She's amazing. She's just carrying on as if nothing had happened. By the way, they scheduled her operation for Tuesday, and they're going to keep her overnight. The hospital is going to send her to a hotel where they have a nursing unit, and the room has two beds so I can stay with her. Do you think you could take Ben for Tuesday night?"

"Of course. I would be delighted to have him."

She rewarded him with a smile. "Thanks, Daniel. You're a brick."

A brick? She thought he was a brick? He didn't want her to think of him as a brick. He wanted her to think he was a sexy guy whom she wanted to go to bed with.

She was going on, "You can stay at our house if you like. That way the school bus will pick Ben up. If you stay at your house, you'll have to pick him up at school on Monday and take him to school on Tuesday morning."

"I don't mind driving him to school, and I would like him to stay in my house."

"Fine."

As they were talking, the riders in the ring had gone from a walk to a trot to a canter. Nancy Kakos came cantering by on a horse that looked as if he'd like to gallop, and Kate said in a low voice, "Take your leg *off* him, Nancy. You're pushing him forward!"

Nancy nodded and swept by.

"I was talking to Nancy for a while, and she told me that this horse is too much for her."

"Yes, he is. I love him myself, but Nancy gets nervous when he gets going, and she grips with her legs for security, but it only results in the horse going faster."

"What kind of a bit are you using with him?"

She gave him a delighted smile. "You do know something about horses."

"I do," he returned modestly.

She laughed. "We've tried a whole succession of bits, and what she has for the show is a kimberwicke. When I ride him I ride him in a snaffle, and he's just fine. But Nancy can't control him with the lighter bit."

He changed the subject. "Can you come with Ben and me on a ride tomorrow?"

She hesitated. "I thought you might want him to yourself."

"I would like a family outing even better."

Her face lighted, and he felt the bottom drop out of his stomach. "All right then. What time do you want to go?"

"Whatever time is best for you."

"One in the afternoon?"

"Fine."

The class was over, but the riders stayed in the ring for the second class in the division. Everyone watched Rafael, as he made notes on his clipboard. Then he gave the board to George, who called out, "The blue ribbon goes to Marissa Canty on Leopold."

"Good choice," Kate said, as a rider on a sleek gray went

out to take her ribbon from George. "Marissa is one of my best students."

"Second place goes to Tom Helvia."

Kate frowned.

"What's the matter? Don't you agree?"

She shrugged. "I thought Kim had a better ride. I think Tom gets preference sometimes because he's male."

The remainder of the ribbons were called out, and Daniel noticed that Nancy Kakos did not get one.

"What's this I hear about you not charging commissions on horses you are buying and selling?" he asked Kate.

"You *were* talking to Nancy," she said.

"You'll never make it as a businesswoman, Kata, if you give away your services for free."

"I charged her a commission when I bought the horse, and the horse was wrong for her. She hired me to buy her a suitable horse and I didn't do that. I'm certainly not going to charge her a commission to sell the unsuitable horse and to buy her the horse that I should have bought her in the first place."

"Have you sold the horse yet?"

"Not yet. I have someone coming to look at him this week. I'd like to place him with a professional if I could. He's very talented, but he needs a light touch. Adam Saunders is a professional eventer, and I think he might like Aladdin a lot."

"Well, good luck."

"Thanks. I have my eye on a horse for Nancy, but she can't afford to buy it until I sell Aladdin."

"Do you often waive your commission?"

"Not often, no."

"Hmmm," said Daniel, who still didn't agree with her.

"You have a lot of students," he said instead.

"Thank God. That's what makes the difference between red and black ink in the account books. I just about break even on the boarding, but I make money on the lessons."

"If you're so profitable, why don't you hire someone to help you with the water buckets?"

She raised an eyebrow. "The reason I make a profit is that I do almost everything myself. If I took on paid help, my profit margin would diminish considerably."

Inside the ring, the riders were beginning the next class. Kate said, "I'd better check the barn to make sure the kids aren't terrifying the horses with the costumes they've created."

Kate left, and Daniel stayed to watch. At the last class of the adult divisions, Ben came to join his father. "The costume show is going to be inside, Daddy," he said. "It's the best part of the whole day. You have to come and watch."

"I was planning to," Daniel assured him.

"Did you get something to eat? We have time to go to the caterer's truck to get something before we go inside."

Daniel squelched a smile. "Your mother sent me some food while I was parking cars. And I think you have probably had quite enough treats for the day."

Ben looked a little crestfallen. "I was only thinking of you."

"Well that was very nice of you, Ben, but I don't need any food. Do you want to go inside?"

"Okay."

This is so nice, Daniel thought as he walked across the grass with Ben in the direction of the indoor arena. A little girl came up to him and shyly asked for his autograph, and he signed her program with a smile.

Ben said, "Have a lot of people asked for your autograph, Daddy?"

"A few."

"Do you like it when people ask for your autograph?"

"Most of the time I don't mind. Sometimes it can be a nuisance."

"Grandpapa must know a lot about horses if he judged the show."

"He knows a great deal about horses. He is one of the most accomplished horsemen in all of Colombia, Ben."

"Do a lot of men ride horses in Colombia?"

"Those who can afford it, yes. By the way, your mother and I are going for a trail ride tomorrow. Would you like to come with us?"

"Sure," Ben said buoyantly.

"Great." A girl passed by leading a small white Arabian who was swathed in a floating white garment. "Wow," Daniel said. "That looks great."

"His name is Ghost," Ben said. "Rebecca Wiley, a girl from my class, rides him. She told me they were going to dress him like a ghost. I guess that's why they have all that white stuff on him."

"This costume show should be fun."

"It is," Ben said. "The funniest part is when the horses dunk for apples. Most of them won't put their faces all the way in the water and Shane—he's Mommy's horse—always wins because he just dives right in. Mommy says it's because he's the greediest."

Daniel lengthened his stride. "We'd better hurry, then, so we can get a good spot to see from."

"Okay," said Ben, and scrambled to keep up.

17

*K*ate, Daniel, and Ben had a fine day for their trail ride, and they started out from High Meadow under a blue sky with enough of a nip in the air to make the horses feel energetic. Kate was riding Shane, Daniel was on Abraham, the big bay gelding he had ridden previously, and Ben was on Tucker, a chestnut pony who was one of Kate's most trusted school horses.

High Meadow Farm adjoined a large expanse of land that belonged to the New England Water Company. This land surrounded a reservoir and was crisscrossed with numerous bridle paths that were available to people who had a water company permit. Easy access to these trails was a big selling point for High Meadow when it came to attracting boarders.

The peak for autumn foliage had passed, but the woods still looked beautiful as they rode along, and Kate inhaled deeply the rich, slightly musty odor given off by the leaves at this time of year. She tried to get Shane out into the woods at least twice a week, but this last week she had been so busy they hadn't gotten out at all. From the bounce in his stride, she knew that Shane was as happy as she to be outdoors.

She glanced over her shoulder at Ben, who was riding directly behind her, sandwiched between Shane and Abraham. "Aren't the woods pretty, Ben?"

"Yep."

"Is Tucker behaving himself?"

"He's okay."

The moment Kate finished speaking a squirrel darted across the path in front of Tucker, and he jumped. "Wow," Ben said.

"The squirrel just startled him," Kate explained. "He wasn't going to run away or anything."

"I wasn't scared, Mommy," Ben said scornfully.

"Excuse me," Kate said, and, smiling, she turned around.

When they got to the trail around the reservoir they were able to ride three abreast, and Ben said to Daniel, "Mommy says that I'm going to your house on Tuesday for a sleepover."

Daniel, who had a wonderful, gaucho-style seat, erect with his legs hanging straight under him, answered, "Yes. I'll pick you up at school on Monday, you'll spend the night with me, and I'll take you to school on Tuesday morning."

"Cool."

From the beginning, Ben had seemed perfectly comfortable with the news of Molly's operation. Of course, they had downplayed it so that it sounded like a routine thing, but still Kate was a little surprised that Ben was so unconcerned.

She looked at Daniel. "We should be back by the early afternoon, so Ben can take the bus home."

"I will get him. That way, if you are delayed, you won't be worried."

"Are you sure?"

"Yes. But I do have something to do Wednesday night, so I can't keep him for you."

"What do you have to do, Daddy?"

Daniel smiled at his son, who was riding in between him and Kate. "I have a party to go to."

"A party?"

A *party*? Kate thought.

Daniel said to Ben, "I'm going with a lady, so I can't cancel—even for your sake, Ben. It would be rude, and a gentleman is never rude to a lady."

Ben, bless him, asked, "Who is the lady, Daddy?"

"You wouldn't know her, Ben."

"What's her name?"

"Alicia Peterson."

Ben continued his interrogation. "Is she pretty?"

"Very pretty. She has her picture in lots of magazines."

Kate said before she could stop herself, "She's a model, then?"

He looked at her with amusement. "You constantly amaze me, Kata. Yes, she's a model. In fact, she's probably the best-known model in the country right now."

"I bet she's not as pretty as Mommy," Ben said.

Kate could feel her cheeks grow warm. "Don't be silly, Ben."

"She isn't as pretty as your mother," Daniel told Ben. "Nobody is as pretty as your mother."

Kate's cheeks grew warmer. *He's only saying that to please Ben*, she thought. Then, *Good God, why should I care if he thinks I'm pretty or not? I despise people who are hung up on looks.*

"Don't worry about Wednesday night," she said a little gruffly. "The doctor assured us that Mom would be able to go home in the morning."

"Good."

How well does he know Alicia Peterson? Are they dating? Are they a couple? Kate was perturbed by these questions, and even more perturbed by her own perturbation. *Why should I care whom Daniel goes out with? Why should I be surprised that he does go out? I only see him in relationship to Ben and the family. I forget that he has a whole life that doesn't include us at all.*

This was not a thought that made her happy, and she worried, *I can't get too dependent on this man. I automatically assumed he would take care of Ben on Tuesday, but I can't do that. I can't rely on him like that. It's dangerous.*

"How about a little trot?" Daniel asked.

"Do you want to try a trot, Ben?"

"Yes," Ben said. "Walking is boring."

"Remember," Daniel said. "You have to stand and sit in rhythm with the horse. It's one-two-sit, one-two-sit. Got it?"

"Did you trot when you went out before?" Kate asked.

"Yes. And Ben did very well."

"All right," Kate said, "Let's go."

The horses moved into a trot, and, between the two big horses, Ben's pony began to trot as well. He held the horn of his Western saddle and followed Daniel's instruction, "One-two-sit, one-two-sit, one-two-sit. Very good, Ben. It's harder to do this on a pony than it is on a horse because a pony's gait is so much quicker. You're doing great."

He was doing very well. One of the reasons that Kate was so keen to have Ben ride was that whenever he had deigned to sit in a saddle he had looked like a natural. As he did now, holding the horn for balance but rising and falling by himself. Halfway around the lake he bugged them to go faster. Kate wanted to keep to a trot, but Daniel said, "Oh come on, Kata. A little canter won't hurt him."

"I'm not a baby!"

So they cantered, and Ben loved it. He stood in his stirrups, and held on to the saddle horn, and laughed as Tucker stretched out between the two bigger horses.

"That was fun," he said when they finally slowed down. "If I could do that all the time, I'd like horseback riding."

Daniel said, "Galloping through the woods is only a part of horsemanship, Ben, like rushing straight down a hill is only a part of skiing. To ski properly you have to learn to steer and manage your skis. The same thing applies to horseback riding; you must learn to steer and manage your horse."

"Do you ski, Daddy?"

"I have skied, yes."

"Could we go sometime?"

"Perhaps."

"Do you like skiing?"

"Not as much as I like horseback riding."

Kate smiled at him over Ben's head.

When they returned to the farm, they found Molly sitting at the kitchen table, still dressed in the deep purple suit she had worn to church. She was reading the *Times*.

"Why are you still dressed up, Nana?" Ben asked.

"I'm going into the city with Alberto, Ben. We're going to a concert."

"I didn't know that," Kate said sharply.

"He only got the tickets yesterday. I guess I forgot to tell you."

Kate frowned. "You could have told me this morning while we were going to church."

"I'm sorry, dear, I forgot." Molly gave her an inquiring look. "Did you need me to watch Ben this afternoon?"

"No." But the frown remained on her face.

"Alberto is a great music lover," Daniel said. "He likes classical best, but he'll listen to anything."

Ben said, "Everybody's going out but Mommy."

This fact had not been lost on Kate. She said, "I'm the lucky one. I get to stay home with you."

Ben beamed. "Do you want to play cards?"

Before she could answer, someone knocked on the door. Molly went to answer it, then she and Alberto came back into the kitchen together. "Did you enjoy your ride?" he asked Kate courteously.

"Very much. The woods are still beautiful."

"Yes. In another two weeks, though, all the trees will be bare."

Molly said, "I'm ready, Alberto. We had better go if we want to make the concert."

"We will make it, Molly," he returned imperturbably. "Do you have a coat? It will be chilly by the time the concert lets out."

"My suit jacket is warm enough."

"Are you sure?"

Molly smiled at him. "I'm sure."

"Very well. Let us go then."

As the couple made their good-byes to the three who were staying, Kate wiped the frown from her face, though she was still frowning inside. There was something about Alberto that was almost too smooth, she thought. *I hope Mom isn't going to fall for all that Latin charm. We don't know anything about this guy, really. I hope she's going to be careful.*

It wasn't that Molly had never gone out with a man since her husband's death, Kate ruminated, but the man had always been a fellow teacher, and they had mostly gone to school functions. These outings with Alberto were *dates.*

Mentally, Kate shook her head. *So what? Mom has a lot on her mind right now, and going to a concert will be a good distraction for her. I shouldn't make more out of this than is there.*

"Earth to Kate," Daniel said.

She snapped to attention. "I'm sorry. Were you talking to me?"

"Ben and I were exploring the possibility of going to Friendly's for an ice cream. What do you think?"

Kate's eyes focused on Daniel. His long length was encased in jeans and a khaki golf jacket, a strand of black hair was hanging over his forehead, and his eyes were glinting with an emotion she couldn't place.

I see too much of him. I'm getting used to having him around, getting used to relying upon him, and that's a mistake. I have to remember that he has a relationship to Ben, but not to me.

She glanced at the kitchen clock. "It's awfully close to dinnertime."

"What are you doing for dinner?" Daniel asked.

"Good question. I'm sure there's something in the freezer I can cook."

"Save yourself the trouble of cooking, Kate, and come out to dinner with me. We can go to Franco's in Westport. Ben can have a small pizza all to himself and you and I can have the best lasagna in Connecticut. We'll have the ice cream for dessert."

The lasagna sounded terrific. "Well . . ." Kate said.

"Please, Mommy. Let's go. It will be fun."

She didn't have the heart to deny Ben, so she said, "Okay, Franco's it is."

Daniel smiled at her, and a little butterfly seemed to flutter in her stomach. She frowned. "Do you want to go now?"

"Sure. We're all hungry enough after the ride."

Kate had skipped lunch and was in fact starving. "Okay. The lasagna sounds great."

When Molly came back from her concert, Kate was waiting up for her. "How was the concert?" she asked, as Molly looked into the living room.

"It was lovely. It was a chamber music concert. Alberto knew one of the musicians."

"That's nice. I'm glad you had a good time."

"What did you do, dear?"

"Ben and I went out to Franco's with Daniel, then we went for ice cream for dessert. I'm still feeling stuffed."

Molly laughed.

"You really seem to like Alberto," Kate said.

"I do. I must confess, it's nice to have a man fussing over me. My femininity definitely feels threatened by this operation."

Kate said earnestly, "It shouldn't, Mom. It's not as if they're taking your whole breast. This is just a little lump."

"I know, but there will be scarring. And the shape of my breast will change."

"It doesn't matter."

"Maybe it doesn't matter to you, Kate, but it matters to me."

Kate had no answer.

Molly came over to where Kate was curled on the sofa and kissed her cheek. "I'm going to bed. It's late, and I'm tired."

Kate managed a smile. "See you in the morning."

She listened to Molly's footsteps on the stairs, then stared for a long time at the same page of her book. Finally, she, too, went up to bed.

18

The first thing Molly and Kate did on the morning of Molly's operation was to check into the hotel where Molly would be staying overnight. The hotel lobby looked like any other hotel lobby, and as they went up in the elevator to the hospital floor, Kate said, "This sure beats checking into a hospital."

"It certainly does."

Molly's room was the first room after the elevator. It contained a hospital bed, with all the appurtenances, and a regular twin bed as well. The window looked out on the street. Kate put their joint suitcase down on the small dresser. "This is great, Mom. I'll be right here beside you in case you need anything."

Someone knocked on the door, and a nurse with smooth brown hair tied at the nape of her neck came in. "Mrs. Foley? I'm Sarah. The nurses' station is just down the hall. Why don't you make yourselves comfortable, and I'll let you know when you're needed in the hospital."

"Thank you," Molly said.

"I know you can't eat anything, but there is quite a good restaurant downstairs if your daughter gets hungry."

"Thank you," Molly said again.

"There's a menu on the bedside table. You can order dinner from room service this evening. Your meal is paid for, but your daughter will have to pay for hers."

"Fine," Molly said, and wondered if she would possibly feel like eating just after an operation.

The nurse smiled at both of them and left.

"Well, we might as well make ourselves comfortable, Mom. You take the chair, and I'll take the bed."

Molly obediently sat in the upholstered wooden chair and Kate perched on the side of the bed.

Kate said, "You know, I was thinking that instead of fixing the roof, we should go for the new furnace first."

Molly, who understood that her daughter was trying to take her mind off the coming operation, played along. They were still debating the virtues of the furnace replacement over the roof when another nurse came to get Molly. Kate was allowed to accompany them.

They went down the elevator, through several long, windowless corridors, through a heavy fire door and into the hospital. The first stop was a dressing area, where Molly changed into a gown. The nurse gave her a bathrobe to cover the gown and nonslippery socks for her feet. Then she and Kate sat in the corridor and waited.

Some patients wandered by, others came by on gurneys. Molly felt perfectly calm. This was something that had to be done, and she was going to do it. Surreptitiously, she slipped her hand under her bathrobe and tenderly cupped her breast. "Good-bye," she thought half-humorously, half-sorrowfully.

Then the surgeon was coming down the hall. "Your time has come," she said with a smile. "We're all ready for you."

Molly stood up.

Kate kissed her. "Good luck, Mom. I'll be waiting for you."

"Thank you, dear."

"This way," the surgeon said, and Molly went with her along another long windowless corridor, down a second hall, and into a room with a table surrounded by all sorts of monitors. There were three people in the room, all dressed in surgical attire and wearing masks.

"If you'll just lie down on the table, Molly," one of them said pleasantly.

Molly said, "What a gyp. On *ER* you get to ride to the operation room on a gurney, and you most certainly don't have to climb onto the table yourself."

Everyone laughed, and Molly got on the table.

The woman who was the anesthesiologist introduced herself and explained that she was going to start the anesthetic and Molly was to count backward from five. She made it to three, and was out.

A nurse was standing next to her bed when she awoke. "She's coming around now," Molly heard her say. Then Kate was there.

"Mom? Mom? Can you hear me?"

"Yes."

Kate squeezed her hand and gave her a tremulous smile. "How do you feel?"

"I don't know," Molly returned. "The operation is over?"

"Yes."

The nurse said to Kate, "We'll keep her here for a little bit longer, then you can go back to the hotel."

She didn't know how long she remained in the recovery room, with Kate standing next to her like an archangel guarding paradise. Finally, though, they put her in a wheelchair and took her back to her hotel room, which looked positively cozy and welcoming after the vast, impersonality of the hospital.

She got out of the wheelchair and into bed perfectly easily. "I don't feel wobbly at all," she told the nurse.

"That's good. When you feel like it, you can call down to the restaurant and order dinner."

"All right."

The nurse left. Kate came over to kiss her cheek. "Just rest for a while, Mom. Then we'll see if you feel like eating."

"All right, Kate. But first I want to see what they've done." She opened the front of her hospital coat and looked down.

Thank God, was her first thought. She still had her breast. The two-inch incision had been made about a half inch above her nipple, but the nipple was still perfect. And the shape of the breast didn't look much changed. "This isn't bad at all."

Her sense of relief was huge.

Kate came over to look. The line of the incision was visible through the tape that covered it. "Wow," she said. "It looks great."

Molly smiled tremulously. "It does, doesn't it?"

Kate bent and kissed her cheek. "Get some rest, Mom."

She closed her eyes and an hour later she opened them and discovered that she was hungry. They had an excellent meal brought up from the restaurant, the nurse came in twice to check the IV that was in Molly's arm and the drain that was in her breast, then it was time for bed.

As she tried to find a comfortable sleeping position that would not compromise her breast, Molly said, "Thank you, Kate, for being with me today."

"Mom! Where else would I be?"

"I know. I'm lucky to have a daughter like you."

"You're always there for me when I need help. That's what we do. We help each other."

Molly smiled. "Yes. That's what we do."

"Good night, Mom."

"Good night, Kate."

They both settled down to sleep.

Molly got home at noon the following day and at twelve-thirty a delivery of a dozen magnificent red roses came from Alberto. Then came a beautiful floral arrangement from Daniel. Then came a lovely plant from the Monteros, which Daniel must have sent. Finally, a floral tribute from the English Department at Glendale High School arrived.

"My goodness," Molly said a little breathlessly.

"The place smells like a funeral home," Kate said.

"Kate! What a thing to say. It smells wonderful."

Kate, who had never once thought of sending her mother flowers, smiled wryly.

But she was hugely relieved by how well her mother seemed. Molly slept for part of the afternoon, but she was up soon after Daniel dropped Ben off from school. The three of them ate a snack in the kitchen, and Ben asked, "Would you like to sit quietly, and I'll read you a book, Nana?"

Molly said, "I would love to have you read me a book."

"Okay. And then maybe we can play cards."

"That sounds like fun."

Kate said, "Well, it looks as if I can safely leave you in Ben's hands, Mom. I have a lesson to teach."

"Go ahead, dear. I'll do just fine."

"Send Ben to fetch me if you need me."

"I won't need you."

"I hope not, but if you do . . ."

"If I do, I'll send Ben."

Kate went down to the riding ring to give her lesson.

Molly did not have to take any of the painkillers that the surgeon had prescribed, and two days after the operation she had the drain taken out of the wound. Kate was as relieved as Molly by how easily the operation had gone.

"Mom's doing great," she told George on the afternoon after Molly had had the drain removed. She was over at his farm because his prize golden retriever had given birth recently, and Kate had not yet seen the puppies.

The puppies were as beautiful as George had said they were, and after Kate had admired them they went into George's kitchen for a cup of coffee. Nothing in the kitchen had been changed since George's wife had died fifteen years earlier, with the exception that George had added a microwave in which he cooked the TV dinners that he existed on, and he had a new coffeemaker.

"Glad to hear that," George replied as he filled the coffeemaker with water.

"Is Tom Marshall going to take one of the puppies?" she asked, and they talked comfortably about the puppies' prospective homes as the coffee dripped. Then George poured two cups, put one in front of Kate at the kitchen table, and brought one over for himself. Before he sat down he said, "You didn't by any chance see a copy of today's *Daily News* did you?"

"We don't get the *News*. Why?"

"There was a picture of Daniel in it, that's all. He was at some big shindig in the city."

"Oh."

"He had a very glamorous-looking woman on his arm."

Kate took a swallow of coffee. "Do you have the paper handy?"

"It's right in the living room. Hold on."

George came back with the paper and plopped it on the table in front of Kate. It was already open to the page that sported Daniel's picture.

The photographer had caught him on his way into the dance. He was dressed in a tuxedo, and the woman on his arm wore an evening gown. Kate looked at the sculpted face of Alicia Peterson, at her mass of blond hair, at the fur wrap she was clutching around her bare shoulders, and felt a stab of intense dislike.

George said blandly, "I imagine he didn't ask you because he knew you wouldn't leave Molly."

"Don't be silly, George. Why would Daniel ask me to a dance, for God's sake? We don't have that kind of a relationship."

"What kind of a relationship do you have, Kate?" George asked gravely.

If anyone other than George or her mother had asked her that question, she would have told them in no uncertain terms that it was none of their business. To George she said truthfully, "I don't really know. I never expected to be spending this amount of time with Daniel. I see him or talk to him almost every single day. It's because of Ben, I know, but I hadn't expected him to be so . . . involved . . . with my own life."

George looked at her in silence. His skin looked like wrinkled leather under the hanging kitchen lamp fixture.

"Do you have something to say?" she asked finally.

"I do, but I don't know if I should say it. I don't want to scare you."

"Scare me? What on earth could scare me, George? You

had better tell me, or I'll be imagining all kinds of awful things."

"Daniel is interested in you, Kate. Interested in the way a man is interested in a woman he finds attractive. The question is, are you interested back?"

Kate stared at him. Finally, she said, "Do you mean you think Daniel is . . . romantically . . . interested in me?"

"That is exactly what I mean."

She shook her head. "I don't think so, George. Our relationship hinges on Ben. There's nothing beyond that."

George reached across the table and put a hand over hers. "Kate, I love you as if you were my own daughter. It's hurt me over these years to see how hard you've had to work." She tried to break in, but he tightened his hold on her hand and went on, "No, listen to me. I know you don't mind hard work. But the farm has deprived you of any kind of a normal social life. You've been so focused on getting it in the black that you haven't let anything else compete for your attention. Now that the farm is in the black, do you intend to continue devoting your entire life to it? Do you ever plan to get married? To have children other than Ben?"

Kate dropped her eyes. "I haven't had time to think about that much."

"That is precisely my point. Your father would have been proud of the way you dug in and made a success of High Meadow. But he wouldn't want you to make a slave of yourself to the farm, and that is what you have done, Kate. It's time you started to think of yourself and your own future."

Kate didn't say anything.

"Daniel seems to be a fine young man. He's interested in you. All I'm saying is: Give him a chance. Don't automatically shut him out, as I've seen you do to any number of men over the years."

"That's not true! What men have I shut out?"

"How about Dr. Winwood?"

"He's one of my vets!"

"He's one of your vets, and there was a time when he was interested in becoming something more, but you never saw it. I'll bet he asked you out, and you said no."

Kate frowned. "He might have invited me to dinner, but I like to have dinner on the weekend with Ben. I don't get much of a chance to do that during the week."

"I rest my case."

"I don't know about all of this, George. I don't think it would be a good idea for me to become involved that way with Daniel."

"Whyever not?"

"Because if it didn't work out, and we didn't end up getting married, it would be horribly awkward. I mean, we would have to see each other over Ben, and it would be well . . . awkward."

"Kate Foley, I never thought I'd see the day that you were a chicken heart."

"I'm not a chicken heart. I'm just being sensible."

"You're being a chicken."

Kate drew a long breath. "I'll tell you what I'm a chicken about, George. I'm a chicken about Mom. Every time I think that she has cancer, I get sick to my stomach. What would happen if she died? What would I do? I can't imagine my life without her."

George countered, "What if Molly doesn't die? What if she marries this Alberto fellow, who seems to be so keen on her? What if she goes to live in Colombia?"

"Mom isn't going to marry Alberto!"

"How do you know, young lady? Your mother has been a widow for a long time. How do you know that she might not want a new man in her life? She's still a mighty fine-looking woman."

Kate just stared at him.

"And one of these days, Ben will be all grown-up, Kate. He won't need you anymore. What are you going to do then? Muck out stalls and feed horses day in and day out? By yourself?"

Kate's face got very pale.

"You listen to me and give Daniel a chance. I worry about you, and I'm too old to have to worry like that."

Kate still didn't reply.

"Will you do it for me, Kate? If Daniel asks you out, will you go?"

She said faintly, "What if he doesn't ask me out?"

"He will," George said positively. "Believe me, he will."

19

$\mathcal{A}$ week after the operation, Molly went back to see the surgeon to get her pathology report. The big issue in this report was whether or not cancer had been found in the margins around the lump and/or in the lymph nodes the doctor had removed from under her arm. If the nodes were positive, it meant the cancer had spread. If they were negative, and the margins were negative, that meant that the cancer was probably localized in the lump. And the lump was gone.

Molly was far more nervous about the pathology report than she had been about the operation. If there was cancer in the lymph nodes, the chances of her beating the disease went way down. *This, not the surgery, is the life-and-death part*, she thought for the umpteenth time as Kate drove her to the surgeon's office. She knew, from the strained look on Kate's face, that her daughter was feeling the same way.

They reported to the reception desk and were told to take a seat in the small waiting room. A copy of the *New Haven Register* was on the table, and Kate asked if she'd like to look at it.

"No thanks, dear," Molly said.

A nurse came into the waiting room and called the overweight man who had been sitting with them.

Molly stared at the art museum print of Degas that hung on the wall across from her. *When I leave here, I'll know. I'll either be celebrating, or I'll be wishing I could turn back time to this minute, when I didn't know.*

The receptionist called her name. Molly got up and went to the desk. "I'm so sorry, Mrs. Foley, but the lab hasn't sent over your report yet." Molly's stomach twisted. *They can't expect me to wait another day!* "Dr. Rose has called, however, and they are going to fax it over. We'll let you know when it's here."

"Thank you," Molly said faintly, and went back to sit beside Kate.

"I can't believe it," Kate said, when Molly told her what had happened. She made no attempt to lower her voice. "They had a whole bloody week! What the hell were those people at the lab doing?"

"These things happen, Kate," Molly said.

Kate was implacable. "Well they shouldn't. If the lab didn't send the reports, someone in this office should have noticed that you had an appointment for today and made sure the pathology report was here."

The receptionist was studiously ignoring Kate's tirade.

"I'm one of many patients, Kate," Molly said.

"You're the only *you*. You're the only person who's my mother, who's Ben's grandmother. You're important, Mom. And so is everybody else who comes in here. You're not numbers, for God's sake."

Molly said, "I know, dear. I'm not happy about having to wait any longer, but there's nothing to be done. So calm down and read the newspaper."

They waited for half an hour. Molly memorized the details of the ballerinas in the Degas print and watched five patients come in and four be called. Finally, someone came to fetch her; she followed the nurse down a corridor and into a waiting room.

"Dr. Rose will be right with you," the nurse said pleasantly, giving her a gown to put on "open side in front."

"Thank you."

Left alone in the examination room, Molly broke into a sweat. *I'll know soon. I won't be able to hide behind not knowing anymore.*

She had changed into the gown and was sitting on the edge of the examining table, her hands clenched tightly in her lap, when Dr. Rose came in. The surgeon smiled at her, and said, "I have good news for you. The lymph nodes and the margins around the lump were clear."

Molly's stomach relaxed for the first time in days. She shut her eyes, and said softly, "Thank you, God."

"I thought you'd be happy to hear that. I took out the sentinel node and six more just to be sure, which is a lot less than we had to take just a few years ago. But we've discovered that when the sentinel node is clear, it usually means the cancer has not spread."

Molly raised her left arm, which had an incision under it. "My arm feels pretty good."

"Yes, but you're going to have to be careful. You don't want to get lymphedema, so be sure you don't lift any heavy weights with your left arm."

"What is lymphedema?"

"It's a blockage in the lymph system—in your case, to the arm. It causes swelling. You most definitely do not want to get lymphedema, so be careful you don't let any heavy weights hang on your arm either. The lymph system in that arm is compromised."

"Permanently?"

"Yes, permanently."

"I'm a high school teacher. I carry a lot of books."

"Then carry them in your right arm."

Molly sighed. "All right."

"The next thing for you to do is to make an appointment with an oncologist."

Molly was surprised. She had assumed that, since the cancer was localized, she wouldn't have to undergo further treatment. "Why? Isn't the cancer gone? You just told me it was confined to the lump."

"As far as we know, it's gone. But cancer can travel in the blood as well as the lymph, and there is no way to screen for that. That's why we use chemotherapy, even on patients like you, where the cancer seems to be localized."

"Oh," Molly said dismally. "Then I'm going to have to have chemotherapy?"

"It's much safer to have it, Mrs. Foley."

"I see."

"Do you have an oncologist you'd prefer?"

"No. The oncologist who treated my husband has since retired. Can you recommend someone to me, Doctor?"

"I usually recommend Anna Golden. She's well-known in her field, and she's empathetic as well. She works out of the MacGahren Cancer Center at St. Thomas's."

"She sounds fine."

"I'll make an appointment for you if you like."

"I don't like, but I suppose I must," Molly said with resignation.

The doctor examined her breast and told her everything looked fine. Then Molly went back to the reception room. Before she went to the desk, she turned to Kate, whose eyes were glued to her, and made the V for victory sign. Kate's smile could have lighted the whole of New Haven.

"I'm going to have to have chemotherapy anyway," Molly

explained to Kate in the car on the way home. "Apparently a few cells might have escaped from the lump, and they don't want to take the chance of them metastasizing anywhere else."

"I'm sorry, Mom. That's not going to be fun."

"No. Well. I have to do what I have to do, I suppose."

They weren't home half an hour before the telephone rang. Kate answered and it was Alberto. "I am calling about your mother's pathology report, Kate. Was it all right?"

"Yes, it was. Hold on, and I'll put Mom on herself."

Molly came to the phone and smiled when she heard the voice on the other end. "Yes. Both the margins and the lymph nodes were clear," she said.

Kate walked out of the kitchen in order to give her mother privacy. As she went upstairs to change into her barn clothes she thought of George's comment that Molly might marry Alberto.

She wouldn't. I know Mom, and she would never leave Ben. He needs her.

She sat down to lace up her paddock boots, paused, folded her hands, and closed her eyes. *Thank you, God, for Mom's good report. Thank you, thank you, thank you, thank you.* She opened her eyes, let out her breath, and went down to the barn.

Thanksgiving fell two days after Molly got the results of her pathology report. Molly had one sister, but she lived in California, and Tim Foley had been an only child, so the three Foleys had usually celebrated the holiday by themselves. This year Molly invited Daniel and Alberto to join them.

Kate spent the morning riding and doing her usual barn chores, but she cut the horses' turnout short so that she could be finished by one o'clock. When she got back to the house, the smell of roasting turkey filled the whole downstairs.

"It smells fabulous, Mom," she said as she came into the kitchen.

Cyrus went over to the stove and sniffed.

Kate laughed. "Cyrus agrees with me."

Molly smiled.

"Daniel and Ben will be here soon, I should think." Kate said. Daniel had taken Ben to New York to see the Macy's Thanksgiving Day Parade.

The doorbell rang. "I'll get it," Kate said, and went to let Alberto in. He was carrying two bottles of champagne.

"Wow," Kate said when she saw the labels.

"We have much to celebrate," Alberto said.

"Yes, we do." Kate watched Molly smile and accept the champagne to put in the refrigerator, and, for the first time, she tried to see her mother as others saw her, as Alberto must see her.

She saw a slim woman of average height, with short, silvery blond hair, and large blue-gray eyes. Her cheekbones were less sharp than Kate's, and there was great sweetness in her smile. Lines fanned out from her eyes, and there were fine lines around her mouth as well, but she did not look her fifty-five years.

Alberto said in an admonishing voice, "I hope you did not lift that turkey."

"No, Kate put it into the oven for me. I have been behaving myself, Alberto."

The two of them acted as if Alberto had every right to question Molly's actions. Kate frowned.

At this point, Ben came rushing into the kitchen. "I was on television! Did you see me?"

He was followed by Daniel, who said, "When are you going to start locking your front door, Kata?"

How did this happen? How did we become so familiar with these men?

"You're paranoid," she answered. Then, to Ben, "I'm afraid I was at the barn all during the parade."

"Did you see me, Nana?"

"I did indeed," Molly replied. "It was a lucky catch because I only had the TV on for a short time."

"I hope Connor saw me."

"How was the parade?" Kate asked her son.

"It was awesome," Ben informed her. "The balloons are *huge*."

"My father took Colleen and me to the parade once," Kate said reminiscently. "Remember, Mom? It was the coldest November on record, and we froze. When we got home, Dad gave us a shot of whiskey to warm up. He said it was an old Irish remedy. You were horrified."

"Maybe I should have a sip of whiskey," Ben said. "I'm cold."

"No way," Kate retorted. "I'll make you some hot cocoa."

"Hot cocoa sounds very appealing," Daniel said. "I think I'll have some, too."

Kate ended up making cocoa for everyone, and they sat around the kitchen table, talking and waiting for the turkey to be cooked.

"What a nice Thanksgiving," Molly said after Daniel and Alberto had left. The two women were at the kitchen sink, with Molly washing her prized Waterford wineglasses and Kate drying them.

"Yes, it was," Kate agreed.

"It's nice to have family to cook for."

"Alberto isn't exactly family."

"He feels like it," Molly said.

Kate said carefully, "Do you think that maybe we're getting too close to Daniel and Alberto, Mom?"

Molly rinsed a glass under running water. "What do you mean by *too close*?"

"It's just that, in a short period of time, they seem to have become very important in our lives. We were fine before they came along. It just makes me uneasy to think that we might be becoming . . . well, dependent . . . on them."

Molly handed the rinsed glass to Kate. "There's nothing wrong with our broadening our circle, Kate. When Ben was an infant, and the farm was in the red, then we had to have tunnel vision to achieve what we needed to achieve. But things are better now. At least, they will be better when I am finished with my cancer treatment."

Kate dried the glass and didn't answer.

"You are such a creature of habit," Molly said, half in exasperation, half in humor. "I think it's wonderful that these men have come into our lives. I think it's good for Ben, it's good for you, and it's good for me."

Kate put the glass on the table with the others she had dried.

Molly said, "Don't you like Alberto?"

"I like Alberto fine."

Molly soaped the last glass. "Good. I like him, too. I enjoy his company. We have a lot in common."

"What do you have in common?"

"Well, we both love music, and we both love the romantic poets."

"Can't you talk about music and the romantic poets at school?"

Molly rinsed the glass. "I can, but I particularly like talking about them to Alberto."

"Oh."

"He said he would be happy to take me to some of my chemotherapy appointments, so that will spare you trying to cram me into your busy schedule, Kate." She handed Kate the glass.

"Mom, I don't mind taking you to your chemotherapy appointments."

"I know you don't, dear, but it will be easier if you have someone to share the load. Alberto said he would help, as did Daniel."

"See—we're becoming dependent upon them."

"What's wrong with that?"

Kate dried the glass slowly. "I don't think it's . . . safe."

Molly untied her apron. "Are you still afraid that Daniel is going to drop Ben?"

"No. I'm not afraid of that. It's not Daniel's relationship to Ben that is bothering me. It's his relationship to *us*."

"To you, you mean."

Kate put the last glass on the table, and she and Molly began to carry them into the dining room to put back in the china closet. Molly opened the glass door, put her two glasses in, and turned to get the two glasses Kate was holding. Kate said abruptly, "This afternoon Daniel asked me to go with him to a party in a fancy hotel in New York."

"And what did you say?"

"I was so surprised I said yes. Then he told me I'd need a gown. I tried to beg off, but then he insulted me by saying he'd buy me a dress if I didn't have one. I told him that I could buy my own gown, thank you. So it ended up that I was buying a gown and going to this party." She gave her mother a dark look. "I think he outmaneuvered me."

Molly smiled. "Who is going to be at this party?"

"Daniel didn't say, but I assume it's some sort of an affair for the Yankees."

Molly said firmly, "I'm glad you're going. I think it will be good for you to broaden your horizons, dear. You can't spend the rest of your life communicating only to horse people."

"I'm interested in horses."

"Well, it's time you got interested in something besides horses. Young girls, like the ones you teach, are horse-mad; an adult has several interests, not just one."

Kate said stiffly, "Are you calling me a child?"

"Of course you're not a child, Kate. You are an excellent mother and businesswoman. But I do think a part of your growth has been . . . well, stunted . . . because of the responsibilities you took on when your father died."

"So now I'm stunted?"

Molly pushed back a silvery feather of hair. "You know what I mean. You've never really gone out with a man, dear, and you're twenty-seven years old. It's time you started to broaden your horizons. Go with Daniel to this party."

"It looks like I'm stuck with it," Kate said. She glanced at her watch. "I think I'll go up to bed, Mom. Six o'clock comes early."

"Yes, it does. Good night, dear."

"Good night."

Kate went up the stairs to her room, but instead of undressing, she sat on the edge of her full-sized bed staring at the picture of her sixteen-year-old self and Shane that hung on the wall. *Mom doesn't see what I see*, she thought. *She doesn't understand.*

The fact was, Kate herself did not fully understand the trauma that her father's death had inflicted on her. Tim Foley had been the biggest thing in Kate's life; he had represented everything to her that she would like to be. Most of all, he had represented security. There was nothing her father didn't know, nothing he couldn't do. And then he died, and left his widow and daughters with a debt-ridden, failing business and $10,000 worth of life insurance.

It was a blow from which Kate had never fully recovered. It accounted for her iron determination to do everything herself. She relied on her mother, but she trusted Molly. She didn't trust men very much. If her father, who had been her bulwark of security, could fail her, what could she expect from any other man?

Then Daniel had come along, and she could feel him slipping in under her guard, insinuating himself into her life. And she didn't . . . couldn't . . . trust him.

Why in the name of God did he invite me to this party? I have nothing to say to any of his friends. Mom is right, all I know is horses. I have no social conversation. I think I'd better tell Daniel that I can't go.

This decision, instead of making her feel satisfied, only made her feel irritable. *Maybe I should go. Maybe I should simply show Daniel that I'm not the type of woman who fits into his world. He should stick to the supermodels who know the game.*

She debated the question of her acceptance or rejection back and forth the whole time she was getting undressed. By the time she got into bed she had decided that she would go with Daniel because she didn't want him to think that she was afraid of going. Then she reached over, flicked the switch on her alarm to *on*, turned off her light, and settled down to sleep.

20

On the Tuesday after Thanksgiving, Molly had her appointment with Dr. Anna Golden, oncologist. Kate went with her.

The MacGahren Cancer Center was a relatively new building and one of its perks was that a whole area of free parking had been provided for patients right in the front of the center. Kate parked her Toyota Corolla, and she and Molly proceeded in the front door of the building after giving Molly's name to the parking attendant, who crossed it off on his list.

They had to walk down three corridors before they reached Dr. Golden's office. There was nothing to distinguish the oncologist's waiting room from the waiting rooms of any other doctors Molly had seen, except perhaps for the fact that two of the women waiting with her were wearing scarves on their heads.

They've lost their hair, Molly thought. *Will I lose mine? What will l look like without my hair? What will Alberto think?*

Kate perched motionless on the edge of her chair, like a falcon in a cage. Her antagonism to her surroundings was very clear by the set expression on her face.

How did Tim and I ever come to have such an intense child? It was not the first time that Molly had had that thought. She was a quiet, gentle woman, and Tim had been an easygoing Irishman with a great sense of humor. Where had Kate come from?

"Mrs. Foley?" A nurse was looking at her inquiringly.

"Yes."

"The doctor will see you now."

Molly got up and, accompanied by Kate, went through the door, down a hall, and into a doctor's office. The woman at the desk was writing something, but she looked up when Kate and Molly came in and smiled. "Please sit down. I'm Dr. Golden."

Molly and Kate sat in the two chairs that were placed next to Dr. Golden's desk. Molly looked at the doctor as she wrote and saw a sturdy woman of about forty-five, with wiry black hair and a determined nose. She put down her pen and looked at Molly.

"I have your report from Dr. Rose, and your surgery went very well. She is recommending chemotherapy to systemically destroy any cancer cells that might be lingering somewhere in your body. Only a small percentage of women have this problem but, unfortunately, we don't have a means of testing to discover in whom the cancer has spread and in whom it hasn't. Consequently, we give chemotherapy to all patients in your position."

"It sounds like using a bomb to kill a fly," Kate said.

"Unfortunately, yes, that's what it's like. Regrettably, at the moment, I don't have any other treatment I can offer you."

Molly said, "I understand."

The doctor continued, "There are three things we look at on the pathology report to determine which drugs to use on

you. The first is the size of the tumor. Yours was over a cen-
timeter, and we consider that large, but the other two evalu-
ating factors are positive. The HER2 gene, which signifies an
aggressive cancer, was not present in your tumor. This is a
good thing. If you tested positive for this gene, I would have
to put you on Adriamycin, which is a harsh drug. People on
Adriamycin tend to get very sick to their stomachs and have
complete hair loss."

"How delightful," Molly murmured faintly.

Kate looked fierce.

The doctor went on, "Third, your tumor tested positive for
estrogen receptive, which is also a good sign that the tumor
is less aggressive. It also means that, when we're finished
with these treatments, I'll probably put you on Tamoxifen,
which has had great success in preventing recurrences."

"I've read about Tamoxifen," Molly said.

Dr. Golden nodded. "So I'll offer you a choice. I can put
you on Adriamycin, which would be four treatments at three
weeks apart, or I can put you on the less aggressive cocktail
of Cytoxan, Methotrexate, and Fluorouracil. This combo is
given eight times at three-week intervals and, combined with
some good antinausea medication, will keep you more comfortable than the Adriamycin. You also don't have a complete
hair loss."

"Is this treatment as effective as the Adriamycin?"

"The difference between them is infinitesimal."

Molly said ironically, "So you're asking me if I want a
drug that will make me violently ill and cause all my hair to
fall out, or one that will be gentler and will let me keep my
hair."

The doctor smiled. "Basically."

"I would say that's a no-brainer. I'll take the Cytox . . .
whatever."

"Absolutely," Kate said. "As long as it gives Mom the same chance as the other would."

"I've used CMF for years, and I'm perfectly comfortable offering it to you."

"Okay, then," Kate said.

"We should get started as soon as possible."

Molly asked, "Will I be able to work?"

"You should."

"I think I'd like to schedule my treatments on a Friday. That will give me the weekend to recuperate before I have to go back to school on Monday."

"We can do that for you. You're a teacher, Molly?"

"Yes."

"One of the things that can happen when you're on chemotherapy is that your white blood count can get very low. This leaves you open to infection. That's why I would like you to get any dental work that you may need done before you start treatment. While you're in treatment I also want you to avoid anything that may give infection a chance to get in. No flossing your teeth, no using Q-Tips to clean your ears—things like that. If you get sick, if you get a fever, I'll have to put you in the hospital. So keep as far away from people with colds as possible."

"My goodness," Molly said faintly.

"All I can tell you is that it's not a pleasant treatment, but the results are excellent."

"That's what counts, I suppose," Molly said.

"Do you have any other questions?"

Molly looked at Kate, who shook her head.

"I don't think so, Dr. Golden. Thank you very much."

The doctor stood up. "Come with me, and I'll give you a flu shot before you go."

"Okay," Molly said.

"I'll wait outside, Mom."

Molly nodded. Kate waited until the doctor and her mother had left the room before going back to the outer office.

Kate took the ice blue dress she had bought at Lord & Taylor on Sunday out of her closet and looked at it. It was strapless and fell in a slim, straight line to her ankles. There was a slit up the back so she could walk. Molly had insisted that she buy it because it complemented her eyes.

What on earth possessed me to tell Daniel I would go with him to this party? I should have just told him to take the model. She put the dress down and went to her dresser drawer to take out the strapless brà and panty hose she had also bought on Sunday. She put everything on the bed and stared at it. *What if I can't think of a single thing to say to Daniel's friends? They'll think I'm a moron. Daniel will think I'm a moron. Why in hell did I say I would go to this party?*

Kate was not used to feeling unsure of herself, and she didn't like it one bit. She liked even less the sneaky feeling she had that the reason she had agreed to go with Daniel was to keep him from going with someone else.

"Damn," she said out loud, stripped down to her white cotton panties, and began to dress.

Her hair and makeup took a minute. Nothing needed to be done with her short cut except to brush it, and she dusted blush on her cheeks and put on lipstick. Cyrus watched all this activity with the air of a dog that is witnessing something new.

As she was coming out of the bathroom she ran into Molly in the hall. "Come into my bedroom so I can see you properly," Molly said.

Kate obediently followed her mother into the pretty

peach-colored master bedroom. Tears brimmed in Molly's eyes as she regarded her daughter. "You look beautiful, dear."

"I'm nervous as hell, Mom. What am I going to talk about?"

"I'm sure the rest of the Yankees will have their wives there. You can talk about children. Now, you need some jewelry, and I want you to wear my diamond earrings and my diamond pendant."

"Are you sure?"

"Positive." Molly went to the jewelry box that was on her dresser, opened it, and took some items out. "Come over here and put these on."

Kate obeyed, and when next she looked in the mirror that hung over Molly's dresser she nodded approval. "They look great. Thanks, Mom."

"You're welcome, dear."

Ben was watching television when Kate went downstairs, but he turned to look at her when she came into the living room. "Mommy! You look pretty."

"Thank you, Ben. Do you like my dress?"

"It's pretty."

She smiled at him.

"When is Daddy coming to get you?"

"He should be here shortly."

Ben went back to his television show, and Kate sat on the sofa, folded her hands with their polished nails in her lap, and thought, *This is a big mistake. I can't believe I did this to myself. I wish the evening were over, and I was just coming home instead of just going out.*

The doorbell rang.

"I'll get it!" Ben said.

Half a minute later he came back into the room hanging on to Daniel's hand. "Daddy's here, Mommy."

Slowly Kate stood up, looking at Ben and avoiding Daniel's eyes. With a shock of surprise she realized that she felt shy. She never felt shy.

"That is a very lovely dress, Kata," Daniel said.

"It's appropriate?"

"Very appropriate."

She looked at him for the first time. He was wearing a tuxedo. Something fluttered in her stomach. He said, "Don't worry. No one will ever guess that it's the first gown you've worn since your senior prom."

There was a smile in his brown eyes and, for some reason, the flutter in her stomach became more pronounced.

"Are you ready?" he asked.

"Yes."

"Where is your coat?"

"In the closet. I'll get it."

Kate came back in her Sunday coat, which was long and single-breasted and black. It was seven years old, but Molly had picked it up for her at a Talbot's sale and, as Kate kept telling Molly whenever her mother mentioned the possibility of her getting a new coat, Talbot's clothes never went out of style.

Molly came into the room right after Kate. "How are you, Daniel?" she asked pleasantly.

"Fine. I'll try not to be too late, Molly. I know that Kata has to get up early in the morning."

"Good grief," Kate said. "You sound like a prom date making promises to a worried mom."

Molly laughed.

Ben, who had caught only one word, said, "Are you going to a prom, Mommy?"

"I feel like it," Kate said.

"I can safely promise that the food will be much better than what is served at a prom," Daniel promised.

Molly laughed again.

Kate said mournfully, "I suppose we'd better go."

Daniel said with amusement, "You sound as if I'm escorting you to the guillotine."

"Frankly, I don't know why you asked me to this party, Daniel, and I don't know why I said yes. But it's too late to change our minds now."

"Yes. It is definitely too late. Come along before you really do chicken out on me."

Kate nodded.

"Have fun, Mommy," Ben said. "I'm glad Daddy is going with you and not that other lady."

There was a brief silence as the adults took in his words. Then Daniel said, "Good night Molly, good night, Ben."

I shouldn't have done this, Kate thought. *Now Ben will be expecting Daniel and me to be a couple. Damn. How stupid have I been?*

They went down the steps, and Kate stopped when she saw the black limousine parked in front of the house. "What's this?"

Daniel put a hand under her elbow and started walking her forward again. "What does it look like?"

"It looks like a limo. Where is your Mercedes?"

"I have an arrangement with Liam, the limo driver. He chauffeurs me when I go into New York so I don't have to worry about finding a parking space."

"You don't have to worry about drinking either," Kate said shrewdly.

"True." A wiry man of about thirty had gotten out of the car and was now holding the passenger door open for her.

Daniel said, "Kate Foley, this is Liam, the best chauffeur in New York City."

"I am that," the chauffeur responded in a pronounced Irish accent. "Pleased to meet you, Miss Foley."

"I'm pleased to meet you, Liam," Kate responded.

Daniel nodded for Kate to get in, which she did, and he went around to the other door and got in next to her. Liam established himself behind the wheel, started the car, and they were off.

It was dark in the backseat. Kate couldn't see Daniel clearly, but she sensed him with all the nerve endings of her body. She wanted to talk, to shatter with everyday chatter this feeling she had of being alone with him in the dark, but she couldn't think of a single thing to say. She crossed her arms in a gesture of protection.

They were on the Merritt Parkway before Daniel spoke. "How did Molly's appointment with the oncologist go?"

It was with great relief that Kate replied, "Haven't you heard?"

"I heard from Alberto, who talked to Molly, but I'd like to hear it from you as well."

Kate was delighted to have a topic of conversation to throw up between them and proceeded to tell him all about Molly's visit to the oncologist. She ended, "The doctor said that in 80 percent of women, chemotherapy is not needed at all. So Mom may have to undergo all of this unnecessarily."

"They have no test to discover if some cancer cells got loose?"

"No. So they hammer everybody."

"Molly's treatment sounds like what my mother had. She lost a lot of her hair, but she wasn't bald. And she wasn't too sick to her stomach, either. Exhaustion was the biggest side effect she had. I remember her telling me that her legs felt like rubber bands."

"Poor Mom. I feel so bad for her, Daniel. She's had so much hardship in her life. She lost her husband, she lost her daughter, and now this. It just doesn't seem fair."

"No, it doesn't," he agreed. "I told Molly I will be happy to help her with the chemo treatments. I'm off, and my time is relatively free."

"I can get Mom to her treatments," Kate said firmly. "Thank you anyway, though."

There was a slight pause, then Daniel said, "Well if you run into trouble, please call on me. I wasn't able to be there for my mother when she was undergoing treatment, and it would make me feel good to be able to help your mother."

Kate looked at him suspiciously, but it was too dark to make out his expression. Was he just trying to couch his offer in terms he knew she would find hard to reject? "All right. Thank you."

There was a pause, then he said, "I don't remember if I told you what this benefit is for."

Kate frowned. "You didn't tell me it was a benefit. You told me it was a party and I should wear a long dress."

His voice was casual. "It's the annual Elizabeth Taylor Benefit for AIDS. I go because it's a good cause. She raises a lot of money every year for AIDS research."

Kate said in a higher voice than usual, "Daniel. Please don't tell me that this party is going to be packed with celebrities."

"A lot of different kinds of people will be there, Kata."

She was getting angry. "You got me to go under false pretences! I thought it was a party for the Yankees!"

He said calmly, "I never told you that."

"You let me think it." She clenched her fists. "I could kill you. Are there going to be photographers there?"

He said, in a sane and reasonable voice that only made her more angry, "Look, Kata, it won't be so bad. There will be plenty of people more important than I am for the photographers to concentrate on."

"You lied to me."

"No, I didn't. I simply withheld a little information."

Kate stared at his shadowy face. "I hate people who lie."

"I'm sorry. I didn't think it would upset you so much."

"Why did you ask me? Why didn't you just take the supermodel?"

"I didn't want to spend an evening in the company of the supermodel. I wanted to spend an evening with you."

"And you expect me to be flattered by that?"

"I don't expect you to be anything. I simply hope that you will try very hard to enjoy the party. The food will be fabulous."

"Mom's cooking is fabulous. I don't have to go to a benefit to eat well."

"Do you want me to take you home?"

"No. But don't expect much of anything from me. I am totally clueless about the newest movies or the latest Broadway shows."

"Don't worry about it."

Kate's voice was bitter. "Easy for you to say. You're not facing an evening where you feel like you're in a foreign country and everyone is speaking a language you don't know."

For the first time there was an edge in Daniel's voice. "No, I am facing an evening with an unnecessarily shrill young woman who is rapidly getting on my nerves."

Good grief, Kate thought, taken aback by that edge. *I've upset him.* She said in a milder voice, "You should have told me the truth."

"I can see that." The edge was still there in his voice.

Kate let out her breath. She had never seen Daniel upset. He just hadn't realized how like a duck out of water she would feel. "I'm sorry I went off on you. You took me by surprise."

He said forcefully, "Kata, believe me when I say that you will be fine. These are only people, after all, no matter how much money they may make. Just as I am only a person."

"You're different."

"How?"

"I don't know, but you are."

"I will take that as a compliment."

She let out her breath. "All right, I'll go to this bloody benefit with you. But I still think it was a dirty trick not to tell me what I was getting myself into."

The edge was gone from his voice as he said, "It's a *party,* Kata, not a torture session."

It would be a torture session for her, but she didn't say that out loud. She didn't want to upset him again.

21

There was a crush of people and photographers around the hotel entrance when Daniel's limo pulled up.

"Good God," Kate said.

"They're here to ogle the movie stars," Daniel said. "You just have to get out of the car and walk into the hotel with me."

The limo pulled up in front of the hotel canopy, Liam came around to open the door, and Kate got out. Daniel slid across the seat and got out behind her. Strobes flashed and somewhere a girl screamed. Kate looked at the throng of fans as if they were creatures from another planet.

"Why would someone want to hang around in the cold to see a movie star get out of a car and go into a hotel?" she asked Daniel, as they hurried up the path between the police barricades. "It just seems so pointless."

"Would you hang around if it meant seeing Nuno Oliviero?"

"If he was going to ride, I'd wait forever. But not just to see him walk into a hotel."

Daniel smiled. "I can't disagree with you, Kata."

A female voice called "Marry me, Daniel!"

"Good God," Kate said.

Daniel laughed.

The tables in the ballroom were all covered in pale pink tablecloths, and the floral arrangements were breathtaking. Daniel got his table number from a man holding a list, and he and Kate made their way across the empty polished dance floor. Two couples were already seated at their table when they arrived.

"Daniel," a blond woman said. "How marvelous. You're at our table."

"Hello, Pam," Daniel said.

Kate looked at the blond young woman in the black gown who had greeted Daniel, and her eyes widened. "Are you Pam Alcott?" she asked.

The other woman gave a little shriek. "My God. Kate Foley. I can't believe it. Are you here with Daniel?"

"Yes, I am."

"How marvelous."

"I can see that I don't have to introduce you two," Daniel said.

"Kate and I competed against each other all through the junior equitation ranks," Pam said.

Kate was delighted to see a familiar face, and the tension in her stomach relaxed a little as she sat down and Daniel introduced them all around. The other couple at the table was in their early thirties and Daniel discovered he had once played in the same golf tournament with the man.

A waiter came to ask them what they would have to drink, and both Kate and Daniel asked for wine. Pam said, "I've been out of the horse world for a while now, Kate, but I hear you're doing very well at High Meadow. The children of several of my friends take lessons with you."

The three men started to talk about golf, and Kate and Pam talked about the horse business. It was a few minutes before Kate realized that the third woman at the table was completely left out of both conversations. Thinking, *There but for the grace of God go I*, she smiled at her, and said, "Do you ride?"

"No, but my daughter does."

"Where does she take lessons?"

"She takes lessons at Hunterly, in Morris County, New Jersey, near where we live."

The women chatted amiably until the last couple arrived at the table. Kate looked up to see a very tall, very thin, very stunning red-haired woman looking at Daniel. "Hello, Daniel," she said.

He made a motion to stand up. "Alicia. How are you?"

The name set off an alarm in Kate's mind. *This must be the supermodel.*

Her eyes, which Kate saw were green, flicked once around the table, stopping briefly at Kate. Then she said to Daniel, "Introduce us, won't you."

"Are you sitting with us?" Daniel's voice sounded courteous, but Kate could see his hand tense around the stem of his wineglass.

"Yes. Isn't it nice? We'll have a chance to catch up with each other."

Daniel leaned over to shake the hand of Alicia's escort. "Daniel Montero," he introduced himself.

"Guy Williams." The escort looked as if he had just stepped out of the page of a Ralph Lauren Polo commercial.

Introductions went around the table, and the newly arrived couple sat down in the two empty chairs, which were next to Daniel. "Have you heard from Jason yet about the photography commercial?" Alicia asked him.

"Yes. They want me to do it."

The conversation went back and forth between the two of

them for almost a minute, with the others listening. Then, when it became clear that Alicia had every intention of monopolizing Daniel, Pam said to Kate, "How old does a child have to be before you take her into your program?"

Kate answered, then the others at the table also began to talk among themselves.

The first course of the meal, grilled asparagus and smoked salmon, was served, and Alicia continued to monopolize Daniel. Kate could feel herself getting annoyed. The woman was being inexcusably rude. The orchestra began to play, and Daniel said firmly, "Please excuse me, Alicia," and turned to Kate. "Would you like to dance, Kata?"

Kate was more than happy to remove Daniel from the clutches of the supermodel, and she accompanied him to the dance floor, where the orchestra was playing an old George Harrison song, "Something in the Way She Moves." When he held out his arms she went into them.

He was so big compared to her. The top of her head fit neatly under his chin and, if she wanted to, she could rest her cheek against his heart. He held her hand with one hand and the other rested on her waist. She felt something inside her go very still.

He bent his head and said, "I'm sorry about Alicia. I had no idea that she would be at our table."

"She's very rude," Kate murmured.

"Yes, she is. She's always been this way; she just focuses on me and tunes everyone else out. At first, I thought it was flattering. Now it's just tiresome."

They danced for a few steps. Kate had no difficulty following him; her body seemed to fit so easily into his. Dreamily, she closed her eyes.

He said, "I could extricate myself from her if I was rude

enough, but I hate to have to do that. It will make everyone at the table uncomfortable."

It took Kate a moment to follow the conversation. Then she said, "She's very beautiful."

"She's too skinny."

Kate wished he would stop talking and just dance. Then someone said, "Kate Foley, I never expected to see you here."

Kate blinked at the silver-haired man who had just spoken to her. "Oh," she said. "Dr. Madison." She blinked again. "I could say the same thing about you."

Richard Madison was the top partner in Turnpike Equine, which was Kate's veterinary group. Recently his availability to local farms had been severely restricted by his job as vet to the United States Equestrian Team, but he had been a good friend of Kate's father, and he always came out to a High Meadow call if he was in Connecticut. Now he nodded toward his wife, and said, "Vera does volunteer work for AIDS research. That's why we're here."

Kate said, "I'm here with Daniel." The music stopped and people started to leave the floor. Kate introduced Daniel to Dr. and Mrs. Madison, and they talked for a few moments before returning to their respective places.

As they threaded their way through the tables, Daniel said, "I think you know more people here than I do."

Kate gave him a wondering look. "Isn't it strange?"

They sat down in time to be served a lovely Caesar salad. Alicia immediately monopolized Daniel, and Kate talked to the two other women about the reading programs in their children's schools. The orchestra played a Latin-sounding song, and Alicia said, "Let's rumba, Daniel."

"No thank you, Alicia," Daniel replied pleasantly.

"Oh come on, don't be a pain. You know you love to dance."

"I do, but it is not polite for me to leave the woman I came with, Alicia."

Alicia looked at Kate. "You don't mind, do you?"

Kate, who had been growing progressively more annoyed with the supermodel, said evenly, "Yes, I do."

Alicia blinked. "My God. It's only a dance."

"You have your own escort," Kate said bluntly. "Dance with him."

"Good for you," the man next to Kate muttered under his breath.

"An excellent idea," the Ralph Lauren type said. "Come along, darling, and behave yourself."

There was a little silence at the table as the two of them left for the dance floor. Then Kate said to Daniel, "Sorry, but she ticked me off."

He gave her a look she couldn't read. "I'm happy that you felt the need to protect me."

Everyone laughed.

The third woman at the table said to Daniel, "Have you ever been to Margarita Island? My husband and I were thinking of going there on vacation, but I've never met anyone who's actually been there."

Daniel responded, and the conversation became general, with people talking about the best beaches and the best resorts. Kate sipped her wine and listened.

"Have you ever been to the Caribbean, Kata?"

"No. The only ocean I've ever seen is in Rhode Island. I'm not much of a beach person. My skin can't take the sun."

"You have gorgeous skin," Pam said.

Kate, who was always uncomfortable accepting compliments about her looks, muttered, "Thank you."

The orchestra stopped playing, Alicia came back to the table and once again monopolized Daniel's attention. Dinner was served and a few of the other people at the table attempted to involve Daniel in their conversations, but Alicia steamrolled right through them.

What a bitch, Kate thought. *I wonder if he was ever serious about her?*

The orchestra struck up a slow song and Daniel turned away from Alicia, and said, "Do you care to dance, Kata?"

She had been waiting to dance with him again. "Sure," she said agreeably, and followed him out to the floor.

"I'm sorry," he said as he held out his arms to her. "Alicia is behaving very badly."

"Yes, she is. Why are you letting her behave so badly?"

He shrugged and looked as helpless as it was possible for him to look. "I was brought up to be polite to women."

"By being polite to her, you're being rude to the rest of us," she pointed out.

"Let's not talk about Alicia. Let's just dance."

That was okay by Kate, and she moved into his arms. The orchestra was playing an old song that Kate knew from her mother, and the words floated around in her brain as she moved to the music with Daniel. *Moon River, wider than a mile, I'm crossing you in style one day . . .*

She felt his big body moving in rhythm with hers, and the stillness she had experienced before enveloped her again. All of the surrounding dancers seemed to fade away, and it was just she and Daniel, dancing to the strains of "Moon River." When the dance was finally over she looked up at him and smiled. She expected him to smile back, but his face wore a hard, narrow-eyed look, which surprised her. She was just going to ask him what he was thinking when the look was replaced by his usual good-humored smile.

They solved the problem of Alicia by staying out on the dance floor and dancing again.

The rest of the evening went by uneventfully, and by twelve-thirty Daniel and Kate were in the limo on their way home to Connecticut. In the darkness of the backseat, Kate yawned hugely.

"Did you enjoy yourself?" Daniel asked, his voice coming out of the darkness next to her.

"It was fine. It ended just in time, though. I was starting to run out of conversation."

"I usually don't go to these formal affairs, but I felt I had to attend this one."

"I didn't know you were so concerned about AIDS."

"Well . . . I do have a college friend who has it."

"That's too bad."

He didn't reply. The backseat was enshrouded in darkness and, even though she couldn't see him, Kate was acutely conscious of his closeness. It was as if her skin had peeled off and all of her nerve endings were exposed. She sat very still and breathed shallowly. *What is happening here?*

He said softly, "I know you're exhausted from the effort of making conversation all night, so I won't go on talking. Go to sleep, Kata, if you're tired." Before she realized what was happening, he had reached an arm around her and brought her head to rest against his shoulder. "There, that's better. I'll wake you when we're home."

Part of Kate wanted to pull away instantly, and part of her wanted intensely to stay. "I'll muss your tuxedo," she said lamely.

"That doesn't matter."

I will never in a million years be able to sleep, she thought. She felt the silk of his lapel under her cheek and the hardness of his shoulder beneath it.

"Relax," he said. "Relax and go to sleep."

Hah. Fat chance. But as the moments ticked by, she did relax. He was so warm, and it was so comfortable in the circle of his arm. Within six minutes, Kate was asleep.

Daniel woke her when they were at the front door of High Meadow. "Wake up, Kata. You're home."

"Wha . . . ?" She jerked away from him and sat bolt upright.

"You're home," he repeated.

"My goodness. I fell asleep."

"Yes, you did. And you didn't snore."

"I never snore," she said indignantly.

"I'm glad to hear that."

Liam had opened the door for her to get out, and Daniel followed her. When she realized that he was going to walk her to her door she said, "Stay here, Daniel. I'm perfectly safe."

"I was brought up to walk ladies to their doors," he said imperturbably, and took her arm.

Molly had actually locked the door, and Kate had to use her key. Once the door was open, she looked up at Daniel and produced a smile. "Thank you for inviting me."

The light on the porch threw a slanting yellowish light on his face. She couldn't read his expression. He said, "Do you know why I really went to that benefit tonight?"

"No."

"I wanted to dance with you."

Her eyes widened.

He bent, took her chin in his fingers, and tilted her face up to his. He kissed her lightly on the lips. "See you tomorrow," he murmured, and went back to the car.

Kate let herself into the house and stood for a moment in the hallway trying to pull herself together. What was Daniel trying to say to her? That he wanted a romantic relationship between them? *I've never had a romantic relationship with anybody*, Kate thought. *When it comes to romantic relationships I'm utterly clueless.*

I could squash this. I could simply tell Daniel that I don't think it's a good idea, and I'm sure he would respect my wishes. But . . . do I want to do that?

Kate pondered this question as she walked slowly up the stairs and into her bedroom. She switched on the light and looked around the room that had been hers since she was an infant. It was a blue-and-white room, like the living room, with a Wedgwood blue comforter on her full-sized bed. The walls were pale blue, and the woodwork was painted white. Kate unzipped her dress and stepped out of it. *Best not to do anything right now. Best just to let things take their course and see how they develop.*

It was cold in her bedroom, and she jumped into her pajamas quickly, washed her face, brushed her teeth, set her alarm, and fell into bed.

22

Molly worked until noon on Friday, then she went home, and Kate drove her to the hospital for her first chemotherapy treatment. It took about two hours for the drugs to drip into the vein in her arm, then Kate took her home.

She felt tired and vaguely nauseated, and when Kate told her to lie down, she didn't protest. Ben had gone over to Connor's house after school, and Kate had lessons, so the house was quiet, and Molly went to sleep. When she awoke it was dark outside.

She lay still for a moment, taking stock of how she felt. There was an unpleasant taste in her mouth and she felt generally unwell, as if she were hungover after a drinking bout. The thought of food made her queasy, but she thought a cup of tea would be good.

She made the tea and sat at the kitchen table. *So it's started*, she thought. *One down and seven more to go*. The months stretched before her like an eon of time. And after that, she had to go through radiation.

I can't look that far ahead, or I'll get discouraged. I need to get through one treatment at a time. The first one is done, and now I have to concentrate on getting better from it.

She was sitting over a second cup of tea when Kate came in. "How's it going, Mom?"

"Not too bad, dear. I haven't had to throw up, or anything like that."

"That's great. Did you eat anything?"

"I had a slice of toast with my tea."

"Do you want anything else?"

"No."

"Okay." Kate went over to the refrigerator, took a Lean Cuisine out of the freezer, and popped it in the micro. When the buzzer rang, she removed it, came and set it down on one of the hunting-print place mats that lay on the table. Molly saw that it was some kind of a pasta and chicken meal, and Kate tucked into it with her usual hearty appetite. Molly repressed a shudder. The sight of frozen dinners always made her shudder, even when she was feeling well. Today it looked even less appetizing than usual.

Kate had finished her dinner and was putting the kettle on for more tea when the phone rang. She picked up the kitchen extension. "Oh, hello, Alberto." She listened for a moment then said, "She's right here; I'll put her on, and she can tell you yourself."

She brought the phone over to where Molly was sitting, and said, "It's Alberto."

Molly put the phone to her ear. "Hello, Alberto. How nice of you to call."

They spoke briefly and as soon as Molly hung up, the phone rang again. This time it was Ben, who was staying over at Connor's for the night. "How are you, Nana?" he asked when Kate put her on. "Are you sick?"

"I'm just tired, Ben. I think I'll go to bed early tonight. Otherwise, I'm fine. When are you coming home?"

"Daddy is coming to get me tomorrow, and he's taking me

and Connor to see the eagle sanctuary. I'll be home after that."

"Good. I hope you have fun."

"I will. I love you, Nana."

Tears stung behind Molly's eyes. "I love you, too, Ben. Don't stay up all night now."

"Okay."

"See you tomorrow."

"Bye, Nana."

Molly hung up. "He is just the sweetest child."

Kate smiled. "I know. He takes after Colleen that way."

"Yes, Colleen was sweet."

"Unlike me."

"You were always much too intense to be sweet. Even when you were a tiny infant, you were so determined. I used to feel sometimes as if I was holding a tiger cub in my arms."

Kate laughed.

"I think I'm going to go back to bed, dear. I really do feel wiped out."

Kate came to kiss her cheek. "Okay, Mom. I hope you'll feel better tomorrow."

"I hope so, too."

Molly climbed the stairs feeling like an old woman. Inside her bedroom, she looked at her rumpled queen-sized bed. She had lain down on top of the quilt earlier, and the blanket she had used was still thrown across the peach-colored quilt. She went to fold it and lay it neatly across the chest that was at the bottom of the bed.

It was nice of Alberto to call. He's a very nice man. I thought perhaps the cancer might have driven him away. He went through this once with his wife, and I certainly wouldn't blame him if he didn't want to go through it again.

But he had called, and he had mentioned going out together when she felt better. Molly felt pleased. Alberto was as different from Tim as a man could be, but she liked him very much.

It can never come to anything; after all, he lives in Colombia, and I couldn't leave Kate and Ben. But it's fun after all these years to go out to dinner with a man.

Molly turned down the bed and began to undress.

Molly felt fairly well on Saturday, the day after the treatment, but on Sunday she had to leave church before the consecration. Kate took her home, and she went to bed and stayed there for the rest of the day. "I feel like I have the flu," she told Kate. "I simply feel like a rag."

"Stay in bed, then," Kate advised.

"I hope I can go to school tomorrow."

"If you can't, you can't, and that's all there is to it, Mom. Don't worry. Just rest."

Daniel brought Ben home, and her grandson came in to kiss her and ask how she felt. He was holding a bouquet of flowers. "Daddy bought you these, Nana. He says he hopes you feel better."

"Thank you, sweetheart. Take them downstairs and have Mommy put them in some water."

Kate brought them upstairs again, this time in a vase. "Can I get you something, Mom? A cup of tea? Some ginger ale?"

"No thank you, dear. I'm just going to rest."

She dozed on and off for the rest of the day, slept through the night and woke to the sound of her alarm on Monday morning. She got out of bed, got dressed, and went down to the kitchen. By the time Kate came in from feeding the horses, Molly was making Ben his breakfast.

"Mom! Are you sure you're well enough to go to school?"

"If I can't make it through, I'll leave, but I want to keep my life as normal as possible, Kate. It will help me to cope."

"All right," Kate said doubtfully. "But you were pretty wiped out yesterday."

"I feel better this morning."

Molly made it through the school day, but by the time she got home she was exhausted. She waved to Kate, who was standing at the bottom of the drive waiting for Ben's bus to drop him off, and went on up to the house. She didn't even take her school bag in with her; the effort of lifting it seemed too much.

I'll have a cup of tea, then I'll tackle the stairs and go to bed, she thought. She was sipping tea at the kitchen table when Kate and Ben came in.

"Guess what, Nana? I'm in the Christmas play at school."

"That's wonderful, Ben. What kind of a play is it?"

"It's about a crippled boy named Tiny Tim."

"And are you playing Tiny Tim?"

"Yes, I am. But I didn't get picked because I'm tiny; I got picked because I can talk real loud, and everyone will be able to hear me."

"I can't wait to see it."

Kate said, "Wash your hands, Ben, and you can have some milk and a granola bar."

Ben went out into the hallway to use the downstairs bathroom, and Kate looked at her mother closely. "You look beat, Mom. How did the day go?"

"I got through it, but I'm tired. I think I'll take a nap before I start dinner."

"Don't worry about dinner, Alberto is having it delivered."

"What?"

"He called last night and said he was ordering dinner from a caterer's for us, and it would be delivered at six o'clock."

Molly felt a rush of relief that she wouldn't have to cook. "He shouldn't have done that," she said weakly.

"Well, he did it, so we might as well enjoy it. I just hope he didn't order something too fancy, or Ben won't eat it."

Molly went upstairs to lie down. *How kind of Alberto. He could have just sent flowers, and I would have been pleased. But to think of having dinner sent over! That was truly thoughtful.*

On an impulse, she picked up the phone and dialed Daniel's number. Alberto answered.

"It's Molly. I just called to say thank you for the dinner. What a lovely surprise to find out I don't have to cook tonight."

"I am happy it will be helpful to you. How are you feeling?"

"Tired and a little nauseated. It could be much worse."

"I ordered chicken in a plain wine sauce. It's very mild, so perhaps you will be able to eat something."

"I'm sure I will. It was so thoughtful of you, Alberto."

"You are most welcome, Molly. And now I think that you should lie down."

She smiled. "All right."

"I'll call tomorrow to see how you are doing."

"Wonderful."

Molly hung up the phone, crawled in under her quilt, and went to sleep. She woke at five and went down to the kitchen, where she found Ben doing his homework.

"Have you been working for long?" she asked him.

"No. I was down at the barn with Mommy. She sent me home to do my homework before dinner."

"Is it anything you need help with?"

"It's arithmetic, Nana. I'm good at arithmetic."

"Yes, you are."

"You can check my answers if you want," he said generously.

"I'd love to do that."

The dinner came promptly at six, and Molly and Ben had a feast on chicken in wine sauce, small roasted potatoes, green beans, rolls, and salad. Molly made a plate for Kate and put it in the refrigerator to be warmed up when she came in. Then she checked Ben's homework, which was correct.

She sent Ben into the living room to do his nightly half hour of reading and cleared away the aluminum baking dishes the dinner had come in. Then she sat at the kitchen table with the newspaper, but she didn't read it. Instead, she thought.

How deeply considerate of Alberto to send over dinner. Tim would have sent flowers. Alberto really thought about what would be most helpful to me.

It seems as if I'm spending a lot of time lately thinking about Alberto. We've only been out a few times; I can't let myself get carried away because he's been kind.

But I like him, I like him a lot. He feels about things the way I feel. He's real. He makes me feel alive. He makes me feel attractive, like I'm somebody besides Kate's mother and Ben's grandmother.

Unfortunately, I won't be attractive when most of my hair falls out.

What am I going to do about that? Get a wig? A wig is going to dig into my head and bother me, but I suppose I'll have to get something. I can't go to school looking bald; I'll scare the kids.

What will Alberto think when my hair falls out?

Do I care what Alberto thinks?

Yes, I do.

Do I care what Daniel thinks?

Not really.

Oh dear. I think I'm falling for Alberto.

Is that such a bad thing?

It's not that it's a bad thing, it's that it's a pointless thing. Alberto is planning to go back to his family in Colombia. His book will be published in Colombia. His life is in Colombia.

I can't possibly go and live in Colombia.

Maybe I should stop seeing him. There's no point in setting myself up for heartbreak.

Damn, damn, damn. After all these years I meet a man I really like, and he has to be Colombian.

"I finished my chapter, Nana. Can I put the television on now?"

She smiled at her grandson, "Yes, Ben. You can watch television."

Ben needs me. Kate needs me. I'm not free to please myself right now.

I think I had better explain that to Alberto.

23

The phone in the barn rang while Kate was mucking out Shane's stall. It was Dr. Madison. "Kate, I'm over at George Murray's place, and they've just taken him off in an ambulance. I think he had a heart attack."

"Oh my God."

"It's a miracle that I happened to be here; he went down like a tree. I called 911 and started CPR, but I can't stay here. Someone is going to have to look after these horses until . . . well, until George can do it himself."

"I'll look after the horses. Were you able to start him breathing again?"

"No."

"Shit."

"Yes."

"All right, Dr. Madison. Thanks for calling me. I'll look after George's horses. Which hospital did they take him to?"

"I think they went to Bridgeport."

"Okay."

Kate hung up the phone and went back to finish mucking Shane's stall. *I'll bring my horses in early, then I'll go over to George's and get his horses in. Then I'll call the hospital. What lessons do I have scheduled for this afternoon?*

She wheeled the wheelbarrow to the muck heap, emptied it, returned to the barn, and started on her last stall. Then she let her school horses in by simply opening the big door at the back of the indoor arena. The herd came racing in, Max in front as always, the others meticulously in the order of their herd status. All the animals knew their own stalls and were eager for the hay they knew awaited them, so all Kate had to do was go around and close the stall doors. After she walked in the private horses, she went up to the house, left a note for her mother, and drove over to George's.

George's was a smaller property than High Meadow. The stable was a four-stall barn, which housed three horses: George's old hunter and two Morgans, which he drove. The hunter was already in his stall; evidently he had been the subject of the vet's ministrations. Kate brought the Morgans in, gave all the horses hay and made sure their water buckets were full, then went to call the hospital.

There was no information available on George Murray.

The hospital was only fifteen minutes away, and Kate decided to simply go. She put George's Jack Russell, Samson, in the car with Cyrus and drove to the emergency entrance, where she parked the car. She went inside and asked for George.

The receptionist told her to wait and, after a few minutes, a blond young man in scrubs came out to talk to her. "I'm Dr. Fowler," he said. "Are you Mr. Murray's daughter?"

"No, I'm a good friend."

"Do you know how we can contact his family?"

"He has one son, and he's a doctor in Massachusetts."

"Would you have his phone number?"

"I probably have it at home." She gripped her hands together hard. "What's going on? Is George going to be okay?"

"I'm very sorry," Dr. Fowler replied, "but he was dead on arrival. It was impossible to resuscitate him."

No, Kate thought numbly. *I can't believe it. George isn't dead. He can't be dead. He's only sixty-eight.*

She said this last thought out loud.

"I'm sorry," the doctor repeated. "Would it be possible for you to give us his son's phone number so we can notify him?"

"I'll have to go home and call you. I don't have it with me."

"I would appreciate that, Miss Foley."

Kate drove home and looked up Ken Murray's phone numbers. There were two of them, one for home and one for the office. She dialed the office number and got a receptionist.

"This is Kate Foley. I'm calling about Dr. Murray's father. I'm afraid I have bad news. Will you put him on, please?"

She waited for perhaps a minute and a half, then she heard Ken's voice speaking her name. "Kate?"

"Ken, I'm so sorry to have to tell you this, but George had a heart attack this morning. He was dead by the time they got him to the hospital."

"My God."

"I know. It's a shock."

"There was no warning?"

"Not that I know of. He seemed perfectly normal the last time I saw him. He was talking about showing the Morgans at Fox Ridge this spring."

"I'll come down tonight."

"The hospital wants you to call—to make dispositions for the . . . the body."

"Do you have the number?"

She gave it to him.

"Is anyone looking after the horses?

"I am. And I have Samson with me, so you don't have to worry about him."

"Thanks, Kate. Is . . . is Kirby White still in business?"

"Yes. Do you want their number?"

"If you wouldn't mind. I'll have to make arrangements for a wake. Dad had a lot of friends who will want to say good-bye."

"Here's the number," Kate said.

She hung up and glanced at her watch. It was time for Ben's bus.

"Cyrus!" The shepherd lifted his head from his paws.

"Go get Ben, Cyrus." She opened the kitchen door. "Go get Ben."

The shepherd trotted out the door, then began to lope down the driveway. Kate closed the door to keep the heat in the house, sat down at the table, and buried her face in her hands.

Oh George. I can't believe that this has happened. It shouldn't have happened. You were in great shape.

A cloud of depression so thick it was almost palpable engulfed her.

When Cyrus and Ben came into the kitchen she looked at her son and said, "I've had bad news, Ben. George had a heart attack this morning."

"Is he okay, Mommy?"

"No, he's not okay. He died."

"Oh." Ben's eyes were even larger than usual.

Kate managed a small smile. "I'm feeling very sad. I'll miss him terribly."

Ben came over and put his small hand over hers on the table. "I'm sorry, Mommy."

Kate put her arms around him and hugged him. "Thank

you, Ben." It was so sweet to feel his strong little body pressed against her. She bent her head and kissed the top of his head. "I'm going to have to take care of his horses."

"I'll help you, Mommy."

"Thank you, sweetheart. I appreciate that."

Ben was sitting at the kitchen table eating a peanut butter cookie when Molly came in. Kate gave her the news.

"Oh, Kate. Oh no. I'm so sorry, darling."

Kate nodded. "I talked to Ken, and he's coming down tonight. I told him I'd look after George's horses."

Molly looked as if she was going to protest, but then she said nothing.

Kate looked at the kitchen clock. "I have a lesson in fifteen minutes. Mom, do you think you could call the people in my six o'clock lesson and tell them it's canceled? That way, I can feed here a little early and get over to feed at George's before his horses get too anxious."

"Of course I can call for you, Kate."

"I wrote down the names for you. The numbers are on the Rolodex in my office."

"Okay."

Ben said, "Have another cup of tea, Mommy. It will make you feel better."

Both women laughed. Kate said, "I haven't time, Ben. But I will have a cookie."

Ben passed her the tin, and she took one and went out. Cyrus followed her and, after the briefest of pauses, Samson went out after Cyrus.

Kate was just finishing up in George's barn when Ken Murray's car pulled in. His wife and two sons went into the house, but he walked over to the barn to talk to Kate.

"The wake will be Thursday and the funeral on Friday,"

he said to her. "I made arrangements with Kirby White in town."

Kate nodded. "Have you notified the newspapers?"

"Kirby White did that for me."

Kate nodded again. Ken Murray was six years older than she and they had never been close friends, but they had known each other for a long time. "I'm so sorry, Ken," she said now. "He was a wonderful man."

"You're going to miss him more than I will, Kate. He was part of your life in a way that he wasn't part of mine anymore."

Kate knew that this was true and didn't try to deny it.

Ken looked down at the small terrier that was standing next to Kate. He bent to pet him. "Hey there, fellow. What's going to become of you, eh?"

"I can take him home with me tonight, if he'll be too much trouble for you," Kate said.

"Do you think you could keep him permanently, Kate? Jason, my younger son, is allergic to animals."

"Of course I'll keep him."

"Thank you. I wish the horses could be disposed of so easily."

Kate stiffened at his use of the word "disposed." "George loved his horses almost as much as he loved Samson. You can't be thinking of putting them down?"

"I can probably sell the Morgans. Dad showed them, and they did pretty well. But Sebastian is ancient. Who will take him?"

"I will," Kate said promptly. "I just lost a boarder the other day—the owner moved to Maryland—so I have an empty stall. I would be honored to take Sebastian."

"Thank you, Kate. I'll pay his boarding fee for as long as you have him, I promise you."

Kate nodded.

They spoke for a few more minutes, then Ken went up to the house, and Kate got in her car to go home.

Kate didn't cry when she gave the news to Daniel, nor did she cry when she saw the obituary notice in the local paper. She didn't even cry when she was petting Samson and trying to reassure him. Nor did she cry when she walked into the funeral home and saw George lying in a coffin.

The wake was crowded. Ken had asked Kate to stand with the family. "You're the daughter Dad never had. Besides, you'll know more people than I will," he had said. So she stood from three to five in the afternoon and from seven to nine at night, shaking hands and being kissed by all of George's friends.

Daniel came in the evening. "I came for you," he said when she told him she was surprised to see him. "Molly had to stay home with Ben tonight, and I thought you should have someone here. I know you cared for him deeply. I am so sorry, Kata. All I can say is that he didn't suffer."

Everybody had been saying that, and it was even true, but it didn't make Kate feel much better. "Thank you," she said now. "I appreciate your coming, Daniel."

She didn't cry until the wake was over and she went up to say a prayer in front of the casket. She looked at George. *God. I can't believe this is happening.* And the dam that she had built against grief ruptured, and she started to sob.

Someone put an arm around her shoulders. "Go ahead and cry, Kata."

She turned her face into Daniel's shoulder, to shield herself from the rest of the room, and deep, wracking sobs tore through her.

"Who's that?" she heard someone say.

"It's Kate," came the response.

Ken's voice said, "Kate . . ."

She looked up from Daniel's shoulder and saw Ken. He was crying. "Oh, Ken." They hugged each other.

Then Daniel was helping her into her black Talbot's coat. "I'll drive you home," he said. She was in no condition to drive, and she knew it. "Thank you, Daniel."

"He was only sixty-eight," she said to Daniel through her tears. "He wasn't ready to die."

"Is anyone ever really ready to die?"

"My father was. By the time the cancer got finished with him, he was ready to die."

"Just think that George didn't have to go through that ordeal. One minute he was here, feeling fine and healthy, and the next minute he was gone. I hope I'll be so lucky when my time comes."

Kate crushed the handkerchief she had been using in her hand. "Maybe what I meant was that *I* wasn't ready for him to die."

"I know you were fond of him, Kata. I'm sorry."

Fond of him? Are those the words to describe my feelings for George?

She pondered this question later, when she was alone in her room, undressing for bed. She felt as if a huge part of her life had just been ripped away from her. No more George. It didn't seem possible. Who would she discuss the day-to-day operations of the barn with? Who else would be as interested, as knowledgeable, as George?

Ever since she had taken over running the business from her father, George had been there for her. Once, when she was in a real tight spot, he had even lent her money.

I've been so proud of standing alone, she thought. *I forgot that George was always there, standing behind me, ready to catch me if I fell. I thought I didn't depend on anyone, but I depended on him. And now he's gone.*

George is gone, and Mom has cancer.

A feeling that felt suspiciously like panic tightened Kate's stomach. *I'm a sham. I convinced myself that I was self-sufficient, that I could take care of the barn and take care of Ben by myself. But all the while I was relying on George and Mom to back me up.*

"*No man is an island, entire of itself; every man is a piece of the continent, a part of the main . . .*" The quote, which she had heard her mother use a number of times, came to her mind.

I guess it's true, but it seems as if all my bridges to the main are being cut away from me.

She buttoned up her flannel pajama top and got into bed. Daniel had been there for her tonight, she thought. Was she building another bridge to Daniel? And if she was, would it be reliable?

If he can get me to marry him, then he has Ben. Isn't that what this romancing me is all about? Getting control of Ben?

I don't know. I don't seem to know anything anymore. And now I have to call Caroline Douglas and tell her that the empty stall I offered her is filled. She's not going to be a happy camper. She'll probably change instructors.

Well, there's nothing I can do about it. I wouldn't trust Sebastian to anybody else. George loved that horse, and I'm going to take care of him the way George would want. And the same goes for poor little Samson.

Kate turned over on her side, pulled the covers up over her shoulders, and shut her eyes. She was half-asleep when an incident from her childhood popped into her mind. She had been eight years old and at a horse show with her father when she had gotten lost. She could still remember the terror that had possessed her when she realized that he was nowhere in sight. Everywhere she looked there were strange people and strange horses. Frantically, she had started to dart through the crowd of people, looking for the familiar black hair and broad shoulders of her father. She couldn't find him.

She didn't hear the announcement when it was made the first time, but when it was repeated she got it: "Kate Foley, please come to the blue-striped tent."

She went up to a woman who was standing at the training ring watching a horse warm up, and said, "Excuse me, where is the blue-striped tent?"

The woman, who was obviously an exhibitor as she had on breeches and boots, looked down at Kate. "Are you lost, honey?"

"My father is waiting for me at the blue-striped tent, but I don't know where it is."

"I'll take you." Kate had walked with the woman through the crowd of people until the tent came into sight. Standing there, in front of where exhibitors were signing in and getting their numbers, was her father.

"Daddy!" She ran to him and threw herself into his arms.

"Where have you been, Kate?" He sounded angry, but she knew he was only frightened.

"You lost me," she said. "I was looking at the horses, and you lost me."

The woman who had helped her came up to them both. "I guess this is your dad, honey."

"Yes," her father had said. "Did you show her the way?"

"Yes. I'm glad she's safe."

"Thank you very much. She had me scared. Kate, say thank you to the lady."

The child Kate had taken her face out of her father's coat and looked at the woman. "Thank you for helping me."

The woman Kate opened her eyes. *Good grief, where did that memory come from? I haven't thought about that in years and years.*

Daddy. I tried so hard to please him. And I did please him. He was proud of me.

God. George is dead.

Nothing is going to be the same anymore.

24

*K*ate ordered most of Ben's Christmas presents from the JCPenney Christmas catalogue, which featured almost all of the things he had asked for. She bought Molly a cashmere sweater and a scarf at Lord & Taylor, then wondered if she should buy a present for Daniel.

"Are you getting something for Daniel and Alberto, Mom? They're coming over Christmas morning to watch Ben open his gifts. I suppose we should have something under the tree for them, too."

"I was planning to get them each something," Molly said.

"What can we possibly get Daniel? He has everything. He's a multimillionaire, for God's sake."

"I was going to give them both a book."

Kate broke into an affectionate smile. "You're so predictable, Mom. You always give people books."

"A book makes a nice present."

"Yes, it does. But if you're giving him a book, I can't give him a book, too."

"How about a scarf? Or a shirt?"

"I don't want to give him clothing. It's too personal."

"A CD?"

"That's a thought. I could give them both a CD."

"Alberto loves Mozart."

"Great. And I'll ask Alberto for a suggestion about what to get Daniel."

"Why don't you do that, dear?"

Kate and Molly took Ben to the children's mass at five o'clock on Christmas Eve. Connor's family always had a Christmas Eve open house, and they were there until nine o'clock, at which time they came home and put a very excited Ben to bed.

"This will be the first year that he doesn't believe in Santa Claus," Kate said as she came into the living room where Molly was reading a book. "I was hoping to get another year, but the kids on the bus put a period to that."

Molly looked up. "Everything has its season, dear. It will be fun having Daniel and Alberto here. I think they'll both get a lot of enjoyment out of watching Ben."

"I'm surprised that Alberto didn't go back to Colombia."

Molly raised an eyebrow. "I could say the same thing about Daniel."

"He usually goes to Colombia for Christmas, but he said that this year he wanted to spend Christmas with Ben."

"It will be nice for Ben to have him here."

Kate perched on the sofa arm. "Mom, I'm afraid we're becoming too dependent on Daniel. He's around so much. Good grief, he even fixed the broken microwave for us."

"It wasn't broken. The circuit breaker had just flipped."

"We didn't know that. We would have called a repair service."

"True."

"And Alberto is over a lot, too. Is there something serious between you two?"

Molly parried, "I could ask the same thing about you and Daniel."

"Daniel comes to see Ben."

"Does he?"

"Yes."

"He's asked you out without Ben."

"He asks me out because I'm Ben's mom." There was a note of finality in Kate's voice. "But Alberto doesn't ask you out because of Ben."

"As I believe I told you once before, Alberto and I have a lot in common. We both love books and music. We just have a lot to talk about."

"Dad mostly read news magazines and things like *Equus*."

Molly thought for a minute, then answered quietly, "I loved your father dearly, but we did not share many interests outside you children."

"Do you think you might marry Alberto?"

"I have no plans to marry anyone, Kate. I'm simply enjoying Alberto's company. I'm sure he feels the same way about me."

"Well, if you have a good time with him, Mom, then go ahead. You deserve to have some fun."

"So do you, Kate. I'm glad to see you getting out a little. Daniel has been good for you."

"It's amazing, but we seem to have a lot to talk about, too. And it's not just Ben and horses."

Molly smiled. "That's nice."

"Do you think we can put Ben's presents out now? It's going to take a while to get them up from the basement. I told him he was not to come downstairs on pain of death."

Molly laughed and closed her book. "Okay, let's get started then."

*   *   *

It snowed during the night, and the world was glistening white when Daniel awoke on Christmas morning. He looked at his bedside clock, turned off the alarm he would not need, and got out of bed. After he had dressed he went along to the kitchen for breakfast. Alberto was there before him and had made coffee.

"*Feliz Navidad*," he said to Daniel, and held out his arms. The two men embraced. "Do you want to eat breakfast here or go over to the Foleys' first?" Alberto asked.

"Let's have a cup of coffee and then go over to see Ben. Kata said to come at eight, and it's almost seven-thirty now."

"All right."

It was still snowing lightly when they were leaving, and Daniel drove his Lexus SUV with the four-wheel drive, a car he had bought for just such occasions as this. The plows had been out, and the main roads were clear, although the road to High Meadow was still clogged with snow. Daniel needed his SUV to get down it, and to get up the Foleys' driveway. They arrived at eight-fifteen.

Daniel could hear Ben's voice as he rang the bell. "They're here! They're here! I'll get the door, Mommy. They're here."

Daniel smiled. "Is he so joyful to see us, or is it that now he gets to open his presents?"

"A little bit of both perhaps," Alberto replied tactfully.

The door swung open, and Ben stood there in his blue pajamas. "Daddy!" He looked at the shopping bag Daniel was carrying. "More presents?"

Daniel laughed. "Yes, more presents."

"Come in," Molly said as she came out into the hall from the living room. "Let me take your coats."

"I still have one more present in the car, Molly," Daniel said. "I'll just get it now." He came back in carrying an enormous box wrapped in holiday paper.

"Is that for me?" Ben asked in awe.

"It's for you."

"Wow."

The coats were disposed of, and they all made their way into the living room, where Kate was sitting on the sofa drinking a cup of coffee. She got up when they came in and Daniel went to kiss her cheek. Her skin felt like a flower petal under his lips. "*Feliz Navidad*, Kata," he said.

She looked up at him with those beautiful aquamarine eyes, "Merry Christmas, Daniel. You're fifteen minutes late. Ben has been having heart failure."

"It took us a little longer because of the snow."

"Your tree is beautiful with all the presents under it," Alberto said.

The tree was the largest the Foleys had had since Kate's father died. Daniel and Alberto had gone with Kate, Ben, and Molly to cut it down and, since they had the men to carry it, they were able to get a big tree. When they had finished decorating it, it took up almost a quarter of the room.

"Can we open the presents now?" Ben asked.

All of the adults looked at his eager face. "Pick a present and open it," Kate said.

"Can I open Daddy's present first? It's the biggest."

"Go ahead," Kate said. She was wearing her usual uniform of jeans and a sweater, but she had moccasins on her feet instead of shoes.

Ben began to rip at the wrapping paper, peeling it off and throwing it. Molly said, "I'd better get a garbage bag before we have paper all over the living room."

"What is it?" Ben said, as he looked at the huge cardboard box that was revealed to him.

"Is it a computer?" Kate asked.

"Yes," Daniel said. "It's a computer, Ben."

Ben's eyes were huge. "You mean I have my very own computer? Like Connor?"

"I'm sure you'll be glad to share it with your mother and grandmother."

"Is it like the computers we have in school?"

Daniel looked at Kate, "It's a standard PC from Gateway. I hope it's okay."

"It's fine." He couldn't quite read the expression on her face.

"Can I open it up so I can see it?" Ben asked.

"I will help you, Ben," Alberto said.

Daniel said to Kate in a low voice, "Perhaps I should have consulted you first, but I knew you didn't have a computer in the house, and in this day and age . . ."

"It's a great present," she said. She wrinkled her nose. He wondered if she knew how charming she looked when she did that. "It's just . . . all his friends at school are into video games and I've been able to stave him off because we didn't have a computer. Now we do."

"Surely some video games are acceptable. And the computer has an encyclopedia on it as well as a dictionary, a thesaurus, and an assortment of other things that will help with his schoolwork."

She smiled. Did she know how gorgeous she was when she smiled? "Thanks, Daniel. It was a thoughtful gift."

The computer had been unveiled, and Daniel said, "If there's time later on, I'll set it up for you."

Kate looked at Molly. "Where can we put it?"

Molly said, "In the spare bedroom. But we'll have to get a computer desk."

Kate, who did not want it in Ben's bedroom, nodded her approval.

The next hour was spent in an orgy of gift opening. Daniel

gave Kate a silver necklace set with a single aquamarine. It was very lovely, very simple, and the kind of gift she could accept without worrying about the cost.

"Thank you," she said. "It's beautiful."

"It matches your eyes," he said lightly.

"It's lovely, dear," Molly said.

Kate gave Daniel the Bach recording that Alberto had suggested, and he seemed very pleased with it. Molly and Alberto exchanged books. Ben also got some books from the Captain Underpants series.

Daniel was incredulous. "Captain Underpants?"

"They're all the rage," Kate assured him. "Ben loves them."

But clearly what Ben loved the most were the Bionicle Legos. He quickly became absorbed in looking at the designs and the kinds of things he could build with them.

"Well, we've all had quite a haul," Molly said, when all the wrapping paper had been stuffed into a plastic trash bag. "How about breakfast?"

"Sounds good to me," Daniel said.

"Pancakes?"

"Delicious."

Molly started for the kitchen, and Alberto said, "I will help you, Molly," and went with her.

Daniel, who had been sitting on the other end of the sofa from Kate, turned to her, and said softly, "Thank you, Kata, for having us this morning. This was one of the best Christmases of my life."

"I'm glad. He's a wonderful little boy, isn't he?"

"He is. Would you give me your hand?" With a puzzled look, she held it out to him. He took it, raised it to his lips, kissed the palm, then folded her fingers over the kiss. "It was one of the best Christmases because I spent it with my son, but also because I spent it with you."

Kate looked at him uncertainly as she took back her hand.

"I have one more present for Ben, but I don't want to announce it until I clear it with you."

"What is it?"

"I have booked a trip to Disney World for Ben, you, and me. We leave tomorrow and come back Sunday—we'll be there four nights."

"I can't go," Kate said immediately. "I can't leave the horses."

"Yes, you can. I worked this all out with Molly. It's vacation week, and we have got a roster of your students who are going to muck out stalls and bring the horses in and out from turnout. Jean Stewart is going to do your beginner lessons, and your advanced lessons will get a day off."

Kate closed her mouth. "Did you talk to all these people behind my back?"

"I'm afraid that we did."

She shook her head decisively. "Well, I can't do it. I have Sebastian to look after, as well as George's two Morgans."

"Ken is sending the Morgans to a sale barn to be sold."

She said carefully, "Daniel, this was very kind of you, but I can't go. Ben would love to go, however. Why don't you take him?"

"You'd trust me with him by myself?"

"Yes."

"That makes me glad, but if you won't go, then we won't go either."

"Don't be silly, Daniel. You would adore to have Ben to yourself for five days."

"I would adore to have Ben and *you* to myself for five

days. I mean it, Kata, if you won't come, then I'll call the trip off."

She frowned at him. "That isn't fair."

"It's why I told you before I told Ben. I knew you would make trouble about coming. But think, Kata. I've booked us into the Villas, into a two-bedroom apartment with a full kitchen. You and Ben can have one bedroom, and I'll take the other. You're fully covered on all farm chores—your students were more than happy to work for you. They all seemed to think that you needed a vacation. Why not just do it?"

"We would leave tomorrow?" She appeared to be weakening.

"Yes. Just throw some things in a suitcase—if you forget something we can buy it there. It will be fun."

"It would be fun." Then her great light eyes clouded. "I can't. Mom has her second chemo treatment on Friday. I have to be here for her."

"Alberto will take her to her treatment, and he said he would spend the night here with her to make certain everything is all right."

"You cleared this with Mom?"

"Yes. She will be very upset if you make her an excuse for not going. She wants you to go on this vacation."

Kate said a little breathlessly, "It's a conspiracy."

"That it is. We wanted to back you into a corner where you couldn't say no without looking churlish."

She laughed. "Well, you were successful. And, since I don't want to sound churlish, I'll have to say yes. Thank you, Daniel. Ben and I will go to Disney World with you."

25

After breakfast, Daniel took Ben outside to build a snowman while Kate did her barn chores. Then he sat with Ben and helped him build with his Legos. When Kate came in from the barn, she found the two of them on the floor beside the Christmas tree, intent on what they were doing. She stopped in the doorway, and the sight of those two dark heads bent close together caused something to turn over in her heart.

It was Daniel who first sensed her presence in the doorway. "Kate, these Legos are terrific. We didn't have anything like this when we were kids."

He was so genuinely enthusiastic that she had to smile. "I always thought I'd be an architect if I wasn't a baseball player," he confessed. "I loved building stuff when I was a child."

"Well you can't be a baseball player forever," she said practically. "Maybe you can be an architect in the next part of your life."

"What's an architect?" Ben wanted to know.

"An architect designs buildings," Daniel explained.

"I'd like to be an architect, too. I'm real good at building, aren't I, Mommy?"

"Yes, you are." Then, to Daniel, "What did you major in in college?"

"Political science."

"That's a long way from architecture."

"My father wanted me to be a lawyer."

"Just what this country needs," Kate said ironically. "Another lawyer."

"If people didn't sue so much in the United States, there wouldn't be enough work for all the lawyers, and their numbers would drop."

"This is true."

"What did you major in, Kata?"

"I never finished college."

"Well, what did you major in?"

"I was going to major in animal science at UConn, but when Dad died I decided to stay at home and commute to Southern Connecticut. They didn't have animal science so I majored in business."

Ben looked up from his Legos. "Do you want to sit with us, Mommy?"

"No thank you, sweetheart. I'm going to rout Nana out of the kitchen and finish cooking the dinner."

"Tell Nana to take a nap," Ben said.

Kate and Daniel exchanged a tenderly amused look.

"I will," Kate said, and went along the hallway to the kitchen.

Molly was sitting at the table with a glass of eggnog in front of her, and Alberto was at the stove.

"My goodness," Kate said. "Are you cooking, Alberto?"

"I learned to cook when my wife died, and I discovered that I was a very good cook. I told your mother to rest and that I would do the dinner."

"I was going to tell her the same thing."

"He won't turn over the stove," Molly said. Her eyes looked bluer than usual. "The man is a tyrant."

"It is kind of you to offer to help, but I don't need you," Alberto said. "It will be another hour at least until dinner is ready, and I think you should convince your mother to take a nap."

Kate stiffened. That was precisely what she was about to do, but she wasn't sure she liked this man giving Molly and her orders. After a second's pause, she said, "Yes, why don't you lie down for a while, Mom? You were up early this morning."

"It's a conspiracy," Molly said. Her eyes were still looking very blue.

"Go ahead," Kate said.

Molly stood up. "All right. I will go and take a nap. But this dinner had better be good, Alberto."

He replied in a mild voice, "It will be."

After Molly had left the room, Kate said, "Really, Alberto, you're the guest. You don't have to cook the dinner. I was planning to do it."

"I like to cook," Alberto said, "and I get very little opportunity at Daniel's. Maria, his housekeeper, is a wonderful cook, and she won't let me near her kitchen."

Kate sat down at the table and took a sip of Molly's half-finished eggnog. "I would have thought you'd go home for Christmas. Mom says you have a daughter and grandchildren in Colombia."

"I decided that I would spend Christmas here."

Kate, who only knew how to be direct, asked, "Why?"

He turned from the stove to look at her. Even with a wooden spoon in his hand, he was a distinguished-looking man, slim and elegant with brown eyes the color of sherry wine. He was very different from her big, broad-shouldered father.

He said, "I wanted to spend Christmas with your mother."

Kate scowled.

"Is there a reason for that horrible frown?"

"I just don't want to see Mom hurt. She likes you, Alberto, but she would never leave Ben to go and live in Colombia. I think you should know that."

"I had already figured that out for myself, but thank you for the advice."

His voice was perfectly pleasant, perfectly courteous, but Kate heard the warning. She said, "It *is* my business, you know. Mom and I have worked out our lives to suit Ben and to suit us. We've done just fine for eight years. We don't need anyone else to help us."

Alberto put down the wooden spoon he had been holding. "You are right that you have worked out your lives to suit Ben. And you have done a splendid job with Ben. He is a healthy, happy child, and you are to be congratulated for that. But, as women, you and your mother have needs beyond those satisfied by caring for Ben."

Kate said defensively, "I have my barn and my horses; Mom has her teaching. We are doing just fine."

"Are you saying that there is no room in your life for anyone beyond the three of you?"

Kate's scowl returned. "I don't mean that."

"It seems to me that that is what you are saying."

"It's not that there's no room; it's that there's no need."

There was a little silence as he contemplated her face. Then he said gently, "How many people do you love, Kate?"

She blinked, surprised by the question. "What do you mean?"

"I mean just what I said. How many people do you love?"

"Ben and Mom."

"And that is all the room you have in your heart—room for two people? There is no place to add someone else? You are going to go through your life loving two people only?"

"I loved George, too."

"George is dead. You're down to two people. It seems to me that you could make room for more."

Kate did not like the way this conversation was going. Alberto had managed to put her on the defensive. "Are you saying you want me to make room for you?"

"No. I want your mother to make room for me. You need to make room for Daniel."

Color stained Kate's cheeks. "I have been very nice to Daniel."

Alberto smiled. "Yes, you have. And I know it has been hard for you to accept such a change in your life. But life is change, Kate. If we don't change, we die."

"Mommy!" It was Ben in the doorway. "We've finished. Come and see my space station."

Kate tried to disguise her relief at the interruption as she turned to welcome Ben. "That's great, sweetheart. I'm coming."

Alberto's dinner of roast beef, roasted potatoes, broccoli, and buttered carrots was delicious. Over dinner, Daniel broke the news to Ben that they were going to Disney World the next day.

The little boy was ecstatic. "Can I call Connor and tell him, Mommy?"

"After dinner," Kate replied.

Once Alberto's dinner had been eaten, and the dishes cleared and packed into the dishwasher, Kate let Daniel and

Alberto have one more cup of coffee, then she sent them home.

"I have to pack, and Mom has had enough excitement for the day. Go home."

"Are you always this tactless, Kata, or is it just with me?" Daniel complained, as she handed him his jacket.

"I believe in saying what I mean."

"So I have noticed."

"What is the weather likely to be at Disney? Should I pack summer clothes?"

"Pack a little bit of both."

"You're a help."

He shrugged. "The weather could go either way."

Alberto kissed Molly's cheek. "I will talk to you tomorrow."

Kate closed the door behind the men and turned to her mother. "That was certainly an exciting Christmas. Ben and I are going to Disney, and you didn't have to cook dinner."

"Alberto did a good job, didn't he?"

"Dinner was great." Kate looked at Ben, and said, "You can read for half an hour, then it's bed for you, chum. We have to get up early tomorrow to catch a plane."

Ben's brown eyes were sparkling. "This was the *best* Christmas—even though I didn't believe in Santa Claus."

Kate gave him a hug. "You certainly did all right for yourself."

"When can we put the computer up?"

"When we get a desk to put it on."

"When can we do that?"

"You and I are going to be busy for the next few days, remember?"

"Nana can buy the desk. Can't you, Nana?"

Kate said, "Your father said he would pick up the desk,

Ben, so you're going to have to wait until you get home from Florida."

Molly said, "Alberto can pick it up. That way the computer will be all ready when you get home."

"Forget it," Kate said. "You've got enough to keep you occupied without setting the computer up."

Ben looked at her anxiously. "But you are going to put it up, aren't you, Mommy?"

"Yes."

The worry cleared away from his face. "I think I'll start to read one of my new Captain Underpants books."

"Good idea. And you can take it on the plane with you tomorrow."

"I've never been on a plane," Ben said. "Do you think I'll be scared?"

"There's nothing to be scared about."

"There was that plane that crashed into the building, Mommy."

"That was a terrible thing, but there's little likelihood of that happening to us, Ben. In fact, it's been proven that it's more dangerous to get in a car than it is to get on a plane."

After Ben had gone upstairs, Kate turned to Molly. "I have a bone to pick with you. You conspired with Daniel behind my back."

Molly smiled. "I know I did. And it was wonderful how willing people were to help out. You're completely covered through the thirtieth."

"I want to see the list of people you've got lined up."

"I will be happy to show you. Jean Stewart is doing most of the work, with Amy Sanderson and Beth Hendricks coming in second and third."

"They're all good kids."

"You should bring something back for Jean. She's actually the one who made the schedule and got the people."

"I will."

Molly sat down on the sofa. "You should go and pack, dear. I'm going to start the book that Alberto gave me."

Kate said, "I didn't want to go, you know. I told Daniel to go with Ben, and he said that he wouldn't go unless I went too."

"He knows how stubborn you are, and he also knows that you wouldn't want to deprive Ben of such a treat."

"When did the idea for this vacation come up?"

"Two weeks ago, a few days before I went for my first chemo treatment."

"Are you all right going with Alberto to the next treatment, Mom? I feel as if I'm deserting you."

"I'm fine with it, and Alberto assures me that he is fine with it, too. His wife did not have breast cancer—she had pancreatic cancer, and she went too quickly for them even to start chemo treatments—so coming with me will not bring back sad memories."

"He said he would sleep here the night of your treatment. Do you really want that?"

"It's completely unnecessary, but he insisted. I don't mind having him, if that's what you mean. I'll probably be sleeping most of the time anyway."

"I just feel badly about being away."

"Kate, if you stayed home because of me, I would be very upset. When Daniel broached the subject of the Disney trip to me, I jumped for joy. You haven't had a vacation in over ten years. It's more than time for you to take some time for yourself."

"You haven't had a vacation in ten years either."

"When this cancer treatment is finished with, I plan to take one."

"That's a great idea."

"Instead of talking about this vacation, dear, you should be packing for it."

"I know, I know. I'm going to have to rout out the bathing suits. Will it be warm enough to swim?"

"I have no idea, but you most certainly should take them. Now get moving. Daniel is picking you up at six o'clock tomorrow morning."

"It will seem strange not to be feeding the horses."

"Don't even think about the horses. Jean is feeding them in the morning, and Beth and Amy are sharing the evening feeding. They'll manage to exist without you for a few days, believe me. And so will the dogs."

Kate smiled. "Okay, ma'am. I'll go and pack."

She went up the stairs, and Molly picked up her book.

26

$\mathcal{W}$hen Daniel, Kate, and Ben stepped off the plane in Orlando, it was seventy degrees. Daniel smiled as he felt the balmy air touch his face. "Ah, now this feels good."

"Coming from Colombia, you must be used to warm weather," Kate said.

"Bogotá is not that warm. It's near the equator, but it's also eight thousand feet high. We get cold enough for a coat in the winter, and the summer is cooler than it is in Connecticut."

"Wow. I always assumed Colombia was warm."

"Colombia's weather depends upon what altitude you are at. At the beach, it is very warm indeed."

Between them, Ben gave a little skip. "How long does it take to fly to Colombia?"

"It's another couple of hours from here."

"Someday can I go and see it?"

"Someday."

They picked up the car Daniel had rented, a modest Ford Taurus, and drove to the resort hotel on the Disney property where they were staying. The style of the hotel was Spanish, and it was located next to a small but scenic lake.

Their lakefront town house unit was lovely. The living room had French doors looking out on the lake, and there was a fully equipped kitchen on the first floor as well. Upstairs were two bedrooms, one with a view of the lake and the other with a view of a gorgeous garden. The lakefront room had a king-sized bed and the other one had two twins. Each bedroom had its own bathroom, although the king-sized room's bathroom was larger.

"Do you and Ben want to share the bigger bedroom, Kata?" Daniel asked. "The bed is as large as two twins put together."

"No thank you, we'll take the other room."

"Daddy's bedroom has a television," Ben pointed out.

"A good reason for us not to take it," Kate replied.

"When can we go to Disney?" Ben asked.

"As soon as we have unpacked and had some lunch," Daniel said.

Kate asked, "Do we need passes to get into the park?"

"We have Ultimate Park Hopper tickets," Daniel informed her. "We can go anywhere."

"Where shall we start?"

"I recommend that we start with the Magic Kingdom."

They unpacked and had lunch within their complex, then they got on the tram and went to the Magic Kingdom.

The two adults got their greatest pleasure from watching Ben. Most of his friends had been to Disney, some of them twice, and he was so excited to be there himself, going on the rides he had heard about and getting the various characters to sign his autograph book, that his feet scarcely seemed to touch the ground.

He adored Splash Mountain, and Kate and Daniel got exceedingly wet from having to go on it twice.

They ate dinner at Tony's Town Square Restaurant and

didn't get home until eight o'clock. Ben stayed up until nine, then Kate put him to bed. "This was the best day of my life," he confided to her as she kissed him good night.

"I'm glad you had such a good time, sweetheart."

"It makes it even funner that Daddy is here."

"Yes, it does."

"Can I go swimming in the pool tomorrow?"

"If the weather is good enough. Now go to sleep. You've had a very exciting day, and you must be tired."

"Good night, Mommy."

"Good night, Ben."

Daniel was sitting in the living room when Kate came down the stairs. Unself-consciously, she went to sit next to him on the flowered sofa. "He said that this was the best day of his life. Wasn't that sweet?"

He lowered the newspaper he had been reading. "I'm glad he had a good time."

"What's on the program for tomorrow?"

"How about Epcot?"

"You seem to know your way around. Have you been here before?"

"My parents took me a few times when I was a kid. I gather you never got here?"

"My mother took Colleen once. I didn't want to go because I had a horse show to ride in."

He smiled faintly, and murmured, "Why am I not surprised?"

"He did mention that he wanted to go swimming in the pool."

Daniel put his folded newspaper on the table next to him. "We could come back to the hotel in the middle of the day, when it's warmest. He could swim then."

"That sounds good." She looked at the blank TV screen. "Is there anything you want to watch?"

"The Knicks are playing Miami. Do you like basketball?"

"Sure."

Daniel switched on the TV and found the right channel just as Alan Houston sank a three-pointer. "Good going," Daniel said, as the two teams raced back up the floor.

Daniel quickly became absorbed by the game, and Kate gradually became absorbed by Daniel's closeness. It had seemed so natural to choose a seat next to him on the sofa, but now she wished that she had sat in the matching chair.

The game continued, with Daniel occasionally muttering comments about the play. Kate was silent. He was so close that she could feel the warmth from his body. *I'm sexually attracted to him*, she realized with dismay. *My God. This is terrible.*

Daniel said a word in Spanish that Kate suspected wasn't very nice. "They have a genius for giving up leads," he said. "They have no toughness anymore."

Kate looked at the men in basketball shorts passing the ball around and thought, *This is so awkward. How am I ever going to behave normally around him now?*

Halftime came, and Daniel turned down the sound on the TV. He turned to look at her. "We don't have to watch the second half if there's something else you would enjoy more. You'd have to be a masochist to enjoy the Knicks this season."

"The basketball game is fine," Kate said in a subdued voice.

With the sound turned down on the TV, everything suddenly seemed very quiet. Kate's heart was beating so loudly that she was afraid it would be audible to Daniel. She forced a smile. "Or maybe there's a comedy that we could watch."

He had pushed the coffee table forward to accommodate his long legs, and now he turned to look at her. His knit shirt was open at the throat, and the light from the lamp shone on the smoothness of his hair. Suddenly he seemed very big. "What do you usually do in the evening, Kata?"

"I finish up at the barn at a little before eight, then I go home and eat dinner, then I spend some time with Ben before he goes to bed."

"And after he goes to bed?"

"Sometimes I work on barn business, sometimes I read a book, sometimes I watch TV. It all depends on how tired I am."

He nodded as if that was the answer he had expected. Then, without warning, he reached out and took her hand into his. "Kata darling," he said, "do you think it could ever work between you and me?"

Her heart gave a single loud thump. "I don't know."

He smiled wryly. "Every other woman in the world would have said, 'What do you mean?' But not you."

"I assumed you meant would it ever work romantically between us two. Was I right?"

"You were exactly right."

Kate made no move to pull her hand away. "We're friends, and it's good for Ben that we're friends. I'm afraid that we might spoil that."

He said gravely, "I don't want to be just your friend."

"I don't know what I want," she confessed. "This is all so new to me, Daniel."

"I know." He smiled tenderly. "You never had time for romance."

"I never had the inclination, either."

"Do you have the inclination with me?"

"I don't know."

"Kiss me and find out."

Her eyes clung to his, and she took a deep steadying breath. "All right."

"You are so brave, Kata," he said softly. Using the hand he held, he drew her toward him. "I think you are the bravest person that I know."

"Because I said I would kiss you? Is it going to be that bad?"

He laughed deep in his throat. "You tell me." And then his mouth was coming down on hers.

It was the sweetest thing he had ever known, the feel of her mouth under his. Her lips were soft, and he increased the pressure of his mouth. Slowly, hesitantly, her mouth opened, yielding, unsure of what he wanted, but trusting him. When he found her tongue she stiffened for a moment then relaxed against him. He could feel the swell of her breast against his chest. He reached up to cup and support the back of her head. Her hair felt like silk under his fingers. He fought his desire to push her down on the sofa and make love to her, and lifted his face. "Well?" he said huskily. "Was it bad?"

Her aquamarine eyes looked dazed. "My goodness," she said. "My prom dates both kissed me, and I didn't like it at all. This was very different."

He smiled with genuine amusement. "I'm glad I'm better than your prom dates."

"I've never had sex, Daniel. I think you should know that."

"I already know. You never had the time."

She smiled back at him. "I never had the time for a vacation either, yet here I am. You are making an awful lot of changes in my life."

"Some change is necessary, Kata. All living things change."

"Alberto said the same thing to me yesterday."

"Alberto is a very wise man."

She frowned. "I think he's after Mom."

"And you don't approve?"

"It's not that I don't approve, it's that I don't want to see Mom get hurt. She would never leave Ben to marry Alberto and go back to Colombia."

"She might if you and I married."

The blue-green eyes searched his. "Are you thinking along those lines?"

"After that kiss? I most certainly am."

He could see the conflict on her face. "It would probably be the best thing for Ben . . ."

"Kata," he said strongly, "if you ever marry me for Ben's sake, I will be furious with you. If we marry, it has to be for our sakes, not Ben's."

She looked uncertain. *But she kissed me back*, he thought. *She most definitely kissed me back.*

"Think about it," he said.

"A-all right. I will."

Later that night, Daniel lay in his enormous king-sized bed and listened to the rustle of palm trees outside the open sliding-glass door that led to his balcony. He could not exorcise the tension from his body. He could not banish Kate from his mind.

Daniel was in what was for him an unusual situation. Women had been chasing him ever since he was a teenager, and sex had been a part of most of his relationships. It had taken a heroic act of self-discipline to back away from Kate tonight, but he had been afraid that if he didn't break the kiss, he wouldn't be able to stop. He wondered how long he could exist on kisses alone. He wanted her so badly.

And yet . . . alongside his carnal passion for Kate there bloomed the softer emotions of protectiveness and care. There was a gallantry about her that stirred him profoundly. He thought it was unspeakably courageous the way she had shouldered the load of her father's business and her sister's child.

He thought of the way her lips had felt under his tonight, the way her breast had pressed against his chest, and he groaned and rolled over in bed.

This is a perfect chance for us to be together. Ben is so tired when he goes to bed that he sleeps like the dead. It's a perfect chance for Kata and me. But will Kata be willing?

He finally went to sleep and dreamed that he was making love to her in a grassy meadow where horses were grazing.

Kate also lay awake, listening to the wind in the palms. In the other bed, Ben slept soundly.

Daniel's kiss this evening had been as different from what she thought of as the wet sloppiness of her prom dates' kisses as sunlight was from darkness.

I was sorry when Daniel let me go, she thought in wonder. *I wanted him to go on kissing me. I wanted him to go on holding me. I wanted him to make love to me.*

She thought about what he had said about Ben. *He's right. I can't think of anything more terrible than to be locked in the intimacy of marriage with someone you don't love. But do I love Daniel? Or is it just a physical attraction?*

I don't know. I've never been in this situation before. I don't know.

Kate was someone who had always known her own mind, and this uncertainty made her feel uneasy. She thought of Alberto's words, that she only loved two people in the world, and she thought that he was right. But those two people had always been enough for her. Was that still true?

What if Mom wants to marry Alberto? What would I do then?

Damn. Life was going along so smoothly until Daniel came along.

The scariest thing was that she wasn't sure if she wished that things could return to the comfortable past or if she preferred to venture forth into the future. Finally, she fell asleep and dreamed she was being chased down a long, dark hallway by something terrible. Then she was in a room with Daniel, and the terror subsided. Somehow, she knew she was safe as long as she was with him.

27

*B*efore they left for the park the next morning, Kate and Daniel made a stop at Publix to get some food and snacks into the kitchen. Then they headed to Disney, getting off the tram at Epcot. There was so much to see that Ben decided not to break up the day with a swim in the pool. They started at Spaceship Earth, then methodically saw most of the other exhibits available. Kate particularly liked the Living Seas exhibit.

"I never realized how educational Disney was," she said to Daniel, as they came out of the exhibit. "This is a great opportunity for Ben to learn."

She and Daniel were almost identically dressed in khaki pants, blue knit shirts, and moccasins. They had laughed when they saw each other at breakfast in the morning.

"The Connecticut influence," Daniel had said wryly.

"The comfort influence," Kate had returned.

They were together all day long, united in their enjoyment of their son. They got home at five o'clock and, even though it was a little chilly, there were some children in the pool, and Ben wanted to go in. So Daniel took him to the pool while Kate stayed behind. She had picked up some pasta and sauce in the morning and was going to make it for dinner.

Daniel had objected when she had done so, but she had said it would be easier than dragging a tired Ben out to a restaurant for dinner, and he had given in.

When Ben finally returned to the unit, wrapped in a big towel, he was shivering. "Daddy will fix a hot shower for you," Kate said. "Then get dressed and come down for dinner."

Daniel took him upstairs, then returned to talk to Kate. "I'm sorry we were so long, but he was playing with the oldest boy from the other family, and he was having so much fun that I hated to pull him away."

"Couldn't you see that he was shivering?"

"He was moving too fast for me to notice."

"Well, he'll survive, I suppose. I'll put the pot of water on the stove to boil."

"Are you sure you wouldn't rather eat out?"

"I'm sure. We can eat out tomorrow night if you like."

"Can I do anything for you?"

"Nope. Why don't you go and watch the news or something?"

"Yes, ma'am." A few moments later, Kate heard the sound of the television come on.

They ate dinner, then Ben and Daniel played checkers. "Can we go swimming again tomorrow morning, Daddy?"

"I'd rather not, Ben. It's too chilly in the mornings."

At that moment Kate came downstairs from the bedroom, where she had been telephoning Jean to make sure everything was going all right in the barn. "Your father's right," she said. "You were freezing when you came in tonight. It is December, after all."

"But I told Todd I would meet him at the pool."

"Todd's mother will probably say the same thing I did."

"No, she won't. He's *expecting* me, Mommy. I have to be there."

"No, you don't," Daniel said authoritatively. "We're going to the Animal Kingdom tomorrow, and that will keep you occupied enough."

Ben scowled.

Kate said, "This discussion is over, Ben. It's time you got into your pajamas."

As an unhappy Ben trooped up the stairs to the bedroom, Daniel said to Kate, "I can take him if you think it will be okay."

"No. You were absolutely right to tell him no. He was almost blue when he came in tonight. He never has enough sense to come out when he's cold."

"He was having a great time."

"He will have a great time at the Animal Kingdom, too."

They put Ben to bed, then went downstairs to the living room and watched *CSI* on television. At ten o'clock, Daniel switched the TV off and came back to sit on the sofa. He stretched his legs out in front of him comfortably, and asked, "Would you like to make love with me tonight?"

Kate's head turned. "I beg your pardon?"

"I asked if you would like to make love with me tonight." He spoke almost lazily, contemplating the feet stretched so comfortably in front of him.

"Are you serious?"

He turned and she saw his eyes. "Perfectly."

Kate's heart began to pound. She said uncertainly, "I've never done it before."

"I know. You told me. Would you like to try it with me?"

Kate bent her head and looked at her hands in her lap. He looked at the exposed nape of her neck and enclosed it with his hand. "Your skin is so beautiful," he said. "You are so beautiful, Kata."

She looked up from the contemplation of her hands and stuck her chin in the air. "All right. Let's do it."

His eyes sparkled. "I always said you were brave."

"I don't feel very brave," she confessed.

"It will be all right, darling. Believe me, everything will be all right." And he bent his head and kissed her.

This kiss was different from the one they had exchanged the previous night. That had been careful and tender. This was urgent and intense, and it seemed to ignite something inside her, and she wasn't afraid anymore. She accepted his kiss, and then, sliding her arms around his neck, she returned it. One of his hands slid under her shirt and cupped her breast. Kate murmured with pleasure, and, after a minute, her hand began to caress the shiny dark hair at the back of his head.

"Let's go upstairs," he said. The touch of his hand on her breast was exquisite.

"Yes," she said.

He rose with his usual grace and, bending for a minute, picked her up as easily as if she had been a child. He carried her easily, too, up the stairs and into his bedroom, where he set her on her feet beside the bed.

"You should know this," he said. His hands were on her shoulders and he was standing so close that Kate had to tilt her head far back to look up into his face. "I don't think I've ever wanted anything the way I want you right now." His voice sounded normal, but she could see, above the opened collar of his shirt, a pulse beating rapidly under the warm olive skin.

Kate asked, trying to sound natural, "Should I get undressed?"

"Why don't we both get undressed?"

Kate pulled her shirt out from her pants, then pulled it over her head. She tossed it on a chair, then she unhooked her bra. Daniel also pulled his knit shirt over his head and Kate gazed at him, for a moment almost unconscious of her own naked flesh, so interested was she in the smoothly muscled expanse of Daniel's chest, shoulders, and upper arms. Without his shirt he didn't look as slim as he did with his clothes on.

When she was just wearing her panties he took her hand. "Come to bed, Kata," and she went.

For one of the few times in her life, her clever brain was stilled, and all she was aware of was Daniel's hands touching her, his mouth caressing her. She arched up against him, her slender body pressing against the strength of his. He buried his lips in the short silk of her hair.

"Kata." He made her name sound like a love word.

She kissed his shoulder. His fingers moved caressingly along her inner thigh. Then he touched her, and her breath caught and her body tensed and feeling flooded through her. She looked up into his face and, as their eyes met, something passed between them—something so intimate, so tender, that Kate's throat ached.

"Okay?" he asked softly.

"Okay," she replied.

He continued to touch and caress her, and Kate felt her body ripen in response. Soon fire was running through her veins, and an incredible tension was building in her loins. "Daniel," she said. "Daniel."

"Hold on," he muttered, "this might hurt." And then he was coming into her.

She climaxed just as he entered her, so the cascading pleasure of orgasm was mixed with the burning pain of his penetration. She cried out but did not try to pull away. She heard him say her name, heard the love words he was using. She felt the power of him within her and, even though it hurt, it was splendid. Without realizing it, her nails dug into his shoulders. She would see the marks of them the following day.

When he had got his breath back and his heart was no longer hammering, he held her in the crook of his arm, and she nestled her cheek into the slightly damp hollow of his shoulder. He kissed the top of her head and she turned her lips to the smooth bare skin of his chest. "Wow," she said.

"I'm sorry I hurt you."

"It wasn't too bad."

"I can't believe you were still intact after all those years of riding horses."

"I think I'm bleeding. I'd better go and clean up."

"Do you have to leave?"

"Yes."

Kate went into the bathroom and discovered she was indeed bleeding. She did a cleanup job, enveloped herself in the robe that was hanging on the hook, went back into the bedroom, and sat on the edge of the bed. She said, "I begin to see why sex is so popular."

His eyes were half-closed and he looked as if he were going to fall asleep. "Is that a compliment?"

"It is."

One eye opened all the way. "Wait until we try it the next time, after you've healed a bit."

"Mmm."

The other eye opened. "Come here."

She crawled into the middle of the bed, next to him, and once more he cradled her in his arm. "Sleep with me."

"I can't. If Ben wakes up and I'm not there, he'll come looking for me."

"He won't wake up."

"He might."

He made a sound of frustration.

"I'll stay for a little while."

"Okay," and he buried his lips in her hair.

He was so warm, so big, so comforting. Kate actually fell asleep and didn't migrate back to her own bedroom until four o'clock in the morning.

Kate did not awaken until eight o'clock, an unheard of time for her. Ben's bed was already empty. She got up, took a shower, and went downstairs about eight-twenty. Daniel was sitting at the table with a cup of coffee and the morning newspaper, which had been left at their door.

"Where's Ben?" she asked.

"Isn't he in his bed?"

Fear caused Kate's heart to thud. "No, I woke up at eight, and he wasn't there. I thought he would be down here with you."

"I haven't seen him." Daniel put down his newspaper. "The little brat has gone to swim in the pool."

Relief flooded through Kate. "That must be it. He went to swim with that boy."

"Let's go get him."

"All right."

The two of them half walked, half ran the short distance to the swimming pool, but all they found there was a bald man swimming laps. "Have you seen any children?" Daniel asked him.

"There were two boys swimming here when I came, but they left," the man told him.

"Which way did they go? Did you notice?"

"Actually, I think they went with someone."

Kate's hand flew to her mouth.

Daniel asked, "Who did they go with?"

The man, who had been treading water, swam over to the side of the pool. "Are you missing your children?"

"Yes." So far Daniel had done all the talking. Kate just stood there in frozen silence.

"Jesus," the man said. "They went with a guy I thought must be their grandfather."

"Maybe he was Todd's grandfather," Kate said in a voice even she didn't recognize. "Do you know where Todd's family are staying, Daniel?"

"I don't know the unit number, and I don't know his last name either."

"What are we going to do?"

"You go back to the apartment and wait by the telephone. I imagine that Todd's parents will either telephone to tell us where Ben is, or they'll bring him home. I'll wait here by the pool in case his father comes looking for him like we went looking for Ben."

"All right." Kate felt incapable of thought. Terror had petrified every other faculty. She had actually turned to leave when a man dressed in jeans and a red knit shirt came into the pool enclosure.

"Shit," Daniel said.

The man recognized Daniel and came over to him. "I'm looking for my son. He slipped away from the unit this morning, and I think he might have come here to swim with your son."

Oh my God, Kate thought. *Oh my God. He's been kidnapped.*

Daniel was looking very grim. "You didn't send him here with his grandfather?"

"His grandfather? His grandfather isn't with us. Apparently he made plans with your boy yesterday and, when we said he couldn't swim so early, he sneaked out on us."

"My son did the exact same thing. This man here saw the two boys go off with a man he assumed to be their grandfather."

"Oh no. Oh God. Do you think they've been kidnapped?"

"It looks that way," Daniel said.

I don't believe it. I can't believe it. This isn't happening. Jesus, Mary, and Joseph make it not be true. Watch out for Ben. Keep him safe. Please, please, please keep him safe.

Daniel said, "I think we had better call the police." He looked at the man in the bathing suit, who by now had climbed out of the pool. "Will you tell the police what you have told us?"

"Of course." He had draped a towel around himself but he was looking cold. "I'll need to let my wife know what's happened, though. She's expecting me to return for breakfast."

"Come to my apartment," Daniel said commandingly. "We can make the phone calls from there."

The two men and Kate automatically began to follow him as he turned and headed toward the exit from the pool enclosure.

It took the police about five minutes to respond. Almost the first thing they asked was, "Do you think the kidnapper knew the boy was your son, Mr. Montero?"

"I have no idea," Daniel replied evenly. "I was with him at the pool yesterday, and anyone who bothered to notice would have known he was with me. But the only other people at the pool were Tom Robbins and his kids."

"Yeah, nobody else came by," Tom Robbins agreed.

The policeman said, "Still, that doesn't mean someone

wasn't watching. The pool is visible from any number of rooms." He turned to the man in the bathing suit, whose name had turned out to be Ron Blake. "Are you sure the boys went with him willingly?"

"Yes. It's why I didn't take much notice."

"Would you be able to identify the man?"

"You know, I don't think so. I saw him only briefly. I have to confess my thoughts were that I was happy the kids were going, that I would have the pool to myself to swim laps."

The burly cop who was in charge said, "There are two possibilities here. The boys were taken by a pervert, or the main target was the Montero boy, and the purpose was ransom."

Kate felt dizzy. It was scarcely a second before Daniel's arm was around her. "Come and sit down, Kata," he said. "Let me get you some water."

Kate sat down because if she didn't, she was afraid she was going to fall down. *What will I do if Ben is killed? How can I go on living?*

Daniel said strongly, "We'll get him back, Kata."

She looked up at him and nodded. She forced her brain to function. "I hope it's ransom and not the other."

He put his hand on her shoulder and said to the cop in charge, "What do we do first?"

"First I'll put out an alarm for my men to look for an elderly man with the two boys we'll describe. Then we'll get a tap on your phone, in case the kidnapper tries to get in touch with you."

Kidnapper, Kate thought. *Ben has been kidnapped. Oh my dear God. Ben has really been kidnapped.*

"I have to call Mom," she said to Daniel.

"Why don't you give it a few hours? There's no point in scaring her if it's not necessary."

"Do you think they'll be found in a few hours?"

"Every cop in the area will be looking for him, Kata. There's a good chance he'll be found."

"Okay. I'll wait, then."

But the hours went by, and nothing happened. Two policemen as well as Tom Robbins waited by the phone, but there was no ransom call. There was no report that a policeman had found the boys. All there was, was silence.

Kate was in anguish. Her worst nightmare had come true. She had lost Ben.

She said to Daniel, "If only we had let him swim this morning, you would have gone with him and he would have been safe."

"I know, Kata. It just never occurred to me that he would sneak out on us. He's usually such an accommodating child."

"If I hadn't been so tired from last night, I would have heard him get up. I never sleep until eight o'clock."

He didn't try to reassure her. "I've thought of that, too. But it's pointless to keep going over the past. What's done is done. We have to concentrate now on finding him."

"Do you think we will find him, Daniel?"

"I do." He sounded calm and confident. "I just have a feeling that this will come out all right, and we'll be looking to hand Ben his head for scaring us this way."

It helped enormously to hear that confidence from him. She gave a wobbly laugh. "I'll kill him when I get my hands on him."

"We both will."

But the day passed into the evening, and still they heard nothing. Two policemen remained in the apartment monitoring the phone, which never rang.

Kate mentioned calling Molly once more, but Daniel said, "Isn't this the day for her chemo treatment?"

"Is this Friday?"

"Yes."

"You're right. She had chemo today. Maybe I'll wait until tomorrow."

"Good idea."

The police got a call that a man and two boys had been picked up, and Kate started to hope. But then word came through that the boys weren't Ben and Todd, and she started to despair.

The night crept on. Kate was exhausted, but she couldn't think of trying to sleep. She curled up in the corner of the sofa and, on and off, Daniel held her.

When Kate was under great stress, her response had always been to retreat into herself. Yet the feel of Daniel's arms, the warmth of Daniel's presence, was a comfort. She knew that he was as distraught as she was, that his loss would be almost as great as hers, and it helped to have him close.

The sun rose, and the second day of waiting began.

28

When the grandfatherly-looking man had asked Ben and Todd if they wanted to use his pool basketball hoop, the boys had said, "Cool." When the man said his unit was on the other side of the resort and they'd have to go in his car to get it, the boys had thoughtlessly hopped in the car. It wasn't until the car had left the grounds of the resort that it occurred to Ben that he had done the very thing he had always promised his mother he would never do: He had gotten into a car with a stranger.

"Hey!" he called. "Mister! You told us you were taking us to your room."

"I will, boys, I will. I just need to make a little side trip first."

"We can't make any side trips. Our parents will be looking for us."

"Just sit tight, sonny, and everything will be okay."

Todd said loudly, "Take us home!"

"I will, I will. I just want to get a few pictures of you first."

By then Ben was really scared. "Stop the car," he said.

"I'll stop soon," and the man kept on driving.

In the backseat, Ben and Todd looked at each other out of

frightened eyes. "We're being kidnapped," Ben said in a low voice.

"I'm scared," Todd said.

"I'll open the window and yell," Ben said, and put his hand on the window button. He pressed, but nothing happened. The windows had been locked from the front.

"Maybe we should jump out," Todd said.

But the door was locked as well.

"Let us go, or we'll tell the police on you," Ben said.

"No one's going to hurt you, boys, so just settle down back there."

Ben sat in tense silence, thinking. At last he whispered to Todd, "When he slows down for a light, let's both of us jump on him."

Todd nodded, but the car suddenly swerved into the front parking lot of a Holiday Inn. A man who had been standing there jumped into the front seat. It all happened so fast that Ben and Todd didn't have time to react. The car was driving off before they thought to do anything.

The new man was younger than the driver, and he looked like a disgruntled vulture. "Good. You've got them."

Ben felt his heart sink. It would be hard to jump the driver with this second man in the car. "Where are you taking us?" he demanded. "What do you want?"

"Relax, kid," the vulture said. "No one's going to hurt you."

Ben and Todd sat side by side, their shoulders touching for comfort.

"They're gorgeous," the vulture said to the driver. "One blond and one dark. Perfect."

"What are you going to do with us?" Todd asked in a quavering voice.

"I told you, we're not going to hurt you. We're just going

to take some pictures of you, then we'll take you home. There's nothing to be scared about. Just cooperate, and you won't get hurt." He turned to give them an evil stare. "I've got a gun in my pocket. Don't make me use it."

Todd shrank even closer to Ben.

These are very bad men, Ben thought. *I have to pay attention to where we're going so I can tell Daddy.*

So it was when the car finally pulled off the highway, Ben noted the number and street name on the exit sign.

"When they let us get out of the car, let's make a run for it," Ben whispered to Todd. Todd nodded.

The car pulled up in front of a large warehouse-style building. There was no one in sight. "All right," the vulture said, "we get out here."

Ben got out of the car first and, as the vulture grabbed his arm, he bent his head and bit him.

"Ahhhh . . ." the vulture cried. "The little bastard's bitten me."

In the split second that the man's grip had loosened, Ben broke away and began to run down the street. The man was after him in a flash, overtaking him with his longer stride, and jerking his arm behind his back as he returned up the street.

"We've got a fiery one, eh?" the grandfatherly-looking man said. "If that translates to the movie screen, we'll have a real winner."

With both boys under firm control, they marched them into the building. The door opened on a cavernous, almost-empty room with high windows and plywood flooring. In one corner were pushed together a bed, a sofa, and a bathtub. Another corner held an assortment of lights on stands. The room also contained what looked like a very large dog crate, about five feet high and five feet in diameter. The two boys were hustled into the crate, and the door was locked behind them.

"There's a bucket in there if you have to pee," the vulture said. "And there are two bottles of water and some power bars in there also. We'll see you tomorrow."

"Tomorrow?" Todd said in a panicky voice. "You can't leave us here until tomorrow!"

The grandfatherly man said, "Don't worry none, sonny. You just do what we want you to do in front of the camera, and you'll be back with your families in no time."

The men went out and the warehouse door closed behind them. Todd started to cry.

Ben said, "We have to get out of here, Todd. These men are going to make us do something bad."

"How are we supposed to get out? They've locked us in a cage!"

"I don't know," Ben said. He felt like crying, too. He said, "We won't do what they want us to do, and maybe then they'll give up and let us go."

The day dragged on. Their captors had thoughtfully provided them with two soiled-looking sleeping bags, which the boys sat on. Solemnly they recited the Lord's Prayer and asked God to help them. Then, when it grew dark and the light ceased to come in through the windows, they crawled into the sleeping bags and tried to sleep. Ben prayed some more.

The sun had been up two hours when the big doors to the building crashed open and five men, all holding guns, came in in a rush.

"Jesus Christ," one of them said when he saw the boys in the cage.

Ben and Todd pressed against each other.

"Is anyone here besides you?" one of the other men demanded.

"No," Ben managed to say. "They went away yesterday and left us alone. Who are you?"

"It's all right, kid," the man said. "You're safe now. We're the police."

It was an hour later when the parents of both boys showed up at the police station.

"Mommy!" Ben cried, and ran straight into her arms, wrapping his own arms around her waist and pressing his face into her breast. "Some bad men kidnapped me, Mommy. I'm sorry. I'm sorry I got in the car with them."

"I could murder you," Kate said, holding him so tightly that he could scarcely breathe. "Do you know what you've put us through?"

"I'm sorry. I was so scared. But I prayed, and the police came."

"Oh God. Oh Ben. I am so glad to have you back."

Daniel said, "We've been praying too, son."

"Daddy!"

"Give me a hug," Daniel said huskily, and Ben went into his arms.

The Robbins family was going through a similar reunion scene and when both families had calmed down, an officer in plain clothes said, "We need to get a statement from each of the boys. You can be present when we do it."

They took the two boys separately, and Ben and Kate and Daniel went into a small room that held a table, four chairs, and a tape recorder. Ben said anxiously, "I'm sorry I got in the car with that man, but he looked nice. He was *old.* I didn't mean to do anything wrong."

"You didn't do anything wrong, Ben," the policeman,

whose name was Brown, assured him. "It's the men who took you who did something wrong. We need you to tell us all about them so we can catch them."

"Ben will be happy to cooperate, Officer," Daniel said.

Kate said, "Has Ben eaten anything this morning?"

"The policemen bought us donuts, Mommy."

The detective said, "Begin from the time you got into the car, Ben."

"The man said he had a pool basketball game that Todd and me could play with. That's why we got into the car, to go and get it. But when he drove outside the resort, we got scared. But he wouldn't stop to let us out. We tried to open the windows and the doors, but they were locked. Then the other man got into the car and told us he had a gun."

"Would you know these men if you saw them again, Ben?"

"Yes."

"Good. Then what happened?"

"They took us into the building and put us into that cage. They said they would be back in the morning to take pictures of us and after they did that we could go home."

Kate interrupted, "You were in a cage?"

"Yes."

"My God."

"The night was very long," Ben said. "I prayed and prayed that God would help us. Then, in the morning, the policemen came."

A tall man in a blue blazer came into the room and the policeman with them shut the tape recorder off. "I'm Lieutenant Tiffany," the new man said. "We picked up the two men who kidnapped the boys. Does Ben think he would recognize them?"

"Ben," Detective Brown said gravely, "would you be able

to pick those men out if they were shown to you with a group of other men?"

"Sure."

"Good," said Lieutenant Tiffany. "I'll arrange for the lineup then."

"I gather that this was a pornography ring," Daniel said.

"Yes. They produce videos of children engaging in sexual activity and market them for big bucks. We've been on their trail for a while, and this morning we staged a raid on the warehouse where we'd been told they shoot the films. It was just luck that we happened to find your boys."

"I think it was God," Ben said.

Kate said softly, "I think it was, too."

They had to wait while the lineups were being arranged, then Todd went first to view them. Ben seemed to have recovered some of his old confidence now that he realized he wasn't in trouble with the law for what he had done. When it was his turn to look at the lineups, he picked the two men out instantly.

"Those are the guys Todd picked, too," Lieutenant Tiffany told them. "Good job, Ben."

Finally, they were free to return to the resort. Once they were inside their unit, Kate said to Ben, "Never ever do anything like that again."

He hung his head. "I won't, Mommy."

"I can't believe you got in that car!"

"He was an old man, Mommy. I didn't think he was bad."

Daniel said, "I don't think there's any point in dwelling on this any more than we have to. I'm sure that Ben has learned his lesson."

"I'm sorry, Mommy. I'm sorry I scared you."

Kate hugged him. "Thank God you're safe." She let him go and sniffled. "Let's have some lunch."

"Good idea," Daniel said. "Particularly since we didn't have any breakfast."

"I can make us peanut butter and jelly sandwiches."

"Sounds good to me. Unless you'd like to go out?"

Kate shook her head vehemently. "I want to stay right here."

"Okay, then peanut butter and jelly it is."

They sat around the table, eating their sandwiches, and Ben said, "Why did those men want to take pictures of us?"

Kate and Daniel exchanged a look.

You tell him, Kate thought.

Daniel said, "They wanted to take videos of you with your clothes off. Then they would sell the videos to bad people who like to look at naked children."

"They were going to make us take our clothes off?"

"Yes."

"Yuck."

"Precisely."

"Why would anyone want to look at videos of naked children?"

"Some people are just sick, Ben. It's hard to explain."

"I knew those men wanted us to do something bad. They were happy that Todd was blond and I was dark."

"*God*," Kate said.

Daniel looked at her. "We were very lucky."

"Yes, we were."

"Are the police going to put those men in jail?"

"They'd better," Kate said.

Ben said with concern, "If they don't, they might kidnap more boys."

Daniel said, "I'm sure they'll put them in jail, Ben. And your being able to pick them out of the lineup will be a big part of their evidence. You went through a frightening ordeal, but the good thing is that you will have helped to put two very bad men in jail."

Once lunch was over, Daniel said to Kate, "Why don't you take a nap? You didn't get any sleep last night, and you must be exhausted. I'll keep Ben under my eagle eye, I promise."

"You didn't get any sleep, either."

"I'm used to it. Sometimes our flights don't get into places until three or four in the morning. I'll be fine, and Ben will be fine. Take a nap."

"Nana takes naps, but Mommy doesn't," Ben said.

"Well she's going to take a nap today."

Kate looked at Ben, then she looked at Daniel. "I feel as if someone has just hit me over the head with a sledgehammer, but I don't think I could sleep."

"Then lie down and rest. Ben and I will go down to the pool, and I won't let him out of my sight."

Her great light eyes searched his face. "All right," she said at last. "I'll rest."

"Good girl."

"Will you swim with me, Daddy?"

"Sure thing. Let's go and get our bathing suits on."

When Kate finally lay down her brain was filled with frightening images of Ben in a cage. She was afraid to think of what might have happened if the police hadn't arrived.

Thank you, God, for saving him. Thank you, thank you, thank you.

She didn't think she would be able to sleep, but sheer exhaustion eventually took over and she did.

They went out to a restaurant for dinner. "I never got to the Animal Kingdom," Ben said sorrowfully. "Or to MGM."

"We'll come back again someday," Daniel said.

"We will? Promise?"

"I promise." Daniel looked at Kate. "It was a random kidnapping, Kata. Those men never knew he was my son."

She nodded. "To think that I was afraid to send him to Colombia, and this happens—at Disney World!"

"When we get home, I think Ben should get some counseling," Daniel said. "I was almost kidnapped once, and it's an experience that stays with you." He looked at Ben. "I still get nightmares about it once in a while."

"You were almost kidnapped, Daddy?"

"Yes. I was much older than you, though, and I was able to get free and run away before they could get me in the car."

"How old were you?" Kate asked.

"Nineteen. It was during the war against Pablo Escobar, when he was kidnapping people to force the Assembly to vote against extradition to the United States. As I said, I got away. But the experience stayed with me, which is why I think Ben should get counseling."

"What is counseling?" Ben asked.

"You just talk to a doctor about what happened and the doctor makes you feel better about it."

"Did you go for counseling, Daddy?"

"No, but I wish I had."

"Okay, I'll go."

Kate said, "We'll have to pack when we get home. Our flight leaves at ten in the morning and we have to be there two hours in advance."

They put Ben to bed at eight o'clock, then Daniel returned with Kate to the living room. She looked at him and said, "They almost made a pornographic video of him, Daniel."

He reached out and drew her close. "I know. I know. God was very good to us." He could feel her trembling and held her closer. "He will be all right, Kata. But I do think we should get him some counseling."

"I think that's a good idea." She rested her cheek against his shoulder. "It's always been my greatest fear—losing Ben. And then it happened."

"It happened, and no permanent harm has been done." His hand came up to caress her hair. "You can relax now. Ben is safe."

"I'll bet he won't ever sneak out on us again."

He loved the feel of her hair under his fingers. He curved his fingers around the nape of her neck. It was so tender and vulnerable, her nape. He loved it.

She said, "Thank God you were with me. If I'd had to go through that alone . . . well, I don't know how I would have done it."

He slid his hand along the line of her jaw to her chin and tilted her head up. Then he kissed her.

Her mouth opened for him as soon as he asked, yielding, responding, telling him without words that whatever he wanted of her he could have.

"Kata. Love." His voice was almost a croak, and his mouth moved over her face, kissing her eyelids, her cheeks, then coming back once again to her mouth. She was arched up against him, her slender body taut and trembling. He slid a hand beneath her white shirt and touched her breast. He felt her nipple stand up hard against the palm of his hand, and he groaned.

He tried to regain his self-control, but it was fast slipping away. She leaned back from him a little and gazed up into his face. Her eyes were purely aquamarine, her mouth was a little swollen from his kisses. He put his hand on her arm, pulled her off the sofa, and led her upstairs to his bedroom.

The feel of her under him was exquisite. He kissed her again and again and her body arched to the demanding urgency of his.

All he wanted was to have her. But he had to be careful. He had to be gentle. This was Kata, who had given him her virginity. He couldn't hurt her.

But he could feel the passion ignite in her. He took her nipple into his mouth, and she cried out. Her eyes were closed. "Kata?" he panted.

She opened herself to take him in even as she held on to him tightly. The last time he had made sure she had an orgasm before he entered, but this time he couldn't wait. He drove in, deep into the heart of her, and her heat and her moisture welcomed him. He drove her up the bed and she took him even deeper, as if the joining of their bodies could heal the suffering of these last two days.

After, she lay nestled quietly in his arms, and he felt his heart would break with love for her. She was his. She had never been anyone else's. He held her close against him, and he knew the course of his life had somehow changed. Nothing would ever be the same now that he had held Kata in his arms.

She stirred against him and kissed his collarbone. "I love you, Daniel," she breathed.

Happiness flooded through him. "I love you, too," he said. "I love you, too."

29

The day before Molly's second chemotherapy session, Alberto took her out to dinner. They went to an excellent Italian restaurant in Greenwich.

"Is this the last meal of the condemned?" Molly asked humorously as she looked at the impressive menu.

He smiled. "Surely it is not as bad as that."

She sighed. "It feels that way. The last treatment I was out of commission for two whole days, and I'm afraid it's only going to get worse."

"It is very unpleasant, I agree. But you must remember that your prognosis is for a cure. Keep your eye on the prize, Molly."

"You're right. I'm being a baby. I'm not this way with anyone else. What is it about you that brings out the complainer in me, Alberto?"

"You feel you have to be strong for Kate and Ben. With me you can be honest."

The waiter came with their drinks. Molly, who didn't usually drink anything but wine, had ordered a scotch sour. Alberto had a glass of red wine.

Molly took a sip of her drink and closed her eyes. "My, this brings back memories. When Tim and I went out to dinner, I would always order a scotch sour. I haven't had one in years."

"Why did you stop drinking them?"

She lifted an eyebrow. "I stopped going out to dinner."

"Why?"

She took another sip of her drink. "There wasn't any money, Alberto. It was pretty bad when Tim died. He had gone through all our savings to keep the farm running. The only income we had was my salary. We could have lived on my salary, but we couldn't keep the farm going on it. I would have sold the farm, but Kate wouldn't hear of it. And Tim had left the farm to her."

"He didn't leave you the farm?" Alberto was incredulous.

"I never had anything to do with the horses, really, and Colleen was like me. He knew I would sell it, and he knew that Kate wouldn't."

Alberto took a sip of his cabernet sauvignon. "She seems to have saved it."

"She did an unbelievable job. She carried the farm on her back for years; in fact, she's still carrying it on her back. She does almost all of the work herself. Even now, when she could afford to hire help, she insists on doing most of the work herself."

"She has a lot of energy."

"She does, but she has nothing left over for the rest of her life. She's a beautiful girl, and she's never had a boyfriend. All of her being has been invested in that farm. And in Ben."

The waiter came with their salads. Alberto picked up his fork. "It seems to me, Molly, that you are in the same circumstances as your daughter. You carried the household with your teaching job, and you took on the job of baby-sitting for Ben. What time did you have for the rest of your life?"

Molly smiled and tasted her salad. "We're just two boring women, I'm afraid."

"I would say that you are two very strong and dedicated women. And that is very admirable. But I think it may be time for you to expand your lives."

"Are you talking about Kate and Daniel?"

After the slightest pause, Alberto said, "Yes."

"It would be so wonderful if they married," Molly said wistfully. "It would be perfect for Ben, of course, but it would also be perfect for Kate. She relates to Daniel. She *sees* him. She's never really seen any other man. And I think he cares for her."

"I think he does also."

Molly laughed. "I must sound like a matchmaking mama."

"Do you know what amazes me most about you, Molly?"

"What?"

"You never seem to think of yourself."

She flushed. "I think of myself when it's necessary."

He put his salad fork down for a moment. "Have you ever thought about what your life would be if Daniel and Kate do marry? Would you plan to live with them?"

She looked at him in horror. "Of course not."

"Then what will you do? You have invested your life in your daughter and grandson. What life will you have left if they start to lead lives that don't include you?"

She said a little defensively, "I have my teaching."

He took a bite of his salad and watched her. Then he said, "I'll wager that you're eligible to retire."

She shook her head impatiently. "I can't retire. We need my full salary, not what a pension would bring in."

"If Kate marries Daniel, she won't need your salary at all."

The waiter arrived to collect their salad dishes. Molly took another sip of her scotch sour, and said, "Did you take me out to dinner just to harangue me, Alberto?"

His lips smiled slightly, but his eyes remained grave. "I am just pointing out to you things that I don't think you have ever bothered to think about for yourself."

"I've thought about them," Molly said tightly. "But that's the way things are."

"They don't need to stay that way."

Molly looked at him warily.

He smiled. "All right. I'll stop and let you enjoy your dinner. But let me end this 'harangue' by saying that you are a very lovely woman, Molly Foley."

"Thank you, Alberto," she said, and took the last long swallow of her scotch.

Alberto took Molly to her chemo treatment and when she came home she lay down while he cooked some dinner.

He's such a dear man, Molly thought. *I can't believe how important he has become in my life. And in such a short time! I will miss him dreadfully when he goes back to Colombia.*

She lay curled up on her side under a fleece blanket and thought about Alberto. *I think he feels about me the way I feel about him.* She thought of their dinner conversation the previous evening. Alberto had not said anything that Molly didn't already know for herself, but she had never thought there was anything to be done about it.

We talked about Kate and Daniel getting married. What about Alberto and me?

The answer was immediate: *I can't marry Alberto. His life is in Colombia, and my life is here, with my daughter and my grandson. Daniel lives in the United States. Kate's and my situations are not comparable.*

But Alberto had made her life sound so . . . bleak. As bleak as she made Kate's life sound to her.

There's not much to choose between us, I'm afraid, she thought wryly. *The Foley girls will never make anyone's list of top ten Women on the Town.*

Her mind drifted to the afternoon's chemotherapy session. *It's far from certain that I'll even have a future.*

But deep in her heart, Molly believed she would be cured. She had stage one breast cancer that had not spread to the lymph system. Her prognosis for recovery was excellent.

Am I going to be alone for the rest of my life? Do I want to be alone for the rest of my life?

I don't, she thought. *But I don't see what l can do about it.*

"Nana! Nana! Nana! You'll never guess what happened to me. I was kidnapped!"

Molly caught Ben in her arms and hugged him. His hard little-boy body felt so wonderful. She looked at Kate in amusement, expecting an explanation of this extraordinary statement, but Kate's face was grave.

"It's true," she said. "He was kidnapped. But, as you can see, we got him back."

"I will carry these bags upstairs for you, Kata," Daniel said.

"Tell Nana, Mommy. Tell her what happened."

"First let me find out how Nana is feeling, Ben. She had her treatment while we were gone."

"I'm tired," Molly admitted. "But not too tired to hear your story. I'll make us some tea."

Kate hung up her coat, then Ben's, and, when Daniel returned downstairs, she hung up his. Then they went into the kitchen, and Molly poured tea.

When they were all sitting around the kitchen table, Kate said to Daniel, "You tell Mom. I can hardly talk about it yet."

So Daniel told the story, interrupted periodically by Ben; "They put me in a big dog cage, Nana!" and "The police had guns, Nana!"

Molly was horrified. "And they never knew that Ben was your son, Daniel?"

"No. They were looking for children to use in their porn flicks."

Molly felt even sicker to her stomach than she already was.

"Do you know what a porn flick is, Nana?"

She looked at her grandson cautiously. "What is it?"

"It's pictures of children without their clothes on. Isn't that weird?"

"Very weird," Molly said faintly.

"Daddy says I should have a . . . what's it called, Daddy?"

"A counselor," Daniel replied.

"Is that necessary?" Molly asked. She looked at her grandson's animated face. "Ben seems to regard this whole thing as a big adventure."

"Daddy says I might have nightmares," Ben said.

"I think a counselor would be a good idea," Daniel said quietly.

"So do I," said Kate.

"All right, then," Molly said.

Kate said, "So, tell me, how did the second chemo session go?"

"Very much like the first. Alberto sat with me and we talked while I was getting the IV. Then I came home and went to bed. He cooked a wonderful dinner, which I was able to eat, and then I went back to bed. Like the last time, I feel worse the second day than I did yesterday."

"You don't have any color in your face."

"I know. I've been trying not to look in the mirror."

"I wish you could have come to Disney with us, Nana. You would have liked Epcot."

She smiled with her heart. "I wish I could have gone too, Ben. I'll bet you had a great time. Tell me about some of the things that you saw."

Ben, who never had a problem with talking, proceeded to do just that. After fifteen minutes, Kate said, "I think you should go lie down, Mom. Ben can tell you the rest later."

"I think you're right," Molly said. She got up and went around the table to kiss Ben. "I'll hear the rest when I wake up. Okay?"

"Okay. I hope you feel better soon, Nana."

"Thank you, honey."

Molly went upstairs to bed. She slept for a while, and when she awoke she still didn't have the energy to get up. *I'll feel better tomorrow*, she told herself. *If I can get through today, tomorrow will be better.*

She thought of what had happened to Ben, and she shuddered. How could people be so evil? *I must have led a very sheltered life, but the most evil person I ever met is Marty Lockwood. And he's more irresponsible than he is evil. Of course, I've always known there's evil in the world, it's just that it never directly touched me.*

Her bedroom door opened and Kate looked in.

"I'm awake," Molly called.

Kate came over and sat down on the edge of her bed. "How are you feeling, Mom?"

"Tired. I'm tired of feeling tired."

"Why don't you stay home from school tomorrow?"

"I'll see how I feel in the morning."

Kate's eye fell on the bouquet of flowers on her dresser. "Where did the flowers come from? Alberto?"

"Yes. He has been so thoughtful."

"He's a nice man."

"Yes, he is."

Kate said gravely, "Ben's kidnapping was the worst thing that ever happened to me. It was . . . oh, it's indescribable how I felt. The worst feeling in the world."

"I can believe it."

"At first I thought that he was taken because he's Daniel's son, but that wouldn't account for them taking the other boy, too. And there was no ransom demand. I didn't know whether I should hope that there would be one—because at least then we'd know that Ben was alive. But we waited all day and the telephone never rang. It was horrible."

"It makes going through chemo sound like a piece of cake," Molly said soberly.

"I would rather go through chemo a hundred times than go through that again."

"Why didn't you call me?"

"I would have called you if we hadn't found him when we did."

Molly sighed. "What awful people live in the world."

"I know."

"Have you checked on your beloved horses?"

Kate smiled. "Yes, I have. And everything went smoothly. No one colicked or foundered or anything like that. Jean was wonderful."

"Ben sounded as if he had a good time in spite of the kidnapping."

"The first two days were great. He had a blast."

"And you?"

"It was fun. It was fun watching Ben have fun. And the Epcot exhibits really were interesting."

Kate was keeping something from her. Molly asked, "Did you and Daniel get along all right?"

"Sure," Kate replied.

She stood up and leaned over to kiss Molly's cheek. "Rest some more, Mom. Do you think you'll be up to eating some dinner?"

"I'll try."

"Great. I'm just roasting a chicken."

"Sounds good."

Kate closed the door quietly as she left.

30

It was New Year's Eve and Kate sat in her office and looked at the framed picture of George and Sebastian she had hanging on her wall. *I can't believe he's gone. I can't believe that he's never going to walk in this door, that I'm never going to see him again.*

Can you hear me, George? I miss you. I miss you very much. And Sebastian misses you, too. He's grieving, and I wish I could help him. But it's you he wants.

Maybe I'll turn Sebastian out in the same paddock with Shane. They're both old horses; it might help Sebastian to have a buddy.

So many changes . . . nothing will ever be the same again.

For some reason, Alberto's words popped into her mind. "Change is life."

"I suppose it is," she said out loud. "But that doesn't mean I have to like it."

Some other words of Alberto's came to her mind. "And that is all the room you have in your heart—room for two people? There is no place to add someone else?"

Daniel would be moving into the spare room at High Meadow for the month of January, his custody month for Ben. That would be another big change in her life.

She thought of those two nights in Florida, and the way he had made her feel. When she was eighteen she had once watched the brutally elemental mating of stallion with mare, and she had always vaguely thought that human mating must be something like that.

What she had experienced might have been elemental, but it had been far from brutal. It had been profoundly moving, and not just physically. She had felt herself drawn to Daniel by ties of the heart as well as the flesh.

What is going to happen to us?

Because, as intensely as she felt about him, Kate couldn't see herself married to Daniel. She couldn't see herself giving up her business and moving to Greenwich.

What would I do with myself if I didn't have my horses?

And yet, could she see herself giving up Daniel?

How did it happen that he's become the biggest thing in my life next to Ben? What will we do when he's living in the house with me? Will we make love under the same roof as Mom and Ben?

Ben's presence didn't stop us in Florida.

Someone knocked on the office door, and Jean Stewart came into the room. "Could I go over a few things with you, Kate?"

"Sure thing," Kate said, and prepared to give her attention to matters of the farm.

Daniel had been invited to several New Year's Eve parties, but instead he made a reservation to take Kate out to dinner. Then they would see the new year in at home. At the last minute, Kate managed to snag Jean Stewart to baby-sit for Ben, and Alberto and Molly decided to join them.

The restaurant in Westport was packed, and there was the usual stir as they walked in and Daniel was recognized.

"I have some news," Daniel said after they had all been seated and given menus.

"What?" Kate asked.

"I'm not sure if you'll consider it good news or bad, but my parents are coming to stay. I got a call this morning. They said that since I didn't go to Colombia for Christmas, they would come to America to spend the beginning of the new year with me."

"How lovely," Molly said sincerely.

Kate said, "But you're supposed to be staying with us for January."

He looked at her. "I know, but I think I had better stay in Greenwich until my parents leave. They'll probably only stay for a week." His voice was deeply regretful.

She nodded slowly. He thought that she was looking like an angel tonight, in a blue dress that made her eyes look more blue than green. Her short hair showed off her long lovely throat and small, elegant ears. He felt desire stir and resolutely drank some of his water and tried to pay attention to the conversation.

Alberto was saying, "We may be crossing in the air. I have to go back to Colombia, and I managed to get a flight out tomorrow."

Molly didn't say anything, but she looked dismayed.

Kate said, "Is everything okay?"

"Everything is fine, but I have to talk to my publishers about the book, and it will be easier to do it in person than on the telephone. I also understand that an American publisher is interested in buying the book in translation."

Molly's face lit. "Alberto! How marvelous."

"That's great," Kate said.

"When did this come about?" Daniel asked.

"I heard while you were down in Florida."

"Will . . . will you be coming back?" Molly asked.

He looked at her. "I am not ready to return to Colombia permanently. Yet."

A little color flushed into Molly's pale face.

Kate said, "Do you mean you're thinking of quitting your job with Daniel?"

"It was always going to be a temporary thing," Alberto said. "In fact, I stayed longer than I planned. My daughter is very annoyed with me"—his eyes went once again to Molly—"but I am glad that I remained."

Molly didn't say anything.

"You've spoiled me, Alberto," Daniel said. "You managed to get my life more organized than it has ever been, and you did it part-time while you worked on your book. I won't be able to replace you."

"You probably won't," Alberto agreed mildly.

Both Molly and Kate laughed.

Kate said, "What about Ben? I know you said you wanted to take him to school, but it might be easier for him to take the bus while your parents are here."

"It would definitely be easier for him to take the bus."

"Okay."

Molly said, "Are you going to tell your parents about Ben's kidnapping?"

Daniel said, "You know Ben will blurt it all out. It's better that they hear the story from me, first."

Molly smiled. "Discretion is not one of Ben's virtues, bless him."

"You mean he's a big mouth," Kate said.

"He's a very self-confident child," Alberto said. "You two ladies are to be congratulated."

Molly and Kate exchanged a look.

"Self-confident," Kate said. "I like that better than conceited."

"What are you going to do with your parents during their visit?" Molly asked Daniel.

"My mother will shop and my father will hang out at Kate's barn," Daniel returned easily.

Kate smiled. "I'll be glad to have him. If I'm lucky, he'll give me another lesson. I learned so much from him the last time he was here."

When she smiled like that she was breathtaking.

Daniel said, his eyes still on Kate, "I thought maybe I would stay over at High Meadow tonight. My parents don't get in until late in the afternoon, and this way I can have the morning with Ben."

"Of course you can stay over, Daniel," Molly said. "The spare room is all ready for you."

Kate's lashes lowered to conceal her eyes.

The waiter came to take their drinks order.

The four of them toasted the new year in with champagne, then Alberto left to go back to Greenwich and the two Foleys and Daniel climbed the stairs to go to bed.

Molly left them in the hall, going into her bedroom and firmly closing the door. Daniel said to Kate gravely, "Your place or mine?"

"The spare room shares a wall with Ben's room."

"Why don't we make it your place, then?"

"Okay. But wait a half an hour until Mom's asleep. I'll get in the bathroom now, then you can have it."

"Okay."

The upstairs in the old house was chilly, and Kate wrapped a fleece bathrobe around her nakedness and got into her double bed with the flannel sheets and pulled the covers up over her head. She breathed in and out in the tentlike darkness, trying to warm the bed up with her breath. Gradually she got warmer and poked her nose out into the chilly air of her bedroom.

Precisely half an hour after she had left him in the hall, Daniel knocked softly on her door and came in. He was wearing a robe over his pajamas.

"I think this room is even colder than mine," he said as he came over to the bed and got in beside her.

"The thermostat is set to go down at eleven because we're usually in bed by then."

"Come here and let's get warm together."

Kate moved into his arms.

"Ai!" she yipped. "Your feet are freezing. Keep them to yourself, please."

"How are they going to get warm if you don't let them touch you?"

"That's your problem, buddy."

"Such tenderness," he said. "Such care."

"Such cold feet," she retorted.

He chuckled. "Let's see what I've got here. I feel a fleece bathrobe, but what is under it?" He slid a hand between the folds of her robe and touched her bare breast. "Ah," he said. "How nice."

"You have pajamas on," Kate said. "I didn't put pajamas on."

"I didn't want to meet your mother or Ben in the hallway and be wearing only my robe. It would be a little embarrassing."

"True."

"Ben would be sure to say, 'Daddy, why are you naked?'"

Kate giggled.

"Do that again," he said.

"Do what?"

"Make that little laughing sound. It's enchanting."

"It's a spontaneous sound. I can't make it at will."

"Are you warm enough for me to kiss you?"

"I think kissing would help the warming process."

"All right." And he lowered his mouth to hers.

He kissed her, and the very touch of her mouth made him shudder. She opened her lips and kissed him back.

As soon as his tongue entered her mouth, desire washed over her like a surge of warm water, and she clung to him in the darkness that did not feel cold anymore. He pushed her robe away and his mouth was moving all over her and she could feel the pulse between her legs beating more and more intensely.

"Daniel," she said as her hands spread flat against his back. "Daniel."

Then he was entering her, and it felt so good. The feel of him inside her was so good. Back and forth he went, back and forth, until she thought she could endure the tension no more, then the explosion of pleasure came, rocking her whole body with its power.

When it was over she lay still against him, absorbing the heat from his body. "Daniel?" she murmured after a while.

"Yes?"

"Is it always like that?"

"No, Kata, it's not always like that. It's only like that with you."

"I'm glad."

She rested her cheek against his chest and listened to the slowing beat of his heart. He was so warm.

"You don't have to go back to your cold bed right away," she said. "You can stay here for the night. But you have to get back to the spare room before Ben or my mother get up."

"Perhaps we should set the alarm."

"I have it set for six because I have to feed the horses. That should be safe enough."

She felt his lips on her hair. "I love you, Kata," he said.

"I love you, too."

"Will you marry me?"

"Let's not talk about that right now, Daniel. It's too late. Let's just go to sleep."

"All right, if that's what you want."

"It is. Didn't we get this bed nice and warm?"

"It feels wonderful. But I have to go to sleep facing the other way. I never go to sleep on my back."

"Okay."

Daniel turned over and punched his pillow into shape. Kate curled up behind him and, briefly, rested her cheek against him. She could feel the movement of his back as he breathed. "I do love you," she murmured.

"Good," he said.

"Good night, Daniel."

"Good night, Kata."

Within five minutes they were both asleep.

31

*B*en went back to school the day after New Year's Day and at midafternoon Daniel came over to the barn with his father. Kate had just finished cleaning out the last stall when they arrived. The men were dressed in coats and scarves, but Kate wore only a sweater.

"Aren't you cold?" Daniel asked.

"I have on long underwear," she explained. "And I've been mucking stalls."

"I forgot how cold it gets in America," Rafael said. "I had to borrow one of Daniel's mufflers."

"If it's too cold, we can skip the lesson," Kate said.

"Not at all. I was thinking we would work on your seat today."

"Great," said Kate. "Shane is very good on the lunge line, if that's what you want to do."

"I will be happy to lunge you."

As they walked to Shane's stall, Rafael said, "What happened to the horse you rode the last time?"

"He's been sold. He was too much for his rider, so we got her a new horse."

"That's too bad. He was a nice animal."

"Yes, he was. I miss riding him."

She saddled up Shane while Daniel and Rafael sipped the coffee they had brought. They had thoughtfully brought a cup of Starbucks for Kate, too, but she put it aside for later. "If I drink it now, it will only make me want to go to the bathroom in the middle of my lesson," she explained.

Once they were in the ring, Rafael began, "The classical seat is vital to any work you might do in dressage. Over two thousand years ago Xenophon wrote, 'I do not approve of a seat which is as though the man were on a chair, but rather as though he were standing upright with his legs apart.' That is the classical seat—not the forward seat which you use for your jumping, and not the chair seat you see often used incorrectly in dressage tests."

Kate had borrowed a dressage saddle from one of her clients who did combined training. Rafael put her on the lunge line and watched in silence as she went around him in a circle.

"Stop," he said, and went to lower her stirrups two holes.

"Good grief," Kate said. "I feel like I'm reaching for them."

"You can't achieve the feeling of standing on the ground if your knee is too bent. Let your legs grow long from the hip. Let gravity carry them right down into your foot, then into the ground. But sit proudly with your upper body."

Kate went back to circling him, concentrating on dropping her legs down. Once Rafael decided she was sitting correctly, she moved into a trot. "Keep your shoulders still, your back straight, then move from the hip with the horse."

They worked for forty minutes and by the end of the session Kate was sitting more deeply, and more erectly, with her heels, hips, and head all lined up so that a straight line could be drawn through them.

"That was great," she said as she got off of Shane. "Could we do another session tomorrow?"

"I don't see why not. It is a pleasure to work with such a responsive student."

They took Shane back into the barn and Kate didn't bother to put him on crossties to unsaddle him. She and Rafael were talking enthusiastically about Rafael's Andalusians when a white towel that had been perched precariously on the rack of the stall door just behind Shane fell to the ground. Without thinking, Daniel bent to pick it up. His gloved hand was flat on the ground at the same moment that Shane stepped back. Shane's hoof, shod in steel and bearing his full weight, came down on Daniel's hand.

Daniel exclaimed in Spanish. Shane, feeling something under his foot, lifted it immediately and Daniel pulled his hand away.

"Oh no," said Kate. "Your hand!"

Daniel was cradling his right hand, his pitching hand, with the left. "Shit," he said. "I think it's broken."

Rafael asked Daniel a question in Spanish.

"*Sí,*" Daniel responded.

Kate said, "We better get you to the emergency room right away."

"Yes," Daniel said a trifle grimly. "The sooner this is attended to, the less swelling there will be."

"I will drive you," Rafael said. "Come. Let us go."

"I'll come with you," Kate said.

"You can't," Daniel said. He was very pale. "You have to be here for Ben."

"Will you call me, Daniel? Please?"

"I will call you as soon as we know something. Come on, Papa. We need to go."

Kate stood next to her horse and watched the two men

leave the barn. *My God, my God, my God. How did Daniel's hand ever get under Shane's hoof?*

She brushed Shane and put him out in the paddock with Sebastian. Then she cleaned the water buckets. But her mind was not on her work; it was with Daniel.

It was his right hand, his pitching hand. What if it's permanently damaged? What if Daniel can't ever pitch again?

The thought petrified her. Daniel wasn't thirty yet. He had years of pitching before him. It would be too cruel to have his career cut short due to an accident like this.

But career-ending injuries happened all the time in sports. Why shouldn't it happen to Daniel?

She walked down to the bus stop to meet Ben and debated whether or not to tell him about what had happened. They were in the kitchen, and she still hadn't decided, when the phone rang. She picked up the kitchen extension. "Hello."

"Kata."

She shut her eyes at the sound of his voice. "How are you? Have you seen a doctor?"

"They've X-rayed my hand and two bones are broken."

"Oh my God."

"The treatment is not to use the hand until they're healed. Then I'll need physical therapy to gain the hand's strength back."

"Will this . . . will this affect your pitching?"

"I don't know, Kata," he said gravely. "We'll just have to wait and see."

"Daniel, how can I tell you how sorry I am that this happened. I should have put Shane on the crossties . . ."

He cut in, "Don't blame yourself. I should have had enough sense to keep my hand away from the vicinity of a horse's hoof."

"It wasn't your fault . . ."

"That's the point, Kata. It wasn't anybody's fault."

"Have you contacted the Yankees yet?"

"Not yet." He sounded grim. "That's next on my list of things to do. They'll want me looked at by a specialist, not just an emergency room doctor."

"A specialist is a good idea."

"Yes. Listen, I'm calling you from a pay phone at the hospital. I'll talk to you again tonight."

"Okay. Take care of yourself."

"Right. Good-bye."

"Good-bye," and Kate hung up the phone.

Ben was looking at her with very bright eyes. "Was that Daddy?"

"Yes."

"Did something happen?"

"Yes. By accident, Shane stepped on your father's hand."

Ben's large brown eyes grew even larger. "Did he break it?"

"Yes, he did. And it was his right hand, his pitching hand, so everyone is very upset."

"Is Daddy in the hospital?"

"Grandpapa took him to the hospital, and they fixed the broken bones, but Daddy can't use his hand for a while."

"But they fixed it?"

"Yes."

"Well, that's good then." Ben went back to his glass of milk. "It's a good thing Daddy's not playing baseball now."

Kate responded hollowly, "Yes, it's a very good thing."

Half an hour later, she went through the same explanation with Molly, who was horrified.

"Shane is such a sensible horse. However did this happen?"

"Claire left a towel on her door and when it fell down,

Daniel stooped to pick it up. His hand was on the ground at the exact moment that Shane decided to back up."

"Oh my dear." Molly came to put an arm around Kate's shoulders. "It was an accident, but you must feel terrible."

"I feel horrible, Mom. What if it doesn't heal properly? What if Daniel can never pitch again?"

"That's not likely to happen."

"How do we know? And we won't know until the bones are healed and the physical therapy is finished and he can start throwing again. Can you imagine the worry he is going to carry for all that time?"

"It's not going to be fun," Molly admitted.

"I feel like it was my fault. Shane is my horse."

"It's not as if Shane did it deliberately, dear. It was an accident. I'm sure Daniel knows that."

"He told me it was nobody's fault; it was just one of those things that happen."

Ben said, "I'll pray that Daddy's hand gets better." After the kidnapping incident, Ben had become a great believer in prayer.

"That would be wonderful," Molly told him. "I'm sure your prayers will help."

That evening, as Kate was walking back to the house after her lessons, she saw Daniel's car coming up the driveway. Rafael was driving.

She began to run.

Daniel was closing the car door behind him when she reached the driveway. "Daniel! How are you doing?"

"Oh there you are, Kata. I can't stay, I only stopped by to let you know that I'm okay."

She stopped next to him and looked up. "Did you see a specialist?"

"I've seen a specialist, I've had an MRI, and the conclusion is the same as that of the emergency room doctor. I've broken two bones in my hand."

He lifted his hand for her to see it. "It's taped, and I have to wear this protective glove." The glove covered the palm of his hand and left the tops of his fingers free.

"Can you use your fingers?"

He wiggled them to show her that he could. "I think it's going to be all right, Kata."

"I am sure it will be all right," Rafael said. He hadn't gotten out of the car and was speaking through the open window. "Now that you have seen Kate, Daniel, and she knows that you are not permanently maimed, can we please go home?"

"All right, Papa." He gave Kate an apologetic smile. "I'd better go. My mother wants to see me, too."

"Of course you should go. Thank you for coming. The hand doesn't look half as bad as I imagined it would."

"That is exactly the reason I came by. I didn't want you imagining all sorts of horrible things."

The light from the front porch showed her his face. He looked tired, she thought. And, for all his brave words, worried.

She wanted desperately to kiss him, but Rafael was there.

"Good night," she said.

"I'll call you in the morning about our lesson," Rafael said.

"Great."

Daniel got back in the car, which Rafael turned so he could go forward down the long narrow driveway. Kate felt a pain in the region of her heart as she watched them go.

That night, Daniel had a nightmare that when he tried to pitch he couldn't properly grip the ball. He tried to throw pitches but all his balls went into the dirt or sailed overhead into the backstop. And his hand hurt all the time. He woke up sweating, with his heart hammering in his chest. And his hand hurt.

"*Dios*," he muttered as he realized he was safely in bed. He thrust his good hand through his tousled hair, pushing it back off his forehead. The pain pills had worn off, and his injured hand was throbbing. "*Damn.*"

He should be snug in bed with Kata and not lying here alone with a broken hand. *What rotten luck. If the damn horse had stepped back one second later, my hand would have been out of the way.*

But he knew that that was how accidents happened: fast. One minute you were safe, and the next minute you had torn an ACL, or gotten a concussion, or broken a hand.

It wouldn't be so bad if I was a position player, but pitching is so exact. If my grip changes at all, I won't be the pitcher that I was. I have to be able to hold the ball the exact way I held it before the hand was broken.

What are the chances of that happening?

No one would tell him the answer to that question. All the doctors would say was, "Wait and see."

It would be three weeks before they could take X-rays again. The doctor had told him that broken bones were better than torn ligaments, that bones generally heal cleaner.

What will I do with myself if I can't pitch? I'm not ready to give it up yet. I'm too young.

He got out of bed, went into the bathroom, and took more pain pills. While he was waiting for them to kick in, his mind turned to Kate.

Kata said she loved me, but she didn't say she'd marry me. How will she feel if I can't pitch anymore?

The answer was immediate: Whether he pitched or not

would make no difference to Kate. But it would most certainly matter to him.

It isn't fair to ask her to marry me when my life is in such turmoil. I have a nerve asking her to marry me at all when I can't give her children.

It was the deepest wound to his manhood, the fact that he could not father children. The puniest guy in the stands could have a child, but he could not. It had been a bitter blow. The only people who knew were his parents and Alberto . . . and Kate. He had never told any of the women he dated his secret; he had only told Kate.

How can I love her the way I do, how can I pour myself into the very heart of her, and not be able to give her a child?

And now, to add to that, there was the doubt about whether he would be able to pitch again.

He was a power pitcher. He had been the top strikeout pitcher in his league for the last four years. His starts had been like baseball rock concerts. If his hand didn't heal properly, all of that was in jeopardy.

What will I do with myself if I can't pitch?

His mind went blank at that question. He couldn't imagine himself not pitching.

How can I ask Kata to marry a broken-down pitcher who can't give her a child? It's impossible.

Not that she jumped at the chance when I proposed. She said she loved me, but when I mentioned marriage she said, "Let's talk about it later."

It would be better not to mention marriage again until he knew about his hand. Once he knew where he stood, then he would decide what it was that he should do.

32

The day before Daniel's parents were due to leave for Colombia, Daniel invited Kate, Molly, and Ben to his house for dinner. It was January 6, and the Monteros had presents for Ben. Rafael explained to him the Spanish tradition of giving gifts on the day of the wise men's visit while Victoria took Molly aside and asked her how her treatments were progressing.

"I'm tired and I'm starting to lose my hair," Molly said. "And, to top it off, my blood count is too low, and I have to go to the hospital for shots to bring it up before they can give me the next chemo treatment."

"Yes, that happened to me also," Victoria said. "I am so sorry for you, Molly. It is a wretched experience to go through."

Molly sighed. "Everyone has been very supportive."

"Are you sick to your stomach?"

"Not really. But food doesn't interest me all that much."

"I know. I lost ten pounds while I was in treatment."

"But you're okay now?"

"I am okay, and I must tell you that I rarely think of that time in my life. Oh, I think about it when I go for my yearly mammogram, but otherwise it doesn't come to my mind. I consider myself cured."

"That's great, Victoria. And I feel optimistic that I will be all right also. I just have to get through this miserable treatment first."

"You will get through it, Molly. And you will be better. That is what counts."

Ben came over to join them. "Grandmama, come and hear about how I was kidnapped."

"What?"

"Come on, Daddy is telling Grandpapa."

Victoria went to join the group sitting around the coffee table. "What is this about Ben being kidnapped?"

Daniel told the story of what had happened in Florida.

His parents were horrified. Ben was pleased to find himself the center of attention.

Kate, who was sitting on the sofa next to Daniel, murmured, "How can we get him to stop telling everyone he was kidnapped?"

Daniel smiled. "I don't know. Maybe it's cathartic for him to keep hearing the story."

Ben, who was sitting on the second sofa with Daniel's cat in his lap, said, "I prayed, Grandmama, and the police came."

"God was looking out for you," Victoria said.

Ben nodded.

Maria came to the door and said to Victoria in Spanish that the dinner was ready.

"Come along," Victoria said. "It's time for us to move to the dining room."

Rafael spent the better part of the dinner trying to convince Kate to come to visit his ranch in Colombia.

"I have a beautiful young horse I think you would love. If you come and visit and like him, I will give him to you."

Kate, who wasn't very good at hiding her feelings, looked stunned. "You would?"

"Yes. I am sure you will love him."

"I would love to come, Rafael, but, to be honest, there's so much political unrest in Colombia that I'm afraid."

"My ranch is in the government-controlled area of the country."

"Even so . . ." She glanced at Ben.

"You would be safe on my ranch, I swear to you. Safer than you were at Disney World."

"Well . . . I'll think about it."

Rafael looked as if he would say more, but Daniel cut in, "Don't push her, Papa."

"I am just not certain that Kate understands how safe the ranch is."

"You've told her, now let's drop the subject."

Molly said, "It's nice that Alberto is returning on Monday."

Everyone looked at her in surprise.

Daniel said, "I didn't know that."

Molly looked a little embarrassed. "He called me earlier. I'm sure he will be calling you as well, Daniel."

Victoria looked interested. "Alberto called you, Molly?"

"Yes," Molly said.

"Have you and Alberto become . . . er friends?"

"Yes," Molly said.

"How interesting. Alberto is a wonderful man, you know."

"Yes," Molly said.

Rafael said, "I was at a party with Alberto's publisher last week, and he is very excited about the book. They have sold it in Chile and Argentina and Peru, and they were in negotiations for the English translation rights to be sold to America. Gabriel García Márquez gave him a great quote for the cover."

"I didn't know that," Molly said. "That's fabulous."

"Who is Gabriel García Márquez?" Kate asked.

Daniel answered, "He's Colombia's Nobel Prize-winning novelist."

"Wow. That *is* great."

"It certainly is," Victoria said.

"What is this, Mommy?" Ben asked, holding a piece of food up on his fork.

"That is a scallop, a kind of a fish," Kate answered.

"You are eating *Arroz con Mariscos*, Ben," Victoria said. "Maria makes it perfectly." She looked at Molly. "The secret is in cooking the shellfish just until they are done and not a second longer."

"It's delicious," Molly said.

"It certainly is," Kate agreed. "But the closest Ben has come to this at home is fish sticks."

"I like fish sticks," Ben said.

Victoria visibly suppressed a shudder. "Well, if you like fish sticks, Ben, you ought to like *Arroz con Mariscos*."

"What does that mean, Grandmama?"

"Rice with shellfish."

"I like the rice," Ben said.

"Try a shrimp . . . that one there."

Ben gave Kate a look.

She smiled, "It won't hurt you to take a little bite. It's good, really."

Ben nibbled a tiny piece of the shrimp. "It's okay."

"Then finish it," Victoria said.

Ben heroically took another bite.

Rafael said consolingly, "There is cake for dessert. You will like that."

Ben brightened noticeably.

Daniel's glove was open-fingered, so he was able to use his hand to eat, albeit a bit awkwardly.

Kate said, "I hope Alberto's book does come out in English. I'd like to read it."

Molly said with amusement, "Considering that you never read anything that isn't about horses, he will be honored."

"I read things that aren't about horses," Kate said huffily.

"Oh yes? What?"

"I read the newspaper."

"You read Captain Underpants, Mommy," Ben said helpfully.

Rafael and Victoria looked at Kate in amazement.

Kate grinned. "I know it sounds bad, but it's a series of children's books that Ben likes."

"What else have you read, Ben?" Victoria asked.

All the adults gave him their attention as he replied.

Kate went to bed feeling unsatisfied. Just to see Daniel brought such a hunger that it frightened her.

I love him, she thought.

What to do? What to do? He wanted her to marry him, but she was certain he would expect her to fit her life into his. After all, he was the one making the big money.

It would work if Daniel would live at High Meadow and let me keep my business.

But she couldn't see that happening. The commute to the Bronx from Greenwich, the first town in Connecticut, was bad enough. Moving to Glendale would add a half an hour to his trip either way. Plus, his house was gorgeous and the farmhouse was . . . well, a farmhouse.

So what do I do? Give him up?

I can't give him up. He's mine.

If I lived in Greenwich, I could continue to ride. I could stable a horse at what I'm sure would be a fabulous stable and I could even take dressage lessons. Ben could go to the Greenwich schools, which are wonderful.

But I don't want to give up my business. I've worked hard to establish it, and I love it. I don't want to give it up.

Can my life and Daniel's coexist?

They could if we just continued the way we are now.

But Kate didn't want that either. It would send all the wrong messages to Ben, for one thing. And she wanted the closeness that she thought marriage to Daniel would give her.

But . . . I don't want to have to choose between my business and Daniel. It isn't fair that I should have to make such a choice. Other women marry and keep their work.

But her job wasn't just a job; it was a vocation, a twenty-four-hour commitment. And she loved it. But Daniel's job wasn't ordinary either.

He'd be away half the time. What would I do with myself, with Ben in school and only one horse to take care of? I'd go nuts.

I could get another kind of a job.

But she rejected that idea immediately. The very thought of being cooped up in the same place all day made her feel suffocated.

We could adopt children.

But that wasn't the answer, either. She would love to have more children, but the idea of who she was so intimately connected to the farm, and had been for so many years, that the thought of losing it felt like an amputation.

I'll have to explain to Daniel how I feel. Maybe he will have a solution. Maybe he will volunteer to live at High Meadow . . .

Don't get your hopes up, Kate warned herself. *Daniel is a*

*Latin male. I'm sure he will expect his wife to fit her life into
his and not the other way around.*

It took Kate quite a while before she finally fell asleep.

The following day Daniel took his parents to the airport,
then he packed a suitcase and drove to High Meadow. It was
three in the afternoon, and Kate was waiting at the bus stop
for Ben, with Cyrus beside her. Daniel pulled his car into the
driveway and went to join her.

It was a cold day, and Kate was wearing her Mountain
Horse jacket, fleece riding breeches, and lined boots. Daniel
flipped the hood of his parka over his head to protect himself
from the wind and jammed his hands in his pockets.

"Florida looks good right now," he commented as he
stopped beside her.

"I don't mind cold weather, but I object to frigid," Kate
said. "There is a finite amount of clothes that you can put
on."

He didn't smile. "I have never before minded going to
Florida for spring training, but this year I don't want to go
because I'll miss you and Ben."

"When does spring training begin?"

"The end of February."

"So soon? It seems as if you just finished playing!"

"There's four months between the end of the old season
and spring training. It's more vacation than most men get."

"If you consider the fact that you don't get any Saturdays
or Sundays off during the season, I don't think the days off
come out in your favor," Kate said.

"When you are doing what you love, you don't mind
working long hours."

"That's true. Mom is always after me to cut back my
schedule, but I don't mind it. I love it, in fact."

There was brilliant color in her cheeks, and her eyes were very blue, their whites very white. She was so damn beautiful.

"What would you do, Kata, if you hurt your leg and couldn't ride anymore?"

"It would break my heart," she said simply.

"Yes," he said. "I thought it would."

There was a little silence, then she said, "Are you worrying about pitching again, Daniel?"

"Yes."

"I suppose you can't help it."

"It's my pitching hand, and two bones are broken."

"I feel so terrible about the accident . . ."

"Please don't blame yourself. That's not what this is all about."

"All right."

"I keep wondering what I would do with myself if I can't pitch again."

She looked at him gravely. "I wish I had an answer for you, Daniel. But I have been asking myself a similar question. What would I do with myself if I didn't have my horses and my business?"

He smiled wryly. "We're evidently a pair with very little imagination."

She didn't smile back. "So it seems."

A yellow school bus turned the corner and began to come up the street. Cyrus's tail began to wave as he saw it, and Samson came over to stand next to Kate.

"I brought a suitcase with me," Daniel said. "I thought I'd begin my father-in-residence stint tonight."

"Great."

The bus came to a stop in front of them, and after a moment Ben came down the stairs, his backpack dangling off one shoulder.

"Daddy," he said with delight when he saw Daniel. "I didn't know you'd be waiting for me, too."

"You're just lucky I happened to come along," Daniel said. "Come on and hop in the car, and I'll save you a cold walk back to the house."

Ben and Cyrus and Samson got into the backseat of Daniel's Mercedes and Kate got in the front. In under a minute they were all getting out and filing in through the front door of the farmhouse.

"Go change your clothes, then you can have milk and cookies," Kate said to Ben. Then, to Daniel, "You can take your suitcase upstairs to the spare room."

"Do I get milk and cookies too?"

She smiled. "Certainly."

When they returned back downstairs, Kate had taken off several layers plus her heavy boots. Daniel had a sweater on over jeans, and Ben came down dressed in a sweatshirt and jeans. Daniel said, "You keep this house colder than I keep mine."

"If it was any warmer, I'd be suffocating," Kate said. "I have long underwear under these fleece pants and turtle-neck."

"I got an invitation today to Josh's birthday party, Mommy," Ben said as he took his seat at the table. "He invited the whole class."

"That was very nice of him," Kate said. "Where is it going to be?"

"At the Video Game Parlor."

"A birthday party at a video parlor?" Daniel said.

"No one has birthday parties in the house anymore," Kate said. "One of the parties he went to was actually on a yacht.

Can you imagine anyone dumb enough to coop ten boys up together on a boat?"

"No," said Daniel.

"I had a pony party, Daddy," Ben said. "Everyone got to ride Tucker and Scout and then we played musical chairs and then we had ice cream and cake and I opened my presents."

"It sounds like a great party," Daniel said.

"It was. I think it was the best party of all."

"It was certainly the cheapest," Kate muttered under her breath.

"What's on the agenda for today?"

Kate gave him a beatific smile. "There's a Cub Scout pack meeting tonight that you can take Ben to."

He looked at her warily. "Cub Scout pack meeting? As in a large number of boys locked up together in a gymnasium?"

"You got it."

"Can you really take me, Daddy? It will be so fun!"

"What time is it at?"

"Seven o'clock," Kate said.

"Are you coming too?" Daniel asked Kate.

"Oh I think it will be fun for Ben to have his daddy to himself for the evening."

"All the other boys' fathers come," Ben said, which clinched it, of course.

Kate said, "If you're going to the Cub Scout meeting, then you have to get your homework done this afternoon. Perhaps Daddy can help you with it."

"Will you, Daddy?"

"I would be pleased to help you, Ben."

"Great," Kate said brightly. "I'll be down at the barn if you need me. Mom should be coming in soon."

As she went out into the hall to put on her discarded layers, she was smiling.

33

Molly came in while Ben and Daniel were working on Ben's homework. She smiled when she saw the two of them sitting at the table.

Daniel got up and went to take the bag of groceries she was carrying from her hands.

"Thank you, Daniel," she said.

"What's for dinner, Nana?" Ben asked.

"Meatballs and spaghetti."

"Yeah! I love meatballs and spaghetti."

"I know. That is why we have it as frequently as we do." Daniel laughed.

"You have your Cub Scout meeting tonight, so we have to eat by six," Molly said. "How are you coming with the homework?"

Daniel said, "Very well. We're almost finished. And I hardly had to help at all."

"Wait until he gets a project. You can help then," Molly said.

"Is that a threat?"

Molly laughed. "Yes, I'm afraid it is. These teachers! The things they come up with! We're very boring in high school; we just assign papers. Of course, they learn something from doing a paper; sometimes I wonder about these projects. The parents wind up doing them half the time because they're so involved."

"I can't wait," Daniel said, and Molly laughed again.

It was five o'clock and Molly was rolling meatballs when the telephone rang. She picked it up, and it was Alberto.

"Molly?"

"Yes." Her voice sounded a little breathless. "Are you back, Alberto?"

"Yes. I am calling you from Daniel's."

"How was your flight?"

"There was the usual delay going through Customs, but otherwise it was fine."

"How was your visit?"

"Good, but I missed you."

Molly glanced into the hallway, but Daniel and Ben were in the living room. "I missed you, too. How did the discussion about your book go?"

"Very well, indeed. It looks as if I might make some good money out of this book."

"That's wonderful, Alberto. I am so pleased for you."

"Yes. It is very nice."

"I wish I could read it."

"It is going to be translated into English, and you can read it then."

"Wonderful."

"When can I see you? Can you go out to dinner with me tomorrow?"

"I have to make dinner for Ben and Daniel. Kate has a late night. But I can go out after that. Daniel is here to be with Ben."

"Shall I pick you up at seven?"

"Seven would be fine."

"I'll see you then."

"Okay. Good-bye, Alberto."

"Good-bye, Molly."

Molly hung up and went to stand at the kitchen window, hugging her elbows and looking down at the barn. She had been surprised by how much she missed Alberto. In a very short time he had woven himself into the fabric of her life, and when he was gone he left a hole.

Where is this friendship going? she wondered. *Alberto is not the kind of man to have casual relationships.*

There had been nothing physical between them except for the last time, when Alberto had kissed her hand. It had been a surprisingly erotic gesture, and Molly had been shocked by the strength of her own response. She had lived a celibate life since Tim's death, and if she sometimes missed the presence of a man, the feel of a man, she had not let herself dwell on those absences. She had too many responsibilities to be thinking about men.

Then Alberto had come along. She had never met anyone like him. Their thoughts matched so closely that sometimes listening to him was like listening to herself.

It had not been that way with Tim. Their relationship had been a paradigm of "opposites attract."

Am I falling in love with Alberto? Have I already fallen in love with him? And if I have, what can I do about it?

These were questions she had no answers to.

I need to see him again. I need to see how l feel when I am with him once again. Then, perhaps, I will know.

They went to a seafood restaurant in Norwalk. As they sat across from each other at the candlelit table, Molly looked at Alberto's face. It was a fine face, she thought, masculine yet sensitive, with an appealing gravity in the intelligent brown eyes.

What would Tim think of him? she wondered.

The answer was immediate. *They wouldn't have a thought in common.*

How could I have loved Tim the way I did, then turn around and love someone who is his complete opposite? Because I think I do love Alberto. I certainly care about him and . . . and I would like to go to bed with him.

Molly flushed as she had this last thought and concentrated her attention on what Alberto was saying about the horrors of going through Customs at JFK if you were a Colombian.

The waiter took their drinks order, and she said, "Ben is so excited about having Daniel to live with us."

"Daniel was looking forward to it as well."

"I don't know how happy he was after the Cub Scout meeting last night. I gather it was pretty raucous."

Alberto smiled. "It is good for Daniel to see the difficult side of being a father. So far he has had only the good times."

"He took it pretty well," Molly said. "His only comment when he came home was that he had better be a good person because if he wasn't, and he got sent to hell, his punishment would be to spend all of eternity at a Cub Scout pack meeting."

Alberto laughed out loud.

"Kate agreed with him. She was delighted that she didn't have to go."

"You don't take him to his Cub Scout meetings?"

"I take him to the den meeting once a week, but I leave him there and pick him up. I refused to do the pack meetings. I'm too old. Kate arranged her schedule to be able to go with him."

Their drinks came and Molly took a sip of her wine.

Alberto said, "I missed you while I was in Colombia. I didn't expect to miss you so much."

Molly looked at him in surprise. "I felt the same way."

"We haven't known each other for that long, but I feel that there is a connection between us, Molly. I wonder if you feel it, too?"

"Yes."

"It is wonderful, but it is a little disrupting, too."

"I know what you mean."

"My daughter kept asking me when I was coming home to stay."

Molly looked at him over the rim of her wineglass. "And what did you tell her?"

"I told her that I didn't know. I told her that there was a woman in Connecticut that I cared about."

"And what did your daughter say?"

"She was a little dismayed. She has been the only woman in my life for several years now, and her children have been one of the focal points of my existence. She's afraid that all that may change."

Molly put her glass down. "Will it?"

"Nothing will ever lessen my daughter's and my grand-children's importance to me. But they may have to learn to share their premier places with someone else."

Molly nodded gravely.

"And then there is my book. I am seriously thinking of giving up teaching and going into writing full-time."

"Can you afford to do that, Alberto?"

"I think I can. I think the foreign rights money from my book is going to be substantial."

"Would you continue to work for Daniel?"

The waiter came to take their orders, and Alberto told him

they weren't ready yet. Then he said, "I am very fond of Daniel, but I need my own space."

"Yes," Molly said.

"I have been thinking about asking you to marry me."

"I have cancer, Alberto."

"You are going to beat the cancer."

"I hope so, but there's no guarantee."

"I feel in my heart that you are going to be healthy again, Molly. I did not feel that way when my wife got sick, but she had a different kind of cancer."

"Well . . . I have to admit that I've been thinking about the possibility of marrying you."

"Do you think it could work?"

She shook her head. "I couldn't leave Kate and Ben, Alberto. They need me too much."

"Kate will marry Daniel. It is written in the cards."

"I think she might. I hope she does. But even if she does, Kate will still need me to help her with Ben. Daniel is away too much for her to count on him."

"Kate can get a baby-sitter, like every other working mother."

"Ben has never had baby-sitters. He's always had us."

"Then it's time he learned to live with a baby-sitter."

Molly gave a forced laugh. "Are you really asking me to marry you, Alberto?"

"Yes, I am. What do you say?"

"I'm going to have to think about it. I don't know if I could turn my back on Kate and Ben and go to live in Colombia."

"What if we split our time between Colombia and the States? Six months in each place. How would that be?"

"You would do that?"

"For you, I would do that."

"I don't know, Alberto. I'll have to think about it."

"Of course. I won't rush you, *querida*."

"Good grief," Molly said. "Here comes the waiter again. We had better look at this menu and decide what we're going to eat."

Molly went to sleep right away that night, but she woke up at one and went to the bathroom. As she was coming out of the bathroom she heard the sound of voices in Kate's room. She stopped short.

It was barely more than a murmur, but Molly's hearing was very acute.

It's Daniel and Kate, she thought.

She moved quietly back to her bed.

Daniel and Kate. So something really is happening between them.

She smiled, but as she lay there the smile slowly faded. *And where does that leave me? What kind of a future can I see for myself if Daniel and Kate do marry?*

If Kate and Daniel married, everything would be changed. She would no longer be living with Kate and Ben.

Do I want to live by myself? Do I want to grow old by myself? Do I want to grow old with Alberto?

If he were an American, it wouldn't be so hard to make a decision.

What a stupid thought. Being Colombian is part of who Alberto is, and it's Alberto that I love.

It could be an exciting life. If Alberto turned into a literary lion, she would have the opportunity to mix in circles she had never dreamed of. That would be fun. Living in Colombia for half the year might be fun as well. She liked Rafael and Victoria very much, and presumably she would like Alberto's other friends too.

What if Kate and Daniel don't marry?

That won't happen, she thought. For other people their ages, sex might not mean commitment, but Molly was certain that for her daughter and Daniel it did. Kate had never had any other relationship, and Daniel must know that. He would take a relationship between them very seriously.

They would marry, and have more children, and Molly would be an ordinary grandma, not the principal caregiver she had been to Ben. There would be a big space in her life that could not be filled by her teaching.

Perhaps I shouldn't give Alberto an answer until there is an announcement from Kate and Daniel.

Is that fair to Alberto? "I can't marry you, Alberto, until I am certain that my daughter's future is settled." How will he take a comment like that?

She thought of his response at dinner when she had brought this subject up: "Let Kate get a baby-sitter like other working mothers."

He was right.

Would Kate even continue to work once she was married? Somehow, Molly couldn't picture a multimillionaire like Daniel living in the farmhouse.

Perhaps she'll have babies and stay home.

Molly smiled into her pillow. Impossible. Children at home would never be enough to take up all of Kate's energy. And it was simply impossible to picture Kate without her horses.

I should make this decision independently of Kate, as I'm sure Kate will make her decision independently of me.

So? Do I or don't I?

I think . . . I think maybe I will.

34

It was a cold, overcast day and Kate looked up at the sky, a frown on her face. She was running a little low on wood shavings, and her next delivery wasn't until the following week, so she was planning to take the pickup over to Agway to pick up some bags.

I'll take a tarp, she decided. *That way, if it rains, the bedding will be okay.*

She made the run and had driven into the stable yard with the pickup when Daniel's Mercedes came up the driveway. He parked in front of the house and came down to the stable area as she was unloading the truck.

"Whoa," he said. "Let me do that. Those bags are heavy."

"I do this all the time," Kate said. "You've seen the muscles in my arms and back. I'm fine. And you can't lift these because of your hand."

"It won't hurt my hand . . ."

"Daniel, don't be an idiot. Of course it could hurt your hand. You have broken bones. Now go away and let me get on with my work."

His mouth tightened, then he turned on his heel and went back up to the house.

I've hurt his feelings, Kate thought. *But really. Any child would know enough not to pick up a weight like this with a broken hand.*

She spent the next forty minutes unloading the truck and stacking the bedding in the space in front of the wash stall. When she went back to the house, Daniel was having a cup of coffee in the kitchen.

"Any left?" she asked cheerfully as she went to the coffeemaker.

"Yes."

She poured herself a cup and came to sit across from him at the table. "When you sulk you look just like Ben."

"I am not sulking."

"It sure looks like that's what you're doing."

He said through his teeth, "It's this damn hand."

"You've got two more weeks, Daniel, and then the tape can come off."

"I hate to see you doing these strenuous things, Kata. I know I'm being chauvinistic about it, but it hurts my pride."

"It's my job, Daniel. I will hate you going away to spring training, but that's your job. We have to learn to live with each other's jobs."

"I suppose you're right," he said grumpily. "But you should employ a man around here to do the heavy work."

"I can't afford to hire a man."

He scowled at her.

"Are you going to be home for dinner tonight, or is tonight the night you're speaking at the Little League dinner?"

"Tonight is the Little League dinner. I told Molly this morning that I wouldn't be here for dinner."

"Okay."

He stood up. "If you will excuse me, I have some work to do on my computer."

Kate watched him leave the kitchen, a faint frown on her face.

Something was wrong with Daniel.

He's worried about his hand.

Well, so am I. But it's not as bad as Mom's cancer. It's not like his life is being threatened.

But in a way it was. His life as a baseball player, as a pitcher, was being threatened. He hadn't said much to Kate about his feelings on this subject, but she could guess what they must be. Perhaps in six or seven years, when his skills were lessening, he would be tired of the grueling schedule. Perhaps then he would be ready to retire. He wasn't ready yet.

She could see the moment again, Daniel's hand on the ground, poised to pick up the towel, and Shane's hoof coming down right on it.

God. What an uncanny thing to have happened.

She poured more coffee into her cup, stirred in a little sugar, and sat back down at the table.

Daniel hadn't mentioned marriage again. He had asked her to marry him once, and she had put him off, and he hadn't asked again.

He loves me. I know he loves me. Then why hasn't he asked me to marry him again?

Is it his hand?

In a few weeks he would be leaving for spring training. She would miss him desperately. And it was not just the love-making that she would miss. She would miss coming into the kitchen or the living room and unexpectedly finding him there; she would miss the way he said her name; she would miss the nights they didn't make love, but just slept together in the same bed—peaceful, because they were with each other.

It was February, and Daniel was still living at High Meadow. Kate had asked him to stay on, and he had told her that it would take a bomb to get him out.

She had laughed. It was the first attempt at levity that he had made in quite some time, and she wanted to reward it. Most of the time he was . . . preoccupied. Even Ben had to say sometimes, "Daddy are you listening to me?"

It was his hand. The closer they got to spring training, the closer he came to the moment when he would know if he would still be the pitcher that he had been, the tenser he got.

And there was nothing she could do. If there was a feeling of desperation in his lovemaking sometimes, all she could do was to respond with the ardor he so clearly needed from her. The rest of it was in God's hands.

As February progressed, George's Morgans were sold to a horse farm in Bethany, so Kate did not have to keep running over to his place twice a day to feed and to turnout. Ben's Cub Scouts had their annual Pinewood Derby and Daniel helped Ben to make the car that came in second. And Molly slept with Alberto.

It was not something that either of them had planned. They had gone out to dinner and returned to Daniel's house to listen to a new album that Alberto had bought. They were sitting on the sofa, listening to the strains of Bach, when Alberto suddenly covered her hand with his, and said softly, "Shall it be tonight, Molly? Maria has gone to bed."

Molly turned and looked into his face. She didn't pretend to misunderstand him. "All right . . . but it's been a very long time for me, Alberto. Tim has been dead for nine years."

"I, too, have been alone since my wife died. But I'm tired of being alone. I want you Molly. I love you, and I want you."

She smiled. "I love you and I want you, too."

"Then come to my bedroom with me."

"All right."

He stood up and held out a hand to help her. She arose and, hand in hand, they walked down the corridor, up the stairs, and into Alberto's bedroom.

Molly had never been in here before, and she looked around curiously. It was furnished with a queen-sized bed with a maple headboard and footboard, and a maple bureau and chest of drawers. The bedspread was a simple white chenille, but the rug was a beautiful oriental. Several pictures were placed on the bureau, and Molly went over to look at them. Alberto followed.

"That was my wife," he said as Molly picked up a portrait of a dark-haired smiling woman with a high-bridged nose and hair pulled back off her face.

"She's lovely."

He picked up another picture. "And this is my daughter and son-in-law with their children."

The young woman in the picture bore a close resemblance to the photo Molly had just put down. "She looks like her mother."

"Yes, she does. And this is Anna and this," he pointed to the baby his daughter was cradling, "is Ricardo."

"They're adorable," Molly said sincerely.

"I think so. Ricardo is walking now; he was only a few months old when that picture was taken."

"You have a lovely family, Alberto."

"Thank you. And now I am going to kiss you."

They had never done more than exchange brief kisses of greeting and departure, but from the moment that his mouth touched hers, Molly knew that this was something different.

She slid her arms around him and gave herself up to the moment.

Time passed blissfully, then he said in a husky voice, "Let us go to bed, *querida*."

"All right." Molly followed him over to the bed and the two of them shed their clothes and Alberto pulled back the covers and they got in.

The feel of his lean body against hers was so different from the muscled bulk of Tim, but the sensations waking in her own body were familiar. She had had an intensely passionate relationship with her husband, and now the passion rose in her again, like a bell clanging throughout her body. Alberto's hands were skillful and gentle, and the more they touched and caressed, the louder the bell rang inside her. When they both were ready, she wrapped her legs around his waist and arched her back so he could enter.

He penetrated and it felt so good. Her body closing around him felt so good. She held on tighter as he drove inside her, softening her, stretching her, until the bell was clanging so loudly that it could not be denied, and she convulsed around him, her body shuddering again and again and again with pleasure.

He held her close, and said huskily, "I love you, Molly."

"I love you, too," she replied.

"Will you make an honest man out of me and marry me?"

She didn't even hesitate. "Yes, Alberto, I will."

Molly waited until the following evening to break her news, when Ben was in bed and she was sitting in the living room with Kate and Daniel. Daniel was reading the *New York Times* and Kate was reading an article about Potomac horse fever in *Equus* when Molly said, "I have something to tell you."

Two sets of eyes looked up. Brown and aqua regarded her with anticipation. Molly took a deep breath then said, "Alberto and I are going to be married."

Kate looked stunned.

Daniel said, "That's wonderful, Molly." He got up and came over to kiss her. "Alberto is a lucky man."

"Thank you, Daniel."

Kate didn't say anything.

"Kata?" Daniel said.

"Are you going to live in Colombia?" Kate asked tensely.

"We will spend half the year in Colombia and half the year here."

"Oh."

Daniel said quietly, "Kata, aren't you going to wish your mother well?"

She looked at him. "Yes. Of course." She also got up and came to kiss Molly. "Congratulations, Mom."

"You're upset," Molly said.

"No! It's just that I'm . . . surprised."

"How can you be surprised, Kata? Molly and Alberto have been smelling like June roses ever since they met."

Kate sat back down on the sofa. Her face looked strained. "I'm just dense, I guess."

"I'll be in Connecticut for half the year, and Colombia is only a plane ride away," Molly said. "It won't be the same because I won't be living with you anymore, but I will still be around."

"It won't be the same," Kate repeated.

"No. It won't be."

Kate looked down at her hands. "Ben will miss you terribly."

"Ben now has a father as well as a mother. And he has two other grandparents. He will get over missing me."

Kate bit her lip and said in a small voice, "I don't know if I will."

"Oh, honey." Molly went over to the sofa, sat beside Kate, and put her arms around her. "Things are changing in our lives, and I know how you hate change. But change is life, Kate."

"So everybody keeps telling me." Kate sounded desolate.

Over her head, Molly's eyes met Daniel's.

He said, "Don't worry about Kata. She will come around. She just needs some time to adjust her thinking."

Kate laughed shakily. "That's true. You know how one-track I am, Mom. It's just hard to think of my life without you."

"I will still be a part of your life, but in a new way."

"Yes." Kate mustered a smile. "I wish every happiness to you and Alberto, Mom. You deserve it."

Molly smiled back. "Thank you, dear."

"Have you set a date?"

"I want to finish my cancer treatment first, and Alberto wants to introduce me to his family."

"Are you going to be married in Colombia?"

"No, we will be married right here in Connecticut."

"So . . . we're talking about June? July?"

"June, if I can make all my chemo appointments. If I even get a little sick, they won't give them to me. Or if my blood count is too low, they won't give them. So the date is tentative."

"Does Alberto want to wait until your cancer treatments are finished?"

"No, I do. I want to feel like my normal self when I embark on a new marriage. On the other hand, we don't have unlimited time to wait. We're neither of us young anymore."

Kate said, "Of course you're young, Mom."

"Thank you. And do you know something? When I'm with Alberto I *feel* young."

"Don't you feel young when you're with us?"

Molly said straight-faced, "Sometimes I feel a million years old."

"Mom!"

Molly laughed. "I'm just kidding." She stood up. "I'm going upstairs to read my book in bed. I'll see you both in the morning."

"Good night, Mom."

"Good night, Molly."

"Good night to the two of you."

When they had heard Molly's door close, Kate and Daniel looked at each other.

Kate said, "I never ever thought that she would marry him."

"I think it's wonderful," Daniel said. "They have a lot in common. I think they will enjoy their life together very much."

Kate pushed her fingers through her short cap of black hair. "This will probably sound colossally selfish, but who is going to watch Ben and give him his dinner while I'm teaching?"

"You will have to hire someone."

Kate puffed up her cheeks and blew out.

"In fact, if I may make a recommendation, you should hire a couple. The woman can act as housekeeper and baby-sitter, and the man can do the heavy work around the house and the barn."

"Oh, right, as if I have the money to do that."

"I will pay for it."

"No, you won't."

"Kata, look ahead. You are young now, and full of energy,

but what are you going to do as you grow older and physical work becomes harder? Someday you are going to have to face the fact that you need paid help."

"Daniel, it isn't all that easy to get paid help."

"Where do the other barns get their workers?"

"Mostly, they hire Mexicans. But frequently there's a language problem. I don't want to hire someone I can't speak to. How would I let him know what it was I wanted him to do?"

"I am sure I can find a couple in Colombia who would be happy to come to the United States and have steady jobs."

She gave him a defiant stare and didn't say anything.

"Will you at least think about it, Kata?"

"I'll think about it." But her expression told him that her mind was made up.

He said, "You are the most stubborn person I have ever met."

"It takes one to know one," Kate returned.

At that, he laughed.

Kate got up, went over to Daniel's chair, sat on his lap, and kissed him. "You have such a sunny disposition. Ben takes after you that way."

"How does he resemble Colleen?"

"When he lifts his head a certain way, I can see her in him. Most of the time I just see you."

He said soberly, "You should have children of your own, Kata. You should be able to look at a child and see yourself."

"I plan to have children of my own. It's called adoption."

"It isn't the same."

"The result is the same. I love Ben as much as I would have if I'd given birth to him."

"Yes, but he's your sister's child."

She put her hands on either side of his face and looked into his eyes. "That doesn't matter. What matters is that, when someone puts a child in your arms, instantly, that child is yours. You don't even think about where he came from. All you know is that he's yours."

"But you miss the whole experience of giving birth."

Kate laughed. "Believe me, that is a bonus, not a hardship. How could I ride if I was pregnant?"

He smiled. "God forbid that you wouldn't be able to ride."

"I would be miserable."

He smoothed his left forefinger along her cheekbone. "I could find a couple to work for you. Please think about it."

"Where would they live, Daniel? I don't want strangers living in the house with me."

"We could find them an apartment."

"And who would pay for the apartment?"

He didn't answer.

"Look, I appreciate your concern for me, but it isn't necessary. The only help I need is someone part-time to be with Ben after school."

"Let's change the subject," he said.

"Good idea."

"How much do you love me?"

She gave him a long, slow kiss, then, when she had lifted her head, she said, "A lot."

The old farmhouse was quiet, with Ben sleeping and Molly reading behind closed doors. The only sound was the occasional hum of the refrigerator. He cupped her face in his hands. "When I'm with you like this, I feel at peace."

He kissed the tip of her nose, and she nestled her head against his shoulder. "Oh? I thought you felt horny."

He chuckled. "That too."

"I feel peaceful when I'm with you, too."

He smoothed her hair away from her forehead. "You should have your own children."

"Is that why you haven't asked me to marry you again? Because you can't have children?"

"It's part of the reason, yes."

She could hear his heart beating steadily against her cheek. "We'll adopt children. I'll bet there are plenty of Colombian children who need a good home."

"I'm sure there are."

"So that's not a problem, Daniel. We'll have children. Ben needs to have a brother and a sister."

"Mmmm."

"So will you ask me to marry you again?"

"Kata, I might not have a job. I can't make plans for my future until I know where I stand in regard to this hand. If I can pitch, then I will ask you again."

"And if you can't?"

"We'll cross that bridge when we come to it."

She stayed silent, listening to the rhythmic beat of his heart. Then, at last, she said, "All right."

35

The end of February came, pitchers and catchers were due to report to spring training camp, and Daniel left for Florida. And Molly and Alberto flew to Bogotá for a long weekend with his family.

"For God's sake, Mom, take care of yourself," Kate urged her mother as they spoke together in the living room the night before Molly's departure. "Colombia is not the safest place on the planet. I wish Alberto's family had come here."

"He wants me to see his country. He feels bad that it has such a terrible reputation. He says that Bogotá is beautiful, that it's built on a plateau and everywhere you look you can see the mountains. The mountains are always green because they're too close to the equator for it to snow."

"It may be beautiful, but it's dangerous," Kate retorted.

"There is potential danger everywhere, Kate. Look at what happened to Ben at Disney World. Ironically, he might have been safer if Daniel had taken you on a vacation to Colombia."

"I suppose . . ." Kate did not sound convinced.

"I'm nervous about going to Bogotá, but not because I'm afraid of being kidnapped. What if Alberto's family doesn't like me?"

Kate snorted. "Like that could happen."

"It could. His daughter might resent his marrying again. He told me she's grown used to being the center of his life."

"Mom, it is impossible not to like you."

Molly smiled. "Thank you, dear, but you are not exactly an unbiased source."

"Everyone likes you, Mom. In school all of the teachers like you; the administration likes you; the students like you; my students like you. Why should Alberto's daughter be any different?"

Molly laughed. "You make me feel better."

"What if you don't like *her*?"

"I'll fake it."

They both had laughed.

Kate thought back to this conversation as she drove home from the airport after seeing Molly and Alberto off.

Mom looked beautiful this morning. There's a glow about her when she's with Alberto. I guess it's a good thing that he's so unlike Daddy. She must love him in a different way.

She arrived home in time to meet the school bus, and she and Ben, shadowed by Cyrus and Samson, walked back to the house together. "Did Nana leave?" Ben asked.

"Yes, I drove her and Alberto to the airport this morning."

"Alberto is nice. It's okay that Nana is going to marry him, isn't it, Mommy?"

"Of course it's okay. In fact, it's wonderful."

"Are you and Daddy going to get married, too?"

"Would it be all right with you if we did?"

"It would be great! It means that Daddy would live with us all the time."

"How would you like it if we went to live at Daddy's house? You would have to change schools and make new friends."

"Wow," said Ben. "Daddy has a pool."

"You wouldn't mind moving then?"

"My friends could visit me, couldn't they?"

"Of course."

"Great. Let's move to Daddy's house."

"What would I do about the horses?"

Ben said sensibly, "You can drive up here to take care of them. Then, when you're finished, you can come back to Daddy's house."

"It's not as easy as that," Kate said grumpily.

"Why not?" His clear, straight, little-boy stare was hard to avoid.

"Because there'd be no one living here, Ben. Suppose a stable fire started in the middle of the night? No one would know until it was too late, and all of the horses had been trapped in the barn. Someone has to be on the premises— someone has to *live* on the premises—when you have stabled horses."

"Oh." Ben shrugged. "Then I guess that Daddy will just have to come and live with us. Maybe he'll miss his pool and build one for us. Wouldn't that be great?"

After a moment, Kate said, "Yes."

"When are you getting married?"

"We haven't decided to get married yet, Ben."

He was crestfallen. "Do you mean you might not?"

"I mean we haven't decided. But you'll be the first person to know when we do decide, I promise."

"I'm going to pray that you and Daddy get married," Ben said.

"You do that," Kate replied. "Now go on upstairs and change your clothes."

*   *   *

Daniel called that night. "I had an X ray today and the bones have healed."

"Thank God," Kate said fervently.

"I have two weeks of physical therapy before I can start throwing again."

"What kind of physical therapy?"

"Strengthening, mainly. I've lost strength in my whole hand because of its being inactive for so long."

"Have you tried to hold a ball?"

"Yes. And it feels different. The doctors say that it could be because of the general weakness of the hand."

"That sounds logical."

"Yes."

"It must feel good to be able to use it again."

"Yes."

"Are you depressed because it's so weak?"

"Yes."

"It will get better, Daniel. Give yourself some time. The first part of rehabilitation is over; the hand is healed. You knew you were going to have to do physical therapy."

"I knew it, but still I hoped that the ball would feel more comfortable in my hand than it did."

Kate didn't know what to say to him, so she said simply, "I love you."

"I love you too, Kata. God, I wish you were here."

"I wish I was there, too. Ben has a pack meeting tomorrow, and I'm the only one here to take him."

That got a laugh out of him.

She said, "Hang in there, Daniel. It will be all right. Your son has been praying for you faithfully every night."

"That's nice."

"Yes, it is. And it might even be efficacious."

"God, I hope so."

"Do you want to talk to him?"

"Is he there?"

"He's in the kitchen, I'll get him."

Daniel and Ben spoke for five minutes, then Kate got back on to say good-bye. She hung up the phone, and said to Ben, "Is your homework done? Do you need help with anything?"

"No, I finished it all. Can I watch television?"

"There's nothing on tonight. Why don't we read our books together?"

"Okay."

"Pack your school bag first," Kate said. "Then go upstairs and get your book."

Daniel worked hard at his therapy and after two weeks, the doctor said he could start to throw.

At first, it felt awkward. The fluidity of windup and pitch that was his signature wasn't there. He threw for three days to one of the catchers and the arm felt better each time he threw.

But would it be the same?

The question had haunted him ever since the accident had happened. It was such a delicate thing, pitching. It depended on how you gripped the ball, how you hid the ball, how you released the ball. A change in any one of those things, and the pitch was off.

What will I do with myself if I can't play baseball?

That was the other question that haunted him. Money wasn't the problem. He had made enough money to last him the rest of his life. But he had to have something to do, some career that he loved. He would never love anything as much as he loved baseball, but surely there was a profession he could take up.

He could go to law school; that was what his father would advise. Or he could earn a degree in architecture. He had once told Kate that he liked to build things, and she had said that in his second life he could be an architect. Perhaps she was right.

But it was hard to generate any enthusiasm for the profession of architecture when it was baseball he wanted with all his heart and soul.

When Daniel wasn't thinking about his hand, he was thinking about Kate. *She loves me. No matter what happens, I have that to hold on to. Kata loves me.*

She was so beautiful; her spirit was so . . . pure. It astounded him that he was the first man to have touched her, both in body and in spirit.

She loved him. She was one of the most self-sufficient people he had ever met, but she loved him. She wanted him to be a part of her life.

If only he weren't damaged goods.

He thought about it every night as he lay in his lonely bed. *What if this hand doesn't come around? Will I have the right to ask Kata to marry me?*

He was damaged goods. He couldn't give her a child, and he was in danger of losing the thing he did best in the world.

He thought that Kate would marry him if he couldn't pitch. She had questioned whether he was going to ask her again. She wouldn't have done that if she wasn't going to accept him.

On the other hand, who knew with Kate? They would have to work out a way for her to keep her business. She wasn't likely to want to give up something she had spilled blood, sweat, and tears to build up. If they could work something out, and he thought they could, then he thought she would marry him, if he stayed in baseball or not.

But he felt as if he was cheating her. At least, if he could pitch, she would have the prestige of being his wife.

As if prestige matters to Kata!

But he wanted it *for* her. He might not be able to give her children, but at least he could give her honor. At least it would mean something to be his wife.

It wasn't a feeling he was proud of, and he knew Kate wouldn't care if he could no longer pitch. But his pride was involved. He wanted Kate to marry the best pitcher in the American League. He did not want her to marry a has-been.

So he toiled diligently, working at strengthening his hand, working at throwing off the mound, and praying that his pitching would come back.

36

$\mathcal{K}$ate kept abreast of Daniel's progress by reading the *New York Daily News*. It was much more informative than Daniel himself was. So she knew when Daniel first threw in a preseason game, and she knew that he had not been able to get the ball over the plate. She knew that his second start showed some improvement, but he still walked far too many men. And she knew when the Yankee manager named Daniel as the starting pitcher for Opening Day at the stadium.

"He's the ace of my staff," the manager was reported as saying. "I think he's going to be ready."

There was a difference in opinions as to the wisdom of this decision among the newspaper's columnists. Mike Lupica thought that Daniel deserved the honor, while two other columnists thought it was putting too much pressure on Daniel, who wasn't ready yet.

Kate agreed with the two other columnists.

"Daniel hasn't managed to pitch two scoreless innings yet," she said hotly. Alberto had just come back from taking Molly to chemotherapy and Kate found him in the kitchen brewing coffee when she came in after taking Ben to play with a friend. "How can Torre expect him to pitch on Opening Day? He'll be humiliated if he gives up a bunch of runs."

"I would not be at all surprised to discover that Daniel asked to pitch the opening game," Alberto said. "It is a matter of pride. The best pitcher on the staff always pitches Opening Day."

"He needs more practice innings before he pitches in a real game."

"You may think that, maybe even Joe Torre thinks that, but clearly Daniel does not. He might surprise everyone and pitch very well."

"God, I hope so."

"If he has to come out, it will not be the end of the world," Alberto said calmly.

After a moment, Kate said, "I suppose you're right. It just feels like a big deal to me."

"It *is* a big deal. I don't mean to downplay it. But if Daniel doesn't do well, it won't mean that he's finished as a pitcher. It will just mean that he needs more work."

Kate nodded. Then she said, "How did Mom do today?"

"The same as usual. Her blood count was just high enough to allow them to give her the treatment."

"That's good. She doesn't need this to be dragged out any longer than necessary."

"She went upstairs to rest. I am cooking dinner tonight."

"Alberto, you are an angel."

"Thank you."

"I'm just going to peek in on her and see if she's awake."

"That's a good idea."

When Kate gently opened the door to Molly's room, Molly said, "Come in, dear. I'm awake."

Kate went over to stand beside her mother. "How did it go, Mom? Are you feeling sick?"

"A little. Mostly, I'm tired."

Kate looked down at her mother, silently noticing the ravages that the chemotherapy treatment had wreaked. Molly had not completely lost her hair, but it was pitifully thin, with her scalp showing through almost all over. She was white as a ghost.

Kate bent down and kissed her on the forehead. "Only two more to go, Mom. Hang in there."

"I don't have much choice," Molly said wryly.

"Alberto is cooking dinner. Do you have the strength to join us?"

"I'll come downstairs. I don't know if I'll be able to eat."

Kate sat on the side of the bed, and said somberly, "I hate it that you have to go through this."

"I know you do, dear. But, as you pointed out, it will be over soon. And people have been so kind."

"Alberto has been a rock. I feel guilty that I've let him do so much."

"You have commitments and, at the moment, Alberto does not. But you're right; he has been a rock." Molly sighed. "On an entirely different matter, do you think you could come with me to buy a wig?"

Kate looked at her mother's hair. It was so thin. "Of course I can. When do you want to go?"

"Perhaps we could go on Monday. You don't have lessons on Monday."

"Monday would be great. Do you know where to go?"

"There were cards at the hospital. There's a place in Orange that specializes in wigs for cancer patients."

Kate leaned down and kissed her mother's cheek. "We'll go Monday. In the meanwhile there's your old faithful baseball hat."

Molly smiled faintly.

Kate got up. "I'll leave you in peace. I'll come back when dinner is ready."

"Thank you, dear."

Once Kate was outside the door she had to stop to blink back tears. It was awful seeing her mother so fragile.

Please, God, let her be all right. Don't let anything happen to her. I don't know what I would do without her.

After a moment, she went downstairs on her way to the barn.

Daniel came home on Tuesday, April 1. He called Kate from his house and left messages on both her office machine and the one in the house. Forty-five minutes later, Kate got the one in the office and called him back.

It was so great to know he was close by. "You're home!"

"Yes, I'm home. I have the rest of the day off. Can I come and see you?"

Just hearing his voice sent shivers up and down her spine. "Of course. I have lessons from four to seven, though."

"What time does your mother get home?"

"She usually gets in about three."

"How about if I come over right away? That would give us time."

"Time for what?" Kate said with genuine curiosity.

"Do I have to spell it out?" he asked dryly.

"Oh. I just got it."

"You never cease to amaze me."

"Hah. Okay, come right over. I'll be finished up here in a half an hour."

"I'm on my way."

Kate was still in the barn when Daniel arrived. "Kate?" he called as he came down the center aisle.

"I'm cleaning the bathroom," she called back.

She was just finishing scrubbing the toilet when he walked in. The first thing he said was, "You shouldn't be cleaning the bathroom."

Kate looked at his face. "It would be disgusting if I didn't clean it."

His frown deepened. "Someone else should be doing this work."

She said reasonably, "Why would it be all right for someone else to do it, but it's not right for me to do it?"

He made an impatient gesture. "You know what I mean."

She had been so happy to see him, and now he was annoying her. "No, I don't know what you mean. You seem to have some elitist idea that manual work is undignified and that only the lower classes should do it. I suppose it comes from growing up in a rich family and in a country where labor is cheap."

He stared at her. She stared back.

"There is absolutely nothing wrong with me cleaning the bathroom. I clean the bathrooms at home as well. Do you think we should have a cleaning woman in to clean our house?"

She could tell from his face that he did.

"You're a snob, Daniel," she said pleasantly.

"Perhaps I am, but the fact remains that I hate to see my . . . my . . ." His voice trickled away as he tried to think of what to call her.

" 'My' what?" Kate asked.

He said with dignity, "The mother of my son doing such heavy labor."

"Definitely, you're a snob. But I love you anyway. And I missed you."

"I missed you, too." He held out his arms and they held each other and kissed.

When Daniel finally raised his head, he said huskily, "I can't feel you at all. All I feel is layer upon layer of clothes."

"Your jacket is pretty bulky too. Let's go up to the house."

They held hands as they went up the path that led to the house, although neither of them spoke. They went in the front door, hung their coats in the closet, went up the stairs and into Kate's room. Daniel closed the door behind them.

"Alone at last," he said.

She smiled and began to unbutton her wool cardigan sweater. Daniel watched as she shed the sweater, a turtleneck, an undershirt, and her bra. Then she peeled off her jeans, socks, and some more long underwear.

"No wonder you're never cold," Daniel said with amusement. It had taken him only a few seconds to pull off his shirt, sweater, and pants.

"It was in the thirties this morning. Even in April, New England can be cold," Kate replied.

"I missed you," he said, moving toward her. "I missed you so much."

"I know."

Then he was kissing her again. Her arms went around his neck and after a moment he straightened, pulling her feet right off the floor, and began to walk toward the bed. He laid her down, then followed her.

They kissed again and again and his hands were all over her. Kate's hands moved over him as well, feeling the strong muscles of his shoulders and back, moving down to caress the smooth skin that covered his lean hips.

He groaned. "Kata. Oh, Kata."

The exquisite tension was building inside of her, and she clung to him more tightly. He kissed her again, driving her head back into the pillow. She felt his terrible urgency and the tension in her loins ratcheted higher. Her body ached for him and when he moved to kneel over her, she arched herself for him, the surge of liquid in her vagina making it easy for him to enter. As he drove into her, the great waves of his coming washed over her, and a multitude of explosions flooded her body. The intensity of feeling was so great that she cried out.

Afterward they held each other, made wordless by the powerful experience they had just shared. Finally Daniel said, "I love you so much."

"I love you, too. But we have to get up. Mom will be home soon."

"I don't want to get up. I don't ever want to get up."

"I know."

More time passed.

"Daniel, we can't stay here any longer. Mom will be scandalized."

"I doubt that."

"Well, I'll be embarrassed. Come on. Move that leg." And she shook the leg that was under his.

"Oh, all right. I'll get up."

Daniel had just finished dressing when Molly's car pulled into the driveway.

"Go downstairs. Don't wait for me," Kate said. She was busy resuming all her discarded layers. "I don't want her to know we've been upstairs together."

"Kata, I'm sure she knows that we've been sleeping together."

"I'm sure she doesn't." She gave him a push. "Go."

"All right, all right. I'll go."

He left the door ajar and Kate listened as Molly came in the door and called, "Kate? Are you home?"

"I'm here, Molly," Daniel called back from the kitchen. "Kata is upstairs."

"Oh Daniel, you're back."

Kate listened as Molly went toward the kitchen. She gave them five minutes together, then she went downstairs herself.

37

Wednesday, April 2, was a bright, cold spring day, with high clouds scudding across the sky. Yankee Stadium was packed for opening day, and when Kate turned on the radio to listen while she was mucking out stalls and cleaning water buckets, the announcer was saying, "This will be a big test for Montero. He's thrown the ball hard but he's been wild in all of the exhibition games he pitched. Whether or not he's ready is an open question."

"You can't blame Joe for going with him on Opening Day," the second announcer said. "The Yankees wouldn't be wearing World Series rings if it wasn't for Montero's pitching."

"That's so. I guess Joe must figure he owes Daniel this start."

Baltimore was up first, so Daniel was the first pitcher to throw. The announcer painted the picture for his listening audience: "Martin is at the plate, Montero is ready to throw. He deals and the pitch is outside. Ball one."

"Come on, Daniel," Kate prayed as she tossed a pile of manure into a wheelbarrow.

"Once again, Montero deals and . . . Whoa! That was so high it almost got away from Posada!"

"Damn," Kate said.

"You can be sure that Martin won't swing until Montero shows that he can get the ball over the plate."

Which was exactly what happened. Martin walked on four pitches. Kate longed to see Daniel's face, but she couldn't go up to the house to watch TV until she had finished her barn chores.

"Montero looks calm," the first announcer said.

"Montero always looks calm. He would look calm if he was being driven to the guillotine."

"Here's the first pitch—and it's a strike!"

"Thank God," Kate said out loud.

But the next four pitches were balls, and the batter walked.

"Men on first and second, nobody out," the announcer said.

The third batter came to the plate and this time Daniel managed to get two pitches over the plate, but the batter ended up walking.

"When is Joe going to take him out?" the announcer wondered. "Are they going to let him give up a run?"

But the manager remained in the dugout and Daniel pitched to the fourth batter, who swung at a ball close to the plate and grounded into a double play.

"Will he get razzed in the dugout," the announcer said. "You'd think a player as experienced as Henderson would know enough not to swing when the pitcher is having such obvious control problems."

The next batter never took the bat off his shoulder and walked on five pitches.

"Here comes Joe," the announcer said. "Hitchcock has been throwing in the bullpen and, yes, Joe just signaled for him to come in. Joe reached the mound, and Daniel has handed him the ball. Now Montero starts for the dugout . . . Listen to that applause! People are beginning to stand! It's a standing ovation from a packed stadium for Daniel Montero as he walks to the dugout."

The second announcer said, "Yankee fans have long memories. They know what Montero has done for them in the past."

Kate had tears in her eyes. The ovation was wonderful. Daniel probably hated it, but it was a wonderful tribute to him.

The first announcer said, "Montero just threw his glove down on the bench. He's upset."

The second announcer said, "I'm sure he's upset with himself, not with Joe for taking him out. Daniel is such a competitor; he gets mad at himself if he isn't perfect."

You've got that right, Kate thought.

She left the game on as she finished her work, but her mind wasn't on it. She was thinking about Daniel and about how he must feel.

He feels humiliated. He shouldn't, but he does.

She brought in the second turnout, dropped hay from the loft for all of the horses, then went up to the house to make a few phone calls before walking to the bus stop to pick up Ben.

Ben was all excited. "Is the game over? Did Daddy win?"

"The game is still on, but Daddy only pitched the first inning. He has to be careful because of his hand, you know."

Cyrus left the drive to investigate a rustle in the woods. After a moment of indecision, Samson followed him.

"I have Little League practice today, Mommy. Do you remember that?"

"I could hardly forget. You have been reminding me about it every day."

"I'm going to be a pitcher."

"I think you'll be hitting off the T, Ben. There aren't any pitchers until you get older."

Having successfully treed a squirrel, the dogs rejoined them on the drive.

"The T is for little kids."

"I hate to break it to you, chum, but you are a little kid."

"I'm not. I'm almost the tallest in my class. I'm taller than Connor."

Kate said curiously, "Why are you always in competition with Connor, Ben? I thought he was your friend."

He gave her a surprised look. "He is. Connor is my best friend."

"Then why are you always so pleased when you can be better than him?"

His surprise deepened to amazement. "I'm happy for me, Mommy; it doesn't mean I don't like Connor."

Kate sighed and muttered, "It must be a boy thing."

"I got a hundred on my math test, Mommy."

"That's wonderful, Ben," she said warmly. "Good for you."

He beamed. "Mrs. Fitzgerald said I have a good brain for math."

"You do. You must take after your father that way."

"Is Daddy good at math?"

"I'm not sure, but I know your mother was not a math person. She was like Nana; she liked to read books."

"Are you a math person, Mommy?"

"A little bit. I can keep the books for my business, anyway."

Ben said generously, "Connor is a good writer. His writing is better than mine."

"It's nice that you give him credit," Kate said, holding back a smile.

"I wish I was on the Yankees and not the Cubs," Ben said.

"You have to go to the team you're assigned to."

"I know, but I wish I was assigned to the Yankees."

"Then you wouldn't be on the same team as Connor."

"I wish Connor was on the Yankees, too."

"Well, you're both on the Cubs. You don't have to play at all if you don't want to."

"I want to play!"

"Then stop complaining."

"Who is going to take me to practice?"

"Nana is going to take you and Connor, and Connor's mom will pick you up and bring you home."

"Okay. I have homework. Do you want me to do it right away?"

"Yes. But you can have a snack first."

The two of them, along with the dogs, went into the house.

When Molly returned from school the first thing she asked Kate was, "How did Daniel do? Is he still pitching?"

Kate was rinsing out the dishes Ben had used for his snack and the look she gave Molly was bleak. "He had to come out in the first inning."

Molly's face fell. "Oh, Kate. I am so sorry."

"I know. I feel so responsible, Mom. If only I had put Shane on the crossties!"

Molly looked at her daughter. "It isn't like you, Kate, to bemoan things that might have been."

Kate laughed shakily, "I just can't help it. Daniel's whole career is on the line."

Molly said, "I have every confidence that Daniel will get his pitching back. There's nothing wrong with the hand; it healed beautifully. At least that is what Daniel told me."

"It's what he told me, too."

"So he just has to get comfortable with pitching again. I am sure he will."

Kate smiled. "You're always so sensible, Mom."

Molly smiled back. "I'm sensible but tired. I think I will lie down until it's time to take Ben to his Little League practice."

"Are you sure you're up to taking him, Mom? If you're not . . ."

Molly picked up the book bag she had put down on a kitchen chair. "I am perfectly capable of taking Ben, and Connor too, but you're going to have to think about the future, Kate. Once I'm married, I won't always be here to chauffeur Ben. Have you given that any thought?"

Kate bit her lip. "Not yet."

Molly said gently, "I will be glad to help you out when I am here, but when I'm in Colombia, you're going to have to find someone else."

"I know. And I will, Mom. Don't worry about it. I'll work something out."

"I feel like I'm letting you down."

Kate came to hug her mother. "Don't feel that way, Mom, please. You're not letting me down. You've been a rock of support to me and Ben for years. It's time for you to have a life of your own again."

"That's what Alberto says."

"And he's right. I think Alberto is very wise, Mom. He understands things about people."

"He does. That is why his book is making such a splash—he has such insight into people."

"I'll read it the minute it comes out in English."

"Thank you, dear."

"Go on upstairs, and I'll bring you a cup of tea."

Molly kissed Kate's cheek. "That would be very nice."

Kate brought Molly her tea, made sure that Ben was doing

his homework, then went back to the barn to meet her first lesson.

Daniel didn't call. At nine o'clock, when Kate still hadn't heard from him, she phoned his house. Alberto answered.

"Alberto, this is Kate. How is Daniel?"

"Very very calm—the way an explosive is calm until somebody sets a match to it."

"Damn. Do you think I should come over?"

"I don't know . . . I don't think so. I think he might need some time by himself. He feels he humiliated himself in front of fifty thousand people—not to mention the whole television audience."

"He must be feeling pretty raw."

"Yes. It would be better to wait until tomorrow to talk to him, when the wound isn't quite so tender. He will not want to feel less than himself when he is with you."

"That's stupid," Kate said. "I won't think less of him because he had a bad outing pitching!"

"I know that, Kate. But I also understand how Daniel must feel. I am a Latin male myself."

"Well . . . will you tell him I called?"

"I will."

Kate felt suddenly reckless. "Tell him I love him."

"I will do that." She could hear the smile in Alberto's voice.

Kate hung up the receiver.

She felt so badly for Daniel. She was glad she hadn't seen the game on television; it would have been anguish to watch him struggling.

I wish I could see him. I wish I could hold him.

The phone rang, and she picked it up.

"Hello?"

"Kata."

Thank God.

"How are you, Daniel?"

"You saw the game?"

"I listened on the radio. I was working in the barn."

"Pretty pitiful, huh?"

"You shouldn't have pitched. You weren't ready."

"I am beginning to wonder if I will ever be ready."

"Sure you will. You had a serious injury."

"But the bones have healed."

"You threw some pitches over the plate. Each time you pitch, you will get more."

"For a hard-throwing pitcher, I have always had good control."

"And you will have good control again. Just give it some time, Daniel."

He said grimly, "I don't have any choice."

"I miss you. I miss having you under the same roof."

"I miss you, too. You and I have to sit down and have a talk; but not until I'm pitching well again."

"Okay."

"Good night, Kata."

"Good night, Daniel."

She hung up the phone and sat frowning at it for almost a minute. If the hand was healed, then why was Daniel having so much trouble throwing the ball?

He hadn't suggested moving back into the farmhouse. Of course, that would add a half an hour to his trip in each direction. Still . . . it would be nice to know that he wanted to be near her.

Why couldn't Daniel throw strikes?

38

The next time Daniel pitched, once again he left in the first inning, having walked the bases full. Afterward, at his locker, he answered the questions of the reporters with ironclad composure and courtesy.

During the following week, it seemed as if the entire world was focused on Daniel's wildness. Newspaper articles were written on the subject. The announcers talked of it constantly. His pitching coach made myriad suggestions. His catcher made suggestions.

Since it was early spring, there were a number of afternoon games, so he had the evenings free, and he spent those evenings with Ben and Kate. Once away from the stadium, he didn't talk about his pitching at all.

He wanted to make love to Kate, but Molly and Ben were always around. He wanted to move back into the farmhouse, but Kate hadn't suggested it.

He was miserable.

His third start came around. It was Monday, and Kate didn't have after-school lessons, so she went back to the house to watch the first inning on television.

How could he stand it? she wondered. How could he

stand up in front of all those people and risk failure? He was such a proud man. This must be horrible for him.

There was silence in the ballpark as Daniel walked to the mound. There was silence as he threw the first pitch. It was too high. The expression on his face never changed.

His second pitch was too far outside. His third pitch caught the corner of the plate—a strike. The stadium applauded. His fourth pitch went over the catcher's head and his fifth pitch hit into the dirt. The first batter had walked.

Kate watched Posada go out to the mound to talk to Daniel. Daniel listened courteously, nodded, and the catcher went back to his place behind the plate.

The second batter walked on six pitches.

The third batter walked on four pitches.

The manager came out to the mound to remove Daniel from the game.

As Daniel walked off the mound, an eerie silence descended over the stadium. *That walk to the dugout must be the longest walk of his life,* Kate thought. Still in the same eerie silence, the new pitcher accepted the ball from Joe Torre, and the manager walked back to the dugout, his head bowed.

Daniel remained in the dugout for the rest of the game.

"He doesn't have to put himself through this," the announcer said. "Any other man would have gone down to the clubhouse."

"Daniel has so much class," the second announcer said. "It would be a tragedy if he can't fix this wildness problem. The game can't afford to lose a player like that."

Kate turned the TV off and went back down to the barn to finish up her chores. She picked up Ben and Connor at school and brought them back to the farm for a play date. Molly came in and asked immediately how Daniel had done.

"Not too well, Mom. He didn't get anybody out."

"Oh no."

"Yeah. It's a real bummer."

"Poor Daniel. He must be very upset."

"He looks like the sphinx on television, but I can imagine what must be going on inside. I don't have lessons today, and I was thinking of going over to Daniel's house. I'll drive Connor home first. Would that be okay with you?"

"Of course, dear. I'll take care of Ben."

It was six o'clock when Kate pulled up in front of Daniel's house. The garage door was closed, so she didn't know if he was home yet, but she parked in the circular driveway and went to ring the bell.

Daniel answered the door himself. He looked as if he had lost weight.

"Kata! What are you doing here?"

"I came to see you."

"Come in." He led her to the family room and sat next to her on the sofa.

Kate took a deep, steadying breath and said, "I think I know what is wrong with your pitching."

He gave her a wary look. "You do?"

"Yes. You're thinking too much."

"What?"

"It's like riding a horse, Daniel. If you constantly see yourself from the outside: Are my heels down? Is my back straight? Are my elbows bent? You don't achieve harmony with your horse. You have to do all of those things, but you have to do them with your body. You have to let your body do your thinking for you."

She picked up his right hand, his pitching hand, and held it tight. "Daniel, I think you're looking at yourself from the outside. You conduct a little clinic every time you pitch, and so the pitch isn't right. Your body knows how to pitch. I think you need to shut off your brain, go out there, and throw the damn ball into Jorge's glove."

He stared at her. "Do you really think that that is it?"

"Try it. Forget about the mechanics and just throw the ball. I'll bet you do just fine."

"Mel thinks I've been aiming the ball."

"Well, he's your pitching coach. Listen to him."

His eyes began to sparkle. "I do have a checklist of things that I go over before each pitch."

"Did you have the checklist before the accident?"

"No. I didn't need it. I was pitching fine."

"Well, I think you'll pitch just fine again if you get rid of the checklist."

He looked at her in dawning wonder. "Do you know, Kata, I think you might have solved the mystery."

"I thought about it when I was riding this morning. Shane was doing so well that I felt like a part of him. I didn't think at all; all I did was feel the movement. It was wonderful—we were so together. Then, afterward, I thought that that was what you had lost, that mindless, fluid motion that you used to have."

He was silent for a long moment, then he said slowly, "I think that is exactly what happened. I have become too mechanical. I've lost the feel of pitching."

"The problem is in your brain, Daniel, not in your hand."

"But can I fix it?"

"Just go out there and throw. Don't even think about how you are holding the ball; just do what comes naturally."

He looked at her. "Kata, you are wonderful."

"Thank you."

He laughed. "I can't wait to get to the ballpark tomorrow."

Kate said a silent prayer that what she had said would help.

Daniel said, "Alberto is out."

She looked at him. He gave her a warm smile, the kind of smile she had not seen since he got back from Florida. Her stomach clenched. *This has got to work.*

"For how long is Alberto out?"

"He went into the city to meet a friend. He won't be home until eleven at least."

"How convenient."

"For us it is. May I invite you to my bedroom, *señorita*?"

"You may indeed."

Hand in hand they walked down the hallway and into Daniel's room. Kate had seen it once before, when Daniel had given her a tour of the house, and now she glanced quickly around at the pale yellow walls and the warm, orange-printed comforter and upholstery.

"I have missed you so much," he said, turning her to face him. "We have had so little chance for privacy."

"You could have moved back to High Meadow."

"You didn't invite me."

"Oh. Were you waiting for an invitation?"

"Yes."

She smiled up at him. "Well, I came to you instead. You know what they say about Mohammed and the mountain."

"No, what do they say?"

"If the mountain won't come to Mohammed, then Mohammed must go to the mountain."

"And you have come to my mountain."

"So I have."

Still smiling, they undressed and got into Daniel's queen-sized bed. Daniel put his arms around her and buried his face between her neck and shoulder. "I have been so afraid, Kata."

"I know, love. But truly, I think you're going to be all right."

She could feel his lips move on her skin as he answered, "I think so, too."

They stayed thus for about a minute, each taking comfort from the closeness of the other, then one of Daniel's hands began to lightly caress her breast. He lifted his head a little and kissed her throat.

His touch sent white lightning all through Kate, and she ran her hands along his back, feeling the muscles beneath her fingers.

Daniel's hand moved from her breast to her stomach and then moved again. She gasped, pressing up against his hand. He kissed her and continued to kiss and caress her until she whimpered.

He said her name and cupped her breasts in both his hands. She opened her eyes and they stared at each other out of passion-narrowed eyes. Then she put her hands on his hips, pulling him toward her, over her. She arched up to meet him, her breasts filling his hands as she urged him to fill her body.

He drove into her, and she answered him, blazing up in a bonfire of sensation as she closed around his powerful penetration.

They stayed connected for a long time, until Daniel said, "I'm too heavy for you," and withdrew. He pulled her to his side and she nestled against him, resting her head on his shoulder. His body felt warm and relaxed.

"I love you so much," she said.

"I love you so much, too."

"Are we going to get married, Daniel?"

"Yes."

"It's going to be complicated."

"Not unless you make it so."

She stiffened. "I intend to keep my business."

"You should keep your business."

She relaxed again. "Do you think you could live at High Meadow?"

"I could, but I have a better idea."

"What's that?"

"I have a friend in Colombia—he works on my father's ranch. We were boys together. He's married, with one child and expecting another. He speaks passable English. What if we employed him and his wife to do the heavy work around the barn? They could live in the farmhouse as part of the deal."

Kate's whole body had tensed while he spoke. "I don't want strangers dealing with my horses."

"Kata. Tomas has worked with horses all his life. He has been at my father's ranch for five years, and my father won't be happy to lose him."

"How do you know he would come?"

"He will jump at the chance to come to America. It will be an opportunity for him to live in a nice house and for his children to get a good education."

Kate was silent.

He said patiently, "I understand that you would not want to move away and leave the horses unattended, but Tomas would be there. And you would be only a phone call away."

"And I would live in your house?"

"Yes. You could commute to the barn for your own riding and your lessons."

"I can't afford to pay a couple."

"Kata, please. I am a multimillionaire. Whatever is mine is yours. Tomas's salary is a trifle."

Kate still hadn't relaxed. "What would I do with myself if I had a man doing all of my work?"

"You would ride and you would train and you would give lessons. Surely that's a busy enough schedule."

She said, "We could adopt a baby."

Now she felt tension in him. "We'll see."

She pulled away from him so she could see his face. "There's no 'we'll see' about it, Daniel. I want children, and I want us to adopt a Colombian child who needs a good home. I'm very good at being an adoptive mother. I've had a lot of practice."

His dark eyes searched her face. "Are you sure about this?"

"Absolutely sure."

"I just wonder if I will be able to love an adopted child the way I love Ben."

"Trust me, once they put that baby in your arms, you'll be lost."

He smiled. "You sound very sure."

"I am."

"All right, then. We will adopt a baby."

"But who will watch Ben and the baby while I teach after-school lessons? I've been worrying about that ever since Mom told us she was getting married."

"We will hire a nanny."

"Another Colombian?"

"I am sure my mother can find us a nice girl. And there is room in my house for her to live in."

She rested against him again. "You have an answer for everything."

He stroked her hair. "I have given this a lot of thought. I

knew you would want to keep your business and, to be honest, I don't want to live at High Meadow. The house is charming, but it is too small. And it is too far from Yankee Stadium. If you like, we could buy a piece of property in Greenwich and you could open a new business."

She was shaking her head emphatically. "All of my customers are in the Glendale area. Besides, High Meadow Horse Farm was my father's pride and joy. I want to keep it."

"I thought that that was what you would say. So we will keep High Meadow, and you will still be the trainer and teacher. All that will differ is that Tomas will be mucking stalls, cleaning water buckets, and doing turnout. This will give you time to be a mother. That doesn't sound so bad, does it?"

"No."

"See? It will all work out."

She nestled her cheek into the hollow of his shoulder. "I love you."

He kissed the top of her head. "I love you, too."

39

When Daniel got to the stadium the following day, the manager called him into his office. "What about going down to Columbus to work on your control?"

Columbus was the Yankee's premiere minor league team.

"No," Daniel said. He was sitting in a comfortable chair on the opposite side of Joe's desk. Joe had swiveled his chair a little to face Daniel.

Joe said, "Well then, how about going back to Tampa to work with one of the pitching coaches there? You'll be able to concentrate better away from all the hoopla the newspapers are making."

Daniel leaned forward slightly. "Give me one more chance, Joe. I think I can fix this problem myself."

"How?"

"I think it's a mental thing, not something physical."

Joe stared at him for a moment. Then he said, "I think it's a mental thing, too. We all think it's a mental thing. You've lost your confidence, and you're aiming the ball. We've all told you that."

"Yes, but no one told me how to fix it. I kept thinking about how I was pitching the whole time I was pitching. I need to just go out there and do it."

"I won't give you any argument about that."

Daniel said earnestly, "It's like horseback riding. When you're a great rider you don't ride with your mind, you ride with your body. You've got all the fundamentals so schooled that you don't have to think anymore; you just feel. And that's the way I was with my pitching. I had all the fundamentals schooled; my body knew them. All I had to do was throw the ball. Let me try just throwing the ball and see how it comes out."

The manager was frowning. "I don't want to have to take you out of another game, Daniel. It's too hard on you."

"Please, Joe. Just give me one more chance."

The manager sighed. "All right. I'll keep you in the rotation for one more start."

Daniel stood. "Thank you. You won't regret it."

"I hope not, Daniel. For all our sakes, I hope not."

It was a bright and sparkly April afternoon the day Daniel made his fourth start. At one o'clock, Kate went up to the house to watch the first inning on television. The game was at Yankee Stadium, and the stands were fairly full for a workday and school day afternoon.

The story of the day was, of course, Daniel.

"Joe has come under some heavy fire for starting Montero again," the announcer said. "A lot of people think he should have sent him down to Columbus to work on his control there."

The second announcer said, "It's just hard to believe that a great pitcher like Montero could lose his control so catastrophically."

"There are precedents. Look at Mark Wohlers."

"I know."

The "Star-Spangled Banner" was played, the players put

their caps back on, and the first batter came to the plate. Daniel finished throwing his warm-up pitches and waited for the batter to get set.

Kate felt sick to her stomach. She clenched her hands as Daniel went into his windup.

The ball thudded into the glove and the umpire called "*Strike.*"

Kate closed her eyes. *Please God, let the next one be a strike too.*

Daniel delivered, and the umpire called, "*Ball.*"

"Shit," Kate said out loud.

The next two pitches were fastballs straight down the middle of the plate. The batter never took his bat off his shoulder. There was one out. Kate started breathing again.

Daniel's first pitch to the next batter sailed over Posada's head. Kate's stomach tightened. The next pitch was over the plate. The batter stood with his bat on his shoulder.

"They're not going to swing at anything until Montero has established he can pitch over the plate," the announcer said.

The next pitch looked like it caught the outside corner, but the umpire called it a ball.

"Moron," Kate hissed at the screen as the crowd booed its disapproval. The replay showed the pitch clearly getting the outside corner. "How can Daniel expect to get his control back when the umpires don't know a ball from a strike?"

The next pitch was a fastball right down the middle of the plate. The batter looked at it. Two balls and two strikes.

Daniel and Posada conferred about the next pitch and then Posada went back to the plate and the batter took up his position. Daniel delivered, the batter swung and missed by a mile.

"It was a change-up!" the announcer said. "Peters was expecting another fastball and instead he got the change. Daniel sure fooled him."

The second batter hit a weak fly to the first baseman, and the third batter struck out.

Daniel was smiling as he walked off the mound. His grinning teammates in the dugout shook his hand as he came in.

Kate looked at her watch and decided she would watch Daniel pitch the second inning as well. She could listen to the game on the radio while she worked in the barn, but she really wanted to see him.

In the bottom of the first, the Yankees got a run when Jeter doubled, stole third, and came in on Williams's long fly.

Then Daniel was back on the mound to start the second inning. His first pitch was a fastball, waist high, right over the plate, and the left-handed cleanup man sent it into the right field stands. The game was tied.

"Guess they're not waiting around for Montero to get the ball over the plate any more," the announcer said. "If he lays one in there, they're going to powder it."

Daniel motioned to his catcher and Posada came to the mound. They talked for a few moments, then Posada returned to his position behind the plate. Daniel's first pitch to the new batter was a sinker and the batter swung and missed. Strike one. The next pitch was near the outside corner and was called a ball. The third pitch was outside again, but this one caught the corner. Strike two. Next, Daniel threw a slider in the dust. Ball two. The batter fouled off the next two pitches, then Daniel threw a fastball inside. The batter swung at it and missed. Strike three.

The next batter who came to the plate was another left-hander. Daniel threw him a cut fastball, a low slider, another cut fastball, and then a rising fastball to get him out.

The third batter of the inning flied out to short left field.

"He's done it," Kate said jubilantly. "He believed me, and he fixed the problem. Isn't that great, Cyrus?"

Cyrus thumped his tail as she looked at him, and she bent down to kiss the top of his head. "I am so happy."

She and the dogs went down to the barn to finish mucking stalls, and once she was there she turned the radio on to the game. She cleaned the stalls with a song in her heart, because Daniel pitched six strong innings without giving up another run.

She was teaching a lesson a couple of hours later when Ben came down to the ring with the portable phone in his hand. "Mommy, Daddy is on the phone for you. He said you would want to talk to him."

"All walk," Kate called to her lesson. "Let the horses take a breather." She ducked under the fence and took the phone from Ben.

"Hi, Daniel. I saw the first two innings and listened on the radio until you came out. Congratulations. You won."

"My control was so much better, Kata!"

"I know. I saw."

"I did what you said, I closed my mind, stared at Jorge's glove, and just threw. And it went over the plate!"

"You let your body do what it knows how to do."

"Exactly. You are a genius."

She laughed. "I'm not, but if you want to think I am, go right ahead."

"I want to see you tonight. We have to celebrate. Why don't we go out to dinner and then back to my house?"

"I have a better idea. Let's go out to dinner and you can stay over at High Meadow."

"That *is* a better idea."

"What did Joe and Mel say about your pitching?"

"They wanted to know what had happened to make me

see the light, and I told them about your horse comparison. They were impressed."

"As well they should be."

He laughed. She had not heard that joyous sound in over a month and she pictured how his brown eyes would be sparkling and his face would be wearing that terrific smile that always made you want to smile back.

He said, "Can we tell Molly that we're going to get married?"

"Yes."

"Can we give her a date?"

"We don't have a date."

"Well, let's make one."

"I don't want a big wedding and a lot of fuss."

"I love you, Kata. Neither do I. We'll have Ben and your mother and Alberto and my mother and father. How does that sound?"

"Perfect. But we're going to have to live at High Meadow until this wonderful couple you have promised me comes to take over."

"Okay. I will pack a suitcase. Unless . . . will it be too much for Molly if I move in?"

"Not if she doesn't have to cook for you."

"I usually get my supper at the ball park."

"Good. Then pack the suitcase and come."

"I will do that."

"I have to get back to my lesson, Daniel."

"Okay. See you around seven-thirty?"

"Okay."

"Ben!" He had been rolling around with Samson while she talked, and now she called him over and gave him back the phone. "Will you tell Nana that Daddy and I are going out to dinner tonight and that Daddy will be staying over with us?"

"Yes!" Ben said. "I can show him the A I got on my math today."

"He'll be very proud of you."

Ben took the phone back to the house, and Kate went back to her lesson.

When Kate and Daniel returned to the house from dinner they found Molly and Alberto in the living room, sitting side by side on the sofa, holding hands and listening to music. Kate felt the familiar catch at her heart when she saw her mother's tired face.

Molly had one more chemo treatment to go, and the longer the therapy had gone on, the more it had sapped her energy. There was a translucence about her skin and a pallor that made her look very fragile. She was still teaching, but she had missed more days of school as the treatment had gone on.

The older couple both smiled at Daniel, and Alberto said, "I hear that you pitched very well. Congratulations."

Daniel grinned. "Kata can take the credit for my resurrection as a pitcher. She told me I was thinking too much."

A voice said from the hall behind Daniel, "Can I say hello to Daddy?"

"Ben." Molly sounded reproachful. "You should be asleep."

"I was waiting for Mommy to come home."

"Well, since you're up, come into the living room," Kate said. "Daniel and I have an announcement to make."

Barefoot, and clad only in pajamas, Ben came into the room.

Kate said simply, "Daniel and I are going to get married."

"Kate. Oh my dear. I am so happy for you." Molly stood up and held out her arms. Kate went to hug her.

Alberto went to shake Daniel's hand.

Ben said excitedly, "Does this mean that Daddy will live with us all the time?"

"How would you and your mother like to come and live with me?" Daniel asked.

"Yeah! You have a pool, Daddy."

"Yes, I do. And I have strict rules about when children can swim in it."

"I know," Ben said wisely. "Only when there's a grown-up watching you."

"Exactly."

"What are you going to do about High Meadow?" Molly asked Kate.

"We are going to hire a Colombian couple to live in the house and take care of the horses. I'll still do the training and teaching, but not the stalls or the turnout."

"What a wonderful idea." Molly looked at Daniel. "Do you have a couple in mind?"

"As a matter of fact, I do." Daniel looked at Alberto. "Tomas and Marta," he said.

"Tomas works for your father."

"I plan to make him an offer he can't refuse."

"Rafael will not be happy."

"It will be his wedding present to us."

Alberto smiled.

Molly said, "There is a bottle of champagne in the refrigerator left over from Easter. Why don't we open it up?"

"I will get it," Alberto said.

The champagne was opened, and they toasted the happiness of Daniel and Kate. Then Kate took Ben up the stairs to bed.

"I'm glad you and Daddy are getting married," he confided as she pulled the comforter up over his shoulders. "Now we can be a real family."

Kate looked into his bright eyes and felt a pang in her heart. "You and Nana and I have been a real family."

"I know, but we didn't have a Daddy."

"That's true. And now we will."

Ben smiled. "Wait until I tell Connor!"

Daniel gave Molly a half an hour to go to sleep, then he went down the hall to Kate's room. She was sitting up in her double bed dressed in a large T-shirt and reading *Equus* magazine. She put the magazine on the night table next to her as Daniel crossed to the bed.

"We never set a wedding date," he said as he stepped out of his jeans and slid his lean length in next to her.

"There are only two more months of school. I think we should let Ben finish up at Glendale Elementary and start him in September in his new school in Greenwich."

"That makes sense. So shall we say the end of June?"

"Sounds good to me."

"On our wedding night, will you wear a sexy nightgown?"

She stared at him. "What's the point? All you'll do is take it off."

"Men like things like sexy nightgowns, Kata."

"Men are funny creatures."

"We are, and we are very grateful to women when they humor us."

She smiled. "All right. I'll buy a sexy nightgown."

"Thank you, *querida*."

"What does *querida* mean?"

"It means 'darling.'"

She cuddled against his shoulder. "That's nice."

"When will you want Tomas and Marta to start?"

"Are you sure this is going to be all right? Your father won't be mad?"

"He will miss Tomas, but he will also see that this is a wonderful opportunity for him to better his family. He won't mind."

"I'm going to be a married woman. It's funny, Daniel, but I never pictured myself married the way most girls do."

He replied in a matter of fact voice, "That's because you are one of the most self-sufficient people that I know."

"I am self-sufficient. I've always taken pride in being self-sufficient. I liked my life the way it was."

He bent his head and kissed her hair. "It won't change all that much, *querida*. Don't get scared."

"It will change a lot," she replied soberly. "And the biggest change has happened already."

"What is that?"

"Before I met you I was never lonely. But now, if you went away, I would be very lonely. I would be lost. It's a scary thought, to have so much of your happiness riding on one person."

"That's the risk you take when you fall in love, Kata."

"I missed you when you were in Florida, and I will miss you when you go on road trips. There's a little emptiness inside me when you aren't there."

"I'm glad, because I feel the same way about you."

They remained silent for a long moment, Kate listening to the beating of his heart under her cheek. Then Daniel said, "So when do you want Tomas and Marta to start? Do you want them right away or do you want to wait until June?"

"We're going to have to wait—there's no place for them to sleep in the house until we move out."

"True. What about Molly? Has she given any indication about when she and Alberto are going to tie the knot?"

"I think they were thinking of getting married in the summer sometime. She finishes her chemo at the beginning of May and then she has to go for radiation. Then she's going to go to Colombia again to meet some more of Alberto's family."

"Is she going to get married before or after she goes to Colombia?"

"I'm not sure."

"We should find out so I'll know when to have Tomas start. There are visas that need to be gotten."

"Okay, I'll find out."

He sighed. "I feel such happiness being here with you, Kata. Such . . . contentment."

She pressed her cheek against his naked chest. "I feel the same way. Isn't it funny? And I didn't like you at all when first we met."

"I thought you were the most beautiful woman I had ever seen."

"Even more beautiful than the supermodel?"

"Much more beautiful."

"Good."

He eased her away from him so that she was lying against the pillow. "Kiss me," he whispered.

She reached up to put her arms around his neck, and then she obliged.

THE EDITOR'S DIARY

Dear Reader,

For this, the most romantic month of the year, treat yourself to two Valentine-worthy heroes, courtesy of Warner Forever.

Joan Wolf's contemporary romance **HIGH MEADOW** offers Daniel Montero, a heartthrob with good looks, old-world charm, and a winning record as a baseball pitcher. He has everything a single guy could ever want. But Daniel's ready to trade in the perks of being a very eligible bachelor for the comforts of hearth and home. When he finds out that he has a child, a seven-year-old boy he never knew about, he couldn't be happier. His son's adoptive mother isn't thrilled, though. It'll take heart-to-heart talks and slow, melting kisses for Daniel to convince her that he has what it takes to be a wonderful father and a loving husband.

Is there anything sexier than a masked bandit who can out-duel and out-seduce every lord in the land? Meet the Black Fox, the hero of **Amanda Scott's** historical romance **THE SECRET CLAN: HIGHLAND BRIDE**. Raised as a gentleman, the outlaw Fox defends fellow Highlanders against those who would destroy their traditional way of life. When he rescues a Scottish beauty from a kidnapper, he leaves her with a kiss that haunts her dreams . . . and a desire to discover his true identity. You'll delight in every page as the matchmaking fairies of the Secret Clan plot to make happily-ever-after come true for this couple.

Don't forget to visit us at www.warnerforever.com. And please turn the page for your chance to be a lucky contest winner!

With warmest wishes,

Karen Kosztolnyik

Karen Kosztolnyik, Senior Editor

P.S. Coming your way in March 2003 is a hearty dose of love and laughter in **THE KISSING GAME** by **Kasey Michaels**, one of today's best-loved historical romance authors writing about Regency England. If you prefer shivers down your spine, look for **LIKE A KNIFE**, the stunning romantic suspense debut of talented newcomer **Annie Solomon**.

Official Contest Rules